REALMS OF
WRATH & RUIN

GATE CHRONICLES BOOK II

REALMS OF
WRATH & RUIN

GATE CHRONICLES BOOK II

ALLI EARNEST

DRAGON PAGE
ENTERTAINMENT

For information contact :
http://www.alliearnest.com

Front Cover Art by Deandra Scicluna @dealuna.art (Instagram) & @dealunart (ArtStation)

Dragon Page Entertainment Logo Design by Ingrid Nordli @arcticpaintbrush (Instagram)

Arrow Brushes on map by Aura_ID at Brusheezy.com

ISBN (paperback) : 979-8-9883292-0-6

First Edition : June 2023

10 9 8 7 6 5 4 3 2 1

THE GATE CHRONICLES

Cities of Smoke & Starlight

Realms of Wrath & Ruin

C O N T E N T S

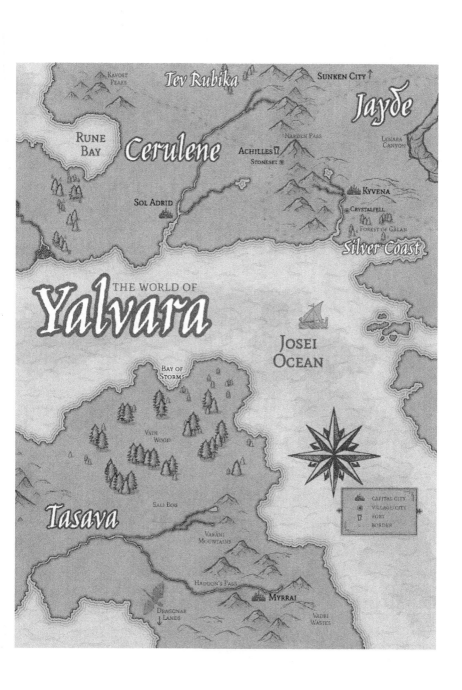

FOLLOW ME!

Join my newsletter:

Instagram:

For Lorelai

PART I: REALMS

CHAPTER 1

EZEKIEL LEE SHACKLEY

Hallie

THE WHITEWASHED STONE BUILDINGS LINING both sides of the lane were lingering specters watching Hallie Walker's every move. She wondered if the errand boy running with erratic footsteps in the opposite direction thought the same. She shivered.

As she strode to the awaiting motorcoach with its low rumble echoing off the stone, the acrid scent of Yalvar fuel burned her nose. She pulled her cracked leather jacket tight, not because of the wind zipping through the cracks between the buildings, but because the smell of the fuel was a firm reminder of where she would spend her evening. A Burning was a ritual with which she was all too familiar. Given the impending war with neighboring Cerulene, it wouldn't be the last she attended. It was a morbid way to remember the dead but customary all the same.

"Hurry, Hals."

Ellis Carrington, the first friend she'd made since moving to the capital, helped her into the coach. He slipped in beside her, shutting the door with a snap. The cab was warm and shadowed, with the only illumination being the setting sun filtering through the front glass. The plush seating was a luxury for a common coach. Ellis must have paid a pretty sum to rent it for such a morose affair.

They set off for the outskirts of Kyvena; nobody much liked the stench of burning flesh inside the city walls. Hallie's hands twisted upon themselves. The gesture felt strange without her right little finger. She had yet to adjust to the odd sensation as it had been a month since she'd lost it in Myrrai.

Even with her friend's comforting presence, she still wished for a pencil in her fingers to sketch away her anxieties. But she hadn't touched any drawing supplies since she'd returned. Hers had fallen through the Gate, and any time she thought about them, she'd remember.

And remembering made her stomach feel like the rolling of sea waves.

Just focus on getting through the night. Losing your composure won't help anyone, most of all yourself.

Ellis smoothed his blond hair back from his narrow face. "Great shocks, of all nights to have a Burning. The walk alone would give me frostbite."

Hallie glanced over at him. The fingers of his left hand were splayed upon his jiggling knee. "Why are you so nervous? These are your people, right?"

Ellis' glare spoke volumes. "We lace our boots same way as you. Maybe it's *you* who needs to rethink things."

Hallie crossed her arms and sank deeper into her jacket. "You have servants to dress you."

"Not me. The Shackleys, maybe."

"Sorry, El. I'm afraid they'll blame me. Maybe I could have done something more. Maybe I should have…"

But she couldn't find the words to finish the sentence. Because what could she have done? Leapt into the line of fire?

"You had no idea a rogue Cerl band would attack you on that research trip. Frankly, it's lucky Zeke was with you. He saved you all."

A research trip. One only she and her pilot, Kase, had returned from. It was a terrible lie, but one Ellis and Petra, her other University friend, believed.

"You weren't there. I *was*. I was right there as he...as he..." she sucked in a breath and brought her hands to her cheeks. "Oh, stars, I don't think I can do this again."

The last Burning she'd attended had been her brother Jack's.

Ellis squeezed her shoulder softly. "I don't think anyone would blame you if you didn't come."

"Kase would."

"If it's anything like his sister's Burning, I doubt he'll notice."

She replayed the memory of Kase sobbing into his hands as he blamed himself for that death. The painful thump of her heart nearly brought tears to her own eyes right there in the motorcoach.

Ellis' hand slipped from her shoulder as he looked out the window. Hallie caught glimpses of the lower city's market square and shops as they passed. The once colorful awnings were wan in the dying winter light. They reflected the numbness that had overtaken her body since her return to Kyvena.

Ellis didn't look at her as he spoke. "Growing up, Kase was brimming with restless energy. Always pulling pranks on the other students and sometimes teachers. Everyone wanted to be his friend. Including me. But his sister's ill-timed death almost killed him."

Hallie knew the feeling all too well.

Ellis' eyes were soft as he turned back to her. "He dropped out after she died."

"He didn't finish school?" Not attending the University was one thing, but failing to graduate from upper school was unheard of in the present day and age—even in somewhere as far removed as Stoneset, where she'd grown up.

"Nope. Point is, I wouldn't worry about what the others think of you. And if you want me to take you home, I will."

Hallie stared at her hands, twisting her fingers once more like an impossible tangle of threads. If only it were so easy. If only she lacked a conscience. "I'll go. It's the right thing to do. Zeke was...Zeke was a good person. And if he'd lived, I might say an even better friend."

Ellis smiled sadly. "You're a good friend, too."

"Thank you."

He sank into the motorcoach seat, the leather creaking as he did. "I don't know how you do it out in the mountains, but *my sort* of people don't like to waste time on something terrible like this, so it won't be a long ordeal. The Shackleys are too important for overzealous public drivel if you ask me. Just a few words about Zeke's military service, his heroism, and such. They'd much rather grieve in private."

Hallie shrugged. She couldn't tell Ellis the rest of what was bothering her. He wouldn't understand.

A day after their arrival in Kyvena, she, Kase, and Saldr, the Yalven emissary sent to barter an alliance with Jayde, had met with the High Council to discuss the mission. She hadn't seen Kase since, and the thought of him awash with the light from his brother's funeral pyre tied her stomach in all sorts of wicked and frayed knots. She hadn't reached out. Neither had he.

The memories of their last week in Myrrai, the Yalven city housing the Gate, were all a blur of meals and books in her mind; but Kase's strong arms folded around her, holding her in the hours after Zeke's death, made Hallie's cheeks heat. She remembered his soft kiss on her messy hair as she soaked his shirt through with tears, his blending with hers.

She was going to see him tonight.

Get a hold of yourself, for moons-sake. It's Kase. And you're going to a Burning.

But it wasn't just him. He'd be there with the rest of his family and the wealthy Jaydian elites.

As the city street lamps faded behind them in the dusky sky, the knots in Hallie's stomach tied themselves ever tighter. She smoothed the creases from her gray skirt. She'd thrown her only black dress in the inn's dining room fireplace after Jack's Burning. She couldn't stand to keep the blasted thing in her wardrobe.

Thinking it would help her fit in better and draw attention

away from the fact she wasn't wearing mourning black, Hallie had also twisted her hair into a proper ladies' bun, free of stray hairs. She ran a shaking hand over it.

"Stop stressing. I promise you, no one's going to be judging your attire or station here. The flames will be a little distracting," Ellis said softly.

Hallie peeked over at him and his still-jiggling his leg. She took a deep breath, the rush of oxygen in her chest calming her nerves for the moment. "Easy for you to say. If Petra was here, you'd be primping your hair in the window reflection the entire time."

He rolled his eyes. "She's getting married in five months. Surely, she hasn't allowed you to forget that fact."

He was trying to lighten the mood, but over the years they'd known each other, she'd learned to read him like a book. His green eyes dulled at her next words: "You could talk to her father."

Ellis rubbed a hand across his face. "That's not how you do it in the city. Especially with a family as eager to rise in society as Petra's. My family doesn't mind being lower than, say, the Shackleys, but that doesn't mean I can have my pick of a bride either. Father might not much care if or whom I choose, but Mother's got her eye on someone."

Hallie chewed the inside of her cheek. "Who?"

Ellis shrugged. "Dunno for sure, but she's been busy planning dozens of dinner parties. I think I'd be happier living life by myself. Somewhere on the coast. Maybe I'll buy a ship and become a captain."

"Didn't you tell me you get seasick?"

"I'd find my sea legs eventually. Imagine spending the rest of your days with the spray of the sea brushing your face as you ride the waves toward the sunset."

"And you'd leave me here with the wolves? How dare you?" Hallie punched him lightly on the shoulder.

"I'll make you my first mate if you want, but you'd have to follow my orders." His eyes were bright for the first time that evening, lifting the somber mood from moments before. "You'd forget I was in charge, so I'd have you walk the plank to the waiting sharks below."

"Except you got us completely lost on that tour of the port

city on school holiday."

"Just because you made a better grade in Geography doesn't mean you get to rub it in," Ellis huffed.

"If you'd studied more instead of flirting with Petra in the library that night before the final, then maybe you would've scored higher."

"Oh, good stars."

Hallie preened a little, relishing her small victory.

The moment didn't last long as the motorcoach slowed to a halt in front of a set of iron gates on the outskirts of the capital. It was time.

Her skirt and blouse were too itchy and laced with ice by the time they trekked through the creaking gates and into Kyvena's Pyrinth. Ellis led her through the maze of white stone walls mixed in with those of mudbrick. A family like Hallie's would rent a lesser one constructed of the latter, but one like the Shackleys would purchase a stone-lined plot with the best money could offer.

However, out in the mountains, it was more traditional to hike to the town's community pyre, which had the best view of Stoneset and the valley below. Hallie preferred that instead of these tight rows like a miniature city left in varying states of decay.

Little spurts of dead grass and clumps of half-melted snow littered the cobblestone path, and as they made their way toward the back of the Pyrinth, most of the plots were gated. You had to have money to spare if you wished to keep your family's pyre plot guarded from trespassers.

Rumor had it some of those who'd lost everything in the fire three years ago had set up camp in the Pyrinth. There wasn't much evidence left behind of inhabitation, but when your life went up in literal flames, you might be desperate enough to live in the place where humanity burned their dead and sent them to the stars above.

At long last, Ellis stopped in front of a towering white wall that shone in the dying orange and golden rays of sunlight. The gate itself was made of a brown, shiny metal.

Like the *Eudora Jayde*.

Zuprium.

Anger licked her insides, but she smothered it best she

could. She'd seen several items made as if they'd been constructed out of the metal to con a patron into paying handsomely, whether it be a locket, ring, or dagger. But with a family like the Shackleys, it might very well be the metal Zeke died to find.

Ellis pushed open the unlocked gate, and Hallie stepped in behind him, swinging it closed once more. The creak echoed off the walls of the pyre plot and in Hallie's head.

In contrast, the small crowd was as silent as the neatly stacked logs in front of them. Hallie and Ellis joined those on the right side, and she glanced up through her lashes at the others. She inspected the faces, but none were Kase. She recognized no one.

Ellis pulled her fingerless-gloved hand into the crook of his elbow and leaned in close. "Looks like we're waiting for the dignitaries and the family. They like to make a grand entrance."

"And the body?"

"That, too."

No sooner were the words out of his mouth than the gate opened once more, and soldiers armed with electropistols and swords at their hips marched inside, fanning out to allow those behind them to enter. Hallie's eyes fell to the sodden hem of her too-long skirts.

She didn't belong among these people.

Men and women in crisp green uniforms, their chests weighed down with military decorations, carried something wrapped in an embroidered shroud. Hallie sucked in a breath as the soldiers carefully lifted Zeke's body and laid it on the pyre before her. She squeezed Ellis' arm tightly when the wind rustled untucked edges of the shroud.

Lieutenant Colonel Ezekiel Lee Shackley

Someone had embroidered the words across what should've been his chest. The Shackley crest underneath was in a dark green thread, a four-pointed star surrounded by interlocking swords. She'd expected a landscape or some other ornamentation upon the white linen, but the simplicity fit the stoic soldier with a shy smile and tender heart.

The corners of her eyes burned as she looked away and found them catching on an elderly gentleman with a snowy-white beard limping in beside a severe woman with a mangled scar across her cheek. Stradats Abram Loffler and Millicent Sarson. Of course, they'd be at such an occasion. Hallie had only glimpsed them at speeches she'd attended at the University, but seeing them this close made her heart stutter a little. They were some of the most powerful people in the world. Loffler appeared quite ancient; perhaps his own Burning wasn't too far in the future.

Before she could continue with that line of thought, a tall man, with closely cropped hair visible under his black bowler and a stern jaw, entered; the man she'd known as High Guardsman Jove Shackley, though he'd renounced that title. He held the hand of a Black woman whose budding stomach was just noticeable through the opening in her fur-lined cloak.

Hallie's mouth went dry when the next figure strode in, his hands tucked into his pilot's jacket and the collar flipped up to fight off the frost-laden evening. His cheeks were ruddy, and his curls were shorter than before.

Kase.

Her stomach somersaulted when he caught her eye as he took up the spot next to his brother. He gave her a tiny, nearly imperceptible nod, which she returned with a slight dip of her head. A bubble of warmth formed in her chest.

I'm glad I came.

The rest of the ceremony passed in a blur, and before Hallie knew it, the flames licked the edge of the pyre. As one, the group of onlookers turned away and gazed toward the heavens.

Hallie closed her eyes tightly as the orator spoke the words of Leaving, the very same ones she herself had choked out at Jack's Burning years before. Silently she mouthed the words with stiff lips.

"Go and find your place among the stars."

And at that moment, Hallie knew with certainty she wasn't the only one tearing up. Her eyes burned, the crisp air bit her cheeks, and the pyre was too warm at her back.

May you find peace at last.

Hallie prayed she'd find some for herself as well.

C H A P T E R   2

FRUSTRATING AS EVER

Hallie

THE SCENT OF ROASTED CHICKEN and the murmuring of the evening meal crowd kept Hallie grounded in the Crown Haven Inn. Many were discussing the latest rumor about some law the City Council wanted to propose. Something about taxes and possible curfews. Hallie wondered if the latter had anything to do with the attack on Fort Achilles at the end of last year, but she didn't dwell on it. It sounded like the measure was unlikely to pass. It would join the other rampant rumors in the papers before dying a quiet death. None of it helped her current situation—socially, scholastically, or financially.

Her own problems were more pressing than paying attention to preening politicians and their machinations. Upon returning to Kyvena, she'd decided to put the fifty gold hunders she'd received from the *Eudora* mission into savings. Once she returned to University, she'd use the funds to finish education and, soon after, purchase the school she intended to open.

But until then, working as a waitress would help make ends meet. At least this sort of job was familiar to her, and she had only been late twice in the month she'd been employed; she had nowhere else to be, and no schoolwork to distract her.

Work helped keep the more intrusive thoughts at bay. The proprietors were a kindly older couple who'd owned the place ever since they'd moved to Kyvena thirty years ago. They reminded her painfully of her parents.

And as each letter she sent to her mother and father went unanswered, her anxiety grew. She needed all the grounding she could get.

The last one had demanded answers.

Who was she?

How had her blood been able to open the door to the Gate chamber? Who in her family had been Yalven? Had that person known the woman in the portrait her great-grandmother had painted? She'd also mentioned she'd lost Jack's pocket watch. Writing out the words in black ink made its absence feel so...final. Either way, she'd paid an icy-eyed trapper a pretty sum to take it through the Narden Pass this time of year.

Hallie's mysterious lineage and the silence from her parents weren't the only things bothering her.

In the month since the Burning, the nightmares hadn't stopped. If she worked herself hard all day, she could get at least an hour of dreamless sleep before the gruesome images set in. Not even her books helped her cope. Because books only made her think of Kase, and that would inevitably spiral into the *Eudora Jayde* mission, and that only brought her back to square one. It was a wicked cycle.

A chilling breeze dashed across her cheeks as the front door of the inn blew open and shut with a sharp snap. She stopped scrubbing a recently-vacated table and looked up. A boy with spots dotting his pale face waited at the entrance. A few black curls peeked out from under his worn cap.

"Miss Hallie Walker?"

"Yes?" she asked as she tucked the rag into her maiden belt. A few of the other patrons glanced at her curiously. The boy held up an envelope, its jade-green wax seal evident even from across the room. Not her parents. They would've used clear wax from leftover candles.

She tried not to slump her shoulders as she met the boy where he still stood at the door. He gave a quick bow and held out the missive. "It's from the Watch."

As soon as Hallie grabbed it, he took his leave, the wind snatching him away. She shivered.

"The Watch?" another server asked, tucking her tray beneath her arm. "What trouble's you in?"

Hallie slipped the missive into the pocket of her apron. "Finish up table seven for me? I'm just gonna..."

The server nodded. "Let me know if you need bail or something. I always pegged ya for the clean sort, but maybe we misjudged you."

"I would never—" but Hallie's coworker had already turned away, golden bun bouncing as she made her way to the half-cleaned mess that was table seven. The diners nearby pretended to be more interested in their food, but their curious stares burned into her from behind.

Stars, what in the blazes was the Watch doing sending her missives during the dinner hour? She would've thought that after the *Eudora*, they would've been more discreet. Or at least sent someone instead of a missive.

The envelope weighed heavily in her pocket as she entered the kitchen. A tall woman with a graying braid looked up from where she scrubbed dishes.

"How's it out there?" Mazie, the proprietor's wife, asked.

"Seems to be slowing." Hallie headed for the stockroom. "We should be able to start cleaning after another half hour or so."

"Wonderful. We can send most of the others home soon, and then we can practice making cinnamon buns for tomorrow."

Hallie laughed outright, the reaction taking an edge off the anxiety flickering through her heart. "You know I'm a terrible cook."

"But how's a pretty young lady like you supposed to get married off if you can't even bake a cinnamon bun?"

Hallie rolled her eyes, but Mazie reminded her so much of her mother—or how her mother had been before Jack died—that it hurt. She hastily changed the subject. "Nole still not back?"

The older woman wiped a bead of sweat from her brow. Her deep brown eyes found Hallie's golden ones. They sparkled a little in the electric lighting. "I told him not to put off renewing our license until the last minute, but he wouldn't listen. He's been in that blasted line all evening!"

Hallie shook her head. "I said I'd go for him."

"That husband of mine is a stubborn one, lass. Make sure you find one who minds ya." She laughed and turned back to the pot. "Holler if you need any help out there. And tell Edith not to flirt too long with that tanner's boy tonight, will you?"

Hallie nodded and pushed open the door to the storage closet with her backside. Mazie started whistling a drinking song as Hallie let the door shut behind her.

The last minute of lightheartedness evaporated as she took the envelope from her pocket and inspected the seal. Four swords surrounded a four-pointed star. The Shackley crest. Was it from the ex-High Guardsman? Or the Stradat Lord Kapitan? From Kase? Stars.

She ripped it open and pulled out the short missive inside.

Miss Walker, you're needed immediately at the Jayde Center. Will explain upon your arrival. - Lord Jove Shackley

Hallie stared at the words. Had something happened with the treaty? Why Hallie was needed for something like that didn't make sense. Saldr didn't require a translator. She stuffed the note into her pocket. It looked like she and Mazie wouldn't be making cinnamon buns that evening after all.

THE JAGGED HONKING OF A horn assaulted Hallie's ears as she passed under the gate to the upper city. The Zuprium doors were wide open like they were most days, but they'd recently been infused with electricity like the hoverships. Power thrummed through them, opening early in the morning, closing late in the evening. Hallie heard it was because of the threat with Cerulene that the doors were infused. She didn't know how late she would be returning to the lower city, but she hoped she'd be able to see the doors in action.

The horn honked again. She looked back at the gleaming motorcoach waiting for her to move off to the side of the street. Hallie groaned but complied.

Kyvena hadn't been built for motorcoaches. The first settlers had lost their technology upon landing on Yalvara a millennium ago, and they didn't know if they would ever have the capability to construct anything as advanced as a motorcoach again. The reason for that had been the Yalvs interfering with the technology, of course, but Hallie wasn't sure how. All she knew was it had to do with Zuprium and the columns Kase had crashed into last autumn.

What if the Essences were somehow involved? Clearly Ben, the Watch agent-turned-traitor on their mission last autumn, had possessed one of them. They weren't all deceased as the records in the University library stated.

When she felt like returning to the University, she would do more research. Hopefully, Professor Christie would have returned by then. He would be a great help—especially since he'd gifted her that book about the Gate. He'd also known about Ben, somehow.

Hallie had so many questions, but Christie was on sabbatical. Probably off searching for more ancient texts.

She waited for the coach to pass and continued up the hill toward the building sitting atop it like a button on an enormous stomach. The Jayde Center shone golden in the dying light. Hallie wondered how easy it would be to break its glass dome. Molding glass in such a way was tedious and expensive. It was just begging for someone to shatter it. She couldn't deny it was beautiful; the University had a similar dome, installed to advertise its progress and wealth.

Back to the University again. Why must everything remind her of her failure?

A few minutes later, she found herself at the bottom of the government building's steps. Her chest burned with the effort of her hike. Even with each breath crystallizing in the air in front of her, she wiped a bit of sweat from her brow with a fingerless-gloved hand. The space where her right little finger should have been felt strange in these gloves, but she couldn't not wear them. Like her lacy blouses, they were more of a comfort than before. All she wanted was to feel whole again, to feel like Hallie.

She held her skirt up above her ankles and climbed the stairs.

Good stars. It took her an embarrassingly long time to do so, and she panted even harder, holding a stitch in her side when she finally reached the top. A man dressed in the green military uniform of the Watch waited at the door, sword and electropistol strapped at his waist and expression stern.

She ignored him and reached for the door, but he stopped her with a curt, "Please show your identification for admittance, Miss."

Hallie fumbled with her satchel but stopped when she processed what he'd said. Identification? She had nothing of the sort. "My name is Hallie Walker. Lord Jove Shackley said I'm needed immediately at the Jayde Center."

The guard's hand rested on the electropistol, his face and eyes like stone. Hallie stumbled back a step. His expression almost reminded her of the murderous statues she and the crew of the *Eudora Jayde* had fought on Tasava. Close, but not quite. Thank the moons.

"Without proper identification, I cannot permit your entrance."

"Please, sir. I'm a Yalven scholar from the University, and I can show you the missive he sent. Here!" She pulled out the crumpled parchment.

"Security is our priority during these times, Miss. I'm sorry."

"I understand that," Hallie said, waving the missive in front of his face, "but I swear I was summoned."

"Is there an issue, soldier?" a cold, detached voice said from behind her.

She whipped around and froze. Two men strode up the stairs toward them. The one in front who'd spoken was tall, and in his military uniform, he was even more imposing, with medals spanning one side of the dark green jacket. The intimidation didn't stop there. The man's steely gray mustache perched sternly above his upper lip, not a whisker out of place, and his eyes were a hardened hazel color. She'd seen him before.

"Stradat Lord Kapitan!" the guard said with a smacking

salute.

Hallie fell into a clumsy curtsy. She had only glimpsed him at Zeke's Burning, but there was no denying who this man was—especially with the rigid way he held himself.

"Hallie?"

Her heart leapt into her throat as she rose from her curtsy. It'd been over a month since she'd last seen the man striding up behind the Stradat Lord Kapitan. His curls were back, the messy, without-a-care strands sticking up every which way even it seemed he'd attempted to comb them. His jacket was still the same brown leather of the Hover Crews, and the beginnings of a beard outlined his strong jaw. Her knees nearly gave out when his blue eyes met hers.

"Kase..." she choked.

For moons-sake, act like a normal human being.

His smile was genuine and showed his straight, white teeth. Her heart fluttered once more. Good stars. It was Kase. Stupid, insufferable Kase. He was the man who'd frustrated her at every turn during the terrifying months they spent searching for the Yalvs. And yet, at the end...

His smile faltered. "You're pale."

She shook her head, a few auburn locks escaping from her hastily done ladies' bun with the movement. "I'm fine. Just, just what are you...are you...um..."

The pointed clearing of a throat froze the words tumbling from her mouth. She looked to the Stradat Lord Kapitan, whose eyes bored into hers. His jaw was firm as he inspected every inch of her in consternation. "And you are?"

"Um..."

"She's Hallie Walker, the scholar Jove hired for the *Eudora* mission," Kase cut in. "And a blasted good one. She's the sole reason the Lord Elder agreed to send an emissary."

The older man's gaze didn't soften at all, but the lines around his mouth relaxed a fraction. "Well, then we appreciate your service to Jayde, but I ask why you've come here. We've already heard your report."

Hallie gulped, but she steeled herself. "Um, well...the High Guards...I mean, Lord Jove Shackley sent me a missive. Said I was needed at the Jayde Center, sir." She held out the parchment.

"My title is Stradat Lord Kapitan." He inspected the note before handing it back. "It is a wonder my eldest son climbed as high as he did. I apologize on his behalf, but I requested Professor Owen Christie's aid, not yours."

Kase opened his mouth for what she was sure would have been a scathing retort, but Hallie held up a hand. Anger at the man's tone flared in her veins. That wiped out any anxiety she'd had before. "I apologize, Stradat Lord Kapitan. I meant no disrespect. The professor is away on sabbatical, so he wouldn't have received your summons. If it has something to do with the Yalvs, then I would be the second-best choice. However, this guardsman will not let me in without identification."

"Sabbatical? I'll be checking with the University, then." The Stradat Lord Kapitan's expression didn't change in the slightest. "Either way, with these uncertain times, we have strict rules in place to protect the nation's leaders and its citizens."

"My record from the *Eudora Jayde* mission should be evidence enough that I can be trusted."

She would've continued her tirade, but she caught sight of the quick jerk of Kase's head and wide eyes. Probably for the best, seeing as the Stradat Lord Kapitan's own eyes narrowed with each successive word she spoke.

"Stradat Lord Kapitan," Kase began, "I can vouch for her..."

The man glared at his son, who shut his mouth faster than Hallie thought possible. Kase's father looked back at her with that icy gaze. "Return here with identification or do not enter at all."

"But, Father—" Kase cut himself off at another deadly glare.

"Have a good evening," the older man said with a nod to Hallie.

With that, the Stradat Lord Kapitan saluted the guard back, who hadn't dropped his pose for the entirety of the conversation, and entered through the front door. Hallie's neck and face burned.

"Come on," Kase said, pulling his jacket more tightly around his shoulders. "I can fix this little problem."

Hallie followed him down the steps, too embarrassed to take her eyes off her boots, the tips peeking out from under her skirts. A waste. She should have simply come in her trousers.

He strode over to the rumbling motorcoach and opened the door. "Hop on in, will you?"

She looked up to catch his eyebrow quirk and said, "I should go. Nole and Mazie could use my help at the inn, and I don't even know why I'm here to begin with."

"All I know is that Saldr sent Father a message saying some other Yalvs had arrived."

"More Yalvs are here? Why?"

"That's what we're here to figure out." He gestured to the open door. She didn't move, so he let out an annoyed sigh. "Shocks, I forgot how stubborn you are. Would you rather walk home and accomplish nothing?"

"And I see you're as frustrating as ever," Hallie growled as she climbed into the motorcoach.

"Always." Kase slid in beside her and shut the door. "Go around the back and park down one of the side streets, Avery, if you would."

"Of course, Master Kase," the chauffeur answered.

"For the umpteenth time, *it's just Kase*, Avery," Kase sighed, running a hand through his hair.

"Yes, Master Kase."

Hallie tried to hold in her laughter, but she wasn't successful. It was a relief from the earlier tension, and she welcomed it. "Sorry."

Kase rolled his eyes. "It'd behoove you to be nice to me right about now."

Hallie choked back the rest of her laughter. "I'm always nice."

"Sure."

The streetlamps lining the road lit up as they passed. Night was upon them. The glow from outside caught on Kase's face as she watched him out of the corner of her eye. Same old Kase, even in his tailored trousers and polished boots. She could hardly believe she sat in his fancy motorcoach after a month of not seeing him. It was strange after spending nearly three months on the same hovership, but their social classes dictated they run in different circles.

After a slightly uneasy silence, Hallie spoke up, "Were you coming up here to help the Yalvs?"

Kase scoffed and tapped out a jagged beat on his knee with

slim fingers. "The illustrious and very dignified Stradat Lord Kapitan has a High Council meeting, and I was going to see if I could help with anything. I was simply forced into the same car by means of necessity."

At Kase's irreverent tone, Hallie peeked up at the driver. "Should you be talking like that?"

"Old Avery agrees with me, I know." Kase smirked. "Not that he'd ever show it. Isn't that right, Avery?"

The driver didn't miss a beat. "I have no say in the matter, Master Kase."

"See?"

"Fine," Hallie said, fiddling with the strap of her new satchel. It didn't fit the same as her old one, but considering that one was somewhere lost in the Gate..."Just tell me what your plan is, and I'll decide if it's worth following or not."

Kase shifted in his seat. They were sitting entirely too close in the space, and Hallie scooted a little further to the left, her cheeks heating. Kase looked out the window as they passed a few buildings and turned down a side street a block from the Jayde Center. "We'll sneak in. Sort of. Tonight's east entrance guard turned me down for drinks. Works in our favor, seeing as the poor bloke got caught snogging the wrong girl last week. Quite egregious, as she wasn't too pretty. Probably the worst bit, that."

"Kase!"

He shrugged. "Do you want to help or not? Besides, I'll twist Jove's arm for your identification papers in the morning. He can push it through, probably within the next week, but I don't know exactly how long it will take. Don't know why the *dulkop* sent for you and didn't think about that."

Hallie ran a hand down her face and sighed. "Fine."

"Glad you finally saw reason."

"But if we get caught, you're taking the blame."

Kase gave a wry laugh. "And I won't even get punished for it. One perk of being the Lord Kapitan's son. Sorry, *Stradat Lord Kapitan*." He chewed on his thumbnail for a moment before continuing. "He's such a blasting *helviter* when he wants to be, which is his every waking, breathing hour. Stars, it was nice to be away from home for so long last fall."

"I don't think you should talk that way about your father..."

He shook his head. "If you knew him like I do, you'd understand I'm being *kind*." He peeked out the window. The chauffeur parked the car, and Kase opened the motorcoach door. He held out his hand. "Hurry, would you?"

"Gracious day," Hallie grumbled as she placed her hand in his. It was a little rough, a few callouses along his palm. Again, she wondered where someone wealthy and city-bred like Kase would've collected them. Once out of the coach, she slipped out of his grip. She prayed the evening hid her blush.

With a quick word to Avery and a tap on the roof, Kase led her down the street and back toward the Jayde Center. His stride was confident, his boots clicking smartly on the cobblestones.

Streetlamps like bobbing candles lit the lane every fifteen feet or so and cast Hallie and Kase's shadows along the empty government buildings. Most of the employees who worked in them had gone home for the evening. That meant there was no one to see them sneak into one of the most important buildings of all.

As they approached the back of the Jayde Center, Hallie spotted a guard standing erect beside a large metal door. In the flickering electric light, Hallie thought it had a brown tint to it.

Pulling something from the pocket of his jacket, Kase strode over to the guard, who put a hand to his electropistol before relaxing. "I'm *not* leaving my post to go get drinks."

Hallie bit back a smile at the hint of exasperation in his voice. Apparently, the curly-haired pilot had that effect on everyone. Kase held out a piece of paper. "I'm on business for the Stradat Lord Kapitan."

"Ah, so that's why you wanted to get drinks." The man glanced at the papers before handing it back. "Fine, and the girl?"

Kase looked back at Hallie and winked. She rolled her eyes. *Mother of ash, he's cocky.* He turned back to the guard. "She's with me."

The guard tightened his hold on the electropistol at his side. "You can't just bring anyone in here. You know that."

"It's all right. Thank you, sir. We'll be on our way." Hallie gave him a smile and started to back away before Kase put a hand on her shoulder.

"Indeed, I do, but like I said, this is on the Stradat Lord Kapitan's orders specifically, and he's part of the High Council, in case you weren't aware."

The man's dark eyes flitted to his shoes and then to Kase once more. "Kase...if I let you in, and someone finds out..."

"Send them to me."

"But that would mean I would still get the stick. So no."

Hand falling from her shoulder, Kase slid what Hallie assumed was his identification papers into his pocket. "And if I were to tell your wife..." he leaned in so close Hallie could barely hear the next words, "what I saw the other night at the tavern? What would you think then?"

Even in the dim lighting, Hallie made out the blush blossoming across the man's entire face. He immediately straightened and let go of the grip of his pistol. "It's your grave, Shackley."

Hallie looked at the ground to avoid saying something incredibly stupid. *Kase is such a...*

"Thank you, Saul. We appreciate your cooperation and silence." Kase held out his arm for Hallie, but she didn't take it. He turned back to her. "Coming?"

Hallie unclenched her fist from around her satchel strap and marched past him, stopping in front of the guard. "I apologize for my companion, but I promise to get proper papers soon."

The man stepped away from the door. "I'd stay far away from that one, Miss. Surely, you can find better with that pretty little face of yours."

Hallie's face burned as Kase stepped up, poking the other man in the chest with each word. "Shocks and bolts, you keep your mouth shut, all right? I always make good on my promises *and* my threats."

The man's eyes narrowed, but he didn't say anything. Kase grabbed Hallie's arm and pulled her through the door before the guard did anything else. He didn't let go until Hallie pulled out of his grip. She crossed her arms when he turned and asked, "What now?"

"You can't treat people like dirt."

Kase rolled his eyes. "He cheated on his wife. He *is* dirt."

Hallie breathed out sharply through her nose, a gesture

Kase seemed to find amusing by his grin. She narrowed her eyes. "Just lead me to where Saldr is."

"Fine, fine, don't get your knickers in a twist." A sharp clacking of boots echoed off the shining marble floor, and Kase whipped his head around before turning back to her. "Just let me do the talking if anyone stops us, okay?"

Hallie ground her teeth, but she nodded. Kase held out his arm again, and she reluctantly took it, placing her hand in the crook of his elbow. Kase nodded to the soldiers on patrol as they passed in the corridors, none of which thought to question Kase. Ridiculous.

He guided her up a few staircases and through another corridor lined with portraits of important people whose names Hallie couldn't remember. Incandescent bulbs housed in simple black-iron sconces flanked them.

At long last, he stopped in front of a set of double doors on the fourth floor. "This is where they should be. Hopefully." He turned to the stoic guard. "Miss Walker and I are here to see Lord Saldr."

Why a guard? Hallie's stomach filled with stone.

The man gave Kase a once over, a flicker of recognition in his eyes, and nodded. "The Stradat Lord Kapitan said you'd be along."

Hesitantly, Hallie released Kase's arm and placed her hands on the doors, pushing them open. The well-oiled hinges were silent as she stepped over the threshold.

The room was larger than she imagined it would be from the outside, but the paint chipping off the beams in the high ceiling made her feel as if she'd stepped into the old rat-infested auditorium no one liked to visit on the University campus.

"Miss Walker and Master Shackley!"

The anguished shout echoed off the dark stone walls. Hallie searched for the speaker.

His hair was mussed instead of in its usual sleek tail, and his golden eyes were red-rimmed and swollen, but there was no mistaking Saldr. Hallie's heartbeat sped up at the sight. Surrounding him were other Yalvs, about a hundred or so. Little children, too, with their miniature robes and snaggletoothed smiles and adults dressed soot-stained in traditional garb.

What in the blazes is going on?

CHAPTER 3

THROUGH THE GATE

Kase

KASE WATCHED FROM THE CORNER of his eye as Hallie embraced Saldr. He hadn't pegged Saldr as the hugging type. None of the Yalvs struck him as touchy feely. They were all tall, willowy, and rather somber at the best of times.

He took in Hallie as she pulled back from the towering Lord Saldr and spoke in a whisper. She hadn't changed much in the month since he'd seen her. Granted, he'd only glimpsed her at the Burning, and his thoughts had been elsewhere. Understandably. It was a miracle he'd been sober for it.

Now, her auburn hair was pulled back in a messy knot, bits of electric light catching a few strands like shattered stars. She shifted her weight a little, and he caught the tip of a leather boot peeking out underneath the hem of her skirts. He smiled. Of course, she'd eschew dainty slippers; and he'd have bet his life she had a sketchpad tucked away in that satchel of hers.

He wiped the smile off his face as soon as she turned

toward him with wide eyes and a bloodless face. Kase's heart sped up. "What's wrong?"

Hallie's hands shook as she smoothed the fabric of her skirt. "What do you know about everything that's happened?"

Kase ran a hand through his hair, his curls finally long enough to do so. Stars, he'd missed them. His mother had forced him to cut them upon his return, saying he looked like an unwashed heathen. "Not much. The Stradat Lord Kapitan was a little stingy with the details."

Hallie's face paled even further. "Someone came through the Gate."

"*What?*" A chill raced up his spine.

Saldr's voice was cloaked in emotion. "From talking with my people, I understand your friend, the one who fell through, is the one who came through. He destroyed our city with a great winged dragonar. The ones who are here..." He spread his hands out toward the Yalvs dotted around the room. "...they escaped through a Passage."

Hallie's knees gave out. Kase and Saldr caught her arms before she fell to the floor. Her voice was tight as she steadied herself, pulling out of their grip. "But the Lord Elder, he told me Ben didn't have the key, that the Essence who could control the Gate was dead."

Kase looked back at the others. They chatted quietly with one another. Some were crying; some slept with their lanky forms curled into balls in the uncomfortable, interconnected seats. What had happened to the others? Had they escaped through other Passages? Or was this...was this all that was left?

"Where is the Lord Elder?" Kase didn't want to think about Ben and what little he recalled from the night Zeke died. That wound was more painful than the sword-inflicted one. He rubbed his side where the scar should have been if not for Saldr's healing.

Saldr clenched a fist and brought it to his chest. "We believe he fell defending our city."

He took a moment to compose himself. Stars, what was the Lord Elder to him but a leader? Sure, Kase had been shocked upon their return to Kyvena to find Stradat Richter had been murdered, but he didn't get choked up over it. The Lord Elder had made Kase feel incredibly uncomfortable—not that he wanted him dead or anything. Hallie gripped her skirts tightly in her fists.

Saldr continued, his golden eyes bleary. "As for your question, Miss Walker, it's complicated and best explained seated."

Kase tilted his head and followed him over to a few seats near the corner of the room, away from the others. He sat on Hallie's other side and leaned forward, elbows on his knees, to hear what Saldr had to say.

"Your friend possesses another Essence power—one we had lost, but alas, he unlocked the Gate and its horrors." The Yalv bent forward, fingers laced.

Kase set his jaw against the overwhelming emotions coursing through his heart and mind. He breathed deeply through his nose, trying to calm himself. While he only remembered bits and pieces of that day, he did recall the fight with Ben. Kase knew there was something wrong with him. He'd acted possessed by something otherworldly, but Kase still couldn't forget his anger. Ben was the reason Zeke was now a pile of forgotten ash. "He's not my friend. Not anymore."

"Kase," Hallie squeaked, "you saw Ben, heard him. I don't think he *wanted* to become one."

"The Essence of Keys, while a pressing problem, is not the worst of it." Saldr's eyes didn't leave Hallie's. "The Essence power the Lord Elder possesses cannot fall into the wrong hands. To do so would be the destruction of our world. After Navara fled, another Chosen has yet to appear."

Hallie gasped, and Kase caught her startled look. He ran a hand through his hair. "I don't understand."

"Essence wielders pass on their power to their Chosen when they deem it acceptable—usually when the wielder has lived a long life and wishes to rejoin Toro in the skies. If the Essence wielder dies before they can pass it on, whether or not a Chosen has appeared, their power will be reborn into someone with Yalven ancestry."

"Is there a way to separate the Essence power from the wielder? Without losing the power to rebirth?" Hallie asked softly. "Or do you lose them both?"

Saldr looked between the two of them, then down at the floor. "If there is a way to separate the two, the knowledge would be hidden deep in the great library of Myrrai. Unfortunately, all the Passages have been destroyed."

Saldr took a deep, steadying breath. "Our people have fled fiery destruction, and we cannot hope to do anything more this evening. I was hoping someone would have secured lodging by now, but alas..."

Hallie's voice wobbled as she spoke, "We'll do whatever we can to help."

Before Saldr could respond, the door swung open once more, and an elderly, limping gentleman strode into the room with two men in the uniforms of the Watch—dark grey with the proper insignia embroidered on their right shoulders. The older man inspected the room.

Kase frowned. Why had ancient Loffler come? He was useless. Did his father believe the situation was not dire enough to appear himself?

"Good evening, Stradat." Kase greeted as the man approached. He shook his hand, two plain bronze-colored bracelets jingling at the older man's wrist. A tiny shock stung Kase.

"Oh dear," Loffler said with a laugh. "I apologize. I seem to shuffle more these days, causing static. Can't lift my old feet properly any longer."

He swatted at the pocket of his button-down shirt. "I've been sent this." He found it on the second try, fishing out a small slip of parchment. Its seal was broken. "Are you helping with the refugees, young lady?" Loffler wheezed, looking at Hallie.

Kase took the missive from the man and nodded to Hallie. "Miss Walker is the leading Yalven scholar at the University, and with Owen Christie not in the city...she's helping out tonight."

Kase caught her glance. She didn't mention his threat to blackmail the guard. Instead, she changed the topic as she gave a quick curtsy. "It's an honor to meet you, Stradat. Lord Saldr has been filling me in on what...what happened in Myrrai."

Kase noted the familiar seal, the swords bordering the four-pointed star. He ripped off the wax, surreptitiously letting it fall to the floor.

"A shame," Loffler said. He limped over to one of the seats

Kase, Hallie, and Saldr had vacated and lowered himself into it. Kase was certain he heard bones pop as he did so. "But what's done is done. No use worrying about it now."

Not even Kase would have been so callous. Neither Hallie nor Saldr spoke. Probably too shocked to know how to respond. Kase covered up his secondhand embarrassment by inspecting the parchment in his hand.

The message was without embellishments. The letters were square and strong. The ink itself seemed to radiate with power. It was the Stradat Lord Kapitan's handwriting.

Take the Yalvs to the Stradat Wing. We will acclimate them into Jaydian society with the help of the University within the next month.

Hallie found her voice. "I mean no disrespect, Stradat. But these people have lost their homes, family, and neighbors. I wouldn't say this is something to treat so flippantly."

Loffler looked up with hooded eyes. "Yes, yes. I didn't mean it that way. I just...well...great stars...young Shackley...what did the missive say?"

"Didn't you help...never mind," Kase fought the urge to roll his eyes. No wonder his father had relegated the man to messenger duty. "The Yalvs will be staying in the Stradat wing until they're acclimated."

"We are grateful for the kindness." Saldr stood and joined a few of his weary countrymen.

"Don't thank us yet," Loffler murmured as the Yalv walked away. He pushed himself out of the chair. "I'm needed back in the council chamber. Young Shackley, work with the guards to get them...well..."

And then he limped back toward the door, never finishing his sentence.

Shocks, that man should have retired ten years ago.

Kase rubbed the stubble on his cheeks before turning back to Hallie. "Let's get these poor people settled, all right? You and Saldr explain to the others what's going on."

Hallie stared for a moment but didn't say anything. Eventually she turned and walked toward the Yalvs.

The rest of the night passed in a dull blur, and three hours later, everyone was settled in their temporary housing. Kase didn't envy the lavish one-room apartments tucked into the private wing of the Jayde Center—overly stuffy and reminiscent of Shackley Manor. However, the refugees hadn't minded. Their hollow faces told Kase they were too worn out to care.

Kase closed the door of the final room and turned at the footsteps coming down the hall.

"Is that the last group?" Hallie asked as she trudged toward him. A few wayward auburn strands clung to her temple.

He nodded. "One family to each room, and the stragglers sharing—"

His own yawn cut him off. Hallie followed suit. "Stars, I'm exhausted, and I still have to walk back." She pressed her palms to her eyes. "But after everything from Saldr, I don't think I'm going to get any sleep even if I tried."

Kase put his hands in his pockets and started down the corridor. Hallie followed silently behind him. He peeked back at her. "I'll have Avery drop you off in the motorcoach. I've heard the lower city's been a little tempestuous as of late."

He'd heard of small skirmishes breaking out where the Watch had to intervene. Jove said something the other day about how they'd arrested at least three instigators who weren't talking much. Kase would rather Hallie not end up on the front page of the paper the next morning as a mugging victim—or worse.

"No, no, really, it's fine."

Kase stopped, and she bumped into him. He caught her arm before she fell.

"Oof, sorry," she said, pulling out of his grip and straightening her skirts.

"Hallie, I know you're not stupid enough to think you can walk alone down to the lower city this time of night."

Her eyes sparked. "I can take care of myself."

"I can see the circles underneath your eyes clear as day. Even your sharp tongue wouldn't be enough to fight off some disgusting lowlife. There are rumors of unrest after everything going on in Cerulene—some ridiculous rabble rousers calling themselves One World or something."

She closed her eyes and took a deep breath, but she didn't tell him off. Yet. Kase tried again. "Let Avery drive you. I swear not to say anything the entire way."

"Just take me home before I run out of the very little

patience I have left." She groaned, pulling at her satchel strap. Kase smirked. Same old Hallie.

"Let's go."

She followed him out of the Jayde Center's east entrance where he'd persuaded Saul to let them in. With a wicked grin and nod to the man, Kase led Hallie out and down the street to the alley where they'd left Avery.

"Like I said earlier, I'll have Jove push through your government identification. That way you can help with the refugees whenever you need—"

He stopped mid-sentence; because when they turned the corner of some nondescript government building Kase had never bothered to learn the name of, he found the alleyway empty. "Where'd he go?"

Hallie turned. "It's fine. I promise I'll be okay."

Her voice was exhausted and sounded very much like she did mind. Kase cursed. "Did that *helviter* of a father not realize I'd need a ride home, too?"

"Kase!"

He shook his head, ignoring her protestation of his language. He breathed deeply and tried to calm his bubbling anger rising to the surface.

Raging at the Stradat Lord Kapitan now would only mean he got to bed later. And Kase was blasting tired.

"Let's see if Avery is in front of the Jayde Center. Otherwise, we'll walk to the Manor and then let him take you home."

"But that will only take longer." Kase quirked an eyebrow, and she sighed loudly. "*Fine.* I'm too tired to argue with you anymore."

"I knew you'd come around if I bothered you enough."

She rolled her eyes. "Prat."

Kase grinned and led her back toward the Jayde Center. Once they'd passed through General Samuel McKenzie Square without any sign of the motorcoach, they made their way down the wide yet quiet avenue. While it was the most important in the city as it ran down to the front gates a few miles away, all the wealthy inhabitants were either out at the theater, some other entertainment venue—acceptable or not—or tucked in their lavish homes away from the lower city's filth.

The electric streetlamps cast flickering shadows on the ground as they walked. Kase tried not to focus too much on Hallie's silhouette. He barely recalled the moments before they'd entered the Gate chamber, but he did vaguely remember bumping heads, and...*shocks.*

His heart picked up speed.

"So..." Hallie started, "Is your father always like that?"

Well, that was one way to distract him. Kase grunted and put his hands in his pockets. "Worse."

Hallie pulled her coat further around her shoulders. The crisp chill of the February night made Kase long for summer. Hallie peeked over at him as they walked. "I don't envy you, then. Though he and my mother might get along."

Kase laughed despite himself. "That, I *highly* doubt."

"You don't know my mother."

"Come on, she can't be so bad. Believe me, the Stradat Lord Kapitan...well, I..." Kase coughed. "I'd rather not spoil this lovely frostbitten evening stroll talking about him."

Kase caught Hallie's reddened cheeks as she muttered, "Sorry. I never seem to know when to shut up. Especially when I'm tired."

Kase fiddled with the ring on his little finger, one of the only bits of Ana he had left. Thoughts of his father always led him back to her. "It's okay."

When she didn't respond, the silence pressed down upon him thick enough to cut with a soldier's sword. Kase wanted to say something, anything to shatter it, but he was at a loss. They had only bonded through their shared nightmare of an autumn, so what did they have in common other than books? What else did she like? He didn't think bringing up the Yalvs would be the smartest idea.

Kase wasn't one to bring home many ladies. There was a short fling with Stradat Richter's daughter, Lavinia. Jove had teased him endlessly about it. She was beautiful, but she'd cared more about her standing in society than anything else. Now that Kase thought about it, she probably only pretended to be interested in him because of who his father was. Blasted woman.

I shouldn't think things like that. Lavinia is dead.

Finding out the Cerls had assassinated Stradat Richter and

his entire family upon his and Hallie's return to Kyvena had been a shock. Yet, everything with Zeke had lessened that blow for him personally. His mother had cried for days after Kase's return.

Think of something else.

He glanced at Hallie. Her tall frame was strong, her shoulders pulled back. She walked with authority, yet her eyes told a different story. They darted from side to side, the dark circles more prominent in the light from the streetlamps. He cleared his throat. "So, read anything good lately?"

Better than discussing the weather, he guessed.

Hallie yawned. "I've been meaning to start a re-reading of *Frankenstein* by Mary Shelley soon, but Mazie and Nole have needed a good bit of help, so I haven't had the time."

A re-read of *Frankenstein*? Kase's heart leapt. "I always felt bad for the monster. He didn't ask for any of that, and I find the novel a fascinating look into First Earth culture. I also love *Le Morte d'Arthur*. Both are behind *The Odyssey*, of course."

Heat blossomed in his chest at her small smile aimed at him and her eyes bright.

Hallie leaned toward him. "Same here. I hate the way Arthur's story ends. But he kind of deserved what he got."

"Yeah, and the whole Lancelot thing...pretty ridiculous, if you ask me."

She nodded. "And Morgan le Fay? I still don't understand how she could betray Arthur like that. He was her brother..."

When she trailed off, he made sure she hadn't fallen behind or been kidnapped by some dirty *kretin*. Instead, she was frozen in place. Her eyes were wide, her mouth open in a silent gasp.

He rubbed the back of his neck and scuffed his boot against the cobblestones below. "Shackley Manor's a little over-the-top, I know." They'd reached the gates with their wrought iron bars and the stone griffins leering over the entrance. He'd always hated them. "I promise the terrifying griffins aren't real, they like to scare the commoners."

"You live here?" she squeaked, coming out of her temporary trance.

"Not by choice."

"I knew you were rich, but I didn't realize you were—" she

cut herself off at his look.

He was glad the night was dark and hoped the streetlamps didn't pick up the blush spreading up his neck. He waved to the guard through the swirling pattern of the gate. "Father forgot I'd ridden with him to the Jayde Center."

Within a minute, the head guard was there with his key and two-toned brown hair. "The Stradat Lord Kapitan has yet to return with Chauffeur Avery."

He unlocked the gate and gestured to one of his men, both grasping the handles and pulling hard. The swirling designs parted, leaving a sizable opening.

His father hadn't returned yet? But then where was the car?

"Are you sure?" Kase asked, rubbing his stubble. "Avery wasn't there, and I couldn't—holy moons. Give me a moment." He turned to Hallie, who had caught sight of the Manor beyond. He scratched his cheek. "As lavishly wealthy as my family is, we don't have a second motorcoach."

She shook her head, her shoulders slumping, and tore her gaze away from the towering estate. "Kase, I could have been halfway there by now."

He held up his hands. Where had his father gone? Why hadn't he come home? "Listen, I'll still walk you. I couldn't live with myself if something happened." He pulled out his new pocket watch, as the other one had perished on the *Eudora Jayde*'s fall from the trees, and popped open the cover. "Actually, it's nearly half-past eleven. I have an idea."

She crossed her arms.

He shook his head. "Stay here for the night. As you can guess, we have an abundance of guest rooms."

She looked down, fiddling with her skirts. "But I have work."

"Avery can take you down in the morning."

If he returns.

Hallie chewed her lip. "I feel like it'd be breaking one of those ridiculous rules of propriety you wealthy people worship."

"Why?"

"Because...I don't know. Stars, I'm so tired."

"Blast the rules. Besides, did you miss the part where I said we have plenty of rooms? It's not like you'd have to share one with—ahem." His ears were on fire at the thought. "Hallie, listen. We're both exhausted. It's late. But if you're really determined, we can either wait until my father returns, or I'll walk you down. But you're not going back alone. Don't argue on that point any further. You won't win."

Even if I just want to crawl in bed and stay there for the next three centuries.

He glanced at the gate guards. They stood alert, hands at their sides like the well-trained soldiers they were. No emotion. Nothing. Hallie looked at Kase at last and waved her hand dismissively toward the mansion. "There'd better not be a gremlin or whatever in my room, watching me sleep. With all that money, couldn't you get different statues to lord over your gates?"

Kase laughed. "It could be worse, believe me. You should see what Lord Stephenson's got over his fireplace in the dining hall. I still haven't decided whether it's a bear or rather ugly wolf."

She mumbled something incoherent as Kase led her through the gates and up the short drive. After knocking on the door, Kase nodded to the butler when he responded. The foyer was dark as they stepped inside, lit only with the candle the spindly man held in long, skeletal fingers. Kase had yet to meet a Rubikan without the latter.

"Avery seems to be with my father still, and I didn't want Miss Walker to walk home this late." His words were rushed, but he didn't know what else to say; something about the appraising look the old butler adopted when he'd spotted Hallie bothered Kase. He couldn't quite place his finger on why, though.

"Of course, I believe the Bellefgrad Suite is prepared. Shall I escort her?"

Kase shook his head. "No need. Please, Thoreau, go to bed and rest. You've been up too long, I'm certain."

Butler Thoreau handed off the candle holder and bowed. "Of course. Goodnight, Master Kase."

Kase took the light and ground his teeth, but he was too tired to correct him for the thousandth time. He held out his other arm. "We have to be quiet. Your room is in the family wing, and Mother's a stickler about her sleep when she can get it."

Hallie's hand grasped the crook of his elbow, and he led her up the slick marble staircase and down the corridor to the family's suites off the first landing. The faint light from the candle spread out before them as their boots tapped lightly on the polished floor.

"Don't you have electricity in a fancy place like this?" she whispered, her breath tickling his ear.

He suppressed a shiver. "The Stradat Lord Kapitan refuses to have it in the house. I think he's simply touched in the head."

"Listen, I understand you might not get along with your father, but he is one of the *highest-ranking members of the government*, in case you weren't aware."

Kase fought the irritation spilling into his bloodstream like a waterfall. They were both exhausted and on edge with everything they'd learned that day. The Yalvs. Ben.

He took a deep breath. "I'm aware, and he makes sure I know it. Now, I'd appreciate it if you'd leave it alone."

Hallie took her hand from his arm. Kase turned toward her, ready for whatever else she might throw at him. She clasped her hands tightly and refused to meet his eyes. "Sorry. You're letting me stay here so I don't get mugged or anything, and here I am lecturing you on how to live your life."

Kase held out his arm once more. "As long as you realize you're being a *dulkop*, I'll accept your apology."

"Just this once."

Kase nodded as she joined him once more. In soft silence only broken by their footsteps, they turned the corner into the family wing. A faint beam of light streamed from a cracked door ahead.

"Blast," he muttered softly.

Hallie tilted her head. "What is it?"

His finger was rough against his lips as he held it there and shook his head. He unwound her hand from his elbow and set the candle on the floor. Kase stepped with light feet toward the opening and with the air of a thief, peeked around the door frame.

His mother with her dark curls generously streaked with glistening silver sipped tea on a plush settee, a book in her lap, floor-to-ceiling mahogany shelves bursting with volumes of all shapes and sizes stretching out behind her. She still wore her jewel encrusted dinner gown. Her blue eyes were intent on the passage in front of her, and if Kase was quiet enough, she wouldn't notice him passing by. Hopefully.

He motioned to Hallie in the near darkness.

"What are you..." she whispered, but the leather of his jacket creaked with his exaggerated arm motions to get her to stop mid-sentence.

"Harlan? Is that you?" his mother asked from the room beyond.

Hallie joined him, and Kase closed his eyes. *Wonderful. Why is Mother blessed with the hearing of a bat?*

He mouthed, *Stay here*, before stepping into his mother's personal library.

She hadn't even looked up from her book. The solitary lantern on the side table cast a golden glow on her unblemished skin. Kase folded his hands behind his back. "It's me, Mother."

She set down her still-steaming teacup on the side table carved with peacocks and held up her book. "I was waiting for you and your father, but I got distracted examining this latest find. The book dealer said it was a genuine First Earth edition of *The Scarlet Letter*, but I have my doubts."

A gasp echoed in the hallway, and Kase winced as his mother paused. He should've known Hallie couldn't keep her mouth shut if books were involved. He cleared his throat. "Um, with it being so late and all...Hallie? You can come in."

His mother raised manicured eyebrows as she closed the book and set it next to the cup of tea. Kase turned when Hallie entered. The scholar had one hand tangled up in the strap of her satchel as she tried to curtsy. If Kase hadn't been so tense, he might've laughed. Not out of derision, but because there wasn't any need to curtsy to his mother.

Waving her hand, his mother stood from her chair. "Oh, please don't trouble yourself with that nonsense."

"My name is Hallie Walker, ma'am, I mean Your Grace...or...um, I know your husband is the Stradat Lord Kapitan, but I'm not sure how I should...I'm terribly sorry for barging in and..."

This time Kase couldn't help the laugh escaping his lips. Hallie glared at him, and he grinned. "Hallie, this is my mother,

Lady Celeste Shackley."

"*Hallie, is it?*" His mother asked with a smile as Kase stumbled a little at her words. "It seems as if my son is on first-name terms with you, I see."

"It's not what you think, Mother," he explained, the heat radiating up from his core and catching his neck in its blaze. One slip of his tongue and his incredibly old-fashioned, high-society mother leapt at the opportunity. "Hallie...er...Miss Walker was on the *Eudora* mission with me, and we were both at the Jayde Center helping with refugees and it was late and Father has the motorcoach and I didn't want her walking home this late and..."

His mother strode up to him and patted his cheek softly, halting his babbling. "It's not a bad thing, dear. Now, Miss Walker, please call me Les. No need for all the other highfalutin titles in my home."

Hallie's face was as red as the plush rug she stood upon, but she relaxed the hold on her satchel. "Thank you, ma'am, I mean...Les. And please, I'm just Hallie. I didn't mean to impose or anything, but Kase, Master Shackley, or, um, he wouldn't let it—um, I mean, I tried to tell him I'd be fine walking home."

"It's all right, dear. I'm happy to meet you. My son isn't one to talk much, but he's mentioned you in such a positive light I wondered when I'd finally meet the woman who has—"

Kase interrupted before she could finish the sentence. "Mother, we're both tired, and we want to get some sleep. Hal...Miss Walker has classes to attend tomorrow, being a University student and all."

If Hallie's face could get any redder, she would have combusted then and there, Kase was sure. He knew his had blown past that point five minutes ago.

Hallie started to speak up, but she quickly turned whatever it was she was about to say into a cough. "Yes, I sincerely apologize, but I really am about to fall asleep on my feet. Not that our conversation is boring or anything."

His mother laughed. "I'll let my Kase show you to your room, and I look forward to conversing with you more at breakfast. Sleep well, dear. It's been a pleasure to meet you at last."

If Kase could have fallen through the floor, he would have

readily accepted his demise. He was nearly twenty-two years old for moons-sake, and his mother still acted as if he were seventeen.

He quickly strode over to Hallie and held out his arm. "Night, Mother."

She nodded and sat back down, pulling her tea and book into her lap once more.

If she's waiting for the Stradat Lord Kapitan to come home any time soon, I have a feeling she'll be waiting a while.

CHAPTER 4

BLASTED STONE

Hallie

HALLIE THOUGHT PETRA'S ROOM AT the Lieber Townhouse was extravagant with its draped canopy bed and silk embroidered curtains, but the Bellefgrad Suite at Shackley Manor put all that to shame. For one, it had its own name. That in and of itself was rather ridiculous, but the floors of polished stone, upholstered and gold-trimmed walls, and chandelier in the shape of a six-tiered cake dripping in diamonds almost made her sick to the stomach. *All that money for a guest suite.* Because it was indeed a suite, complete with its own bathing room and balcony.

However, the fine decor wasn't enough to distract her from the thoughts that kept her up most of the night. The events from the previous day played like a First Earth picture show through her mind until the earliest morning hours. The Yalvs' haggard faces were at the forefront, coupled with the immense guilt of knowing that, by pushing Ben through the Gate, she had caused their distress.

That brought on another host of questions. Was the Essence why Ben betrayed them? Or had he always been a spy for Cerulene? How had he brought a dragonar through the Gate?

And here Hallie was sleeping on silk sheets. Guilt filled her stomach like lead.

The whole conversation with Kase's mother made everything worse. Gracious day, his mother probably thought they'd start courting any day now. Hallie's heart thumped in her chest. It was a ridiculous notion, right? Kase said he barely remembered anything that happened on the night of the Cerl attack. Surely, he didn't remember the almost kiss. Surely, he wouldn't want to court *her*. Hallie was well beneath his social standing. But his mother said he'd mentioned her before, and...well, she hadn't gotten much sleep regardless.

And it doesn't look like I will.

She sat up and stretched, her muscles aching from the hike through the city and lack of sleep. Might as well check out the adjoining bath if she had the time. When else would she get the chance to stay in such lavish arrangements?

Pink fragmented light laced with the gold of sunrise crawled across the floor from the double doors of the balcony. Hopefully, the Shackleys weren't the sort to eat breakfast at the crack of dawn.

She threw off the duvet cover, and as her feet landed on the cold floor, she winced. "Are wooden floors too good for the rich? Blasted stone."

Hobbling over to the bathing room, she peeked out the balcony doors. The grass and tree limbs were glittering with frost. Tempting. She'd go out after her bath. If only she could sketch the scene.

Phantom pain flashed in her Vasa-healed hand. No, she wouldn't sketch it.

After soaking in lavender-infused bath water, she dressed in her pretty clothes from the night before. She would change before she went back up to the—no, she wouldn't be able to get into the Jayde Center without identification. Hadn't Kase said he would talk to Jove that morning and get her the papers? She wouldn't dare allow Kase to blackmail another guard.

Slipping on her boots, she stood and tied her hair up into a loose ladies' bun. Glancing in the mirror, she tried to ignore the dark circles underneath her eyes. Maybe one day they'd disappear.

Pulling open the dainty glass-paned doors, the crisp air of early morning stole through her lungs and came out as small puffs hovering above her lips, but the view was worth the chill. They were in the middle of the city, and yet, the Shackley family had made it feel as if she were in a forgotten wonderland. Each tree was dressed in robes of ice from the morning frost and sparkled in the sunlight. If she were to walk down the little path below, the blades of grass would crunch under her boots with each step.

What would it be like when spring arrived in a month? Would daisies and daffodils line the little trails through the trees? Would those trees reach to the sky with their budding leaves?

A slight cough broke her reverie, and she jumped. To her left was another balcony not ten feet away, where Kase stood. He wasn't wearing a jacket, but he was nearly dressed for an estate dinner. His slacks were dark and held up by matching suspenders over his white collared shirt, and if she was seeing things correctly, he was barefoot.

"Um, good morning," Hallie said at last. Kase waved and then frowned.

"Did you not see the wardrobe in your room? I'm sure you can find something so you don't have to wear your old clothes."

Hallie shook her head. "No, it's fine. I'll go home and change after breakfast."

"Suit yourself."

"Where are your shoes?" Her teeth chattered as she spoke.

Kase shrugged. "It's not too bad. Anyway, I'll show you down to the dining room in a few minutes. Don't want you to get lost."

"If your house wasn't so big, that might not be an issue, Lord Pilot."

"Very funny," Kase said with a roll of his eyes. "Be there in a second."

With that, he went back inside and shut the balcony doors with a muffled thump. Was he right next door? The thought he'd been so close sent a rush of heat through her body, which was stupid as they'd slept a room away while on their mission. Good stars. She hadn't noticed last night because as soon as he'd shown her into the chamber, she'd immediately run over and fallen face first onto the bed. It'd been nice for about three seconds until her anxieties had taken over.

She stepped back into her room and looked at the silk-canopied bed. Maybe one day, her brain would let her actually *sleep* in one like it.

After a barely audible knock on the door, Hallie strode over and tugged the heavy wood open. Kase stood in the hallway, his shoes adding an inch or two to his height. He was still a head taller than she.

Hallie raised a brow. "Do you always dress up for breakfast?"

Kase snorted. "When I don't have flight training. And I have impeccable taste, thank you very much."

"But no frock coat?"

"I said I had *impeccable* taste."

Hallie couldn't conceal her grin. This was a side to him she hadn't seen before. It also looked like he'd attempted to tame his curls by the way his hair was slightly wet on top, except a tuft still stuck up on the right side. It didn't help when he ran a hand through them before holding out his arm.

"Such a gentleman," Hallie teased, taking it. His muscles tensed a little at her touch, and she tried to ignore the uptick in her pulse. She *was* tired. "So, what've you told your mother about me? You didn't tell her how I slapped you that one time or anything?"

"*Twice.* You slapped me twice if I recall," Kase mumbled, and led her down the corridor. "Though the second time is still a little blurry."

Hallie's fingers around his arm flexed. Of course. "Sorry about that. I didn't know what to do to snap you out of...out of..."

"It's all right. I'd have done the same thing if I were you."

Hallie took a breath. "And how are...um, how are you doing? With everything? Zeke?"

"Fine."

His curt response brought back the memory of his breakdown and subsequent confession over his sister. Why couldn't she shut up? Of course, he wouldn't want to talk about it.

They continued in silence, so Hallie took the opportunity to inspect the paintings on the walls, interspersed with candlelit sconces carved with leaves and possibly berries of some sort. One particular portrait caught her eye. It was of a girl who looked to be a few years younger than Hallie, with soft blonde hair and the clearest blue eyes. She wasn't smiling in the portrait, only staring straight ahead like a queen on a gilded throne. The background held a library of books Hallie wished she could read.

Hallie hadn't realized she'd stopped to stare until her arm fell from Kase's. She ran a finger along the gilded frame. Maybe it was the way her nose sloped and turned up slightly at the end, but the younger woman reminded her of Kase. "This is Ana, isn't it?"

When Kase didn't say anything, she looked at him. He twisted something on his finger and, after a moment, met her eyes. His voice was soft when he spoke, "It was painted before my parents announced her betrothal."

Betrothal? How old had she been? Sixteen? Seventeen? Barely old enough to be out on her own.

"Whoever did the painting was a brilliant artist," Hallie whispered as Ana's eyes stared into her soul, much like she felt the Lord Elder's had. "It almost looks as if she's on the other side of a window, not immortalized in brush strokes."

Kase nodded. "Mother would only hire the best, of course. Too bad it doesn't show a bit of her personality."

Hallie tilted her head. "What do you mean?"

"Contrary to the painting, she wasn't ever that serious." Kase held out his arm, and Hallie took it once more. "She was the most spirited person I knew. Though, I guess you could give her a run for her money."

Hallie chewed on the inside of her cheek. She couldn't tell if he was complimenting her or not, but she felt like he might've been. In a rather awkward, strange way. "I would say I'm more annoying than spirited."

Kase chuckled and led her along the winding corridor. "Ana was so alive and willing to see the good in everyone. You're like that, too. I treated you like scum, and yet, you were still kind. Well, most of the time."

"You didn't make it easy."

"It's a talent of mine to be as difficult as possible, as I'm sure Jove or Mother will tell you."

"Doesn't surprise me," Hallie said with a small laugh, but then she stopped cold. They'd reached the top of the grand staircase with its shining steps and gilded railing. About to leave through the front door was the Stradat Lord Kapitan with his straight-edge mustache and pressed uniform.

She peeked at Kase in her peripheral vision. His jaw had tightened, but he only hesitated a moment before descending the steps.

The butler opened the door. Kase's father exited through it with barely a cursory glance at his son. The exchange made arguments with her mother seem like mere banter, and neither had said a word.

Kase was silent the rest of the way down the stairs and through a corridor that ended in a set of towering double doors. They reminded Hallie of the gates out front with their carved, swirling patterns and the impressions of griffins near the handles. The eagle talons on each looked sharp enough to cut Hallie into bite-sized pieces and skewer each one for a rather grotesque kabob.

"Why the griffins?" she asked as a nearby servant reached for the door. Apparently opening a door on their own was such a travesty in such a prestigious household. She wondered if a servant had indeed laced up Kase's boots.

Kase ran a hand through his hair. "Some dead ancestor found them particularly intriguing after reading Johan's Nahamika Tales of the Absurd. Have you read it?"

"Not my cup of tea." Hallie vaguely remembered the griffins, but the gory, ludicrously-described deaths of the main characters had been a more prominent theme in the story collection.

"Mine either, but it proves my love of literature goes back perhaps entirely too far."

The dining table in the room beyond was miles long, and the ceiling soared above her head. A row of windows to her left overlooked the gardens she'd glimpsed from her balcony. The chandelier above was lit with candles, wax dripping down the sides and collecting in the awaiting saucers beneath each, and near the center of the table sat Lady Les, hands folded neatly in her lap.

She looked up and smiled, the diamond drops hanging from her ears glittering as she moved. She wore a fine gown with a soft green maiden belt wrapped around her waist. Hallie's own mother wore the matron belt when she went into town, but it was made from dyed cotton; Lady Les' looked to be of the finest silk.

Hallie tugged at her own humble clothes and wished she'd taken Kase's advice and worn something from the wardrobe. Peeking at the hem of her skirt, a mud stain or two mocked her. She didn't belong here.

"Good morning, Kase, Miss Walker. Please, have a seat," Les said and gestured to the ones across from her. "Breakfast isn't as grand as usual because I have my staff working hard on the menu for an upcoming estate dinner."

With smooth grace she hadn't thought possible from him, Kase pulled out her chair, and once she was seated, pushed it in slightly. Her stomach lurched again. This wasn't normal. Kase didn't pull chairs out for her. And no normal person wore diamond drops in their ears to breakfast.

Once Kase seated himself to her right. Les gestured to a servant at the edge of the room, and within a minute, a man dressed in an immaculate deep-green uniform jacket with gold buttons up the sides served Hallie some sort of pastry with a perfectly golden-brown crust like her mother's. A woman in a matching uniform ladled fruit, eggs, and vegetables onto her plate with dainty silver spoons. The final servant poured black tea into a cup at her left side. Steam rose in little swirls to the ceiling above.

"Cream and sugar, Miss?" the man asked.

Hallie shook her head, and the man retreated with the teapot. Another set a tray overflowing with cheeses and breads in front of her.

Were they planning on feeding an entire village?

As her stomach rumbled loud enough for everyone to hear, she realized she'd neglected dinner the previous evening. Kase laughed, and his mother smiled while taking an impossibly dainty sip of tea.

"My apologies," Hallie mumbled as she balled her hands in

her lap.

Lady Les waved her words away. "Please, don't apologize."

Hallie took up her knife and fork, both polished enough to catch a glimpse of her reflection in their surfaces. She cut off a piece of the pastry and placed the morsel in her mouth. Tangy, sweet berries married with a hint of brown sugar exploded on her tongue. *Mazelberries.*

They were nearly as good as her mother's.

She swallowed the knot that had formed in her throat as well as the pastry. "This is delicious. It might even compete with my mother's turnovers."

Kase took a large bite of his, a few flakes catching on his stubble. His eyebrows disappeared into his curls. "Has Omer been holding out on us?"

His mother smiled and rested her wrists on the edge of the tablecloth, her utensils still clasped in her delicate fingers. "Omer heard about a woman in the Nardens who kept winning a competition for the best turnovers and jam. Last fall, he went in search of her and tried to pry the recipe out of her, but she wouldn't budge. He's been trying to recreate it."

Hallie choked on her hot tea, spilling some on her plate. She set the cup down and turned away to cough.

Lady Les was staring at her in surprise. Kase's mouth was open, his fork hovering in front of it.

Hallie coughed once more. "That would've been my mother. She refuses to even tell me the recipe. Did you say he went last fall?"

That would've been when Hallie was away on the *Eudora* mission. Could she pry information from the chef? How long had he tried to persuade her mother into giving him the recipe?

"Yes, but he returned before all this nasty business with Cerulene started."

Kase set his pastry on his plate. "But your cooking is terrible. There's no way your mother could be so accomplished."

"Kase!" His mother gasped. "That's no way to treat our guest!"

He brushed crumbs from his mouth. "I was being honest, Mother."

Lady Les put her hand over her eyes as Hallie's cheeks

burned. Trying to break the awkward silence that had descended over the table, Hallie cleared her throat. "He's not wrong. I'm quite hopeless."

Les lifted her head. "I apologize for my son's behavior. He tends to forget his manners at the most inconvenient of times."

Hallie snorted, and when she realized what she'd done, she slapped her hands over her mouth. Mother of ash, why must she always embarrass herself?

Kase chuckled. "You keep forgetting I'm not Zeke—I mean..."

He trailed off as Hallie caught the pain whispering across the elegant lady's fine-boned features. Setting her silverware aside, Les blinked before she met Hallie's eyes. "I had hoped with a dignified lady such as yourself in the room, my son would at least pretend he had manners, but it seems I must apologize once more."

Hallie's gaze flitted over to where Kase gripped his utensils hard enough to leave lines in his palms. She looked back down at the food she'd barely touched. She no longer felt hungry. "Thank you, but really, it's fine."

The rest of breakfast was marred by tension. Kase's mother asked about Hallie's studies, responding good-naturedly when she mentioned she wanted to open a school after graduation, but talking about the University only made everything worse. Hallie could only keep up the lies for so long.

"I'm so sorry, but I really must be going. I need to get ready before work this afternoon." Hallie folded her napkin and set it beside the plate. Even with the distraction Les provided, Hallie hadn't been able to get the thoughts of her family out of her mind. "Thank you so much for allowing me to stay the night, and for this wonderful breakfast."

Lady Les smiled, her eyes crinkling. "Of course, dear! I do hope you'll be back soon."

She stared pointedly at her son silently pushing the food around on his plate. At his mother's cough, he looked up and sighed. "I'll escort you."

Hallie stood and shook her head. "No, it's all right. Plenty of people will be out and about at this hour."

"At least let me walk you to the door."

Kase asked a servant to fetch Hallie's satchel and coat from her room. She made it to the door before him and reached for the handle, but it moved on its own accord. Servants, of course.

Hallie walked down the corridor, Kase following in silence until she came to an intersection.

"Listen. I'm sorry if I embarrassed you back there. That wasn't my intention at all."

Hallie closed her eyes and tried to quell her emotions. Kase's fists were clenched as he stared at his boots. The soft leather shone in the dim candlelight.

"It's fine." A little snippy, but it was the best she could do in her current state.

"I just...all this..." he waved his hand at their surroundings, "...it drains me. I don't want it. *Any of it.*"

"That has nothing to do with breakfast."

Running a hand through his hair and down his face, he looked much older than twenty-one. "But it's why I—never mind."

She took a deep breath. It wasn't Kase's fault. Not really. "Listen, show me out, and I'll be on my way."

With a nod, Kase led her to the left and into the cavernous foyer. The chandelier was lit, but the sunlight cascading through the window brightened the room better than it ever could. A servant stood by the door with her jacket and satchel in hand. *They're quick.*

Kase nodded to the man and turned to Hallie. "You said you'd be at the University today? If by some miracle Jove is able to push the documentation through, I could run by and give it to you."

The servant opened the door, but Hallie stopped on the threshold. Kase didn't know. "I didn't go back this semester. I...I just couldn't."

Kase's eyes were earnest as he pulled her back inside. "What about graduation?"

She tugged her hand out of his grip and looked anywhere but at him. Her eyes found the portrait she'd spotted the previous night. The entire Shackley family was arranged around a raven-haired Les, who sat stiffly in a plush red armchair. The Stradat Lord Kapitan stood behind her, his hands folded on the back of his wife's chair, the edges of his lips pulled down into a permanent frown. She picked out Kase immediately; his wild hair hadn't changed one bit. He looked to be about eight. His hand clasped Ana's shoulder in front of him. To the other side stood Jove, his proud chest puffed out, his blue eyes serious. Last was Zeke, his slight smile standing out from everyone else's somber expressions. The smile of a ghost.

"Hallie? Why'd you quit the University?"

She turned back to Kase, her shoulders sagging from exhaustion. "I couldn't do it. After everything."

"Hallie..."

She held up a hand. "Thank you for your hospitality, but I need to get home."

With that, she stepped out the door into the chilly February morning.

CHAPTER 5

FROZEN IN CARBONITE

Kase

IF KASE COULD HAVE GOTTEN out of the Manor as easily as Jove had, he would have considered getting married to the first interested party. But all the women who'd tried to wedge their way into his life were dull, nonsensical, or only wanted the prestigious Shackley name to wave about like a jewel-encrusted flag. Kase wanted someone who'd wait twenty years for him to find his way home after war and peril. He did know a Penelope, but she was sixty-four and had survived three husbands, the last one being Stradat Millicent Sarson's predecessor. Nothing like Odysseus' wife.

Jove had always been the lucky one. While Zeke had been the family favorite after Ana's death, it was Jove who'd earned respect from their father for his work in the Watch. Kase had never understood why Jove had gone into government work, but he understood his decision to get out from underneath Harlan's thumb. What had Jove thought when their father took up the mantle of Stradat upon Forrest Carson's death? He guessed it was one of the factors leading to Jove's resignation.

Jove had yet to divulge the true reason—not that Kase pushed him on the subject.

When Kase and Hallie had returned to Kyvena with Zeke's body in tow, they'd gone straight to Jove's townhouse. Kase hadn't known what else to do. His stomach roiled at the memory of shaking and sweating in the chilly December afternoon. Cracked knuckles rapping on the door, a prayer whispered that his brother was at home. Jove answered, saw Kase, and then the cart behind him...Later, Clara painted a forest landscape to hang over the hole Jove had punched in the wall.

Kase shook his head to dispel the memory, finding himself again at his brother's door. The townhouse exterior was plain with its brown brick facade, but Jove had chosen it, and Kase admired him for that decision.

He knocked on the thick wooden door. Carved stars and moons adorned the corners of its frame; Clara's artistic hand was evident in every detail.

After a few seconds, the door opened. It was the maid whose name Kase always had trouble remembering — possibly Rissa or Missy or perhaps even Lizzie. She smiled and bobbed her head as she curtsied. "Good morning, Master Kase. Please come inside; Lord Shackley is expecting you."

After nearly a week of waiting for the papers to be finalized, Jove better had been expecting him. To think he'd told Hallie it might've been done in a day. Stars-blasted bureaucracy.

Kase dipped his head in response and entered. The two-story living space had a tall ceiling and an open-to-below. Although the large black-trimmed windows were frosted for privacy, sunlight filtered through the glass and bathed the furniture—a well-loved davenport and assorted leather armchairs–in gold. Kase could almost see himself reading in front of the immaculate brick fireplace that soared up and vanished into the dark ceiling.

Her paintbrush held aloft, Clara sat in front of an easel near one of the windows. Her stomach had grown considerably in the time Kase had been home. That had been a surprise when he'd arrived. To think a miniature version of Jove would be running amuck soon made Kase uneasy. The little tike would berate their uncle every chance he or she got.

Clara set down her brush. "Good morning, Kase. Jove is in his study."

"Painting another landscape?"

"Well," Clara said, rubbing her belly as she studied her canvas, "I was going to see if Jove would let me visit my parents' country estate, because I want to paint a particular tree in the rose garden that should be blooming any day now, but he's worried about the baby. I'm contenting myself with what I remember."

"Sounds like him."

Clara chuckled. "Maybe I'll convince him yet."

At that moment, Jove's face appeared from behind the mahogany door of his private study on the far side of the room. Kase nodded to Clara, who picked up her paintbrush again. He strode toward his brother.

"I'm here to pick up Hallie's papers." He didn't feel like staying and chatting. All the conversations he'd had with his eldest brother since returning had been overshadowed with the weight of everything they'd lost.

Jove gave him the look, the one that made it seem as if his right eye was twitching. "*Fine.*"

Kase followed his brother into the study. Jove shut the door behind him. "Want some Scotch?" Jove walked over to the little cart in the corner of the room and picked up a bottle, swishing it a little. "Just enough for a glass."

Kase plopped down into a tufted leather chair in front of the desk and slouched. "It's only eleven in the morning."

Jove scooped out a bit of ice with a tiny shovel. The clinking of the cubes hitting the bottom of the glass was almost deafening in the still room.

Kase rubbed his forehead. "I don't have time to watch you drink yourself into oblivion."

Jove swirled the contents and took a swig. He smacked his lips and leaned back against the wood desk. "I have something to ask you."

Kase pulled himself up and leaned forward on the right arm of the chair. "Ask away, and then I'll take the papers. Thank you for pushing them through, by the way."

Except it took a week.

Jove took another sip. "I'm not sure why she wasn't given them when you all returned. Good thing Heddie always liked me."

High Guardswoman Heddie Koppen was one of the very few bureaucrats Kase tolerated. She was blunt and never needed to hear something twice before she got the task done. "Thank her for me, then."

"You'll see her at the dinner next Friday." Jove finished off the rest of his drink and set it down with a hard smack, the ice rattling.

"That's if I go." Kase ran a hand through his curls. "Don't think I've ever seen anyone drink Scotch that quickly unless someone dared them."

His brother raised a brow. "I just needed a pick-me-up." He wiped his lips with the back of his hand. "And Father will notice if you aren't there."

"Whatever." Kase eyed the empty bottle over on the cart. "So, what's your question?"

Jove clasped his fingers in front of him. He was silent for a moment before he finally looked up, his eyes sober and piercing. "With everything going on in the world right now, I don't know what the next month will look like, much less the next day. Things are happening, and even though I'm no longer High Guardsman, I still hear about them."

Kase ground the toe of his boot into the plush rug. "What do you mean? I thought Achilles' troops pushed the Cerls back across the border."

"And once the weather turns, they'll try it again. Father wanted to go in and assassinate—well, it doesn't matter now." Jove stopped himself and focused on his hands again. "Forget I said that."

"You can't say something like that and not explain."

Jove refused to look Kase in the eye. "Listen, the point I'm trying to make is, with the unrest growing, it's only a matter of time before it all comes crashing down. And with Clara due soon, I've had a lot to consider lately."

Kase groaned inwardly. Leave it to dramatic, self-important Jove to draw this out. It's not like Kase had all the time in the world. He needed to drop off Hallie's papers, pray she didn't slap him for stars knew what, and then squeeze in a little training before getting a jacket fitted for the aforementioned estate dinner—if he decided to go. Instead, Jove droned on about impending doom and gloom; they were par for the course. Did he not realize Kase lived with that every day? "And this affects me how?"

Jove tapped his thumbs together. "Clara and I have been talking, and if something were to happen to us...well, we want to ask you if you'd...you know, if you'd be our little boy or girl's godfather."

Godfather? Jove wanted *Kase* to raise his kid if he died? "Have you lost your ever-twinkling mind?"

"I wouldn't say I've *lost* it necessarily."

"What makes you think I could be a remotely decent father?"

"Well, you see—"

"After all we went through growing up with that blasted *helviter,* and you think I can—I just—" Kase swallowed. His voice choked. He didn't know what a good father did or what they even looked like. How could Kase even imagine being one himself?

Jove slid off the desk and gripped Kase's leather-clad shoulder. "I'm not planning on dying anytime soon, but I want to be prepared. Just in case... just in case the worst does happen. We were going to ask both you and Zeke, but well...now, it's just you."

Jove's grip tightened with his words. His eyes were glassy, but it wasn't only from the alcohol. "You'll be a stars-blasted good father because you know exactly what *not* to do."

His words shook at the beginning but solidified upon reaching the end.

His hand slid from Kase's shoulder, and he turned away, looking out the frosted window. Kase put his face in his hands. "I don't know, Jove. Even the thought just..."

Jove peeked over his shoulder. "Scares you out of your mind? You're not alone, I promise you that." He opened one of his desk drawers and shuffled through a few sheets, the crinkling of papers breaking up the silence. He selected one and inspected it before holding it out. "Other than Clara, I can't think of anyone else I'd want raising my child besides you."

Kase's stomach dropped out. "*Me?* You trust me that much?"

"There's a reason I sent *you* on that mission. No matter how hardheaded you are."

Kase worked his jaw and took the paper, catching sight of Hallie's name in bold calligraphy strokes. He folded it and tucked it inside his jacket. Walking toward the door, he paused, one clammy hand grasping the knob.

He half turned. "I just—I don't think I can—" He took a breath. Two. Three. "I can't be the godfather, Jove. I'm not the person you seem to think I am."

With that, he stepped out and closed the door behind him, shutting out Jove's reaction.

KASE DIDN'T BOTHER CALLING A motorcoach to take him down to the lower city. He hoped the crisp air would clear his head after that conversation. He needed his wits about him when he faced Hallie; they hadn't spoken since breakfast with his mother, and Jove always found a way to irritate him.

Godfather?

If Kase hadn't been so flustered by the question, he might have laughed right in his brother's face. It was nonsensical that anyone could think Kase was qualified to do anything of the sort. He was already nervous about being an uncle. A part of him wanted to teach the little runt how to annoy Jove best, but the other part was terrified he'd contaminate it in some way, and that it'd grow to be as messed up as Kase was.

Kase wove through the crowded streets and the bustling market square. Was it just him, or were there even more people than usual? He'd have thought the threat of all-out war would scare people into staying locked up in their homes, but it seemed to have the opposite effect.

He shrugged his way through, bumping shoulders with more than one person, trying to find his way to the teashop.

They still hadn't put up street signs in since he'd last gone through the market square. Blasting ridiculous. After asking a few shop owners, Kase finally found his way to Havron's Tea and Cafe after taking only three wrong turns.

Conversation swirled around him as he walked, and he caught bits and pieces. Some were worried about a potential draft. Some wondered if the Silver Coast would become involved if war did break out. Kase grimaced. Neither sounded good. Especially the draft. He'd become a pilot because he hadn't wanted to join the Regulars, but that would change if the Stradat Lord Kapitan had his way.

Patting the pocket where he'd stuffed Hallie's identification papers, Kase took a deep breath and opened the arched door.

The teashop's main room was quaint and lined with floor to ceiling bookshelves along the walls. Each shelf had various knick-knacks that Kase would expect to find somewhere in the University's museum, like fossilized fish skeletons and flowers. A little absurd. Several plants, not immortalized in stone, draped over the lips of shelves like twisted waterfalls. The owners had sprinkled the space in front of the shelves with mismatched tables and chairs, all varying stains of brown. The whole feel of the place reminded Kase very much of his old school rooms, sans preserved flora and fauna.

Scanning the room, he spotted the pencil stuck in Hallie's bun. She faced away from him and was leaning back in her chair reading a novel that was entirely too close to her face. Kase allowed himself a relieved sigh.

She must be in a decent mood, then.

He didn't quite know why that would be the case. Despite their relatively short acquaintance, he felt like he'd known her for ages. It was a strange feeling, though not unpleasant.

He slipped his hands in his pockets and wove past the other patrons, many of whom were students with open books and loose parchment strewn about their tables.

He'd chosen not to continue his education, yes, but sometimes he regretted that decision. What he would have done with the extra knowledge or what vocation he might have chosen was a mystery, but a degree would've been nice. And it would have been an excellent excuse to spend hours holed up in the library with dusty tomes.

He came up behind an unsuspecting Hallie, peered over her shoulder, and smirked. "I didn't peg you as the romance type."

She slammed her book shut, twisting in her chair. "Don't you know it's rude to read over someone's shoulder like that?"

Hallie set the book down as Kase took a seat in front of her. He eyed the teacups on the table. "Two? You've already had two cups of tea? I didn't think I was that late."

She rolled her eyes, and Kase bit back a grin. It wasn't going nearly as bad as he'd thought so far. On his way down, he'd imagined a thousand scenarios—most of them ending with a slap. The most entertaining one had been receiving a face full of tea. She scooted one saucer forward. "The barmaid delivered this cup for you. Didn't know what you'd like, but peppermint tea is my favorite."

Kase's fingers were awkwardly bulky around the dainty porcelain. He took a tentative sip, the silky texture of the hot tea warming him. While his purpose for this afternoon had helped get his mind off Jove's words from earlier, this delectable drink drove the remaining guilt away. For the time being. Sitting in the teashop with Hallie, he could forget the deep disappointment in Jove's gaze.

"This is delicious. Shame Mother never made me try it before," Kase said, taking another sip.

Hallie fiddled with the edge of her book. "You always wait for your mother to tell you to do something?"

Kase set the cup down as gently as he could. It was so tiny and the details so intricate that it might break simply thinking about it. "I used to be rather picky."

"I do remember you saying something about how my beef stew was terrible."

He ran a hand through his hair. "About that the other day...I'm sorry."

She shook her head. "I overreacted."

"I still shouldn't have said that."

"Kase, it's fine. I was just...it's been a long few months, and with my parents...I just...I'm sorry."

What's happening with her parents? Kase traced a finger along one of the cracks in the wood. A part of him wanted to push her on the topic, but he didn't want to test how far his luck would take him. "I accept your apology, then. But now, I came to give you something, didn't I?"

He dug in his pocket for her papers and offered them to

her. Before she could grab them, however, an idea hit him, and he pulled back. "Actually, no. I think you still owe me."

"Still owe you?"

"Yeah."

"Weren't you apologizing to me two seconds ago?" Her voice grew thin.

"You also threw in a 'sorry,' if my memory serves, and rightfully so." He smirked. "I've decided my feelings were very hurt. An apology such as yours won't suffice."

"You're impossible."

Her cheeks were a little flushed as her golden eyes flashed, and Kase couldn't deny it was fun teasing her. But he also knew her temper would get the better of her if he pressed her too much more. He slid the papers across the table. She snatched them, giving him a waspish look. He leaned back in his chair. "I'll forgive you only if you come with me to an estate dinner next Friday."

Hallie rifled through the papers, scanning each line. Kase cleared his throat and spoke a little louder. "I said I'll forgive you only if you come with me to an estate dinner at Shackley Manor next Friday."

"No."

Kase's chair legs struck the floor with a bang. A nearby student with round eyeglasses perched on the tip of his nose let out a string of murmured curses as he daubed smudged ink. Kase ignored him. "No?"

"*No.*"

Kase leaned forward, his hands splayed upon the wooden tabletop. The stained surface made his fingers slide a little. "You think you can live with yourself after how you treated me?"

Hallie rolled her eyes. "I got along fine without you before the *Eudora.*"

Kase crossed his arms, a little huff escaping his lips. Then he smiled. "But the food is excellent."

Hallie finished inspecting the papers and placed them carefully in her satchel, which was hung on the back of her chair. "And you expect that to sway me?"

"It's that good."

She lifted the cup to her lips. "Why do you so badly want me to go to a function for rich uppities such as yourself?"

Kase shrugged. "Because otherwise I'll have to suffer alone. I'd much rather spend it with someone who'll make fun of the *uppities* with me."

She stared hard at him. The longer she did so, the more nervous Kase became. She didn't move. Probably didn't breathe. What was she thinking? Was she trying to come up with a better excuse to get out of it?

Great shocks, if Kase had asked anyone else, they wouldn't have even blinked before accepting the offer. He drummed his fingers on the table. Hallie narrowed her eyes, but she didn't speak.

Maybe he'd misread her. He'd done it before. In the beginning, she'd been a pretentious thorn in his side, but near the end, he'd thought they had reached an agreement. A respect for each other. Kase had found he'd missed her during the months they'd spent apart after their return to Kvyena.

What more, he actually enjoyed spending time with her now. Maybe teasing her about forgiving him had been a step too far.

He chewed on the inside of his cheek for a moment before leaning forward. "Look, I'm not trying to pressure you…"

"You swear the food will be worth it?"

Kase's muscles relaxed as warmth spread through his chest. "I swear on the soul of my departed pilot's goggles."

"Fine, but if it's terrible, I'll never forgive you."

Kase chuckled and held out his teacup. She begrudgingly clinked her own cup against his before taking a sip.

"So back to your book. Romance?"

"Sort of. If you're of the opinion that romance involves space, laser swords, and overarching empires, then yes, I'm reading a romance."

Kase raised his eyebrows. "When I looked over your shoulder, someone was confessing their undying love for someone else."

"That was before the receiver of such a confession replied 'I know' and then was frozen in carbonite."

Her small smirk was impossibly cute as her golden eyes sparkled. Kase laughed. But then Hallie's face fell a little. She tapped her fingernails on the table top before looking up at him. "Are you sure it's okay for me to go to the dinner? I don't think I have anything nice enough to wear..."

Kase held up a hand. "Just wear what you usually do to the theater."

She took a deep breath. "All right." She finished off her tea and twisted in her seat to grab her jacket. "I have to get going. I'm needed at the inn."

Kase nodded. "Pick you up at six next Friday?"

"Sure." She stood and pushed her arms through her jacket. "I'm in the building on the same street as the Savine bell tower. Number 12."

Kase watched her leave, a bud of hope blooming in his chest. For once, he wouldn't have to suffer through the night alone. It was a fantastic feeling. Now, if he could use that to fix other lacking areas of his life...

He finished off his own drink, left a few coppers on the table, and strode out into the afternoon.

C H A P T E R   6

MADE OF STONE

Clara

WITH EACH STROKE OF CLARA Shackley's fine sable paintbrush, the wine-colored rose petals materialized. Oh, how she missed the flowers blooming in the gardens of her family's estate. Each new layer of paint—of highlight, of shadow— evoked memories of summer days, paintbrush in hand, easel ready to collect her thoughts. As she sat years later in the parlor of her townhouse, Clara could nearly taste the sweet, warm breeze coming up from the southern river.

The roses themselves were the pride and joy of the Davey name. Clara always loved tending to them when she needed a break from painting. It was a wonder her prim and proper mother allowed her to do either. Maybe she knew her daughter needed an outlet for the life path she would follow.

Painting and gardening kept her hands and mind calm. She'd been taught from a young age that emotions were private and not for the public eye. A lady of the Davey family had to be her husband's strength, his confidant. She must be strong. She must be made of stone.

It was a job Clara cherished, for she'd dreamed of becoming a wife and mother for as long as she could remember.

Her unborn baby rolled in her stomach, its little elbow sliding along the side, hitting something it wasn't supposed to. Clara sucked in a breath, hand going to the spot near her hip.

"You running out of room, little one?"

Blessed stars, she wanted to get this baby out. If it wasn't her ribs, it was her bladder, her kidney, and so forth.

It was an equally joyous and exhausting time in her life.

Her home was quiet in the late afternoon while her husband was away at the office. The vines and blooms of plants surrounded her, making her feel almost as if she were in that garden back home. It was a place she felt comfortable even in the middle of busy Kyvena. She wished Jove could find the same serenity. At least he was going into work instead of holing up in his study, refusing to come out even to eat. While she loved having him home, it was doing terrible things to his mental state. He could barely walk around a corner without stumbling upon yet another reminder of everything he'd lost.

And she loved Jove too much to allow him to spiral down the road he was headed.

She was his rock, his confidant, his strength. They'd gone through this when Ana had passed, but Zeke...Zeke was different.

Clara set her paintbrush aside and wiped the stray tear trickling down her cheek. Seeing Jove drink through his sorrow was almost more than she could bear.

What if he never recovered from this? What if he continued to hide behind the walls he didn't realize he was building, brick by brick?

Her stomach tightened painfully and unexpectedly, putting pressure on her already aching back. She placed a hand over the center of her stomach and pushed the breath out of her lungs through her mouth, forcing her face to relax.

Another few seconds, and the tightness faded. False contraction. Clara was still a month out from when they expected the baby to arrive, yet these practice contractions had only intensified over the last week.

Clara put it down to stress.

She looked over to the window where she'd set her favorite flash portrait. It was a relatively new technology, using light to recreate a scene onto special paper. The history books spoke of more advanced gadgetry that allowed the subjects in the portraits to move, but like almost everything from First Earth, it was also lost to time.

The flash portrait was of her and Jove on the night he'd proposed. They looked so happy, so carefree. Her husband's smile was a bittersweet memory, his arm pulling her to his chest. Wasn't she enough? Couldn't she help him get through this?

She reached out and touched the frame. Everything would be okay. It had to be. She was a Davey by birth, a Shackley by marriage. She was strong.

CHAPTER 7

THE USE OF DINNER FORKS

Hallie

A WEEK AFTER ACCEPTING KASE'S invitation to dinner, Hallie fingered the navy lace cuff of a dress in the tailor's shop. The pattern on this particular one created a swirling design, almost like sea waves all the way up the sleeves and the bodice to a clear mesh-like collar covering the shoulders. She peeked at the price tag and felt ill.

Eight gold tenners? For a dress?

While 'present Hallie' could technically afford it with the sum from the *Eudora* mission, she would need the funds for when she returned to University. Even if she did purchase the dress, where would she wear it? To Kase's fancy dinner the next night?

Her stomach churned at the thought. Why in the blazes had she said yes?

"You've been making that same face for the past half hour. Is it because you still haven't heard back from your parents?"

Petra twisted to the side in front of a trio of floor-length mirrors near the back of the dress shop. Soft, incandescent light flashed off her gemstone earrings as she glanced at Hallie. The pedestal she stood upon brought her to Hallie's height.

Hallie dropped the price tag. "I know the fort's troops defeated that Cerl force, but I can't help but think...I mean, I haven't heard anything. I feel like I should've heard something by now..." She coughed. "But it's not just that."

Hallie stepped around the attendant pinning the hem of Petra's new evening gown. It was a deep red, like the color of late autumn maple leaves, with a standing collar, and showed off her curves. The dress was a nod to Petra's First Earth ancestors. Another beautiful dress for another frivolous party. This one was a betrothal dinner. The wealthy liked their parties, and Hallie couldn't believe she'd been sucked into attending one.

Petra patted back an invisible strand of hair. "What is it?"

Hallie looked down at her own attire. Plain brown trousers tucked into her boots. She pulled at her worn lace shirt cuffs. "Well, it's that...promise you won't freak out?"

"Now I'm nervous."

"It's nothing, really..." Hallie swept her hands behind her back and paced in front of the mirror. "I didn't know what to say at first, but for some reason, I ended up saying yes to a...fancy dinner. And now I'm out of sorts because it's not something I'd ever wanted or even dreamed of going to, and I don't know what I'll wear, nor anything about anything at all, and I'm sure there are proper table manners I don't know and—"

"Hallie! Breathe." Petra held up her hand. "Explain slower, please. You've been invited to a dinner party? Where?"

Hallie watched as the attendant stuck another pin in the dress' hem. "Shackley Manor."

The attendant swore softly as Petra jumped. Her eyes, reflected in the center mirror, were as large as Firstmoon. "Shackley Manor? Did I hear you correctly?" She turned to the attendant, who was sucking on an injured finger. "Oh, I'm so sorry, Moffet. I forgot you were there."

Moffet shook her head. "It's quite all right, Miss Lieber. I didn't expect—"

Petra cut in. "What do you mean you're going to a dinner party at Shackley Manor?"

Hallie gave Moffet an apologetic smile. "Well...um...Kase asked me to go with him. He told me it's to make up for something a little while back."

Petra squealed, and Moffet stuck her finger again. The attendant inhaled sharply and stood, curtsying. "I need to grab a few more pins, Miss Lieber. I shall return shortly."

She whipped out of the room, her dark skirts flipping around the corner as she shut the door to the back room. Petra took Hallie's hands in hers. "You can borrow one of my dinner gowns if you don't have anything."

Hallie eyed Petra's wide hips and pulled her hands back. "I don't think anything you have would fit me."

Petra tapped her chin and hopped down from the pedestal. A small clattering followed as the pins in the hem of her skirt scraped along the stone floor. She led Hallie over to the back wall of dresses. "Tomorrow night?"

Hallie nodded.

Petra shuffled through the garments and paused at the one Hallie had been inspecting earlier. She pulled it off the rack and held it up by its wooden hangar. "What about this one? You've always liked pretty lace, and with this deep blue against your pale skin, you'll look positively divine."

"I don't think you understand."

Petra checked the price tag. "And it's only eight gold tenners. A steal!"

Hallie clenched her fists and tempered her frustration. "You do understand that's enough to pay for three months' rent in the wealthiest part of the lower city, right?"

"Don't you have money now or something? From that research job you did up in the mountains?"

Still an incredibly lame story, but it continued to hold up. Petra and Ellis were too trusting.

"I need to save it for when I go back to school."

Petra shoved the dress in Hallie's arms. "Yes, yes. But this is only one dress. And you need it for tomorrow. If you buy this, I'll let you borrow a pair of my slippers that would match perfectly."

"My boots would be fine."

"Trust me. You'll want to look your best. I'll even bring my maid, and she can do your hair and makeup."

Petra's eyes sparkled in the light, and Hallie sighed. Her friend was trying to be kind, and Hallie knew she hadn't meant to be bossy or insulting.

Hallie studied the dress again. Underneath the deep-blue lace of the bodice was a champagne-colored silk layer that continued into the skirt. With Hallie's pale freckled complexion and red hair, she really would look beautiful in it. The lace was soft and silky under her fingertips, and Hallie couldn't very well show up in her trousers and long leather jacket.

She looked back up into Petra's waiting eyes. "Could I also borrow a cloak?"

Petra's smile lit up the room as she squealed once more. "Of course! Now go put it on. I'll get Moffet to help you button up the back when she returns."

Hallie rolled her eyes but headed toward the small, curtained fitting room. Good stars, she was going to spend eight gold tenners on a dress.

HALLIE KNEW HER BED CHAMBER was rather small, but it was miniscule with three people packed inside. Petra was fretting over the state of Hallie's hair, dress, and whether she should wear the navy or champagne slippers lined with jewels.

Hallie hid her growing irritation as her friend also held up various jeweled drop earrings. "I think the pearls would be best. They bring out the gold in your eyes. Yes, I think that will work. I have a matching necklace, but I don't want it to take away from that gorgeous neckline..."

While Petra fluttered about, her maid, a woman near Hallie's age named Vera, inspected Hallie's eyebrows with metal tweezers. Hallie tried not to flinch as the woman pulled at stray hairs. It wasn't easy. Each pluck was like a tiny bee sting.

After bullying her eyebrows into shape, Vera finished her masterpiece with a few well-placed strokes, defining Hallie's features—a little bit of dark powder lining her eyelids, some light rouge on her cheeks.

Though it was more than Hallie had ever done for herself

in her life, only adding the lid powder herself when attending the theater, she found she didn't necessarily mind. Vera's steady hand proved she'd done this a thousand times, and each addition only brought life to Hallie's complexion. Was this what Petra did each day before heading out? Did she have Vera or someone else make sure she was readily presentable no matter the occasion, whether it be a quick jaunt to class or an estate dinner?

As Vera double-checked her work, a knock sounded at the heavy wooden door in the adjoining common room, a luxury in an apartment this small. *Kase.*

Hallie patted her hair. It looked elegant with its braid-decorated twist. No messy, stray hairs marred her pale skin.

Petra set aside one of the many cloaks she'd brought for Hallie to try. "I'll see to it. You finish up here."

Hallie nodded, and Vera pulled out a slender brush and jar of lip stain for the final touch. Peeking in the cloudy mirror propped up on her side table, Hallie hesitated. "You sure I need that?"

Vera raised a blond eyebrow. "Trust me, Miss Walker."

Hallie waved her hand, and Vera dipped the brush into the deep red stain. The brush tickled as she painted Hallie's lips.

Soft laughter came from behind the door to Hallie's bedchamber before Petra entered and shut the door with a snap. Hallie caught the grin on her face in the looking glass.

Petra's smile only grew as she set the dark blue slippers on the floor so Hallie could step into them. They matched the dress perfectly. "First, you look ravishing, dear. And second, he's here."

Hallie tied on her scarlet maiden belt and tossed the borrowed silk cloak around her shoulders. She dried her sweating hands on the material, though they slid right off. *Blast it.* She turned to Vera. "Thank you for your help."

Vera curtsied. "Wait! Your gloves!"

Hallie shook her head. "No, I don't need any..."

But the woman wasn't to be denied, so Hallie found herself pulling on simple white gloves that reached her elbows. At least no one else would feel how sweaty her palms were, though they might notice the missing little finger.

When Hallie was ready, Petra led the way to the door and

opened it wide.

The common room wasn't anything to speak of, just a small parlor with a woodfire stove, a single fraying sofa Hallie rarely used, and haphazard bookshelves full of tomes she no longer cared enough about. She'd tried again and again, but nothing helped. *Frankenstein* still lay on her bedside table. She truly only cared about one book, and that one was gone. Her copy of The *Odyssey* had been in the satchel that fell through the Gate. Hallie tried not to dwell on its loss nor the empty feeling of not having her brother's hand-me-down pocket watch, which she had lost in the ruins where Ebba died.

The light from the gas lantern on the side table added a soft touch to Kase's features. The bit of warmth from the dying fire in the stove wasn't enough to heat the room, which was what Hallie told herself had sent goosebumps flittering across her skin.

Kase leaned against one of the shelves and fiddled with the rim of his bowler hat. His trousers and suit coat were black as a cloudless night sky, and his dark locks shone with hair gel—though there were still some stubborn pieces trying to escape. Hallie smiled.

Kase answered with his own grin that sent a spark of electricity down to each and every fingertip and toe. "Seems like we both clean up well."

Hallie rolled her eyes, trying to ignore the heat creeping up her neck. He took her offered hand and touched his lips to it. The spot tingled through her gloves. "Vera works wonders."

Kase raised a brow. "I don't think it's solely whoever Vera is."

"Vera's my maid. The best Kyvena Finishing School had to offer." Petra stepped up next to Hallie and put a hand on her shoulder, shaking the girl out of her thoughts. "Take care of my friend here. She's a bit nervous."

"*Petra!*"

"What?" Petra asked, her eyebrows drawing together in a frown.

Hallie tugged at the cloak's tie. "Thank you for your help."

Petra leaned closer to whisper in Hallie's ear, her voice taut with unbridled excitement, each word short and fizzing with energy. "Don't forget a single, solitary detail about tonight."

Hallie clenched her teeth in a pained grimace as Kase smirked, overhearing the words. She went to grab her satchel, but Petra stopped her again. "Hallie, don't take that, for moonssake."

"It's quite all right." Kase said, stepping up to Hallie. "You without your sketchbook wouldn't be right."

Warmth spread across her cheeks. "I need it to carry my key."

Petra rolled her eyes. "Fine, fine. Promise you'll hand it off at the door with your cloak, please?"

Hallie swallowed the retort begging to be unleashed from her painted lips. "Thank you again, Petra."

With that, she slung her satchel over her shoulder and tucked her hand into the crook of Kase's offered arm. His muscles tensed beneath her fingers as he shoved his hat onto his head, messing his hair further, and led her out into the chilly evening.

Hallie gasped at the sight of cotton-like snow falling from the sky, whirling in the light from the lanterns that led to market square. Without thinking of what she might look like, she opened her mouth wide and caught a few snowflakes on her tongue. The cold bite of the ice melted away with her body heat. She caught sight of Kase's smirk. "What?"

"At least you're better at catching those than caramels."

"I feel like I should be offended by that," Hallie grumbled, although she secretly appreciated the banter. She didn't know what to do with the feelings bubbling their way up into her chest as snowflakes danced on the brim of his bowler, the shoulders of his fancy jacket, and the bit of stubble lining his jaw.

"I meant it as the highest of compliments, of course."

"You're in a good mood." Relaxing at his playful tone, Hallie poked his shoulder.

Kase pulled her in the direction of the main street, the heels of his shiny loafers clicking against the wet cobblestones. At the end of the lane, a motorcoach was idling. Kase opened the door and gestured for her to climb inside. "It's the first time I'll have someone joining me in mocking impossibly snooty dignitaries. Specifically the Rubikan ambassador, though this event is technically in his honor."

"These things are usually a bore?"

Kase slid in beside her, closing his eyes for a moment before taking off his hat and fiddling with the brim. "They always are, but like I said the other day, the food is worth it. Most of the time. To the Manor, Avery."

"Of course, Master Kase."

Hallie set her satchel at her feet and smoothed her elegant skirt. She tried not to focus on Kase's cologne. It smelled like wood smoke and sweet tobacco and was doing funny things to her heart. "Will there be chocolate?"

"Mother did mention some sort of chocolate delicacy. It'll be delicious, no doubt."

She smiled. "Then I can't wait."

They made more inconsequential small talk for a good bit of the drive, the buildings casting shadows as they rolled by. The conversation flowed easily, and Hallie's posture relaxed as they drove. Even so, she ran over the plan in her head. She'd only come up with it the day before, and she didn't know if Kase would go for it, but when the conversation lagged at last, she prayed her words were as persuasive as she thought they'd be.

He's impulsive. Surely, he'd be all for flying to Stoneset. And the Yalvs are settling in rather quickly. No need to worry there. Saldr will understand.

As she gathered her fleeting bits of courage, city lights filtering in through the window limned Kase's silhouette with gold. She traced a pattern in the smooth leather of the seat. The motion calmed her. Hallie swallowed. "I have something to ask you."

"Yes?" He turned, the angle of his jaw and cheekbone all the more pronounced in the half-light. The stubble was not long enough to be considered scruffy, as if he'd forgotten to shave for a few days.

Stars, he looks good.

"Well." Her throat tightened. His eyes were dark in the shadowed interior of the motorcoach. Her teeth were sharp as she bit her lip. "It's that my...I mean...um...what I wanted to ask was..."

She stopped when the looming griffins of the Shackley Manor gate leered at her through his window. He looked at her expectantly before turning. "Oh, we're here. Didn't take nearly as long as I thought. What were you trying to say?"

She tore her eyes away from the accusing stone stares. "Never mind. It can wait."

"You sure?"

She gave him the best smile she could muster, though she had an inkling he saw right through it. "It's nothing, really."

Coward.

The dull rumble of a dozen motorcoaches met her ears, and, grateful for the reprieve, she peeked out the window. "Just how many people are here?"

Kase tapped the toe of his loafer on the floor. "Well, the Stradats and their respective families," he turned toward her, ticking them off on his fingers, "and then the Rubikan ambassador and his son, quite ugly if you ask me, someone from the Watch, probably the High Guardswoman Heddie Koppen, then there's several of the City Council members from here in Kyvena..."

With each name, the knots in Hallie's stomach tightened. The entirety of the Jaydian government, their families, and any other important persons in Kyvena would be in attendance. Just lovely. Absolutely *lovely.* Feeling incredibly grateful for the expensive gown hugging her form, and for Petra, Hallie kicked her satchel further under the seat.

She breathed out her nose as calmly as she could.

"Hals?" Kase asked. She looked up into his dark blue eyes. They were soft. "You feeling okay?"

"The entire blasted country is here to watch me use the wrong fork at dinner."

Kase took her gloved hand. He did it without hesitation, as casual as you please, except it only made Hallie's heart hammer even more. All the emotions, all the nerves. *Stars. Stars. Stars.*

"Relax," Kase said gently, giving her hand a slight squeeze. "The beauty of so many people is you won't stand out. We're probably seated near Jove and Clara, so you'll have some normal people to talk to. Besides, I'll stop you before you use the meat fork to eat your salad. An easy mistake to make, but I'm rather accomplished at the use of dinner forks."

Hallie squeezed his hand back. "You swear?"

"On my honor as a gentleman."

Hallie snorted and slipped her hand out of his. It felt cold without his warmth. Kase grinned, his straight white teeth flashing. When Avery pulled to a stop, Kase unlatched the door and stepped out, adjusting his tie and the lapels of his suit jacket. He turned back to Hallie. "You ready?"

She took a deep breath. Everything would be all right. She'd eat dinner, enjoy the night, and on the way back, lay out the details of her plan. She only needed faith.

Slipping her hand into his, he helped her out of the coach and into the gentle glow of the waiting night.

CHAPTER 8

BETTER ME THAN JOVE

Kase

FOR ONCE, WALKING THROUGH SHACKLEY Manor's ornate entrance didn't intimidate Kase. For once, he didn't feel alone. For once, he might enjoy the night spent in the company of the pernicious, wealthy elites. He tucked Hallie's hand in the crook of his elbow and nodded to the butler, Thoreau, after making it over the threshold.

When Hallie had first walked into the sitting room of her apartment, his heart skipped one too many beats. The blue dress set off her eyes, and the lower neckline and intricate hairstyle allowed him to appreciate the natural curve of her neck. He'd had to swallow hard and blink at least once to regain his composure. He'd found many a girl pretty in a nice dress, yet Hallie...Hallie was something more.

Even though he liked the braids and twists, he missed the messy hairstyle with the pencil stuck in it. It was odd not seeing her bent over her sketchpad, a bit of charcoal smudged on her cheek. He hadn't seen her sketching in months, but that picture was just...right. He glanced sideways at her as she handed her cloak and gloves to the butler. She'd left her satchel in the car, but he was sure she'd draw every remembered detail later.

Her face was stone-like and reminded him a little of those animated Yalven statues. Was he wrong for bringing her? Would she hate him after the night ended?

He leaned over and whispered in her ear, "The food will be worth it. Promise. That is, if Mother hasn't ordered that stars-awful lemon basil soup she's been favoring lately."

Hallie inspected him for a moment, maybe to see if he was in earnest or not before she finally gave him the ghost of a smile.

He nodded to the servant who opened the door to the parlor. Judging by the number of people inside, he and Hallie were some of the last guests to arrive. He steered her toward the drink cart, avoiding conversation with everyone. He eyed his father speaking with Stradat Loffler by the roaring fire. Kase was surprised the ancient white-haired man had been able to stay awake so long.

The servant near the drink cart bowed as Kase and Hallie approached. Kase nodded to him. "Gin. What would you like, Hals?"

She shook her head. "No, no, I'm fine."

"Having a drink in hand is the best way to avoid answering an unwanted question in a hover wreck of a conversation."

"Is there a non-alcoholic option?"

Kase raised an eyebrow. "I think we have sparkling cherry water."

"I'll have that."

The servant mixed both drinks, pouring each into a fine-spun glass. He topped Hallie's off with a few cherries for aesthetics. Kase took his, the ice clinking against the sides. He took a sip. The subtle taste of pine and sweet berries wasn't terrible.

I wish Mother would serve ale.

Hallie quietly observed the fray as they wove through the guests. Kase spotted Stradat Millicent Sarson, her facial scar catching in the light from the chandelier above. She entertained the Rubikan ambassador—probably giving him orders on how best to run his country, even though he wasn't part of the oligarchy. Kase and Hallie passed near the fireplace, and his father's stare burned through the back of his head.

Ignore him.

Kase led Hallie over near the freestanding shelves where his mother kept many of her glass figurines. These were the ones not important enough to sit on the side tables next to the many finely-upholstered davenports.

Dark-stained bookshelves and still-life portraits lined the other available wall space in the room. Kase's grandmother had purchased the latter from a famous painter who had an affinity for various fruits and beasts. Kase thought the man must have been drunk on mazelberry rum the entirety of his career, as no one in their right mind would paint tigers posing with apples. Curiously, none of the art contained griffins. His grandmother must've been tired of seeing the things around the manor.

Hallie took an experimental sip of her drink and smiled. "This is the best sparkling water I've ever tasted!"

Kase swigged his gin. "We Shackleys pride ourselves on offering only the best. It would be a shame if you'd only had decent sparkling water."

"An insult, of course."

"Absolutely."

She smiled before taking another drink. Kase's shoulders relaxed a smidge. Tense Hallie unnerved him. It reminded him of the time right after Ebba had died on the mission—and other memories he'd rather not revisit.

She glanced down at the shelves. "Oh, this is a beautiful etagere!" She ran a hand over the carved design of the shelf. She bent slightly and inspected the tiny glass sculptures. "I love these, too."

"After Mother reads a book she particularly enjoys, she has another trilogy commissioned. The etagere they're on is from one of the republics on the other side of Tev Rubika. Can't remember its name."

"The figurines are exquisite," she whispered, bending slightly to inspect one of the creatures from an old Jaydian folk tale Kase had forgotten the name of. He only remembered being horrified by the description of the monsters as his mother read the story to him and his siblings. The vile things had claws, and their too-many eyes reminded him of spiders.

Of course, the story had been one of Ana's favorites, which was another reason Kase tried to forget it. "Where does she commission them from?"

Kase looked over the crowd, trying to spot his brother and Clara. Plenty of beaded gowns and tailored suits decorated the parlor, but no one wore Jove's ever-present scowl. "Clara draws the figures herself and hands the plans off to a glass blower in the lower city."

"Clara?"

"Jove's wife. I think you'd have a lot to talk about with both of you being artists and all. She paints, mostly." Kase turned back to Hallie.

Out of the corner of his eye, he saw his mother weaving around one of the side tables and a few of the important dinner guests. Her elegant yet simple tiara glittered in her dark hair and matched the silver gown brushing the tips of her slippers.

"Miss Walker, what a lovely surprise!" his mother said, setting her own drink on a nearby shelf sans miniature sculptures. "When Kase mentioned he'd be bringing a guest, I didn't realize it was you, dear."

She pulled Hallie in for a quick hug and then held her out at arm's length. Kase blinked. His mother had only met Hallie once. He tapped his fingers on his glass. "I thought I told you I'd asked her."

His mother quirked a dark brow. "I would've remembered if you were bringing a lady to dinner. I thought it might've been Ben or…"

She trailed off, and her words hung in the air like the chill outside. She didn't know details. Only that like Zeke, Skibs hadn't returned. She had no idea he was alive, much less working for the Cerls. Pain rippled across her face, but it was gone in a flash. "What I was trying to say is that it's high time my Kase brought a woman around, and I adore you very much, Miss Walker."

Kase's neck burned as Hallie fumbled for words. "Um, thank…thank you, Lady Celeste."

"Les, please."

Hallie smiled shyly. "Of course, Les. And please, call me Hallie." She nodded to the figurines. "These are lovely, and I like that each has to do with literature."

His mother's hands dropped from Hallie's shoulders as she put a hand to her chest. "I treasure these little baubles nearly as much as the books themselves. I have about a hundred more upstairs in my library, but my favorites are here in the parlor for everyone to admire."

Kase glanced around the tables, searching for the specific one he liked. "Mother, where's King Arthur? I think Hallie would like to see that one."

Another pained look crossed her face as she picked up her drink. "It fell a little while ago. Shattered."

There was something else there. Something his mother didn't want to say. It was the way she said it—like she'd caught a sudden cold—but before he could press the issue, she continued, her voice light and airy once more. "Either way, you must come back to visit soon, Miss Walker! When you do, I'll have Mr. Thoreau give you a tour, as you weren't able to see the rest of the Manor last time you were here."

"Mother," Kase interrupted, trying to get off the topic that made his stomach tighten, "have you seen Jove and Clara yet?"

As if summoned, the door to the parlor opened, and Jove stepped through. He was different than when Kase had seen him earlier in the week. His eyes were less wild. Clara was on his arm, her budding stomach evident even in the loose folds of her purple gown. Jove grabbed a drink before spotting Kase. He guided Clara over.

Les embraced Clara as she took her hand from Jove's elbow. "I didn't know if you'd be able to make it, being so close to your due date, but I'm glad you did."

Clara rubbed her stomach. "For a second, I didn't think I'd be able to, but the baby finally decided to behave."

"Everything all right?" His mother asked, her brows drawing together.

"Yes, yes, the midwife said it was normal, so I'm not worried," Clara responded, her brown eyes soft and earnest. She patted her stomach. "We might have a stubborn one on our hands."

"He wouldn't be a Shackley if he wasn't." Les laughed and gave Clara's arm another squeeze.

"Mother, please." Jove shook his head. "Besides, we won't know the sex until the baby finally arrives." He turned to Hallie.

"Good to see you, Miss Walker."

Hallie dipped into a small curtsy, and Kase snorted. She glared at him and rose, turning back to his brother. "And you as well."

Jove gave Kase an irritated look. "Good stars, Kase. She's just being polite."

"Yeah, but it's you."

A muscle twitched in Jove's jaw before he caught Clara's hand. "Miss Walker, I don't believe you've met my wife. Clara, this is Miss Hallie Walker. She's a renowned scholar at the University and helped the Watch last fall."

The way he described it sounded rather strange, as if he knew he wasn't supposed to say anything but nearly spilled the secret; Kase couldn't help but notice the lean of the Rubikan ambassador's shining bald head at the words.

Kase cleared his throat. "Hallie is an artist, too, Clara."

"Yes," Hallie said, her hands folded in front of her, "Kase was telling me you like to paint?"

Clara's dark brows rose. "First names? My, Kase, you've been holding out on us."

Kase choked on his drink. The alcohol burned his nose and throat as he coughed violently.

Hallie's face was nearly as red as her hair. Her words came out rushed. "We got to know each other really well...where I grew up in Stoneset, you see, we don't—we're not too formal with names." She took a large gulp of her sparkling cherry water.

Clara gave Kase an appraising look before turning back to Hallie. "Oh, I'm teasing. I'm sure Les would agree that it's simply nice to finally meet the woman Kase has spoken so much about."

"It's true," his mother chimed in.

Jove's lip curled. "He even tried to gel his hair."

Hallie's face had now surpassed the color of the cherries in her sparkling water. Kase was certain his mirrored hers. He elbowed his brother in the arm and murmured, "I didn't want a lecture about my curls from Mother."

Jove laughed into his glass.

His mother reached up and twisted one of the curls into place. "It does look nice, dear."

Kase batted her hand away. "*Mother.*"

Clara took Hallie's hand in both of hers. "Anyway, Miss Walker, I do love meeting other creatives such as myself! So, tell me, what medium do you prefer?"

The women's conversation descended into one of paints, charcoals, and types of canvas. Hallie's face returned to its normal color. Kase hoped his would soon. He hadn't thought he'd spoken much about her, but he never shared much about his past relationships. Not that he was in a relationship. No, no. Hallie was just a friend. A very pretty friend whose slim figure was evident in the evening gown she wore, a friend he felt rather comfortable around, but...

Kase finished off his gin.

His mother glanced around, the jewels on her tiara winking like stars in a clear night sky. She turned back to her sons. "In more serious matters, I need to talk with both of you later. Your father...well...I won't go into the details here, obviously, but I'm worried."

"Worried about what?" Jove asked.

Kase rolled his eyes. "She said she can't go into details here, you *dulkop.*"

"Boys..." His mother groaned as Jove opened his mouth to retort, but before she could say anything else, a servant appeared beside her.

The man's green uniform was spotless and unwrinkled as he bowed. "Lady Celeste, dinner is ready. Shall I inform the Stradat Lord Kapitan?"

His mother jumped a little, but she quickly regained her composure. "It wasn't supposed to be served until seven, and it's only..." She checked the mechanical wooden clock tower in the far corner of the room. "...I believe that says fifteen to the hour?"

The serving man's face reddened beneath his ruddy hair. "Of course. I will inform Mr. Thoreau and Chef Omer that you would like to eat in fifteen minutes."

His mother put a hand on his arm. "No, we'll go in now. The Stradat Lord Kapitan will be more upset if the food is cold."

"Shall I inform him?" the servant asked, though Kase could tell from the slight widening of his eyes that he'd much rather face torture in the bowels of the Cerulene king's dungeon than approach the Lord Kapitan with the news dinner would be served fifteen minutes earlier than planned.

"No, no, I'll tell him."

His mother strode toward Harlan, who had joined a group of government officials that included members of Kyvena's City Council. Anderson Enright was among them, the son of the late Reuben Enright. The current rumor was he'd take his father's place on the Council in the next election. He'd been one of Jove's schoolmates and good friends.

As his mother joined the group, Anderson looked up at Jove and Kase. He smiled and walked over with an air of casual grace. "Well, mates, it's been ages!"

Jove's face broke into a smile as he shook the man's umber hand. Kase had always thought Anderson was too happy and too good-looking to be genuine. Maybe it was simply Kase's own dour demeanor.

"And you, Anderson. I don't believe I've seen you since your father's passing."

Jove's sharp elbow jabbed Kase in the arm, and he ground out, "Yes, I was sorry to hear about Lord Reuben."

Kase avoided Jove's glare and put on his best sympathetic expression as Anderson nodded. "Thank you. We've each dealt with it in our own ways—Mother the worst of us—but we're managing. I'm thankful to have learned as much as I did from him, and I'm planning on continuing his legacy in the Council."

Except you must be elected, you dulkop. What makes you think the position is yours already?

Jove held up his glass. "I'm sure the Council would be all the better with you on it. I've heard talk about what you've done for the lower city, and with your impending marriage to the Lieber heiress..."

Kase tuned them out and scanned the room to see if he could find anything more interesting to bide the time until his mother convinced Harlan to go to dinner early—a travesty, of course. It wasn't going well, if Kase were to judge success by the deepening lines on his father's face; but in a moment, his curt nod preceded the subtle relief flooding his mother's shoulders.

Harlan cleared his throat. "We invite you to join us for dinner. Butler, please lead our guests into the dining hall."

Following his words, Thoreau appeared through the doors

leading to the dining hall from the parlor. Hallie whispered something to Clara and joined Kase. "May I take my drink with me?"

Kase smirked. "That good, huh?"

They joined the queue to the dining hall. The conversations around them were like soft murmurs in the dark. Hallie flashed him a quick grin. "Is that a yes?"

"Wine is served at dinner, and it's a breach of etiquette to bring in your 'before dinner' drinks. Normally I'd say blast the rules, but..."

Hallie knocked the rest of it back like a day laborer deep in his cups. Kase laughed as she smacked her lips upon finishing and left the glass with a nearby servant. She gave the woman a small nod. "Thank you."

Kase shook his head as he handed his own glass over. "I didn't know you were such a fan of sparkling water."

"Just one of the many fascinating facets of my personality." She turned slightly toward him as he led her to seats across from Jove and Clara. Kase was forced to sit next to Anderson.

"Glad you aren't so nervous anymore."

She shrugged as servants pulled out their chairs. Hallie sat, lifting her skirt so it didn't get caught in the legs of the chair. A server leaned forward to fill her wine glass. "Oh, I don't—"

But the hush falling over the room like a dusting of new snow cut her off as Harlan stood from his seat at the far end of the table. Kase traced his finger along the rim of his wine glass. The dark liquid caught the light with each tiny ripple.

"I thank you for your presence here to celebrate our most recent accomplishment in the fight against Cerulene. Ambassador Gustave Crozier was vital in our negotiations with the united Rubikan states. Everyone, please join me in a toast to this momentous occasion," Harlan boomed.

As one, every dinner attendee raised their glittering glasses in the air. Harlan followed suit. "Thank you, Ambassador Crozier. With Tev Rubika, we can fight this threat at both our borders. *Procht.*"

"*Procht.*" The murmured echo came soon after, and Kase took a sip of his wine. It was warm across the tongue. Hallie hadn't touched her glass.

"It's not too bad. Has a bit of a walnut taste," he said as

servants brought forth the first course.

Hallie's eyes darted to the servers. "Oh, I just...do you think someone could bring me a sparkling water?"

"The wine is good. I promise."

"It's not that I don't believe you," Hallie whispered as bowls of soup were set before them. "I don't drink alcohol."

Kase raised his eyebrows. "You don't?"

She shook her head. "Not since Jack died."

Kase turned to the servant who'd placed the bowl of soup in front of Anderson. "Would you mind bringing the lady a sparkling cherry water?"

"She does not like the wine?"

Hallie's cheeks pinked as she waved a hand. "I'll be fine."

Kase touched her shoulder. "The man will bring it with the next course. Won't you?"

"Yes, Master Kase."

"Thank you," Hallie said softly.

"You're welcome."

The soup course was served, and Kase noticed specks of basil floating on the pearly surface. He groaned.

Thank the stars and moons he'd only have to eat a little bit of it. He peeked at Hallie. She grabbed the spoon to the left of the porcelain charger. The senior councilman's wife seated to Hallie's left scrunched up her nose. Kase leaned over and whispered, "Right side. Right spoon."

She hastily corrected her error, her fingers gripping the new utensil a little too hard, judging by the whites of her knuckles.

Kase gave her a smile. "The other one is for dessert."

Hallie scooped out a bite and blew on it. "Because reusing the same spoon would be a breach of propriety?"

Kase tasted his own. His lips puckered. *I despise lemon.* "Of course. And make sure you don't finish off the soup. That shows you're too hungry. Granted, with this, it's not going to be difficult."

Hallie blinked at the sour kick to the steaming soup. "And if I'm rather hungry?"

Kase set his spoon beside the bowl. "That makes you look like you're part of the lower...of the...never mind."

Hallie's cheeks pinked, but she didn't say anything else.

The thought of her not fitting into the world he'd grown up in bothered Kase. He couldn't necessarily explain why, seeing as he'd never fit into it either. He didn't want her to have to suffer the looks or the wagging tongues of the ladies who frequented his mother's entertaining parlor. Lady Les didn't much like them either, but she knew she had to play the game. It kept her distracted from...other things.

Conversations fluttered around them like soft bird chatter. Kase couldn't decipher the individual words, and he couldn't think of anything else to say to Hallie. Shocks. Why was this so hard?

The main course arrived along with Hallie's sparkling water. Kase cut into his steak, his knife slicing through the meat like butter. He wished for a less expensive cut because the words coming from the man's mouth made Kase want to keep sawing away.

Anderson leaned toward Kase and lowered his voice so only Kase, Hallie, and Jove could hear. "I've heard the Watch has been keeping tabs on that crazed group of fanatics. I can't remember the name, something about uniting—"

"One World," Jove said a little too loudly.

Kase clenched his silverware in his hands as Jove finished off his glass of wine and signaled for another. "Jove," he hissed, "keep your voice down."

Kase had heard the rumors, same as Anderson. The group had been initially responsible for some demonstrations in a city near the Lenara Canyon out east. Kase hadn't thought much of them until he'd heard of more demonstrations popping up in bigger cities throughout Jayde. Hallie leaned in. "What's One World?"

Jove swirled his newly-poured wine and took a gulp as Anderson and the others waited expectantly. Kase bent down to Hallie's ear. "It's a group of rabble rousers causing a ruckus in some of the other cities. I think I mentioned the other night how they've possibly made their way here."

A bit of her flyaway hair tickled his lips when she nodded, her eyes widening a little. He pulled back and tried not to bring a hand to his tingling lips. He eyed his wine glass, half-full. He didn't think he could blame alcohol for the sensation. He stuffed a bite of steak into his mouth and chewed. The juicy

REALMS OF WRATH & RUIN

smokiness was perfect yet didn't help his predicament.

"Cheeky *dulkops*." Anderson twirled a bite of steak in the juice on his plate. "Does the Watch think this One World will make an appearance here in Kyvena?"

Hesitating, Kase glanced at Jove. His brother set down his glass, the wine sloshing a little, but no drops landed on the cloth. Clara bit her lip, but she didn't say anything as Jove leaned forward, his tie creeping close to what was left of his rosemary potatoes. "I'm not supposed to talk about business outside of the Watch, but..." he glanced down the table. Kase followed his gaze to where Heddie, the Head Guardswoman, conversed with his mother and another member of the City Council. He turned back to Anderson. "I wouldn't be surprised if we saw a little unrest here."

Kase ran a hand through his gelled hair. The goop made it feel like it was made of wax. He made a mental note to never try it again. "I thought the demonstrations were just a bunch of drunkards yelling obscenities and conspiracy theories at passerby."

Anderson shook his head. "There's more than a few injured men in the Lenara region particularly."

"I can't give all the details, of course, but have faith we're doing what we can to prevent anything worse," Jove said.

Hallie shifted in her seat, her arm brushing against Kase's and leaving a wave of heat in its wake. "Would anyone care to explain more about who or what this group is?"

Anderson leaned forward a little more so he could see her around Kase's form. Anderson answered, "According to their manifesto, they don't believe in the division of countries or kingdoms."

"They want to take down the government?" Hallie asked, her food forgotten beneath her hovering silver utensils. She'd used the correct fork without prompting from Kase.

Jove patted his mouth with a cloth napkin. "I wouldn't worry about it, Miss Walker. Groups like that come and go like the tide. Every few years or so another one pops up." His words slurred toward the end.

"Except this one seems to have some momentum," Kase said.

Jove finished off his glass of wine and gestured for a third.

The serving man refilled it, a look of unease skittering across his features.

Harlan's gaze was so incendiary that Kase could feel it burning into him. It moved to Jove, and a pit opened in Kase's stomach. "Jove, I think it's best if you..."

"Nope." Jove plowed on. "We'll take care of anything that gets out of hand."

Clara put a hand on his arm. "Love, I thought this was a celebration."

Jove looked down at her hand, then back up at her. Kase tapped out a slight staccato on his knees with his fingers. Finally, Jove set his glass down. "Of course."

After a few moments in which the silence seemed to be a living, breathing entity, the conversation turned back to frivolous things when the dessert course was served. Anderson talked about how he was tired of snow, Clara shared that she wanted to paint the new species of tiger coming to City Menagerie as soon as it arrived, and Kase and Jove debated the outcome of the most recent groggon sport match.

"It's not like Kyvena had a chance," Kase said, scooping out chocolate mousse from a lily-shaped crystalline bowl. "The Silver Coast has too many aces."

Jove was on his fourth glass of wine, his voice growing louder with each word. "I wish I'd gone pro back in my day."

"Is that so?" Anderson laughed. "Would you say that was before or after you knocked me in the head with the bat?"

"You blocked my shot."

"You admit it was purposeful."

Jove laughed loudly, spilling his wine. The red stain looked eerily like blood on the white linen. Clara plucked the drink from his hand and ignored his small groan. She whispered something in his ear.

"The few Yalvs I've explained the game to want to give groggon a try," Hallie said. "I don't think they'll be professionals any time soon, but I was incredibly thrilled to hear they want to start settling in—especially since they've only been here a few weeks."

Anderson coughed, choking on his dessert. "It's bad enough they're taking jobs in the lower city, but now they want to infiltrate our sports?"

Kase sensed Hallie's tense posture. "Their home was destroyed, and they have nowhere else to go. Would you rather them drain our near-empty coffers?"

"Near empty?" Hallie asked, her voice strained.

Kase kicked himself. Even Jove looked at him accusingly, though he swayed a little.

When will this dinner be over?

Anderson cut in. "But this new deal with Tev Rubika should help. I don't trust the Yalvs one bit, and no matter what the Stradat Lord Kapitan says, I doubt they're truly on our side. They disappeared for twenty years and expect us to welcome them back with open arms? *Please.*"

Kase swallowed hard, but it was the clatter of Hallie's spoon against the delicate bowl that distracted him. Her voice was low. "You have no idea what they've been through."

"I didn't mean to offend. Especially as I have a bit of Yalven blood myself—back a few generations." Anderson raised his hands. "But I'm doing what's best for my constituents. We're having enough trouble with the Rubikan refugees. That's why I'm excited to be on the Council. I can make a difference in people's lives."

"Except you aren't even—" Hallie growled, but Kase put a hand on her forearm. She stopped mid-sentence, her breathing coming fast.

Kase plastered on the politest smile he could muster. "The chocolate mousse is absolutely delicious, and it would be a shame to let it go to waste."

Kase's hand slid down Hallie's arm and gripped her hand. It was small and a little warm, fitting perfectly in his. He gave it a squeeze before letting go.

With a slow breath, she picked up her spoon again. The others followed suit, and Kase was glad for this particular silence. It wouldn't be much longer now. They only had to make it through after-dinner drinks, and then Kase was free.

He'd thought he might enjoy one of these dinners. He almost chuckled to himself at the irony.

Once all the guests had finished the dessert course, Kase led Hallie back into the parlor where more servants poured steaming-hot coffees and after-dinner drinks. Conscious of the alcohol thrumming in his veins, Kase opted for a coffee. Hallie followed suit.

She took the dainty cup and saucer and added a dash of cream to it before migrating over to his mother's figurines. Kase popped a few sugar cubes into his cup and joined her.

Kase was about to ask about her work when her eyes widened slightly. He peeked over his shoulder to see the Rubikan ambassador heading their way. The man had a proud look about him in the way he thrust his chest out with each step. His bald head reflected the light from the chandelier, and his nose was short, ending too early to seem natural, but it was his eyes that were most disconcerting. They were two different colors—the right one blue as the summer sky and the left a dirt brown. Kase set his coffee down on his saucer.

"Ambassador," he greeted.

The man's conflicting eyes brightened as a smile spread across his face. "Young Master Shackley, I presume?"

"Yes, I'm Kase."

"Of course, of course. You look extraordinarily like your father did when he was younger. I've known him since we were about your age."

Kase's nostrils flared as he gripped the handle of his coffee cup tighter. Hallie stepped in, laying a hand on his upper arm, both calming him and releasing a handful of butterflies in his stomach at the same time. "It's so wonderful to meet you, Ambassador Crozier. My name is Hallie Walker. I was a student at the University, and I wanted to say I appreciated your lecture last spring about Rubikan economic policy."

The man's face split into a wide smile that reminded Kase of a perfectly cracked egg. "I'm so glad you enjoyed it! Economics has been a long-time passion of mine, and with our challenges with the civil war, it was interesting to see the shift in various markets."

Hallie's hand left Kase's arm, and it felt cold without it. Kase gulped his coffee to clear his head as Hallie continued, "I was able to do a deeper study on it using the book you wrote about the scarcity of metals and the effect on war itself. My professor even...well, he was extraordinarily pleased with my research. I owe you half my good mark."

The man chuckled and tipped his head. "You're too kind— Miss Walker, was it? Yes, now, if you found that interesting, I'd recommend reading DeFortier's *Conjunction of Conflation*. A riveting read."

Kase very much doubted that.

He set his coffee on a nearby shelf, next to a tome with the title *The History of the Three Earths: How Three Peoples Found Safety on Yalvara*. His head was still fuzzy.

Ambassador Crozier leaned in, his smile growing wider. "I'll let you in on a little secret of mine, dear, if you'd allow me."

"Of course!"

Kase shifted his weight to his other foot. As much as he enjoyed reading, he had never found economics all that engaging. In fact, it reminded him of days spent doodling on spare parchment at the back of his class while the upper schoolmistress' nasally voice threw out inane terms like 'supply' and 'demand'.

"My next book is going to dive into the ancient trade practices of the Yalven nations!"

Cold adrenaline spiked in his chest at the statement, but Hallie's eyes glowed. Her words came out in a rush. "I find the Yalvs and their history most fascinating. When are you expecting the book to be finished?"

The ambassador took a sip of his brandy. "Within the next year. I've been working with Lord Saldr, but he hasn't been as forthcoming as I would have hoped. To think the Yalvs have appeared after so long in hiding? The questions I have!"

The smile on Hallie's face slipped slightly. Like Kase, she was probably remembering the horrific months they'd spent on Tasava trying to find the Yalvs. "It's fascinating, isn't it? I'm thankful the Watch has allowed me to aid Lord Saldr in acclimating them to Jaydian society."

The ambassador tipped his head. "Yes, you have done a fine job from what I hear."

Hallie beamed.

Crozier leaned in. "My dear, I don't mean to be so forward, but I must ask…your eyes. They are a remarkable shade of brown, almost golden, really."

Hallie's breath hitched. The ambassador's question evoked a snippet of a memory in Kase's mind—a metal door and a smear of golden light, bright as a lantern, near where the handle should have been. The image was gone as quickly as it had come. He strained to remember more, but all he could visualize was the door and the glow.

"Yes," Hallie said, her voice quivering slightly, and almost imperceptibly. "My eyes remind me of the color of honey, but that always makes me think of food, and then I inevitably get hungry. I blame my mother for my outrageous sweet tooth."

Her laugh was strained, and Kase glanced at the ambassador. The glimmer in his mismatched eyes wasn't one of mirth.

Kase's heart skipped a beat. He was formulating a plan of escape when Jove stumbled into him.

"Jove!" he hissed, holding his brother up by the shoulder. Shocks, he'd never seen Jove this drunk. In fact, once upon a time, Jove barely touched the stuff. But that was before Kase had returned with Zeke's body in tow. "You're causing a scene."

The ambassador excused himself and strode away. Kase didn't know whether to feel relieved or not. The bittersweet tang of alcohol met his nose as Jove burped into Kase's face.

Hallie caught Jove's other arm. "Here, let's have you sit..."

Jove refused to budge. He pressed his nearly-empty glass of golden brandy to his lips, but Kase snatched it out of his hand. "You've had *enough*."

Kase glanced over to where Clara conversed with his mother and High Guardswoman Heddie Koppen.

"Help me get him to that couch, there," Kase told Hallie, pointing to one nearby.

She nodded and tugged on Jove's arm, but he was an immovable weight.

"Jove," Kase growled. "What in the *blasted holy moons and stars is wrong with you?*"

"I really, really like brandy." He stumbled through the last word.

Hallie tugged on his arm again, and finally Jove followed. Kase steered them to the couch, which Jove fell into gracelessly. Kase ran a hand through his hair, his fingers catching on the waxy texture once more. *Blasted product. Never again.*

Kase stared down at his brother's bloodshot eyes and groaned. "You can't keep covering up what's really bothering you with alcohol."

"Rather rich, coming from you," Jove barked, and Hallie

flinched. Kase winced and peeked around the room.

It'd gone silent.

Kase shushed his brother, but he wasn't ready to be silenced. "I WILL DO WHAT I WANT, NO—"

Kase clamped a hand overs Jove's mouth, the days-old stubble rough underneath his palm. After a tense few moments, chatter filled the void once more, and Kase relaxed his grip on Jove's mouth.

"Hallie?" Kase whispered. She bent down to his level, the lace and gossamer material of her dress rustling. "Would you fetch Clara?"

She was off with a swish of her skirts. Kase glanced around again, and his heart hammered in his chest when he made eye contact with his father. When Harlan excused himself from his conversation, ice flooded Kase's veins. He fisted his hands in Jove's suit jacket, trying to lever him off the couch. "Come on, you need to go home. *Now.*"

Jove stumbled to his feet at Kase's urging. Harlan was only a breath away when Jove's voice rang out again through the parlor. "*You.*"

Kase paused and shut his eyes tight. *Not here.*

Harlan's voice was low and authoritative. "I will not have you make a scene. Leave."

Kase prayed to whoever might have been listening, but it was useless. Hallie and Clara joined them as Jove spat out, "It's your fault Zeke's dead. ALL YOUR BLASTING FAULT."

Spittle flew from Jove's mouth and landed on Harlan's pristine military jacket. He rarely wore anything else. His father's eyes were harder than diamonds. Kase pulled Jove away and turned to Clara. "Take him home, will you?"

"I command you to—" Harlan started, but Jove was too far gone.

"You wanted them to die! All you care about is your pride. Your title."

Clara stepped in between Jove and Harlan, and Jove, in his drunken state, shoved out, trying to get at his father. Hallie gasped, and Kase lunged, but it was Harlan who caught Clara before she fell to the stone floor. Clara murmured a thank you, but it was drowned out in Jove's sobs now bubbling out and overtaking his anger.

"He was my best friend, and you took him from me. *You did this.*"

Kase flinched when Harlan's hand clenched as if he was about to land a blow to Jove's jaw; if the guests hadn't been there, he would have.

He tugged harder on his brother. It was easier now that Jove's tears came freely. Kase gritted his teeth against the pain in his own chest. He understood Jove's anguish more than anyone, but the look in Harlan's eyes... "Come on."

Jove followed, still yelling accusations. Clara grabbed her husband's other arm.

"Love, please. Calm down." Her voice was thick with tears.

Kase finally got Jove to Avery, who was waiting in the motorcoach. His drunken brother slumped over against the far window. Kase was about to help Clara in as well, but she bent over her stomach, sucking in a breath.

"Clara!"

After a moment, she stood and put on a pained smile. "Just a false contraction. I promise, the midwife said it was normal."

Kase shook his head. "I don't know much about stuff like that, but I wouldn't say that was normal."

She held up a hand. "It's all right, Kase. I swear. I'll take Jove home and rest. The excitement tonight was a little too much."

"All right," Kase said, swallowing another argument. "Send word if you need anything."

Clara allowed Kase to help her into the motorcoach. He told Avery to make sure Jove and Clara got home safely.

As the motorcoach trundled down the lane to the gates, Kase plucked up the courage to go back inside; Hallie was still in there, at the mercy of his father. He'd go in and collect her, then walk her home or call another motorcoach out for hire. Anything to make this nightmare of an evening end.

His polished shoes pattered up the stone steps and through the foyer. Jove's words echoed in his head.

You wanted him to die. He was my best friend.

Kase blinked rapidly, trying to get rid of the tears pricking his eyes. In his mind, Zeke was falling again, and the puddle of blood beneath his body just grew and grew.

Kase clenched his jaw tighter. Keep it together for a little while longer.

As he approached the parlor, he looked up, and his heart nearly stopped beating right then and there.

Harlan stood in front of the closed door. With a flick of his head, he gestured toward his study. Kase's stomach churned, but he followed his father down the short hallway and into the room.

Better me than Jove.

C H A P T E R   9

THANK YOU

Hallie

STEAM NO LONGER ROSE FROM Hallie's porcelain cup of coffee. During Jove's outburst, she'd forgotten it until she found herself alone by the tiny glass figurines. She eyed the door, praying Kase would come back soon.

He hadn't.

The Stradat Lord Kapitan had slipped out a few minutes ago, and from her limited experience, that wasn't a good sign. But what could she do? Hallie brought the cup to her lips and took a tentative sip.

"Yech," she spat as she put the coffee back down onto its saucer, then blushed as a few of the nearby guests glanced at her. She gave them an apologetic smile.

"You'd have been better off with a brandy. None of these people know how to make a good batch of coffee," a gruff voice said to her left.

Hallie looked over to find a hawkish woman with her steely

gray hair slicked tightly back into a bun. She wore trousers instead of a gown, and her shoulders told Hallie she wouldn't have needed help lifting the barrels of ale at the inn. She also didn't wear any sort of belt around her waist. Hallie smiled demurely. "I hate cold coffee. It's worse than cold tea, even."

The lady snorted. "Agreed. My name's Heddie Koppen, High Guardswoman of the Watch. We met when you gave your report after returning from the Yalv mission."

She held out a hand, and Hallie took it, giving it a firm shake. Hallie was a little taken back by the gesture, as it wasn't too common among the upper class. A proper peck upon a lady's hand by a gentleman or a small dip of the head were more the style. However, the handshake reminded her of home, where there were no class distinctions based on wealth.

She swallowed to hold back her emotions. How silly of her to nearly tear up over the simplicity of a handshake.

"Of course," Hallie said, hoping the thickness in her voice wasn't noticeable. "I apologize for not saying something earlier. When we gave the report, I was a little distracted."

"You'd been through the blasted fires and back. I don't blame you." She shook her head. "But that's not what I came to talk to you about. Well, not really. I wanted to thank you for your work with the Yalvs in the city."

"Oh!" Hallie said, brightening. "That's no trouble at all!"

The woman shifted her weight. Her shoulders dropped a little. "We've had our hands tied with Cerulene, so you working with Lord Saldr has been helpful. How do you feel they're adjusting?"

"Wonderfully, considering what they've been through. Most of them, that is. Jera, the wife of one of the Lords who..." Hallie thought back to Saldr's brother, Rodr, and his fate. What had happened to the sword in the attack? Ben had flung Rodr into the Gate, using the power as an Essence to summon a sword—the one that had pierced Kase and favored the others Hallie had found in the forest temple. "He, uh, didn't make it to Kyvena. Anyway, Jera was telling me the other day that she and several of the women are interested in finding work in the tailor shops. She's an excellent seamstress from what I understand. I feel horrible for what happened, but I'm glad I've been able to help."

"Of course." The High Guardswoman knocked back her brandy. "Between you and me, I'm even happier to hear it, as their presence has been a thorn in the High Council's side ever since they arrived. I've been trying to talk down the Stradats, but without Jove there, well, it's been an uphill battle."

Hallie wondered if the alcohol had loosened the woman's tongue; her words felt too much like a national secret. Hallie shouldn't be privy to whatever it was the High Council discussed, though it did set a small spark in her blood. "It's not their fault they had to flee their homes. They didn't have anywhere else to go!"

"I know, but I do understand Stradat Sarson's point about the economy being affected by the influx, small as it is. She worries they might start taking the jobs away from those who need it in the lower city, and while that may be true, we should welcome those who are willing to work."

A crimson haze crept in at the edges of her vision. She took a few deep breaths to calm herself before she spoke. It wouldn't do to cause another scene there in the parlor. "These people lost everything they'd ever known, and I'd say the powers that be should appreciate that the Yalvs will no longer drain the government stores if they are able to contribute to society."

With a soft chuckle, the High Guardswoman nodded. "You're not wrong, my dear. Now you see what I'm up against." She drained the last of her brandy. "I didn't mean to get derailed. I wanted to say thank you. However, I must get going. I have to be up at the crack of dawn."

With a short bow of her head, the woman left. Hallie closed her eyes and calmed her racing heart. Was that what the High Council was currently fighting over? Hallie understood the economic ramifications of refugees draining government resources, but if the Yalvs wanted to work, why would anyone deny them that?

Ridiculous blowhards. This is why I never want to go into politics.

Not that the High Guardswoman was one of those. She sounded as if she was truly on Hallie's side. Or at least acknowledged her viewpoint. She now understood what may have led to Jove Shackley's resignation; Hallie didn't think she would have the patience for such pretentious pomposity.

She glanced toward the door once more. Still no Kase. Tapping her nails against the side of her cup, Hallie chewed her lip and looked around the room. She didn't feel like conversing with anyone else, nor did she want the Rubikan ambassador to approach her again. She couldn't pinpoint why the comment about her eyes unnerved her so.

Hallie had always thought their golden color was odd, but now that she knew she had Yalven ancestry? She thought back to the conversation with the ambassador. It'd been thrilling to finally meet Gustave Crozier in person after reading his works and listening to his lectures, but there was something about him asking that question that didn't sit right with her.

Stars. Maybe she was out of sorts after Jove Shackley's outburst. Yes, that's what it was. The guilt of not being able to save Zeke was weighing on her mind. And Anderson Enright had been going on and on at dinner about One World. She was just on edge.

Besides, she still needed to talk to her father about her heritage. His failure to respond only caused more anxiety. Hallie needed to move and do so without the prying eyes of people who could buy Stoneset ten times over.

Had something happened to Kase? He should have been back by now. As she paced behind a couch with a potted tree beside it, she overheard the conversation of the two women sitting there. They didn't acknowledge Hallie, didn't even see her.

"And with Lucy Doyle up and fleeing to their country estate suddenly?" one of the City Councilmen's wives said in a hushed voice, her forehead wrinkled with age. Hallie paused.

Lucy Doyle...Lucy Doyle...

The younger woman with jet-black hair sitting next to her shook her head. "Didn't you hear? She's pregnant, but she's not giving up the father's name. My bet is on a commoner."

Wait...could that be...hadn't Ben said something about a Lucy?

"Well, bless the heavens. No wonder they sent her to Hampshire. And a commoner?" the first one gasped before side-eyeing Les. "My guess would've been Kase Shackley because of the way he chased after Lavinia Richter, may her soul rest among the stars. But he's shown up here with that...girl. Is he trying to make a statement?"

Hallie's face flooded with heat. Dark thoughts squirmed through her mind. She found herself hating a dead girl and wishing she hadn't bought this stupid dress.

It didn't matter. No amount of expensive lace could make her fit in. Snotty uppities with their gossip and...and...

She set her cup down a little too hard on a nearby shelf and scurried off before she said something she'd regret. The women jumped, but Hallie didn't stay to see whether or not they would apologize. She shouldn't have come. There was a sharp pain in her chest.

She didn't belong here.

The green-liveried man with a dark receding hairline bowed as she approached. "May I assist you, Miss?"

"Powder room?"

He walked her toward the door and opened it for her. "Down the hall there," he said as he gestured to the right, past the grand staircase Hallie had descended after that memorable breakfast with Kase and Les. "You should find it on your left."

"Thank you."

The man bowed and went back into the parlor. Hallie leaned against the wall outside the door. She'd been judged before. She'd been looked down upon so many times she'd lost count, so why did their words make her feel so small? She fingered the bump on her nose. Jack would've known what to do. He always had.

She took a deep breath and glanced around the empty foyer. Where had Kase gone? Had he escorted his brother home himself? She wanted to leave. Her chest still felt tight, although the stabbing sensation had dulled now that she was out of that blasted parlor.

The only light in the foyer came from the chandelier hanging from the cathedral-esque ceiling. Damask walls peeked back at her as she stepped forward and inspected the portrait nearest the door once more.

Kase had his hand wrapped around his sister's. His face and hers showed no expression other than abject boredom. She thought back to her own childhood and clenched her fists into the folds of her skirts. She and Jack would never have stood still for so long. In fact, Jack would have probably thrown a tantrum or intentionally messed up the painting process, to Hallie's detriment. She smiled at the idea.

Pulling herself away from the portrait, Hallie returned to the present. Maybe Kase was outside? She eyed the heavy, arched front door. She'd just take a peek. Not long enough to need her cloak and gloves, which were stars knew where.

As soon as she took a step toward the door, a dull clatter broke the silence. She jumped and spun, hand over her heart. "Hello?"

It came from where the man had said the powder room was. She stared apprehensively down the corridor. It had been a rather loud noise. What if someone had fallen?

She went to investigate. The light from the foyer faded. No one had lit the sconces along the walls, and so she traveled deeper into the house in shadow.

A new sound met her ears. Raised voices. Light leaked from under a doorway ahead. As she crept closer, the muffled words became clearer.

"How in the suns is it my fault Jove doused himself in alcohol tonight? Have you lost your mind?" Kase's voice was hard and biting.

Hallie put a hand to her mouth to trap any sounds she might have made as she stopped at the light's edge. The door was slightly ajar. Kase's words hung in the air for a moment. Hallie had never heard the tone he used. Ever. Even at the worst. He'd been rude and inconsiderate and angry over the course of the *Eudora* mission, but those instances paled in comparison to now.

The Stradat Lord Kapitan's voice was the ice to Kase's flame. He didn't yell. He didn't even raise his voice to anything above normal conversation level, but it froze the air in Hallie's lungs. "The only reason I allowed you on that mission was because your drunkard brother assured me you were the only one who could successfully bring the entire crew back home. He was wrong; you're useless. Zeke was the only one who ever came close to earning my respect."

"Like I care about your blasted respect," Kase spat.

Hallie shouldn't have been there. She shouldn't be listening in on this. Hadn't she learned her lesson with the gossiping ladies? But her feet refused to listen. It was as if her dainty slippers were full of stone.

The Stradat Lord Kapitan's laugh was sardonic and had a rough, jagged edge. "It would have been better if *you* had died instead of your brother, for all the good you do."

Hallie's vision blurred; the words almost sounded like he spoke them from the other end of an abandoned mine. They pierced her chest like a dagger. *Oh, Kase.*

"If I could fix it, I would, but you only see—only see—" Raw emotion leaked into Kase's voice. "You've never seen what's right before you!"

"And furthermore, your decision-making has only gotten worse."

"*What in the—*"

"You always knew your marriage would be political, yet you paraded *that girl* in front of the most important people on Yalvara tonight. What a *blasting* disgrace."

Hallie's heartbeat pulsed in her throat. It was one thing for the women in the parlor to think her unworthy. It stung, but frustration was the stronger emotion in that case. To hear this from Kase's father, the Stradat Lord Kapitan...

Just go back to the parlor. Turn around, and whatever you do, don't cry.

But she couldn't even breathe.

"*Don't...you...dare.*" If Kase's tone had been mere flames before, it rose to a blaze. It scalded and scorched. Each word stoked the fire until the inferno raged. "You have no right to say *anything* about her or *anything else* in my life. *I know what you're doing.* I know what the servants are saying. Mother, too. You're a disgusting, blasting *helviter* who thinks it's all right to sleep around with other—"

But whatever else he was going to say was lost in the resounding slap of skin on skin.

Hallie gasped. Someone spit on the floor. Hasty footsteps thundered closer as she scrambled away, but she wasn't fast enough. The door flew open and banged against the wall.

Scarlet blood trickled down Kase's chin from his busted lip. She shook her head. "I didn't—I didn't—"

But whatever she wanted to say evaporated as she met the Stradat Lord Kapitan's steely gaze over Kase's shoulder. He breathed heavily as he wiped his hand upon his military jacket.

She shook her head. "I'm sorry. I didn't mean to..."

Before anything else could be said, Kase grabbed her arm and towed her down the hallway. His grip was like pincers, but she didn't stop him. She could tell that he was struggling to hold in the emotions bubbling beneath the surface. Her arm was the lifeline holding him afloat on a raging sea.

She peeked back down the corridor only to find it empty. "Kase..."

He merely shook his head and pulled her toward the front door. Once outside, he let her arm go and commandeered a car. It wasn't Avery in the driver's seat, but Kase didn't care. He helped Hallie in with a sweaty hand, and after giving curt directions to the man, they were off into the chilly winter night.

IN THE DARKENED MOTORCOACH CAB, the silence was loud enough to drown out everything except Hallie's thoughts. As the streetlamps flashed at regular intervals on their journey through the upper city, Hallie wished she could close her eyes and forget the pain. Kase didn't speak.

Hallie couldn't blame him.

You always knew your marriage would be political, and yet you paraded that girl *in front of the most important people on Yalvara tonight. What a* blasting *disgrace.*

The Stradat Lord Kapitan's voice echoed in her head. He'd said it with such malice, such disgust—as if she were the scum smeared on the edge of his pristine military-style boots.

She hadn't grown up in the city, nor did her family have so much money they didn't know what else to do with it. Her parents did well in Stoneset, but that didn't mean Hallie hadn't had to patch her own clothing growing up. Here in the glittering capital city, even with her University accolades, she still wasn't enough. Not enough for her parents, for the Stradat Lord Kapitan, for Jayde. Not enough for Kase.

She swallowed hard against the lump in her throat and inspected Kase in her peripheral vision.

You have no right to say anything *about her or* anything else *in my life.*

Even though the blood had dried on his swollen bottom lip, Hallie blinked back the tears threatening to fall. She clenched her hands tightly in her lap and wished she hadn't left her satchel in the other motorcoach, which was stupid because she hadn't been able to draw since returning. But maybe simply holding the pencil would've helped her deal with the anxiety and embarrassment still coursing through her veins.

It would also help get her mind off the question that kept coming back up. *How often did something like this happen to him?*

For all her parents' faults, they'd never hit her like that. They'd raised their voices when she and Jack had eaten all the chocolate morsels from the pantry in one sitting. They'd banished her to her room when she'd kicked her brother after some inconsequential argument about who had to sweep up the dining room. They'd nearly forgotten she existed once Jack had died. But they'd never mistreated her in such a terrible, disgusting way.

What horrors had Kase faced in his short life? Jove? Zeke? What nightmares had that monster imposed upon them? Because if that happened once, it happened again. And again. And again.

She wound her fingers into knots until she could no longer feel them.

Soon, they turned onto the lane where her apartment was. A few people milled about, mostly heading off to the taverns near the market. Hallie didn't think there were any troupes playing at Grieg's that evening, though there might be something this weekend she could badger Ellis into taking her to.

She shook her head at the trivial thought. How could she think of a play at a time like this?

When the motorcoach stopped, Kase ran a shaking hand down his face and exited before leaning down to help Hallie out. She took his slightly clammy hand in hers, enveloping his fingers. He mumbled something to the driver as Hallie stood shivering in the crisp night air. She hadn't grabbed Petra's silk cloak before she left. *Blast.*

She didn't particularly want to go back for it, now or ever. Shackley Manor might as well have been cursed.

She and Kase strolled silently along the cobblestone path wide enough for only two, the light from the streetlamps hung off the side of the buildings casting shadows on his features.

Hallie shivered again.

Without a word, Kase shrugged off his jacket and held it up. "Here."

Hallie rubbed her arms. "No, it's all right. We're almost to my apart—" But she stopped herself and cursed softly. "My key. I left it in my satchel, and that's in..."

Kase closed his eyes. "*Blast.*"

The word lacked its usual bite. Instead, it came out in a way that reminded Hallie of the worn leather of her boots, cracked and weary. "I can go get it. Is the car still..."

She glanced back to where the car had been moments earlier to find it gone. Kase inhaled slowly through his nose. "I told him to go back to the Manor."

"I can rent another one ...no, any spare coppers I had are in my bag." Panic clawed its way up her throat. "I guess we can walk back."

"No," Kase spat.

The panic rose even more and bled into irritation. "But I have no other way of getting into my apartment!"

Her breaths were coming faster and faster with each word. She was going to have to walk back alone and possibly face the Stradat Lord Kapitan at the end of it.

Hallie shivered harder, both from cold and frustration, and Kase shoved his jacket in her hands. She pushed it away, but his eyes were hard. "Just take it, will you? And I have some money. I'll lend you a bit, but I'm *not* going back there."

"Fine," she said, taking the jacket and throwing it around her shoulders. Her next shiver was a little less violent, but the stinging bite at the tips of her nose and fingers didn't go away. "Except you can't very well wander around the city this time of night."

He fished a silver out of his pocket and held it between two fingers. "Don't worry about me."

As another chill raced up her spine and rustled her skirts, Hallie tugged the jacket closer, but she didn't take the money. His lip looked like it had gotten larger in the minutes they'd been standing there in front of the building. "Kase..."

He shrugged. "I have enough for a room at an inn."

In his button-up with its overly starched collar tucked over the knot of his skewed tie, he looked exhausted. His eyelids sagged, and the crusted blood of his lip made him look like he'd been in a drunken barfight. His previously slicked-back hair had liberated itself, and with that image, Hallie was transported back to the moments after Zeke sacrificed himself at the entrance to the mountain temple. She could almost hear the pounding of Kase's bloodied fists and feel his wild, untamed gaze.

She eyed the silver fiver still in his fingers. The fare was far too much for a simple cab ride.

She worked her jaw and looked down at the folds of her dress. The navy color seemed even darker. It reflected the myriad of thoughts weighing on her mind. She peeked through her eyelashes at Kase, his hand finally dropping to his side.

"Come on," she said, grabbing the cuff of his sleeve.

"What?" She dragged him behind her, and he stumbled a little before pulling out of her grip. "Hallie, what're you doing?"

"I know a good inn with the best breakfast spread. It's a fair price for a couple rooms."

"But your key."

She stopped and turned, looking him straight in the eyes. The cool light from Firstmoon mixed with the dim streetlamps and warred on his face. "I'll collect my things in the morning. We're both exhausted, and I want to make sure you're somewhere safe."

A low growl erupted from his throat. "I don't need your pity."

"I know," Hallie said. "I know you don't want my pity or my help, but what kind of person would I be if I left you now?"

Kase's stare was hard as mountain stone. His nose was pink from the cold and his face nearly as pale as the Nardens' first snow. He didn't move for a good minute, long enough for a few stray flurries to traipse by on the subtle wind. At last, he sighed. "Fine."

Hallie led them down the street and along the bridge that spanned the Rigamon, a rivulet trickling down from a source somewhere up in the hills. It wasn't much more than a glorified creek, but Hallie had always thought it pretty with the rows of leafless oaks standing sentry on its banks. With the newly fallen snow, the scene looked like a winter wonderland. At least that was one good thing about tonight.

On the other side of the bridge, Hallie pushed open the door to the Crown Haven Inn. Even at this late hour, the dining room was bustling. She hoped Nole didn't ask her to help.

The fiddler's drinking song warbled over the murmur of patrons tightly packed against each other in the limited space. The music was a mountain reel Hallie had danced with Niels a lifetime ago. It was a jumble of short and snappy notes flirting with longer trills that rose until the fiddle ran out of breath. Then it jumped quickly into the next line. A good many men and women were dancing, their smiling faces a contrast to the guests sipping expensive brandy at Shackley Manor.

Kase avoided the middle of the room, weaving his way along the edges toward the bar where Nole was pouring ale. Hallie followed, apologizing whenever Kase bowled through someone without a thought. She gritted her teeth but didn't correct him. He was already on edge. Thankfully, the other patrons were too preoccupied with the evening's entertainment to care.

"Two rooms, please," Kase muttered as he slid a gold tenner across the bar top.

Nole's eyes were as wide as tea saucers. He took the money and shook his head. "That's too much, sir. I couldn't in good faith take that sum from you. Besides, I only got my smallest rooms left. Nothing but a washstand and cot."

Hallie sidestepped a dancing couple and smiled up at her employer. "It's all right, Nole. Just got locked out of my apartment. We'll take two rooms, and I'll fetch us breakfast from the kitchen in the morning. I'm sure the gold tenner will cover that and help you pay the license fee."

Nole set down his rag. "You know I'd let you have the rooms free with all you do around here. Besides, that license fee is already paid."

Hallie smiled wider. "Just take the money. I know you've given away too many free drinks tonight as it is."

Nole chuckled and bent below the bar. Hallie glanced over at Kase, who'd been silent throughout the entire exchange. Whether the toll of the night would come out through his temper was to be determined, but she didn't want that happening there in front of the fiddler, who had finished the reel and began to play her father's favorite drinking song.

If they didn't get to their rooms soon, she might join Kase in his breakdown.

Nole slid two keys across the bar top and scooped up Kase's tenner. "Up the stairs to the top floor, last two rooms on the right. I'll tell Mazie to have cinnamon buns ready at eight bells." He pulled a folded bit of parchment out of his back pocket. "This came with the evening post. Urgent. Said they also sent a copy to your apartment."

Hallie furrowed her brow but grabbed it, both keys, and Kase's arm. "Thank you. See you in the morning."

Avoiding the people who had started a jig to the rousing chorus of the drinking song, Hallie led Kase to the back stairs. They climbed without incident, and with each successive floor, the raucous dining room noise grew fainter until it was barely perceptible.

The upper floors of the inn weren't updated quite yet, and solitary candles flickered in the sconces along the walls. A bit of wax dripped to the dusty wooden floor from the nearest one. Hallie bit back the sting of nostalgia. *Stars.* She needed to keep it together.

Her legs were leaden as she approached the final two doors. She stuck the key into the nearest one.

The lock clicked. She stepped back and handed the key to Kase. "I'll take the one on the end."

Kase stumbled forward, his hand falling on the door frame. The key scraped against the wood as he half turned. "Hal...I'm so...I'm sorry about what...about what..."

But tears choked the words like thorns. They leaked from his eyes, his lashes clumping together as he sucked in several breaths. Hallie's own eyes burned as she caught him by the arm and guided him into the room beyond. She kicked the door closed with her foot.

Nearly tripping over her skirt at least twice, she finally got him to the small cot where he collapsed, his hands hiding his face as more sobs racked his body. "I'm sorry. I'm sorry. I'm so—"

Hallie lit the gas lamp beside the bed and tucked her own key and the telegram into the pocket of Kase's jacket. She didn't want to take it off just yet. Turning back to him, she wiped her stray tears away and fiddled with the cuffs. What could she do?

Leave him to his own misery while she listened to his sobs through the thin walls? Staying was all she could think to do.

The key fell from his hands and clanged against the floor. She fetched it and laid it on the small, crooked wash basin stand.

There was a rough rag next to the wash basin. Hallie dipped it in the stale water and wrung it out. She tiptoed over to the bed and lowered herself down onto the cot next to Kase.

She hesitated, working up the courage, before pulling away his hand. "Here, let me clean your lip."

"*I'm fine.*"

She tightened her grip. "Just be still, would you?"

He closed his eyes, and his muscles relaxed. She tentatively dabbed the damp rag against his busted lip. His breathing evened out as she wiped away the dried blood. She was careful not to press too hard lest it hurt him. When she finished and rinsed out the rag, he finally opened his eyes. They were still wet with tears. She knotted her fingers together as she stood before him. "I don't know what to say, really, but I wanted to thank you...um, for what you said...and..."

The words were too thick for her throat. After a moment, Kase patted the space next to him on the cot, and with slightly shaking knees, she joined him once more. She could feel the heat of his body through the hair's breadth between them. Hallie stared at her hands clasped in her lap.

She didn't know how long they sat there, but it was long enough for the oil in the lamp to burn out, leaving only the soft glow from the street lamps outside. Hallie stared out the small window at the city skyline. Even from here she could make out the glittering dome of the Jayde Center, shining like a beacon in the night.

It made her think about what she'd learned from Anderson Enright. Petra's fiancé was an interesting specimen, and she was sure he and her friend would get along. They both had that air of superiority, though Petra's was more innocent and naïve.

Hallie sometimes wondered why she and Petra were such good friends when they were total opposites. But then she remembered that fateful first day at the University, when, in Biology, she and Petra had been paired up as unwilling lab partners. The professor had assumed they'd want to be friends simply because they were the only two girls in the class.

Hallie smiled at the memory. Both she and Petra had refused to dissect the frog laid before them and had gotten a failing mark. Hallie thought it was disrespectful to the frog, while Petra had simply been disgusted. They then commiserated together at one of the tea shops after class, thinking of all the ways they could get their professor fired. Juvenile, but it'd made them feel better. They'd started studying together and eventually worked up the courage to dissect the next poor creature in class. They'd received perfect marks and had been the best of friends ever since.

Hallie hoped Anderson would make Petra happy. She deserved it. Three times over. But it was his words—or dare she say, even disdain—for the Yalvs that bothered her. She understood his point, but that didn't mean it was right. The refugees had made so much progress, it was astounding. Surely, everyone would stop seeing them as a threat soon.

Lost in her musings, Hallie flinched when something hit her shoulder—but it was only Kase's head. He was fast asleep.

Her heart fluttered. She remembered when he'd come into the bookshop for the first time. She'd been so rude—even though she was loath to admit it. Her cheeks burned at the thoughts she'd had toward him then. How arrogant he was. How privileged and haughty his words had been.

Yet behind all the thorns, he was just a boy abused by the man who was supposed to love him most...and a boy who was unsure of the world and his place in it.

She rubbed her eyes. It was too late if she was waxing poetic in her head.

With the care of one of the beast tamers at the City Menagerie, she eased herself off the cot and laid him gently down. She couldn't very well stay in the same room, and now that her adrenaline had finally calmed, she was about to fall asleep right there.

Thankfully, he only mumbled sleepily. His busted lip was prominent against the rough spun pillow, but it didn't seem to be bothering him now. Hallie eyed his feet hanging off the end of the cot. Too tall. She slipped off his loafers and set them under the cot. She then tugged out the folded blanket from under his feet and spread it across his prone form.

In sleep, he looked so incredibly innocent, the pain from earlier erased. For that, she was grateful. He deserved to sleep so soundly and forget the world for a short time. She wished she could be so lucky. Tonight, her nightmares would return, and she was certain the Stradat Lord Kapitan would join the ensemble cast with his dead son and her dead brother. She tugged at her dress sleeves. She was about to turn away when Kase grabbed her wrist. She let out a soft squeal of surprise.

"Wait," Kase mumbled, the pillow muffling his voice. She could barely discern the word.

Hallie looked down at his fingers around her wrist, his calloused fingertips catching on the lace extending from the dinner jacket sleeve. She knelt down beside him to find his blue eyes peeking out from half-closed lids.

"What is it?" she whispered as his hand fell away and dangled off the edge of the cot.

He blinked blearily.

Hallie sighed. "Kase, rest. I'll see you in the morning."

When he didn't respond, she rose to her feet. She tiptoed toward the door, trying to keep the floorboards from creaking.

"Thank you."

Hallie's hand was on the knob, but she turned back. Kase's eyes were open once more, and her heart wrenched at the depth of his gratitude. He wasn't simply thanking her for putting him to bed, or for making sure he had a blanket to sleep under.

She blinked hard and tucked his jacket closer around her shoulders. "You're welcome."

And with that, she left, shutting the door softly behind her, her heart filled with warmth.

CHAPTER 10

BLASTED LORD PILOT

Hallie

COME HOME. NEED TO TALK.

That was it. That was all the telegram said. The only words she'd heard from her parents in months.

Her mother must've sent it. Papa was always one to use more words than needed. He *did* run the inn and had to converse with all sorts of people. He also helped the town medic when the man was overloaded, which happened more often than it should. That's why Jack had been the one to get the funds for University. Her brother had planned to learn medicine and the healing arts properly.

But then he'd died, and neither the medic, her Pa, nor Hallie could save him.

Hallie woke to knocking on her door. Well, not really. She'd been in and out of sleep all night long after opening the telegram. It didn't help that the smallest rooms at the Crown Haven Inn had the most uncomfortable cots, and it wasn't the best idea to sleep in a fancy gown.

With each successive knock, she grumbled and stumbled from the cot, nearly tripping over the long skirts. She turned the knob and peeked out through the crack. It was Mazie.

"Oh, good. Chose the right door," she said as Hallie opened the door a little wider, letting her inside. She carried a bundle of clothing in one hand. "Nole said you were up here, and in a fancy ball gown." She looked around the room. "He also said something about a gentleman with a busted lip—"

"It's not what you think. And we did get *two rooms*." Heat scorched across Hallie's face.

Mazie cackled and held up the bundle. Her eyebrows rose as she caught sight of Kase's jacket slung over the end of the cot. "Either way, I brought some extra clothes in case you didn't want to wear that fabulous dress into town." Her fingers brushed over the lace at Hallie's wrist.

"Nothing happened." Hallie grabbed the clothes from Mazie's outstretched hand and clutched the bundle to her chest. "Thank you for the clothes!"

She opened the door once more, and Mazie took the hint, but the woman turned before she went over the threshold, a wicked grin creasing her features. "Nole also said the lad was quite the looker!"

"'Bye, Mazie!" Hallie said through gritted teeth.

Hallie shut the door with a snap, but not before she heard the woman's laughter and a muffled, "See you this afternoon!"

Right. Because even after everything that happened last night, Hallie had to work the dinner shift.

Which meant she needed to retrieve her satchel from Shackley Manor.

She changed quickly. Mazie had lent her a wool spun dress that would've fit the older woman nicely, but it swallowed Hallie whole—particularly in the chest area. Well, it was better than wearing the mussed and expensive evening gown while walking to the upper city.

As she grabbed Kase's jacket and slipped into the corridor, she peeked at his door. Probably still asleep. She would bring up a couple cinnamon buns. And coffee. She definitely needed coffee.

The kitchen of the Crown Haven Inn was bustling in the early morning hour. Mazie whisked something in a bowl while

Nole ground coffee beans. The cook girl prepped vegetables and the dish boy pumped out a tub of rinse water while flirting with one of the serving maids. Hallie spotted a plate stacked with hot, fresh cinnamon buns.

Waving to the others, she raked two onto a plate and poured two cups of steaming coffee. Mazie gave her an appraising look, which made Hallie blush before she went back up the stairs, balancing the plate of buns on one of the mug rims. Nodding to a few early risers on their way to breakfast, she finally made it back to Kase's door.

The door looked like any other at the inn, but it still judged her. It reminded her of the terrible evening the night before, all the words she didn't say, the argument she'd overheard. Even the accusations Jove Shackley had flung at his father in a drunken rage.

She knocked with the outside of her foot. Both she and Kase needed to devour these cinnamon buns for their own sanity.

Within a few seconds, the door creaked open. Kase's eyes were red and puffy, his lip bruised. His hair, still slick with gel, stuck out at odd angles. His tie and shirt were rumpled and askew. Stars, she'd never seen him like this, even in the week after Zeke died. Hallie held up the mug without the plate resting on top. "Coffee?"

Kase rubbed a hand down the side of his face and opened the door wider. Hallie took that as an invitation and strode inside. He shut the door behind her and moved the twisted blanket from the cot, bunching it into a ball near the pillow.

"Thanks," he muttered as he grabbed a mug and took a seat on the cot. Hallie followed suit, setting the plate of buns and his jacket between them.

She took a long sip of the hot liquid. It warmed her from the inside out and cleared the fog in her head. "Sorry to wake you so early."

Outside the snow-clouded window, pink fingers stretched across the lightening sky. Kase took a bite out of one of the pastries.

The only sounds in the room were sipping and crunching, but it was far from peaceful. Without meaning to, Hallie had wandered into a part of Kase's life that he'd tried to hide for so many years. She had trouble swallowing the next sip. It was like the guilt had consolidated into a single mass in her throat.

Kase finished his pastry and wiped his fingers on his dark trousers, leaving behind powder streaks. He took one last sip of coffee before setting the cup on the warped floor.

Hallie traced the rim of her mug with her thumbnail "I need to get into my apartment before work this afternoon, so I'll be heading..."

He didn't acknowledge her words, only stared at the ground, the non-injured side of his face smashed into his hand. She couldn't see the expression on his face.

She continued, "I'll have to go by your...house this morning, then. I assume you still would rather not...um, what I'm trying to say is that if you need me to get you anything while I'm there, I can."

He looked over at her. His hand from where he'd been leaning on it had left his cheek red, which evoked the memory of the theater slap so long ago.

She blinked. "I'll grab you a change of clothes? Nole will let you stay here for a day or two if you need it, or you can...um...what is it you want to do? When do you have training? Is there a certain book you want me to fetch?"

Kase's stare was blank.

She cradled the mug in her hands and peered into the depths of the murky liquid. He picked at his fingernails.

"We don't have to talk about what happened last night," Hallie offered, still refusing to make eye contact with him. "Unless you want to, that is."

"I don't."

She swallowed. Well, that was the end of that conversation, then. She chewed her lip. Was there anything else she could say to help him? Could she fix the rift that had been gouged by the night before? For once, she hadn't done anything to provoke it. He hadn't, either. Stars.

Who was Hallie to judge? Hadn't she taken off to Kyvena after Jack died? She suddenly remembered the telegram.

"Kase?"

He looked up at her. His eyes were lifeless. She gave him a half-hearted smile. "I have an idea, but before you answer, you have to hear me out, all right?"

And please say yes.

When he didn't say anything, she continued. "I won't go into the whole thing now, because it'll bore you to death, and I want you to say yes. But I mean, if you want to know more about it, I guess I could..." She trailed off and cleared her throat. "Sorry. I can get carried away."

"It's okay." His voice was raspy.

She set aside her mug. "I need to get to Stoneset, and as you're a pilot, I figured that you might, you know, fly me there? I'd pay you, of course."

More money out of my school fund, though fifty gold hunders should take me a long way...hopefully.

His eyebrows rose into his unruly hair. "The Narden Pass won't be accessible right now."

"I know that." Irritation bled into her voice. She *had* grown up in the mountains. She was aware of what the Pass looked like this time of year. "I could find a trapper to guide me. They do it all the time. I paid one a few weeks ago to take a letter through. All I need is a ride to the Pass itself."

"It's dangerous."

"Please, Kase." Her eyes were burning. "I'd bet you'd do nearly anything to get out of the city after what your father said last night, and I'm giving you the opportunity right now!"

His nostrils flared as he turned away from her. "You shouldn't have been eavesdropping."

Guilt brewed like a storm in her stomach. "I didn't mean to."

"I can't just take off into the mountains. That would mean desertion, along with burglary, treason, and a whole litany of crimes. After last autumn with Trainee Hixon, I'm walking a thin line. He still can't use his legs."

Hallie had heard about that. There'd also been talk Hixon was suing the Crews. Hearsay, but the papers thought it good fodder for the Society section. "But I'd pay you!"

"With war on the horizon, pilots only fly government officials anywhere. That's it. So, no, you can't just pay me. And as much as I would love to leave this blasted city behind, it's not possible"

His words hit her like a ton of bricks, which made her blood heat even more. "Cerulene attacked near Stoneset, so it's not such a far-fetched idea that something could have happened to my parents! The telegram I received from my family sounded serious."

"Jove said Achilles took care of the force. Everyone's fine. You're overreacting."

"I am *not* overreacting!" She stood, her foot knocking over her mug. It was only a quarter of the way full, and a trickle of black liquid spilled onto the floor. "Fine! I'll find a different way. I was trying to help—never mind. You wouldn't understand."

She swiped the other cinnamon bun from the plate and stormed toward the door, ignoring the spilled coffee. Stuffing the pastry in her mouth, she wrenched open the door and slammed it.

Blasted Lord Pilot.

CHAPTER 11

THE CRISP, CLEAN SMELL OF PEPPERMINT

Clara

CLARA BARELY SLEPT. HER EYES didn't—*wouldn't*—close. They ached.

Even before last evening, between insomnia and back pain, her sleep had been riddled with holes, some nights even gaping chasms. But they had been nothing like the one after Jove pushed her in his drunken rage.

He'd been silent on the way home from Shackley Manor, muttering a slurring, shallow apology, before staring out at the houses and streetlamps waving by. Clara refused to talk to him while he was like that, which had happened more often of late. He wouldn't remember the conversation when morning dawned.

After they'd arrived back at the townhouse, the maid quickly turned down the bed with a knowing look. Jove had tumbled into it, snoring loudly as he fell asleep. He hadn't bothered to remove his dinner jacket.

His pounding headache when he woke wouldn't be punishment enough.

After admitting defeat hours later, Clara climbed out of bed, slipping on her embroidered silk dressing gown that had been crafted by Kyvena's best as part of her wedding trousseau. She grabbed the small electric lantern from her bedside table and waddled toward the kitchen. Her bare feet shuffled with each step, the cold wooden floor a welcome relief. Her painted roses from yesterday winked in the lamplight as she passed. Even with the discomfort of carrying a child, she'd managed to create a masterpiece.

I am strong.

The words were empty, but if she said them often enough, they might come true. They had to. She had no choice.

Now only if her mother would arrive, maybe things would get better. Or worse. Maybe having her mother here would deter Jove from drinking. Probably not. What panacea existed for grief so bone-deep, it was a part of you? How could Clara know what that felt like? She'd not lost anyone so close. She had no siblings. Her parents were still young. Her heart gave a painful beat.

Zeke had been an exceptional brother-in-law. He'd been the only one to know of the baby before he left. He'd been so happy, so overjoyed for Jove and Clara, so excited to become an uncle.

And now, he wouldn't.

Clara set the lantern on the round breakfast table and filled the kettle with tap water—a luxury of the upper class—and set it atop the stove, twisting the appropriate metal knob. Tiny blue flames licked the copper sides of the pot. Some tea would do her well. It would calm the raging storm inside her, wash away the lingering pain—physical and emotional.

As a little girl, she'd dreamed of the boy she would one day marry. Of course, her earliest daydreams consisted of a dashing prince riding in on a towering stallion like the old tales her mother used to tell her before she fell asleep. Jove wasn't a prince, but he had once been so much more.

Before Zeke's death, he'd bought her roses every

Wednesday. He'd listen, laying his head on her shoulder, as she read aloud her favorite passages from whatever artist's biography she'd borrowed from the University's library. When her muse waned as it always did in the late winter, he'd take her to the Silver Coast or the foothills of the Nardens just so she could paint. Jove Shackley was her match in every way.

Yet, with Zeke gone, her husband was a shell of the man he once was.

She chose her favorite teacup—one she'd painted with a wintry scene—and some loose-leaf peppermint tea. The kettle chirped twice, the third time turning into a squeal. She lifted it from the burner, twisting the stove knob off. With practiced hands, she poured the water into the cup. Steam rose in delicate swirls as she brought the cup to her lips and blew softly.

The crisp, clean smell of peppermint always grounded her, reminded her of who she was, who she had been. It would fortify her for when her husband woke at last.

She'd reached the dregs by the time Jove stumbled in, eyes bleary and tie crooked. He hadn't shaved or tamed his hair, though he'd changed out of his dinner clothes into appropriate attire for work. He didn't look at her, didn't acknowledge her, as he fell into the chair on the other side of the antique table.

Clara knew what she had to say. She twisted her empty cup in its saucer, the tiny chinking sound not doing much to ward away the looming silence. Jove still slumped in his chair, his right thumb rubbing the floral carving on the table edge.

Setting her teacup aside, Clara pressed her tense fingers against her protruding belly, holding back her agitation as she rubbed a smooth circle. The baby responded with a swift kick, as if goading her into speaking. It gave her courage. Open communication was the only way this marriage would continue to work, and she loved Jove too much to remain quiet.

"Love." Her voice cracked from exhaustion and disuse. Jove didn't take his eyes off his thumb, which was still rubbing the swirled carving, so she cleared her throat. "We need to speak about last night."

Silence.

Clara chewed the edge of her tongue. The lamplight was like the early morning sun, yet it cast untoward shadows on her husband's features. Despite his mere twenty-five years of age, the crow's feet in the corners of his eyes had become chasms in the months gone by.

I am a Davey. I am strong.

She tried again. "Lizzie's tossing out all the alcohol this morning."

His head shot up, eyes bloodshot and wide. His mouth opened.

Clara continued, "It's the only way. You nearly hurt me and the baby last night. You didn't mean to, and I don't even know if you remember everything, but you...you..." She swallowed heavily as her husband cleared his throat, but she cut in before he could speak. "...you're turning into—into someone I no longer—no longer recognize."

She looked down at the table. She didn't want to see the hurt in his eyes. She didn't want to witness the despair that had found its home in their sapphire depths. He'd lost his brother, but she didn't want Jove to lose himself.

"You don't have to get rid of the alcohol." His voice sounded ages away, as if he'd run a race with still too far to go. "I won't drink it."

Clara snapped her head up, blood rushing to her cheeks. "You say that but look where you are now."

Her voice cracked on the last word. The lamplight faded to a golden blur, her husband a dark void as tears flooded her vision. When he didn't say anything at all, she wiped her cheeks with one hand and heaved herself to her feet with the other.

She followed the woodgrain in the floor with her eyes. Jove didn't move to stop her.

Clara left the dregs and her husband in the kitchen, praying he would follow, yet feeling no surprise when he didn't.

CHAPTER 12

LIKE A LADIES' CORSET

Kase

KASE STAGGERED INTO HIS HOVER hangar an hour after Hallie left his room at the inn. To get himself this far without falling over was nothing short of a miracle. It wouldn't help to bust his lip again. What was more, the argument with her had only made his throbbing head worse.

She knew better than he did how dangerous the Pass was, and yet she wanted him to abandon his post and go on another reckless venture that could very well get them killed? Was she insane? Probably.

Except...she had taken care of him last night, and all she'd asked for was a ride to the Pass. He remembered her gentle touch as she'd cleaned him up.

Maybe he shouldn't have reacted so strongly. She didn't deserve that.

Not that the offer hadn't been tempting. But after everything that had happened with the *Eudora* mission, his place was here with the dream of flying for his country. Because that was all he was good for.

Even if Harlan thought he was useless.

Jayde needed him more than Hallie. He also wasn't going to give his father yet another reason to despise his existence, but that might be an impossible task. Maybe he *should* run away with Hallie. Drop her off wherever she wanted and then set out on his own and become a hermit.

He changed out of his bedraggled dinner outfit and shoved his arms through his stiff trainee jacket. His dress slacks and loafers looked funny with the whole ensemble. He dared any of his ground crew to ask about his leather jacket. A few gave him questioning looks while prepping his hover. Ebba would've asked if he'd hired her.

Her death was one of the reasons he'd told Hallie no.

He gave his head mechanic a tight smile before hopping up into the cockpit. The mustachioed man saluted before waving his hands in an 'All Clear.' The hovers were prepared for exiting the hangar.

Once Kase had closed the top, the silence enveloped him. He breathed in the scent of oil and metal and secured his straps. With all the other safety checks completed, Kase flipped a black switch. The resounding hum of the engine embraced him, the tension in his shoulders dripping off at last.

He waved to his crew as he left the hangar. Hopefully, they'd be doing something useful soon instead of flying dignitaries throughout the realm.

Yet hours into training, the peace he'd found in the air melted away. Hallie's words wouldn't leave him alone.

I'd bet you'd do nearly anything to get out of the city after what your father said last night, and I'm giving you the opportunity right now!

She was right, and he hated that. He hated she had to see him look so weak in front of his father. He hated that she had to hear. He hated everything about himself.

Shocks, he needed a distraction, and flying wasn't working. A deluge of memories flooded his mind, increasing his heart rate. He took a deep breath and pressed a button to his left.

Within a few seconds, the fluttering of music notes drifted in the air.

Focus on the music. Focus on the sky. Focus on what I can control.

The electric gramophone wasn't much, but Kase had figured out a way to rig a small one to his hover and play one song. It was one Skibs had teased him about. The violins made it slightly flowery, but the chords always allowed Kase to breathe.

Running through a few more maneuvering drills, Kase checked his fuel gauge. Running low. Blasted thing was one of the older hybrids, and it was days like today he wished he was still flying the *Eudora Jayde*. While also a hybrid, its electrical capacities far outweighed this clunker. That beauty basically flew itself.

Too bad it was a heap of crushed metal on Tasava.

He ignored the nausea creeping up his throat. Kase was in Kyvena, alive and well, yet...yet...

He gripped the steering control until he couldn't feel his fingers. If there was anyone in the world who had an inkling of the way he felt, it was the pretty red-haired scholar who'd seen the worst of the Shackley family and refused to run.

Kase was a terrible human being. He couldn't give her what she needed.

The end of the day's training came as a blessing for once, and Kase hated that even flying couldn't make him feel better. Should he apologize to Hallie? Would that be enough?

After waving goodbye to his ground crew and inwardly thanking them for not commenting on his fat lip, he headed toward the city, a light drizzle beginning. He groaned a little as he stepped out into it, but it did fit his mood.

He'd made it into the city proper, wooden structures giving way to stone, when a figure waved to him. A blond man with a ready grin, the rain soaking the shoulders of his tailored jacket.

Ellis Carrington. Shocks, he hadn't seen him since Zeke's Burning.

"Good to see you again, Kase," Ellis said, the smile never leaving his face. He stuck out his hand. Kase shook it hesitantly.

"And you as well." His words were still a little muffled thanks to his lip.

Ellis gestured for them to walk on, and Kase followed. What in the stars was Ellis doing in this part of town? Wasn't he still at the University? Ellis seemed to hear his thoughts, because he turned and asked, "Wanna grab a drink?"

What? Why? And how in the moons did Ellis know he'd be finished with training at this time? "I should be getting back to..."

Back to where? Kase didn't have anywhere to stay for the night.

"Not to be rude," Kase changed tack, "but we haven't spoken more than a few sentences to each other in years."

Even with the dim light coming from the streetlamps, the blush crawling up Ellis' neck was noticeable.

Blast. Why couldn't Kase keep his thoughts to himself? Why did it matter if he went and got drinks with him? Kase could use an ale or three. "Fine, where to?"

Ellis shrugged. "I know a place around the corner here that boasts it has the best ingleberry wine."

"And the ale?"

"Probably decent."

Weaving in and out of the general population, Ellis led Kase around a corner and down a side street to an establishment busting at the seams, even though it was still early in the evening.

The sign reading 'Estelle's' was shiny from the rain and complete with an overly-rouged woman's face frozen mid wink. Kase hadn't been there before, but he assumed Ellis wouldn't choose anywhere disreputable. Kase pushed open the tavern's heavy oak door, his companion following close behind.

Laughter and boisterous piano notes hit Kase's ears as warmth enveloped him. A group of bearded men to his right were already knee-deep in a game of Hanged Man's Nebula, a version of First Earth's poker. Kase didn't particularly like cards, as he felt like it tempted lower class men without much money to gamble away what little they had. But that wasn't his problem.

He nodded to a rather busty barmaid as he scanned the crowded room for an open table. *This ale better be good.*

He wove his way toward the bar and ordered a mug while Ellis asked for the wine. Kase picked up the mug once the barman had filled it, the wooden grains pressing in on his fingers, and handed over a few coppers before taking a small sip. It wasn't bad. The nutty aftertaste was nice.

"There's a table near the back," Ellis said. He pushed off

from the bar and plunged into the throng. Some couples had left their seats to dance to the pianist's rousing chorus. Ellis took a seat at the secluded table near the back door. "Glad you decided to join me."

Kase grunted and sat. "Sure."

Ellis tasted his wine. "You should try a bit of this once you finish off your ale there. Granted, it tastes a little funny coming out of a mug instead of fine crystal."

Kase raised a brow but didn't comment. "How've you been? Your family doing well?"

Because what else was he supposed to say? Why was he even here?

"Not too bad. Father's excited because they were able to get a troupe from Lenara to perform *The Gilded Lily* this fall. A whole week of shows."

"Don't think I've heard of it." *They're probably wanting to get away, if the rumors in Lenara of One World are indeed true.*

Ellis took a long pull of his wine. "Father says it's made the Violet Opera House over there some very pretty gold. It's about some sailor dying at sea and his fair maiden back home having to deal with the sea monster that killed him. I don't remember the details, but someone told me it was a newer take on *Beowulf.*"

Kase smiled. Finally, something interesting. "*Beowulf,* you say? When can I purchase tickets?"

"Father and the other investors are working out the details now, but hopefully soon. I think it'll be a big hit here. Take everyone's mind off...well, you know..."

Kase stared down at his ale. The golden-brown hue of the liquid glittered in the light from the electric lanterns hung on posts throughout the room. He tugged at the collar of his shirt. "I don't think that's a bad idea."

Ellis was silent for a beat too long. "Have you heard anything? About the Cerls?"

Kase clenched his fist around his mug. "Not really."

"There's a rumor about a draft coming."

Kase shrugged. Could they simply get this over with? Again, why was he here? Could they go back to talking about *Beowulf?* At least that'd been interesting, and it didn't have the side effect of reminding him about the Stradat Lord Kapitan.

But Ellis wasn't to be dissuaded by Kase's silence. "I'd heard enlistment was down, but I didn't think they'd ever enact the draft. Not here. Cerulene, maybe. Or that little strip of land that broke off from Tev Rubika during their civil war. But not Jayde."

"The Stradat Lord Kapitan hasn't said anything about it to me. Neither has Jove, so I don't have an answer for you."

Ellis sat back and inspected the ceiling, mumbling something to himself. "But surely you know something."

Kase waited a moment before answering, if only to keep himself from hurling his mug at the man in front of him. "I told you the *blasted* Stradat Lord Kapitan doesn't tell me anything."

Ellis was quiet. He reached into his pocket and unfolded the parchment, taking a deep breath. "Listen, I know this all came out of the blue, me showing up, but I, uh, well, I thought you'd be interested in this."

He slid the parchment across the table, and a sense of unease descended on the conversation. As Kase grabbed the note, Ellis leaned forward.

"They'd like to meet with you. It's some of our old friends along with a few others. Nothing fancy. We just—well, just listen to what they have to say. They've made some good points."

Kase stared at the word scrawled in dark red ink. It looked painfully like blood.

The Brotherhood of One World cordially invites you to a meeting of minds tonight at dusk.

Karsi va si.

Something had smeared the first part, maybe the rain, but it was still legible. Kase bit the inside of his cheek as a glacial cold raced through his veins. *One World.* Hadn't Jove and Anderson been discussing the group at dinner the previous evening? Hadn't Jove assured everyone they were simply a passing fancy? "El, what is this? It sounds...well, it doesn't sound like anything I should dirty my hands with."

Had Ellis written this? The handwriting was eerily familiar. Old friends of his. Kase wondered...could it be...

No. Not *him.* Eravin wouldn't get involved with something

like this.

He met Ellis' green eyes, which seemed to have solidified into stone—jade, specifically. They weren't the same as the light, happy ones from his school days. Ellis' voice was measured, passion bleeding into each successive word. "But you don't like what's going on, do you? One World works for a better Yalvara. We could be so much more."

Kase crumpled the paper in his fist and leaned in. "I'm the stars-blasted son of the Stradat Lord Kapitan. If my father caught word of this, it would be my neck on the line."

The smile on Ellis' face was small and full of spite. "It won't hurt to talk."

Kase shook his head, a fog of apprehension tinged with fear addling his thoughts. He willed the fog to lift. "I can't. I might not agree with what's going on, but that doesn't mean I'm interested in—whatever it is your friends want to talk about. I've heard things, and..."

"*Our* friends, Kase. *They're our friends.* You know most of them."

"Except I haven't spoken to any school friends in over three years."

"You'll understand once you hear what they have to say. I swear on Tovo's name." Ellis signaled for another round, relaxed and looking almost every bit like the young man Kase knew, except the eyes. Their innocence had dimmed, taken by time and stars knew what else.

The Ellis he knew had been quiet but always willing to join in on the fun, even if it was on the outskirts. Kase and the others allowed him to join their games only because he didn't snitch on them.

And now, the same quiet Ellis was part of a rebellion. What events had led to this moment? What would possess him to join a group of violent rebels? Granted, Kase didn't know much about One World, only what he'd heard through rumors.

He'd told Hallie that One World caused unrest. What he hadn't told her was the tales of brutality, of missing limbs and stolen lives.

Yet, Ellis sat in front of him sans visible bloodstains. Did he know? Ellis was poised, kind, thoughtful, quiet. He wasn't capable of such violence, was he?

Kase didn't understand. Rebels were usually scarred. They were brutes who resorted to killing.

What if the rumors were wrong, spun up by the Jaydian government and disseminated into the populace to keep citizens from joining up? To protect their own power? They'd lied before. The Yalvs were the shining example of that.

Kase relaxed his death grip on his mug, glancing down at the parchment once more.

Karsi va si

We are one. A slogan to rally around—and one derived from a dead language called Cerleze, only taught to the wealthier children of Jayde.

Kase's brain was going a mile a minute. "They just want to talk?"

Ellis took his wine from the barmaid. "Of course."

Kase stared hard at the man in front of him and finished off his ale. "Fine."

"You're certain?" Ellis set down his mug.

"I'll hear what they have to say."

Ellis's lip curled, and he knocked on the wall beside him three times. In a few seconds, the panel slid open. No one waited in the dark. Without looking around, Ellis stood up and entered the space, beckoning for Kase to follow.

No one seemed to care that one of the tavern's patrons disappeared behind a hidden door in the back booth. Heart thumping painfully—either from alcohol or fear—Kase followed Ellis into the dark.

ROOTS DRAPED ACROSS THE CEILING, spindling their way down a corridor that stretched out forever. There was no telling what trees they belonged to. He hadn't thought about how far they'd walked in the sloping, dimly-lit corridor—only that he dreaded what he might find at the end.

Jaydian and First Earth history was full of groups such as One World. At times they were venerated as heroes, others executed as traitors. History was written by the victors after all. So, what's to say One World wasn't the righteous revolutionaries?

That didn't stop the sweat from beading at Kase's hairline.

The room waiting for them was much like the tunnel with its roots and dirt. It was circular, gas lanterns dotting the outer rim of the circular chamber in alcoves. At the center of the room was a table. There was a man sitting at the head, as familiar to Kase as one of his brothers. The handwriting. Kase had been correct.

Eravin Gray.

He hadn't changed much since the days he and Kase stole cigars and liquor from the gentleman's club. His nose was still crooked from the time they'd gotten into a fist fight with the opposing team after a groggon match. Eravin took the punch meant for Kase.

Kase had been there at the top of the city walls, begging Eravin not to jump after finding out his father was running off with his mistress, leaving his ailing wife and son destitute. Yet after Ana's death...after the fire...when Kase had gone to Eravin for help, all he'd received was a door in the face.

He hadn't spoken to or seen Eravin since, and now the ghost of the boy Kase knew stared back, eyes dark as night.

Eravin gestured for Kase to sit at the opposite end of the short table. By the grace of Tovo, Kase's legs didn't give out on him as he walked forward, falling heavily into the seat. Ellis sat beside him.

He'd locked away his memories of Eravin, his life before the fire and Ana's death three years ago, vowing never to think of it all again. It hurt too much. And now, Eravin was here, sitting before him in an underground room.

After minutes of silence, Ellis finally cleared his throat.

Eravin's jaw tightened. He pressed his elbows to the table, his fingers steepled.

"What convinced you to come, Shackley?" His voice was still the overpowering baritone of a man trying to fill the shoes his father left behind. He barely moved his lips.

Kase rested his hand on the edge of the table. He forced himself to be calm, for his muscles to relax though everything in his being begged to run. He swallowed. "To hear what you have to say, a privilege you chose not to grant me three years ago."

The lines around Eravin's mouth deepened, fire lighting in

his eyes. "Such careless words."

Kase let the exchange hover in the air like cigarette smoke. He would not be baited. Did Eravin not realize Kase could go to his father with the very little information he had—Eravin Gray, involved with One World, and this little tavern in the lower city serving as a meeting place?

But the longer the three men sat there, Kase knew he wouldn't. Harlan would never know of this meeting.

"If you think so little of me, then why the invitation?"

Eravin dropped his hands to the table, his fingers splayed upon the surface. "You have the power to make this movement into something more, though inviting you was against my better judgment."

"Ah, yes, I might be more inclined to help if we were friends, but you saw to that, didn't you?"

Ellis cleared his throat, leaning forward and coming into Kase's line of sight. He threw Eravin a look before speaking. "We're fighting for a better Jayde, a better Yalvara. You have connections we don't."

Kase narrowed his eyes, looking from one man to the other. "A better Jayde? By destroying it first? I've heard what One World did in Lenara."

"It's effective."

Kase leaned back, thankful the man's words were no longer venom laced. "The only reason you need me is because I'm the son of the Stradat Lord Kapitan, but you and I both know my father hates me."

"Your brother was once the Head Guardsman of the Watch. You're also the youngest full pilot in history. You devalue yourself, whether that be your father's doing or your own," Ellis said.

The implication brought heat to Kase's neck. No one except Eravin and now Hallie knew about the abuse, yet he'd told Ellis? Kase gritted his teeth. "And you want me to do what?"

Eravin laughed humorlessly. "Tomorrow night, we'll be holding a full meeting to discuss our goals here in the capital. Jagamot is on the horizon, and we need to prepare for the oncoming fight. The High Council refuses to listen to reason. It's time to bring them down."

Jaga-what? "You're not making sense."

"If you want to win, you'll stand at the corner of Kayser and Rath. Alone. Seven tomorrow evening," Eravin said, his voice low.

"And if I don't?"

Eravin smiled. He almost looked like the boy Kase had known. "You'll join. I know you. I know you better than you know yourself."

Kase gritted his teeth. The condescension and arrogance had always been there, but this time, he refused to participate. He'd lived a miserable life these past three years, and then Hallie barged in and yelled at him until he saw what life could be like if he let go of everything—his pain, his anger, and his past.

The man sitting in front of him was not going to bully him. He refused to let go of the life he'd only begun to build, even if it was just barely a foundation.

"You know nothing. The Kase you knew is dead, and I'm not joining. I could tell Jove, my father. I can put a stop to this before it even starts."

Ellis fidgeted in his chair, as if he couldn't find a comfortable position.

Eravin merely leaned back in his own. His smile was more of a sneer as he said, "You could. I wouldn't recommend it, though."

Kase swallowed as Eravin continued, "If you tell anyone about this meeting, anyone at all, I know where to find that pretty redhead you stumble around after."

"Don't you dare." Kase stood so fast, his chair flung back, smacking the ground. "Hallie has nothing to do with this."

The muscles in his arm quivered, his pulse racing, Kase itched for a cocked electropistol in his hand—any weapon at all. Hallie was innocent of Kase's crimes. She was all that was good in his dark world.

And the only light, the budding *whatever it was* with Hallie, had been unwittingly dragged into the room with him, an offering on a plate he didn't realize he'd be sacrificing. He clenched his fingers and glanced at Ellis, whose gaze didn't leave the table. Bile rose in Kase's throat. His lip curled.

That spineless *helviter*. What monster did this to a friend? Heat flushed through his body as he faced Eravin once more.

The man finally shrugged. "Of course not, and she doesn't have to, so long as you keep your mouth shut."

"You involve her, and I'm nowhere near that corner tomorrow night."

Eravin stood, leaning forward, hands on the table. "Again, you could do that, but choosing that path will force me to tell the city exactly what happened three years ago."

Kase saw red. He upended the flimsy table, launching himself at the man. He stopped dead when the cold lips of an electropistol met his damp forehead. Eravin's thumb rested on the hammer.

"You killed my mother in that fire. Did you expect me to simply let that go?"

All the fury thrumming through Kase's veins dissipated in a matter of seconds. "What?"

"Too lost in your own grief to see that you still had people who loved you. I had no one, thanks to you."

Kase stumbled backward, nearly tripping. He caught himself on the leg of the upturned table. "No...no..."

"And the father whom you claim despises you used every string he could to tie up the case like a lady's corset."

Sweat beaded along Kase's hairline. Weakness threaded through his limbs. His hands shook.

Eravin continued. "If you tell, we take the girl. If you don't help, we tell everyone. Either way, our plan for unrest is aided. Everyone will know exactly who killed their friends, their mothers, fathers, and children that night. The city will riot, and you'll be hanged. But at least you wouldn't have to live with it anymore, would you?"

Kase opened his mouth, but nothing came out. He could only see the flames, hear the screams. "I'm sorry. I didn't know...I didn't know...I lost Ana...please, I didn't mean to...my father—"

"I don't care. All I do care about is how we use you." He cocked the electropistol, sparks flaring around the barrel as it came to life. "Seven tomorrow. Corner of Kayser and Rath. Now, get out."

Kase ran.

If he joined, he'd be a traitor to Jayde and his oaths as a pilot. If he told anyone what was going on, Eravin would take

Hallie. If he didn't do anything, he'd hang. His father wouldn't help him this time. Whatever luck Kase had dried up.

Sick and horrified, he left the room and Eravin behind.

CHAPTER 13

FREE AS THE STARS

Hallie

HALLIE HURRIED THROUGH THE STREETS as fast as she could manage. Good stars, so many people got up way too early. She tugged Mazie's old cloak tighter around her shoulders as she made her way to the upper city and through its gate. The electricity in its doors hummed when she passed underneath.

She wondered what Mazie and Nole would say when she told them she'd need to take off for an indefinite amount of time so she could make sure her parents were all right. Surely, they wouldn't mind—since it was for family reasons—but she wasn't sure if they could hold her job until she returned.

Especially if something was wrong.

If she had to hire a motorcoach, it would take nearly two weeks to reach the Pass, and then she'd have to find a trapper to take her through it this time of year. The snows wouldn't begin melting for another month, so the trek would be arduous. And cold. So cold. Avalanches were always a possibility. Stars.

Come home. Need to talk.

Staying in the city, working at the Crown Haven Inn, was a waste of time. She wasn't attending the University. She wasn't doing anything worthwhile now that the Yalvs were adjusting. She was stuck.

Thinking about her myriad of problems didn't help her frazzled nerves as she finally reached Shackley Manor. The griffins adorning the gate leered at her harder than ever. Stony eyes mocked her—they knew she was a fraud. She looked away from the immobile creatures and smiled hesitantly at the guard manning the gate. He looked to be the same one from before, from the night she'd helped Saldr. His two-toned brown and blond hair was even more prominent in the early morning sun.

"Pardon me," she said, her fingers curling around a bar of the ornate gate. She quickly let it go, as it was much too cold for her bare hands. "My name's Hallie Walker. I'm here to retrieve some items I left last evening."

The guard simply stared at her, his gray eyes mirroring the griffins' above. Hallie shifted her weight from foot to foot. Petra's slippers weren't doing much to keep out the cold. She shivered. "I was with Kase, but we had to leave in a hurry."

The guard nodded. "Stand back."

"I promise, I'm telling truth!"

The creaking of the gates cut her off. Relief flooded her chest. *Oh, thank the stars.*

She smiled. "I appreciate it, Mister..."

"Lars." The guard's expression still didn't change, but Hallie took it as a positive. She gave him a swift curtsy.

"Thank you, Mister Lars. I won't be long, I swear."

He nodded again, and she made her way up the drive. She kept her eyes open for any sign of the motorcoach, praying she wouldn't even have to go inside, but the circular drive was empty save for the fountain in the middle. Its waters didn't flow. Like Hallie, the solid cherubs climbing over the lips of each layer looked like they wished for spring to come quickly.

Hallie found herself at the door much too soon. She willed her hand to knock on the door, but it refused to listen. What if the Stradat Lord Kapitan was there? What if they had thrown away Hallie's satchel? What if—

Stop.

If she wanted to get to Stoneset, she needed to knock. She took several deep breaths before rapping smartly on the door with her too-cold knuckles.

The sound echoed in the still air as she buried her hands in the edges of the cloak, and eight heartbeats later, the door opened. The butler stood before her, his face impassive. She curtsied again. "Hello, I'm Hallie Walker. I came last night with Kase, but I believe I left a few of my effects? A cloak, gloves, and satchel."

Please. Please say you still have them. I don't want to have to buy yet another satchel.

With a sharp nod, the man opened the door wider, and Hallie stepped inside with a sigh of relief. He shut the door behind her and strode off down the corridor. Without knowing what else to do, Hallie followed him into the parlor from the previous evening.

"Please make yourself comfortable," the butler said, gesturing with his hand. "I will return shortly."

He shut the door so quietly, Hallie barely heard the latch catch. She took a deep breath and inspected the room. It seemed smaller without so many people filling the space. She spotted the little etagere overladen with glass figurines. That wasn't the only home for them. They were also spread throughout the entire space, like freshly fallen snow.

In addition to the figurines, books stood artfully in the spaces sans glass trinkets. Taking one look at the door to make sure she wasn't going to be disturbed, she meandered over to the bookshelves on the opposite wall.

Hallie's fingers traced the letters embossed on the spines. So many books. She itched to take them from the shelf and read them all, cover to cover. Books on vegetation, politics, and First Earth culture stood on the shelf to her right, but what interested her most was the books below that included histories. Peeking back toward the door, she pulled out *Yalven Continent: Mysteries and Massacres.* The book was small compared to the other volumes, but with everything Hallie had learned before leaving last autumn, it didn't surprise her. In fact, she might be the only one other than Kase who could accurately write a book on the subject.

But all her notes and sketches were gone. Her fingers tightened on the hard leather of the book as she recalled those terrifying moments. The thing that was Ben had nearly killed Kase, and for one horrific moment, she thought he might kill her as well.

She shut her eyes tight and clutched the book to her chest. Reading this might help keep her mind off of her life going up in flames.

For the moment, at least.

She chose a gold-pinstriped couch and opened the book up to the first chapter, "Jagamotian Prophecies."

At the center of Yalven lore sits the prophesied Jagamot. This dark entity is one secret the Yalvs guard zealously for fear of the end of time coming prematurely.

Hallie had read short references to Jagamot in her own studies, but this particular text had an entire chapter devoted to it. Stars, why didn't the University have this on its shelves?

Some texts predict that Zalina, the end of time in the native tongue, will be hailed with fire and brimstone. Others state vast and brutal wars among the nations of Yalvara will precede Zalina. There is one that details the core of Yalvara becoming unstable, causing the planet to implode slowly.

Hallie's stomach turned as she read the gruesome depictions of what would happen to some cities—and that was before Yalvara was destroyed with fire from the heavens. The whole world and everyone left in it would burn.

Some say it only speaks of the Gate's destruction. With the 'Called' Yalvs transforming into holy blades and the 'Chosen' wielding the Essences, one could conclude the Yalven nations are preparing to fight the looming darkness and strife...

A soft clearing of a throat interrupted her. Hallie flinched so hard, the book fell from her fingers and landed with a thud against the stone floor. She whipped her eyes up, trying to find the source and praying it wasn't the Stradat Lord Kapitan.

But it was simply Kase's mother, a demure smile gracing her features. She was dressed in what Hallie would consider pretty clothes, though it wasn't even nine in the morning. Her hair was braided into a crown, the gray strands interwoven and glittering in the light.

"Good morning," Hallie squeaked, picking the book up and

standing. She adjusted the front of her own dress, trying to make it fit a little better. "I didn't hear you come in, I'm so sorry." She held up the book. "I tend to get distracted when books are involved..."

Les' smile finally reached her eyes. "It's all right. My son told me you were something of an avid reader, so having you wait in a room full of stories would be as much of a temptation to you as it is to me."

"Yes," Hallie said. "I used to work at a bookshop before I...before...well, before I went away last fall. I had piles of old and damaged tomes Jess wasn't able to sell. Of course, I haven't been able to read them since...I'm rambling."

Les shook her head. "No, dear. You're perfectly fine. Kase and I are similar in that regard. One of the only good things about our social standing is my library upstairs. You're welcome to peruse it any time you wish."

"Really?" Hallie gasped. She remembered the room from the night before their awkward breakfast. She'd been entirely too exhausted and downtrodden to inspect it thoroughly, but even in her state, she'd admired the shelves overflowing with who knew how many books.

"Of course." Les looked down at her skirts and picked at the beading for a moment. "That book is one I received in the post this week. With the dinner, I hadn't gotten a chance to read it yet."

Hallie ran her fingers over the cover. "It's beautiful. The subject is what I was studying at the University when..."

She trailed off when she realized Les was crying. The older woman put a shaking hand to her brow, the other going to her satin-clad stomach.

"I'm sorry," Les whispered as she fell onto the couch behind her. Hallie shifted her feet from one to the other before she tiptoed to Les' side and sat down next to her. She set the book on her other side, and after a moment's hesitation, rested her hand on Les' softly shaking shoulder.

Hallie didn't know what to do or what to say. She hardly knew what had brought this on.

After another moment of silent tears, Les looked up, her grin forced. "I didn't mean to..." she took a deep breath. "It's just that...have you seen my Kase? Is he all right? He never came home, and after I asked..."

Would Kase care whether or not she told his mother? She probably had an idea of what might have happened, but that didn't mean Hallie could spill Kase's shame out in the open. Even if he'd been an infuriating *dulkop* that morning. But she also knew her own mother prior to Jack's death would have been beside herself if Hallie hadn't come home the night before. She fiddled with her fingers, picking at a particularly annoying hangnail.

"He's fine. I made sure of it." Hallie had to swallow her own tears pooling in her throat, because the words from last night came back to her.

It would have been better if you had died instead of your brother, for all the good you do.

Les wiped her eyes. "I'm glad he has you."

"It's not what you—" Hallie started, but she stopped when she caught Les' watery smile. "We're friends."

"Of course," she said, tucking away stray hairs back into her intricate braid. "That's why I know it will all be fine. I know my husband can be difficult, but he tries to do what's right by us."

"He hit Kase." Hallie's words were stilted, poisoned with anger. Why couldn't she keep her mouth shut? Why couldn't she check her emotions? She was turning into Kase. "And then he said he'd wished Kase had died on our mission to Tasava. How is that *doing right by us?*"

Her breaths came faster, and she couldn't control the tears streaming down her face. All she could think about was Kase and his busted lip. All she could feel was his death-grip on her arm as they fled from the manor. All she could hear were his sobs as the key fell to the inn's floor.

Les' smooth fingers enclosed her own and squeezed them gently. "I never said I agreed with him."

Hallie swiped at her eyes with her other hand. "But how could you allow—"

Her words were cut off by the arrival of the butler, her belongings in his arms. Hallie stood swiftly, taking them from him. Then she noticed another bag, a leather pack, on his shoulder. He held it out as well.

"What is this?" she asked, glancing back at Kase's mother.

Les joined them by the door. "I had Thoreau pack some of

Kase's things." Her words were soft and drowning in bits of sorrow. "I think it's best if he does not return here for a while. I don't know the specifics of what happened last evening, but I know enough. Just..." She paused and pulled an envelope out of her pocket. Her fingers tightened on the parchment, crinkling it slightly. "Just give him this, will you?"

Hallie shook her head. "But I don't..."

"Please." Les' eyes were damp once more. Hallie accepted the letter and nodded, not trusting herself to speak.

She took the extra pack from the butler and slung it over her shoulder with her satchel. Without glancing behind her, she made her way into the foyer and out the front door. But before she stepped over the threshold, she paused. She avoided looking at the family portrait.

"I'll take care of him. I promise you that."

She didn't know if Les heard her not, but it didn't matter. Les trusted her.

And then Hallie was out into the sunny, yet crisp, February morning—with Kase's pack heavy on her shoulder.

HALLIE WIPED A SMALL BIT of sweat from her brow. Not even the steady rain outside could keep people from good food. She would miss the hustle and bustle once she left for Stoneset, but she had to know if her parents were okay. The question plagued her every waking moment since reading the telegram...and then her mind would inevitably drift to practical logistics.

Because that was how her brain worked. And those details and 'what ifs' drove her mad.

Though they did keep her from reliving the morning at Shackley Manor. She'd dropped off Kase's pack at her apartment, hoping—and also sort of not hoping—she'd run into him that night at the inn.

Shaking her head, she thought back to her Stoneset plans. Should she leave on foot? How much would a motorcoach to the Nardens cost? Probably too much. But she didn't fancy riding a horse, mainly because she didn't know the first thing about taking care of one. Jack had always handled the horses back in Stoneset.

She reined in her sorrow and made her way to a table a couple had recently vacated. She began stacking dirty plates, but before she made it back to the kitchen for washing, the front door swung open, the sweet scent of rain joining the aroma of roasted chicken. She glanced up to see a soaking-wet man enter, his jacket dripping onto the dining room floor. She let out a soft gasp. *Kase.*

The dishes clattered as she set them down, and she hurried over before the other barmaid stuck her claws into him. He ran fingers through his wet curls, making them stick up worse than before. He reminded her of the drowned cat she and her brother had found in the creek near the base of the mountains so many years ago.

Kase looked off into the distance, refusing to meet her gaze. "I'd like a table—and keep the ale coming."

She narrowed her eyes. "Are you drunk?"

He ran a hand through his messy curls again and grimaced when it came away with a few strands of hair. He brushed it on his equally soaked trousers and met her gaze. His eyes were clear of drink, but there was something else there, something she couldn't name. "I didn't think barmaids questioned their customers."

She gritted her teeth. "What's wrong with you?"

"*Nothing.* Just want food and something to drink. Shocks, is that too much to ask?"

She glanced around the dining room. The only available table was the one she'd been clearing, but the crowd would be winding down with it being well-past prime dinner hour, and the fiddler wasn't playing tonight.

"Try not to drip on anyone." He followed in silence as she led him to the table and pulled out a chair. "Tonight's special is roasted paprika chicken and steamed vegetables."

He plopped down in the chair, his right hand nearly landing in the leftovers on the plates she'd stacked. "That's fine. And don't forget what I said about the ale."

Hallie grabbed the plates and hissed, "What happened to you?"

"*Please, Hallie.*" This time his eyes didn't focus as he looked somewhere over her shoulder.

"Whatever." She lugged her haul to the kitchen, opening the door with her backside Mazie was placing a batch of pastries in the oven for the breakfast crowd. They'd sell them for a cheaper price than the ones she made fresh in the morning. Hallie had snagged one or two steaming hot ones before walking to the Jayde Center the past few mornings. With the proper identification, she was able to come and go as she pleased. She would miss the pastries when she left for home.

Maybe if all went well with the Yalvs, Hallie could persuade Nole and Mazie to hire a few of the refugees in her stead.

Hallie loaded a plate with food and grabbed a mug of ale. She balanced it all on a tray and headed back out, not saying a word to the others. Nole didn't say anything either, but he was busy monitoring the dish boy's quality of work after one too many plates had come out of the washtub with food still on it.

Back in the dining room, Hallie set her burden in front of Kase with a soft clatter. "Let me know if you need anything else."

Kase looked beside the plate. "A fork would be good."

"Blast. Sorry about that. Hold on." She tucked the tray underneath her arm and scampered back into the kitchen. She grabbed the only fork and knife she saw before Nole stopped her.

"Hals, do you need me at the bar, or does it seem to be slowing down? And we're nearly out of chicken. Anyone else will have to make do with the leftover stew." He stepped away from where he'd been drying the wet plates. "We'll have to start ordering more next week. Without Dunny pickin' tonight, I didn't think we'd have a crowd like this."

Hallie shook her head, a small smile pulling at her lips. "It's winding down. Though my friend from last night stopped in."

"The one who'd been in a fight? I'd hate to see that other guy—"

Hallie sped out of the kitchen before he could finish, utensils gripped in her hand. Once she reached Kase, she set them down.

"Thanks." Kase took up the fork and started on the vegetables, taking liberal sips of ale between each bite.

The rest of the evening passed by with relative ease. By the time the bell tower tolled eleven, all the guests had left, their stomachs full and Nole's money pouch all the heavier. The other barmaid finished cleaning tables, waved, and left for a night of tavern-hopping.

However, Kase still sat at his table, finishing off his fifth ale of the night. Hallie would've cut him off after two, but the other barmaid had gotten to him first. Stars-idiot thought she could flutter her eyelashes and sashay back and forth to get Kase's attention, but he was too far into his cups to notice.

Attempting to keep her temper under control, Hallie had avoided him since. This would prove harder now that there was no one left to serve. She vigorously wiped down a nearby table, and when she was close to stripping off the stain, she folded the rag and set it on the back of the chair.

"Another!" Kase's voice rang through the empty dining room. Hallie took a deep breath and stalked over, ripping the mug from his hands.

"You can barely string three words together."

Kase's eyes narrowed as he looked up at her. "Can too."

"That was only two words."

"But I—" Kase's speech was slurred from the drink and his lip. The swelling had gone down drastically, but it was still there. "I want another."

"No," she hissed. She set the mug aside and put her hands on her hips. What in the blasted suns was wrong with him?

"I have money. Lots of it. Father loves ale. He won't mind if I—" Kase halted mid-sentence and grabbed his head. "Foggy. My brain is full of stars-blasted clouds."

Hallie pulled out the chair beside him and fell into it with a sigh. "You drank five ales. *Five.* Of course you can't think clearly."

"Which is a benefit."

"And where are you staying tonight? You're in no shape to go anywhere else. You'll pass out in a ditch somewhere and someone'll rob you blind."

Kase stood, but his legs wobbled, and he had to sit back down. Footsteps sounded behind Hallie, and Nole put a hand on the back of Kase's chair. Kase looked up with unfocused eyes. "Hello...do I know you?" He asked.

"And hello to you," Nole said, his voice tinged with a laugh. "I know my ale is good, but I think you might've had one too many. I do like to make it strong." He turned to Hallie. "You finish up in here, and I'll make sure he gets to the back sitting room without tripping over his feet. He can sleep it off in there, as we're booked up for the night." Hallie nodded as he turned back to Kase. "Come now, son."

Kase groaned but got up at Nole's urging. Hallie watched him stumble, the innkeeper's hand at his back to catch the pilot if he fell. Once they were out of sight, Hallie made quick work of the mugs and dishes, depositing them with the dish boy. Going back out to the dining room, she locked the front door and did a once over of the space. The only thing out of place was Kase's coat, which he must've removed at some point in the evening. It lay haphazardly on the back of his chair, a fading puddle beneath it. Hallie let that be. The floors were warped already, and she was bone-tired. She grabbed the jacket and realized that it wasn't his leather one. This was some stiff gray material.

"What's going on with you?" she muttered to herself as she pushed the door open to the kitchen. Nole met her at the door.

"He's asking for you. I put a small basin in there for him in case he needs it," he told her as he untied his apron and hung it on the hook beside the stairway that led up to his apartment. Mazie must have already gone up. He looked back toward the dish boy. "Go on home, Cal. Tell your Pa I'll be over tomorrow with that horse."

The boy set aside his towel and scampered out the back door as Hallie turned toward the sitting room. Her legs were frozen in place until Nole put a hand on her shoulder. "I don't know him well enough to judge, but no man drinks that much of my ale just because. If you need any help, holler."

Hallie nodded and untied her own apron, hanging it with Nole's. Wiping the sweat from her palms onto her trousers, she took a deep breath and trudged down the short hall and into the sitting room. They often used the space for things that didn't fit in the pantry, but it had recently been mostly cleared out. Only a crate of potatoes and two barrels of ale were left. Kase sat on a sofa with stuffing sticking out of one of the seams, head buried in his hands and fingers tangled in his hair.

For a moment, she had a flashback of the night after Zeke died, when his hardened exterior had shattered into a thousand pieces, his anguish spilling out like dark blood from a gaping wound.

Her heart squeezed at the present sight. Had something happened to Jove? To his mother? Had his father done something else?

After a moment's hesitation, she crept forward on light feet, but that blasted loose floorboard tore through the silence like a knife through silk. Kase's head jerked up. He relaxed when he realized it was her. "Hey."

Hallie gave him a tight smile as she eased herself into the sagging armchair near him. "Care to tell me why you tried to drown yourself in alcohol?"

"Not really."

Of course. "Is it about last night?"

"I can't tell you."

Hallie pushed herself out of the chair and started toward the door. "Then I'm going home. Try not to get puke on the couch."

"Wait."

Hallie paused with her hand on the door handle. Exhaustion weighed down her bones. "Kase, I have to get up early."

"I can't tell you because you'll hate me for it."

Hallie rubbed her forehead. "Then why tell Nole you wanted to talk to me? You're *smashed.* I'm *tired.* Just go to sleep for moons-sake."

"I did it."

Hallie turned at his words. His face was back in his hands, and he didn't move or make any attempt to continue. Hallie sighed and padded back over, placing her hands on the back of the armchair. "Did what?"

Kase took a shaking breath, the air rattling as he did so. "I did something. A while ago. And I don't think—I don't think I can take it anymore, and if I tell anyone anything...."

He trailed off, hands sinking deeper into his hair.

A feeling akin to what she'd experienced the only time she'd ever been on a boat filled her chest, her stomach, her mouth. "Stop being cryptic. What did you do?"

He shook his head so hard he groaned and clutched it. "I don't want you to hate me."

Hallie tried to swallow the queasiness rising in her throat as she sat on the couch beside him. What was he talking about? She knew he was only this forthcoming as the alcohol ran rampant in his bloodstream. She put a hand on his upper arm. "You're not the only one who's ever messed up before, you know."

Kase tugged out of her grip and slumped forward, his head resting on his forearms. "Not this badly."

Suddenly he sat up, grabbing the sides of Hallie's face. Her skin burned like a torch he held her there. His jaw was firm and his lips taut, but his eyes were alight with fire.

"Do you still want to go to Stoneset?"

"*What?*"

Mumbling to himself, he pulled his hands away and ran them both through his hair. "Yes, yes, that would work. I could sneak into the hangar and get my ship out. Easy."

Hallie shook her head. "Kase? What are you talking about? I thought you couldn't leave. Something about deserting and stealing and something else."

Kase's grin split his face, his teeth gleaming in the soft firelight from the hearth. "Believe me, that's the least of our worries now. I can get you to Stoneset. Easy."

"I don't understand. I didn't think you could get your ship through."

"Didn't you say something about paying a trapper? We can leave tomorrow night. It'll be easy enough to smuggle you onto the airfields. Years of pranking other pilots has its benefits."

Hallie's heart rate picked up, her breathing uneven. "Tomorrow? I don't think I can be ready. I was supposed to go with Petra tomorrow for a fitting, and then—and then—"

Shut up. This is what I wanted, wasn't it?

Kase grabbed her hand and placed a kiss across her knuckles. "This is our only chance. If you want to go, we need to leave. Tomorrow."

"Are you sure?" she asked, snatching her hand from his grasp. It tingled where his lips had brushed her soft skin. Her cheeks flushed. "You're not in the right state of mind to be making decisions like this."

"I thought this was what you wanted. Have you changed your mind that fast?"

I could ask you the same thing.

Hallie sat quietly for a second, fingering a small rip in her trousers on her right knee. This *was* what she'd wanted, wasn't it? But now that she had the opportunity in front of her like a decadent pie waiting to be devoured... "But what do we say? What do I tell everyone?"

Kase shrugged. "What did you plan to say to them in the first place?"

His words weren't slurring so much anymore. Had he really recovered so quickly? Or had it all been an act? Or had the thought of escaping Kyvena—for whatever reasons he refused to tell her—burned away the alcohol clouding his mind?

She bit the inside of her cheek. "I don't know. The truth, I guess? But I need someone to fill in for me here. I'll need to talk with Petra. And then Saldr. Maybe we can leave this weekend instead?"

"I need—*we* need to leave before anyone has a chance to figure out where we've gone. That way we can get a head start, just in case they send someone out to retrieve us."

"Then why not leave now? Why wait? By that logic, we should've left an hour ago."

Kase's laugh was sardonic and riddled with sarcasm. "Because I'm gonna need some of Jove's hangover special before I'm fit to fly. And we need a few supplies. An electropistol or two. Some food. Money. We can stay at a few inns on our way, and it should only take us about a week to make it to the Pass in a hover. Much better than hijacking a blasted motorcoach."

"I have some of your stuff at my apartment." She blushed under his gaze. "I had to go back for my things...and your mother had already packed a bag for you."

Kase's eyebrows shot up, but he didn't say anything. Instead, he stood and paced before the fireplace. Hallie took a deep breath. Would he even remember this when he was sober? Could they pull it off? "Listen, I think I can get Petra to help. Maybe Ellis could fill in for me here, and then—"

"*Not Ellis.*"

"Huh?"

Kase stopped pacing and looked at her, eyes blazing with fire. "He can't know. Promise me. Swear to me you won't tell him."

Hallie sat back, her heart beating a staccato in her chest. "Why not?"

Kase grabbed her hand and squeezed. "*Just trust me.* We leave tomorrow night. I'll meet you in the alleyway behind the inn at ten. And make sure you wear something with a hood."

Hallie shook her head. "You're being irrational."

"Please," he pleaded as he squeezed her hand again. "Please, trust me."

His eyes had fizzled to a simmer. His desperate plea echoed in her head. This was what she wanted. She'd been considering taking off and walking all the way there, and now she had a ride. Why was she hesitating?

She took a deep breath, the smell of charcoal mixed with a tinge of ale drifting in the air. "I can take care of food and other basic supplies. We shouldn't be gone for more than a couple of weeks, right?"

Kase hesitated, but he nodded. "And I'll secure the hover and electropistols. I'll be over first thing in the morning to fetch whatever Mother gave you. She'll have put a sizable purse inside."

Something akin to bubbles filled her stomach as she looked at him. "We're doing this?"

His smile stretched across his face, his eyes crinkling in the corners. "By this time tomorrow night, we'll be free as the stars."

PART II: WRATH

CHAPTER 14

IT'S COMPLICATED

Hallie

THE ONLY SOURCES OF ILLUMINATION in the alleyway were a scattering of windows above Hallie. As she hefted her pack higher on her shoulders, a sense of unease crept up her neck. It was ten o'clock by the bell tolls, and Kase had yet to appear.

She'd left the inn hours earlier to scour the marketplace for a sleeping roll and other supplies. Nole and Mazie had understood her plight, but they'd been a little annoyed by the fact she was leaving so soon. However, the thought of the other barmaid having to work extra shifts also brought Hallie much more delight than it should have.

Her back ached from the weight of her pack. Maybe she should've left *Frankenstein* at home.

No, that was a stupid thought. She'd need something to read when they stopped for the night, something to occupy her mind. She pulled her hood down lower.

As if in answer to her thoughts, clicking boots echoed in the alleyway. She looked up at the entrance and relaxed.

Underneath the hood, she could make out Kase's eyes. He

hadn't abandoned her after all.

"Thought you might have gotten cold feet." Hallie pulled her cloak from where it'd gotten caught in the pack strap. She'd bought it this afternoon and was wearing her leather jacket underneath. It would help if they had a chilly night, but hopefully it wouldn't be needed for much longer with spring just around the corner.

Kase's smile flashed in the shadows as he pulled his hood back. "Course not. Do you have everything?"

"Yes. But it's terribly heavy. I didn't know how much we'd need, and I know how much you hate beef stew,"

Kase chuckled and adjusted his own pack. "Can I carry something? Being a man and all, I'm quite strong."

Hallie gave a nervous titter. "I can carry it myself."

"Suit yourself. You ready? Got your sketchpad?"

Kase didn't know she still couldn't sketch anything. Hallie flexed the remaining fingers on her drawing hand as her thoughts reeled, thinking back to her parents, the Yalvs, the inn...everything. When all this was over, she could go on with her life, maybe even draw something. Maybe.

"Stay close."

Kase headed further down the alleyway. They wove through the city, abandoning the main roads in favor of nooks, crannies, and byways she hadn't realized existed. Every now and then, Kase would pull out a piece of parchment from his pocket. A map, judging by his mutterings as he inspected it.

With each step she took away from the inn, her heart hammered even harder, but not in fear. In anticipation. This was the most exciting thing to happen in weeks. She felt a little guilty leaving the Yalvs behind. She hadn't told Saldr about leaving, and it made her feel like a child again, dreading the chastisement a parent was sure to give for misbehavior. She'd apologize when she returned.

"Okay, we're close," Kase whispered as he halted at the edge of the city.

They hadn't run into many people on their trek, and that included guards of any sort. Probably a good thing if Kase was going to be deserting and all.

"So, what now?" Hallie whispered back. "Are we close? I'm going to have a permanent mark from where this strap has been digging into my shoulder."

Kase looked back. "It's not much further. They have guards stationed at the entrance, but leave the talking to me. Do you have your identification papers?"

Hallie dug in her satchel and pulled them out. "It doesn't say I have authority to access the airfields."

"You won't need it if all goes according to plan. Like I said, follow my lead and keep your hood on." He took a deep breath. "Ready?"

Her heart fluttered uncomfortably. *This is it. There's no going back now.*

Kase unclasped his cloak and folded it over his arm. Underneath, he wore the same jacket from the previous evening, gray and with the Jaydian insignia on his breast. He straightened his uniform and brushed one hand across the brass buttons going up both sides of his chest.

"Where's your leather one?" Hallie took his cloak from him, folding it over her arm.

"Long story."

"If I didn't know any better, I'd say you and the other one were affianced."

"Word to the wise, no one uses 'affianced' anymore."

"Glad you're feeling better."

With a small smirk, Kase left the shelter of the corner where they'd been standing, and Hallie followed a step or two behind. She was curious how he was going to pull this off. Surely, they wouldn't arrest them, but she guessed that all depended on what Kase had up his sleeve.

The night was a crisp one, if silent, outside the city. The airfields weren't too far outside the wall, but to get there, they needed to pass the gate guards. This one wasn't used except for certain military personnel and Crews members, so it didn't need to be as large or well-defended as the gate. A breach would still spell disaster, though.

Kase strutted up to the guards, forming the proper salute as he approached, and Hallie hid any uncertainty. Thankfully, the guards weren't the same ones who'd barred her from accessing the fields before the *Eudora* mission. Sleepy and Rock-Face hadn't been too kind.

"Soldiers, good evening. I'm Pilot Kase Shackley on orders

from the Stradat Lord Kapitan to secure a hover." Kase's voice rang with the confidence of someone who was used to getting his way.

Hallie fidgeted with the papers in her hands as the men before the gate looked her over. She'd pulled her hood up per Kase's orders, but she still squirmed under their scrutiny. The man closest to Kase with the insignia of squad leader on his shoulder spoke first. "We have received no such orders, *Trainee* Pilot Shackley. The airfields are closed."

Hallie's eyes shot to Kase as the muscle in his jaw worked. He adjusted his pack before answering, "I'm a full pilot, soldier."

"Your jacket says otherwise," the squad leader said. His partner's hand went to the electropistol at his side.

"You're new here, aren't you?" Kase pinched the bridge of his nose. "I'm the *son* of the Stradat Lord Kapitan, so my attire is none of your concern. My orders to deliver my client to her assignment come from high up in the military. I cannot disclose anything further than that."

When the squad leader didn't move, Kase undid a few of the buttons on his jacket and reached in, pulling out a folded piece of parchment. "If you doubt me, look at my papers here. I've got express permission to enter the airfields. I apologize for the oversight, but it can't be helped now."

The man took Kase's identification papers and examined them. Hallie caught sight of a pilot's sigil in blazing red ink. The man showed the other guard, whispered something to him, and turned back to Kase, holding the papers out. "I'll be having a word with my superior about this. We can't do our jobs properly if the higher ups don't communicate with us."

Kase returned his papers to the inner pocket of his jacket. "Thank you. Again, I apologize for the confusion. Good evening."

The man signaled up to another on top of the wall, and the door opened. Hallie's heart pounded as the guards eyed them as they passed, but neither stopped them. She hadn't even had to show her own papers still clutched in her hand. They were probably soaked with sweat.

Kase led her to a hangar near the end of the strip and unlocked the side door of the massive structure. Holding it open, he gestured for her to enter. "We don't want those guys to change their minds...or worse, decide to alert anyone at this hour."

Hallie scurried into the dark hangar, and Kase closed the door behind them. In the dim light of Firstmoon filtering through windows on the opposite wall, Hallie glimpsed the silhouette of the hover. Her mouth fell open.

Although not as impressive as the *Eudora Jayde*, this hover—a standard used by the Crews—was still compact, sleek, and a testament to ingenuity.

It wasn't only the size that differed, but the build itself. While the *Eudora* had reminded her of a great sailing vessel, this one was more like a starship out of the history books from First Earth. It had small wings jutting out the sides, and its body was more like a slender horizontal tube, the cockpit covered by a slanting dome. Kase strode over and popped open the top of the cockpit.

"It's not too big. Can seat about three people, not including the pilot. You can put your stuff in the row behind ours. Just make sure they're secure. Loose objects tend to move around mid-flight."

"How am I supposed to get up there?"

Kase laughed. "Oh, right. Hold on." He brought a nearby ladder over, holding it against the side. "Just climb on up and get strapped in. Need to do a few pre-flight checks, so sit tight."

Hallie put her hand on the rung at eye level. It was cold to the touch and smooth underneath her fingertips. She looked up at Kase and took a fortifying breath. "We're doing this."

His eyes were shadowed as he glanced toward the towering hangar doors and then back at her. "Yeah."

"Ma will kill me when I arrive with you in tow. Impropriety and all that. "

Kase smirked. "We're not eloping or anything crazy like that."

"Obviously."

"Then forget society's rules. Besides, you trust me, right?"

She nodded.

"And I trust you. You have a good heart, Hals. That's all that matters."

Heat blossomed across the back of her neck and cheeks. "Thank you."

"You're welcome."

Stars. Had she ever seen Kase that way? So optimistic? So free? She found herself liking this side of him. It also confused her to no end. He'd been a complete wreck the night before, but now he was a different person. Maybe the thought of getting away was enough to push past the terrible memories? She'd certainly found that to be true after Jack died.

Though suppressing one's emotions had never worked for Hallie in the end.

She stepped into the cockpit on unsteady legs, her hands brushing the warm metal of the outer shell and unloaded the pack from her sore shoulders. There were two seats side by side in the front with a small space in the middle, followed by another row where she stowed the bags. At the very back was a tiny cargo compartment just tall enough for a child to stand up straight in. She turned back to the control panel. The left front chair was directly in front of the steering control, and the buttons on the dashboard were dark without the engine running. Attached to the back of the seats were small, tan-colored packs barely wider than the length of her forearm. The *Eudora Jayde* had boasted the same parachutes for each seat.

As Kase tinkered around in the underbelly of the ship, Hallie thrummed her fingers on the back of one seat.

The late-night escape plan, the suspicious guards, and the thought of returning home were all very real reasons her heart was beating a mile a minute. What if they were caught? She wasn't some important diplomat to be whisked away in the dead of night. As soon as their ruse was discovered soldiers would be sent after them. And yet Kase was taking his sweet time preparing the hover for the trip.

The mild frustration allowed the glow in her chest at the thought of this new Kase to dim slightly. It helped clear her head. "How long until we can leave?"

She heard a snap, then a click, and in a few seconds, his face appeared over the lip of the cockpit. "We're good on fuel, and I had to make sure they'd replaced the damaged wires. Go ahead and strap in."

His blue eyes sparkled in the soft moonlight, reflecting the excitement she felt. She nodded. "I don't want to get caught."

"Neither do I." He disappeared. Seconds later, he was

pushing open one steel hangar door with a grunt, then the other. He dashed back to the hover. "Sorry for the delay; I was sabotaging the other hangars. "

"What did you do?"

"Nothing permanent. Just enough to give us a head start if they alert the Crews Colonel or the Stradat Lord Kapitan."

The evening breeze blew Hallie's loose hair into her face. She climbed into the seat beside the pilot's chair and buckled herself in. "But I thought you didn't want to break the law. I distinctly remember you talking about how terrible things would happen if you took me to the Pass."

"Can't you be grateful?"

Hallie sighed. "Fine, fine."

Hallie inspected the dash. There weren't nearly as many buttons as the one on the *Eudora*. She jumped a little as Kase tossed in his own pack, which landed in the seat behind his. Then he removed the ladder from the side of the ship and climbed up into the cockpit using the wing. He stuffed his pack down further and started undoing the buttons on his jacket.

"What are you doing?"

He flung the jacket back toward the cargo area. "I'm not a greenie."

"Greenie?"

"New pilot. That's my old training jacket." He pushed a few buttons and flipped a few switches on the dashboard.

"Not as intimidating."

"Clearly."

The panel came to life, lights flickering like candles in the darkness.

"I'm going to pull us forward, so don't freak out." Kase pushed a pedal with his foot. The craft jerked, and Hallie fell back against her seat.

"Thanks for that."

"I do what I can."

The ship moved at a glacial pace through the open hangar doors and onto the main runway. Hallie bounced a little in her seat as the hover hit a bump or two before coming to rest. Kase pushed another button and hopped out. After closing the doors, he climbed back into the cockpit, grabbed a handle on the slanted dome above, and sealed them in.

"I need to go over a few safety rules. First, don't touch anything unless I tell you to." Hallie rolled her eyes, but Kase didn't seem to notice. "Second, if for some reason we need to eject, grab the lever between your legs and pull up hard. It'll send you skyward and deploy the parachute. Third, if this light starts flashing," he pointed to a big red circular button near the center of the dashboard, "that means something's wrong with the air in the cockpit. If that happens, grab the mask attached to the right and put it over your face like this."

He retrieved his and demonstrated. Hallie laughed. The hose shared a close resemblance to a beak, and the lenses magnified his narrowed eyes. "You look like some sort of deranged bird."

He pulled it off. "Very funny. You won't be laughing when you can't breathe."

"Sorry. Is that all?"

He hooked the mask back into place. "You forgot your second safety strap."

After a moment's hesitation, Kase crossed the distance between them. Hallie didn't breathe as he grabbed the strap over her right shoulder and tugged it across her, clicking it into the adjoining buckle closest to the middle aisle. His Adam's apple bobbed as he sat back and strapped himself in. Hallie fumbled for words only to have a tightness settle in her chest. She cleared her throat. "Anything else?"

Kase tugged a pair of pilot's goggles from beneath his seat. He pulled them down over his eyes. "Lastly, you're not allowed to make fun of my new goggles."

As he pushed the button to start the hover capacities, the ship rising by about ten or fifteen feet, Hallie laughed in relief. She caught Kase's grin as he pushed a pedal with his foot. They approached the edge of the airfield. Hallie didn't let her own smile fall from her face as the tension eased. The gentle hum of the hover was smoothed away any lingering worries.

She was on her way to find the answers she sought. For the first time in months, she allowed herself to relax.

Kase

WITH ONLY FIRSTMOON'S ILLUMINATION, KASE guided the hover at a comfortable if slow pace. Like all hovers, it wasn't designed for flying at night, but Kase knew they didn't have a choice. He needed to get a good lead before anyone realized what he'd done.

This plan had to pan out. Hallie was safe with him.

If he returned to Kyvena, he would be tried as a deserter or an arsonist, maybe even a traitor depending on whatever One World wanted out of him. The only way for Kase to escape was to never go back. His mother probably wouldn't forgive him for leaving without saying a word, but he was doing this for her too. Without him in the picture, she would be much better off.

As for his father, he hoped for nothing but suffering for the Stradat Lord Kapitan.

Jove would be upset. This would show his brother who he really was, and why he couldn't be a blasted godfather.

To shake his melancholy thoughts, he glanced over at Hallie, who stared in wonder at the sky above through the domed cockpit window. The moonlight danced in her eyes as she smiled. "I forgot how breathtaking the stars are away from all the electric lights," she said.

"Isn't it weird that, a thousand years ago, our ancestors came from somewhere up there?"

"And to think we had the technology to survive for years in a hunk of metal hurtling through space. I don't blame the Yalvs one bit for destroying that. I might have done the same thing. They might have the power to manipulate time, but our ancestors sped through the stars."

"Do you think we'll be able to do that again?"

Hugging a knee to her chest, Hallie shifted in her seat. "Half of me wants to see what else is out there, but the other half can only think about how far I'd have to fall."

"There's nothing holding you down up there. They say gravity doesn't exist."

"Yeah, but that means you'd float forever. I don't fancy that either." She was silent for a few moments. When she spoke, her voice was like a whisper in the wind. "Thank you. I don't know why you changed your mind in the first place but thank you."

Kase's hands tightened on the steering control, the leather seams digging into his palms. "Don't thank me yet."

"Why's that?" she asked, her voice almost inaudible over the hum of the engines.

Kase tensed Should he tell her? Would it hurt? He wasn't ever going back to Kyvena anyway. She was already privy to his father's abuse. Besides, Kase had always wanted to live out his days somewhere in the mountains. Maybe make his way to Tev Rubika. Not even his father would find him there.

Hallie fidgeted in her seat, the leather creaking. "I shouldn't pry. I'm sorry."

Kase met her golden-eyed gaze for a moment before turning back. "It's complicated."

With that response, they fell into an uneasy silence. The trees along the road sped past them. They'd only been flying for about an hour, but they had made good progress.

"Aren't you getting tired?" Hallie asked.

Kase shrugged. He was hyped up on adrenaline and a dash of fear, so he knew that would keep him awake long enough. "I want to get as far away from the capital as possible. There's a village about four hours away where pilots usually stop on their missions."

"A decent bed sounds good to me." Hallie waited a moment before she spoke again. "It's a shame we couldn't steal one of the bigger airships like the *Eudora*."

A laugh bubbled up in Kase's throat. "Stradat Sarson's scar popped out when she found out what Jove had done. Of course, my blasted father made Jove take the brunt of the fallout. I think Jove believes he deserved it when he...well when we returned with Zeke's..."

Shocks, it still hurts.

A beat of silence. Hallie's voice softened. "Your father did that?"

Kase shifted a little in his chair, small needles pricked him like knives throughout his leg at the movement. He hadn't sat for this long in a while. Probably not since the *Eudora Jayde.* "You heard what that man...my father...what he did, what he said." He ran his tongue over the healing cut along his lip. "The irony is it was his idea to send us on the mission in the first place. Jove only got off with a steep fine because he'd already

REALMS OF WRATH & RUIN

demoted himself."

"Oh."

An awkward silence descended. Kase felt it in his bones, but he didn't know how to fix it. There wasn't a way he could make her truly understand what it was like to be in a position in society like his. Although she'd grown up without the finer things this life could offer, she'd been more fortunate in many ways.

An hour passed, then another. At last, a cluster of faint lights appeared on the horizon. He pushed a button on his right, bringing the hover lower as they approached. A hundred yards out, he slowed the ship and set it softly onto the dirt road below, using the landing gear to drive it to the edge of town and park it near the walls in a designated area.

The engines whirled to a stop. Kase unbuckled himself and turned to find Hallie had fallen asleep. She looked so peaceful, the lines around her eyes almost nonexistent. He was a little jealous she didn't seem to suffer the same nightmares he did, but he felt bad for waking her.

He smiled sadly and touched her shoulder. She jumped and hastily wiped the side of her mouth with the edge of her sleeve.

"What? What is it?" she gasped, head on a swivel. "Did they catch up to us?"

Kase shook his head. "It's time to find a real bed. Otherwise, you'll have a terrible crick in the morning."

Kase led Hallie to the village's inn. Once he paid the man inside for two rooms, they both trudged up the stairs. After saying a brief goodnight, Kase entered his room and dropped his pack by the door. Without undressing, he fell on the bed and into a fitful sleep.

CHAPTER 15

I DON'T NEED DETAILS

Jove

AS JOVE HEADED TO THE Watch's headquarters, the heavy conversation with Clara didn't leave his shoulders. He didn't have an excuse for his behavior, and he knew it was wrong, but the siren song of alcohol was a powerful thing. When everything was numb, he didn't have to hurt when he remembered that Zeke was dead. Murdered because of the mission Jove had sent him on.

That weight was his constant companion, and he didn't expect it to leave anytime soon. He was the eldest. He was supposed to be the protector.

Smoking was a habit he'd picked up shortly after Ana's death. Nicotine was a small reprieve, a way to calm his frazzled nerves. but he knew it would never cure what was truly causing the pain.

After resigning his Head Guardsman position, the first few weeks had been a relief, even with the Cerls attacking Achilles and his father refusing to speak to him. Jove hadn't minded the latter. It was a taste of what life would've been like if Harlan was no longer a part of it, and it was a beautiful dream.

Stars, Jove was a terrible person.

How could anyone think that? How could Jove, soon to be a father himself, consider how wonderful his life would be if his own wasn't in it?

But the universe had a way of punishing him, and it came in the form of a solitary knock on his townhouse door and a wagon holding his best friend's body. Hallie Walker had held Kase's hand as his youngest brother, now his only brother, explained that Zeke was dead.

The shock had been like fire and ice all at once. His heart forgot to beat. Then he'd punched the wall. The excruciating pain in his newly broken hand had been better than the shock. In fact, Jove might have continued until his hand shattered if Clara hadn't stopped him.

At present, Jove ran his fingers over the fading scabs littering his knuckles as he sat at his small desk, surrounded by Watchmen who had also been delegated to paperwork duties. The room was dark with only two curtained windows, each desk supplied with a small lantern. Jove preferred the silence and dim atmosphere. In the way of personal décor, he had Clara's portrait in a small frame, watching him work. In front of it lay a dusty and blood-speckled pin shaped like the sun. Zeke's. The one he'd received upon his promotion to Lieutenant Colonel. His brother hadn't been cocksure like Kase or proud like Jove, but Zeke had worked hard to accomplish what he did.

Jove kept it as a reminder. His eyes blurred the longer he stared at it.

He fumbled in his pocket for a cigarette and lighter. With the first few inhales and subsequent clouds of smoke floating in front of his face, his heart rate slowed, and the budding tears dried up. He ignored Watchwoman Lois' glare. She was one of the few working at her desk today. Her perfectly round glasses made her look more like a professor than assistant to one of the lower Watch commanders. She slammed a drawer shut on her dark oak desk. When Jove ignored her, she gathered up a pile of papers and left with a huff.

After several puffs, Jove snuffed the cigarette out in his

overflowing ashtray. A cold and scrunched stub fell onto the dark green carpet below.

Just get through this day. Focus on the next minute.

His fingers itched to light another smoke. He coughed. That only made the lingering headache pulse. Shocks, he needed to pull himself together. Composing himself, he inspected the report he was supposed to decipher.

After stepping down as High Guardsman, he'd taken petty roles before finding himself back to where he'd started—in the decoding department.

Except the words he was supposed to comb through to find the hidden message were merely a bunch of spiky symbols. They had no meaning. Nothing did these days. Jove rubbed his eyes.

I can't do this.

As much as Jove blamed his father for Zeke's death, he also blamed himself. His brother had only agreed because Jove had asked him. Sure, Harlan had approved, knowing Zeke was the best choice for the assignment. But it'd been Jove who'd chosen him, sent him to his death.

Any day now he'd have a child; he should be happy. Traitorous tears stained the parchment before him. He never believed he could feel as terrible as he had the night Ana died. But he'd been wrong, so terribly wrong.

Jove had always been the one to take responsibility. He'd been the one who made sure his siblings never took the brunt of their father's anger. It was why he'd stepped in when Harlan had beaten Kase nearly senseless that night. Jove had earned a broken nose and numerous bruises, but his pain was nothing compared to the days after.

It'd been Zeke and Clara who'd gotten him through that.

Jove swiped at his face and lit another cigarette. He picked up Zeke's pin and rubbed the pad of his thumb over the grimy surface. The engraving of a sun and tree decorated the middle of the dirty gold. Speckles of brown dusted the edges and the short green ribbon beneath. Zeke's voice came back to him.

"I don't need details. I'll go because you need me to."

He tucked the pin into his jacket's inner pocket and pushed back from his desk. He needed a bit of fresh air. The Cerls hadn't made a move since attacking Achilles and assassinating the Richter family. It'd been months. The tearstained report could wait.

THE NEXT DAY, JOVE NO longer felt the effects of a hangover, but with the waking hours, his head still hurt. Life was coming at him too quickly. Drowning was the only way to describe what he felt. With each new responsibility, a new stone was added to his back. He was sinking fast, the water above him cloudy and too far from his outstretched fingers.

Clara spent most of her days lounging. She'd much rather be painting all day, but with the baby arriving soon, prolonged amounts of time sitting at her easel only made her back pain worse. Her mother would be arriving from the Davey's country estate in a few weeks to stay until Clara was able to take care of the baby on her own. Lady Davey would be a blessing. Jove couldn't take as much leave as he'd like, and he refused to accept the charity his family name offered. Clara would care for their child when Jove was working—not a nanny or governess.

While he appreciated the invitation to a dinner that night honoring Anderson Enright's impending marriage, Jove felt tired thinking about it. Clara insisted she go with him, though she'd had another spell that day with false contractions. He didn't think it was a good idea for her to attend, but she assured him they would leave if she felt too uncomfortable. Obviously, she wanted to keep an eye on his alcohol consumption.

Would she ever forgive him for his behavior at Shackley Manor? Maybe, but Jove hadn't forgiven himself.

With the sun fading behind the city walls, Jove helped his wife from the hired motorcoach and laced his fingers through hers as they climbed the stairs to Lord Stephenson's city manor. Stephensen was Anderson's uncle by marriage and was the one who'd gotten Anderson's father elected to the City Council ten years ago. Jove hated the practice, but money spoke. Anderson was of a good sort, though. He would do well if he was elected in a few short weeks.

With Anderson's impending election and marriage, Jove hoped his old friend was prepared for the responsibilities of both. He and Clara had been a love match, one even his father had approved of considering his wife's lineage and connections to the sea trade in southern Jayde, but Anderson's situation was quite different. All Jove knew about the woman was that she came from a rising family, her father buying up all sorts of real estate in the lower city.

However, he'd also heard rumor that Miss Petra Lieber was a student at the University of Kyvena, which gave Jove hope. Anderson needed someone to challenge him. Like that Hallie Walker did for Kase. Not that Kase would ever admit to it. He was too much of a loose cannon to settle down. Mother would be sorely disappointed, but Miss Walker was still good for Kase, and Jove had hope. His brother deserved it, especially since Jove was horribly incapable of taking care of him now.

He and Clara handed their outerwear to the butler. Jove brushed his hair, trying to tamper down the wayward strands caused by his bowler. Clara grabbed his hand. "You look fine, love."

He gave her hand a light kiss. "Never as good as you, of course."

She raised an eyebrow. Still no progress. Blast. Jove chewed his lip. When she didn't say anything else, he led her further into the manor. Her deep-russet jeweled gown glittered in the light as they entered the parlor where the rest of the guests waited. He eyed the drink cart.

"Only one glass at dinner," Clara whispered in his ear. She gave his arm a small squeeze as they moved to the hearth. Anderson and the woman who must have been his betrothed stood speaking with a few other members of the City Council, many of whom had witnessed Jove's meltdown at Shackley Manor. He itched to down a bottle of Scotch.

He took a deep breath and ignored the urge.

His parents had declined the invitation that evening. According to his mother, Harlan had other plans. Selfish, of course. There wasn't a High Council meeting that night.

But at least the pressure was off Jove. He could get through the night without embarrassing himself further. He should be able to get a little buzz from the dinner wine without losing his head.

Jove gave a short bow, and Clara a shallow, strained curtsy. Jove kept a tight hold on her fingers so she didn't fall. Anderson bowed back as the other men dispersed. "Thank you for coming, friends. It's a wonderful night to celebrate."

He raised his glass in toast, but without any alcohol in his hand, all Jove could do was nod.

This is going to be difficult.

Jove cleared his throat. "And you must be the lovely Lady Lieber?"

Anderson smiled and put a hand on the woman's back. She was petite and a little curvy, her shiny black hair pulled into an extravagant knot. She executed a flawless curtsy and held out her hand. "Petra Lieber. You must be Lord and Lady Shackley."

Jove gave her hand the customary peck. "Clara and I look forward to getting to know you better."

The woman nodded, but before she could say anything further, the butler strode in and announced dinner would be served in the dining hall. They followed the other guests into the next room, sitting across from Anderson and Petra near the head of the table, a high honor. Only the Stephensens were seated higher.

Lord Stephensen was a portly man with a rather large mustache that shivered with every word he spoke. Tapping his glass, he stood. His happy demeanor didn't match the rather ferocious bear skull hanging above the mantle behind him. "I thank you all for joining us this evening to celebrate the impending nuptials of my nephew and Miss Lieber. Now, let us give thanks for this lovely feast."

Jove wasn't particularly religious, but Clara was. He still bowed his head, focusing on the fact he'd be given a glass of alcohol in mere moments.

Conversation flowed around him as the dinner began. Servants poured white wine for everyone except Clara, who requested sparkling water. Jove's hand itched to down his glass, but Clara kept a hand on his leg, reminding him of what would happen if he went too quickly.

"Miss Lieber," Clara started as she speared a few salad greens onto her fork, "what is it you're studying at the University?"

Jove pushed his own salad around on his plate. He never liked green food.

"I'm studying Languages. I thought it to be the most

interesting pathway," Miss Lieber answered.

Clara's hand left Jove's leg as she leaned forward, though not very far considering her stomach. "Are you focused on modern or ancient?"

"A blend of both, but my favorite to study is the ancient Yalven dialects. I believe we can learn much from their history."

Jove took a sip of wine. He'd sent Zeke to find the Yalvs.

He drained half his glass, and Clara's hand returned to his knee.

"My betrothed is first in her class as well," Anderson said proudly, slipping his arm around Miss Lieber's chair.

Miss Lieber chuckled. "Not really. On paper, yes, but that's only because I don't have to compete with Hallie this semester."

"Hallie?" Clara asked, setting down her fork.

"Hallie Walker," Petra said, a smile lighting her face. "She's my best friend and an absolute genius when it comes to Yalven. In fact, the University sent her on a research trip last fall, but she decided to take this semester off and recover. The poor dear lost a finger in the whole ordeal. Said something about being attacked by a rogue Cerl band." Her smile slipped for a second. "The University should pay her for damages, in my humble opinion. I've taken this to Dean Earlmond already, of course." She blinked before regaining her previous smile. "Either way, being top of my class will look wonderful on my diploma when I graduate in a few months."

Jove finished off his wine and signaled for another. Not only had Jove killed his brother, but he was also the reason Miss Walker had dropped out of the University. *Stars.*

Clara smiled, oblivious to Jove's discomfort. "I didn't realize you knew Miss Walker. She is rather delightful, though I only met her the other evening. She came as my brother-in-law's guest to a dinner party."

"I helped her pick out that divine dress she wore," Miss Lieber said, her back straightening a little. She dabbed her mouth with her napkin. "I'm hoping she'll be my maid of honor, but I have yet to ask her. We've both been rather busy."

"Does the University know when Professor Owen Christie will be returning?" Anderson asked, allowing a servant to take his salad and replace it with soup.

"I'm not aware. We miss his lectures."

Jove recalled the elderly gentleman who'd helped him find a replacement for himself on the *Eudora* mission. Strange that he would take a sabbatical in the middle of the school term. "How long has he been gone?"

Petra Lieber took a sip of her soup. "Since last fall. I assumed he went with Hallie on her research trip, as they left around the same time, but Hallie's back...and he isn't. At first, I thought he might've been injured or killed in that attack."

Strange.

The servant refilled Jove's glass, but before he could take a swig, Clara gave him a pointed look. Jove sighed, setting the glass back down, and finished off his soup.

The meal continued without much interest. The braised lamb drizzled in a white cream sauce was better than Jove expected. Clara particularly enjoyed the potatoes au gratin, a specific pregnancy craving she'd been having. Jove had also managed to sneak in a few sips of wine when Clara wasn't watching. It wasn't until the blueberry tart at the end of the meal that a messenger rushed into the dining hall, nearly stumbling over himself to get to Lord Stephensen.

The man's mustache fluttered as he spoke quietly with the messenger before turning to Jove. "Lord Shackley, I'm afraid you're needed at Shackley Manor. My man here says it's vital you leave now. You'll take my personal coach."

Jove set down his fork, his hand reaching for Clara's. "Why? Is something wrong?"

Lord Stephensen rose from the table and tapped his glass once more to get everyone's attention. "Please, my guests. I apologize for cutting our wonderful evening short, but it seems there's a disturbance within the city. I don't know full details, only that it might be best for us to finish celebrating at another time."

Servants descended upon the guests, pulling out chairs and cleaning up half-eaten dessert plates as the room exploded with noise. Jove helped Clara to her feet. She tucked her hand into the crook of his elbow as they made their way to the foyer, grabbing their effects and sliding into the Stephensens' motorcoach.

"What's happening?" Clara asked after Jove instructed the man to head to his childhood home. She rubbed her stomach

166

with one hand, the other clenching the door handle.

"Not sure," Jove answered, trying not to worry about her body language as he turned toward the window, searching for anything abnormal outside "It must be important, but I'm no longer privy to anything confidential."

Clara was silent, her breathing becoming more strained as the coach traveled through the streets of upper city. Jove looked over. "Clara?"

Her face scrunched up in a painful grimace. She gritted her teeth and sucked in air. "False contraction, I swear."

After about a minute, her face relaxed. Jove brushed a sweaty braid that had escaped her bun behind her ear. He tried to tamp down his rising panic. That wouldn't help anyone. "I'm not a medic, but I would say that looked very real."

"It's too early," Clara breathed, a touch of anxiety in her voice. "I'm supposed to have another four weeks."

Jove smoothed a hand over his stubble. "When we get to the manor, I'm sending for a midwife just in case."

"That's not needed."

Jove wanted to scream. He loved his wife with all his heart, but she was so blasted stubborn sometimes. He clenched his jaw to keep from saying something he'd regret. Did she not see how much he cared for her?

He made sure his voice was calm as he spoke his next words. "Humor me."

The conversation paused as the motorcoach rolled through the gate to Shackley Manor and up the drive. As soon as the driver stopped, his mother sped out the door and down the stairs, her evening gown nearly tripping her.

Jove exited the car and caught her. "What in the blazes are you doing?"

"This arrived a half hour ago." She wheezed as she thrust the note in his hand. "I read it even though it's addressed to your father. I have no idea where he is."

"But why summon me..." Jove looked down at the parchment. The message was scrawled in red ink that looked too much like blood.

We must unite the world before Jagamot comes, and in doing so, we will take down those who are in power.

In one hour, the entire city will know what happened three years ago. They'll understand you must fall when they learn who burned their loved ones. They will want blood, and we're not going to stop them.

Karsi va si

We are one.

One World. Here in Kyvena.

The handwriting seemed familiar, like a forgotten dream. Jove's heart thumped in his ears. It reminded him of Kase's. His brother wasn't a part of One World, was he? No. He wouldn't. He might hate their father, but he would never do something so stupid. "Who sent this?"

"Thoreau said it was a messenger boy from the lower city," his mother answered, wringing her hands. "What does it mean? Are they talking about...the fire? The one with...with Ana?"

"Yes."

"But they're implying that somehow, we're responsible. I thought it was a candle that started it in the lower city. How could we be responsible for that? Jove, what's going on?"

"I don't know." Jove stuffed the letter into his pocket and turned to help Clara out of the car. At the time, not telling his mother what happened the night of the fire had been a mercy. Losing Ana was enough to throw anyone over the deep end. Jove didn't want to make it worse by revealing it was her own son at fault. Of course, Jove had also been recovering from a host of injuries, courtesy of Harlan Shackley's anger.

The Stradat Lord Kapitan and Jove had worked hard to keep the real story from those who would spread it throughout the city. It'd cost a good bit to keep the trial private and lock up the records. *Very* few people knew the truth.

So, who would do this? Who would know? Had Kase told anyone? Surely not. He'd handled Ana's death worse than anyone else. He'd closed himself off, striking out with anger when anyone broached the topic.

Something niggled at the back of his mind. Surely, the government officials Harlan had paid to keep it quiet wouldn't have gone against the Stradat Lord Kapitan. That handwriting. Where had he seen it before?

ALLI EARNEST

Who would Kase have told?

He pulled out the missive again, inspecting the way the writer had formed his letters. He focused on the "J" of Jagamot. Jove wasn't aware of what that was, only that the tail of the letter curled over the stem.

He wracked his brain. Thankfully, he hadn't drunk enough to impair his thinking too much. He put the missive back in his pocket, planning to think more on it once inside. He reached down to help his wife from the motorcoach.

Just as Clara put her hand in Jove's, she yanked it back. She bent over her stomach, grimacing.

"Clara!"

His mother turned back toward the manor. "Thoreau! Call the midwife!"

"I'm...fine." Clara said through heavy breathing. Jove put a hand on her back until the pain passed and her face relaxed.

"Let's get you inside," Jove said, feigning calm. She might have been only eight months pregnant, but she shouldn't be in this much pain with false contractions. Either something was wrong, or Jove would become a father in the next few hours. Neither option made him feel any better.

With his mother's help, they got Clara into the manor and into a guest chamber on the first floor. The stairs would have been too much. The maid fetched a chair for Jove, and his mother busied herself gathering washcloths. He'd helped Clara get out of her evening gown when she doubled over once more. At that point, he scooped her into his arms, carrying her to the bed. He climbed in beside her, holding her until the pain passed once more.

He planted a kiss against her sweaty temple. "You'll be okay."

He helped her slip into a nightgown, washed her face with a damp cloth, and held her hand through the next round of pain.

The midwife arrived in a flurry, and she went right to work inspecting Clara. Jove held his wife as she breathed through another contraction. They were coming closer and closer together.

"I feel pressure. Pressure on my lower back." Clara squeezed her eyes shut and moaned. "It's too soon..."

169

Jove's mother and the midwife spoke in low whispers, the former then ordering the maid to fetch hot water and even more washcloths. The midwife looked at Jove and Clara, her dark eyes glittering. "Everything will be fine, but this baby is coming tonight whether you want it to or not."

Holy blasting stars.

"But my mother, she's not here." Clara breathed, the contraction passing. She laid back in the bed, panting.

Handing him another washcloth, Jove's mother kissed Clara's temple. "I'll send a telegram to Lady Davey. She should be able to catch a hover."

Then she was off.

As Clara squeezed the life out of his hand with the next contraction, all Jove could think was how unprepared he was to become a father. Kase was right.

The elusive missive would have to wait.

CHAPTER 16

COCKY HELVITERS

Kase

EVERY SO OFTEN, KASE COULDN'T help but look back at the road they followed. It was mid-afternoon, three days after they'd escaped Kyvena, but no one tracked them. *Yet.* He was sure someone would've noticed when he hadn't shown up for training, and the absence of his hover, but for now, they were safe. The only ship that could have possibly caught up with them would've been one of the larger hovers, and no one would sanction the use of those to chase after a runaway. That didn't mean he could get cocky, so he kept checking. He'd made sure to damage all the locks to the other hangars, but that wouldn't take them long to get around.

To his right, Hallie fidgeted in her seat. "Can we please stop early for the night? My back is killing me."

"Says the girl who doesn't have to fly this ship," Kase muttered. "We have to get as far as we can before they send out people to hunt us down. We've been over this."

"You think they'd do that?"

Kase shrugged.

Hallie waved her hands in the air. "Except they haven't yet. I feel like if anyone was after us, they'd have caught up by now."

"Well, it depends on who's after us. Besides, if Eravin was..."

Kase winced and cut off mid-sentence, but his words hung in the air like bodies swinging in the guttering wind. His breathing sped up as his foot tensed on the pedal below. "Forget I said anything."

Hallie turned in her seat to look at him, the leather creaking slightly. Kase faced forward, trying to ignore the concern etched across her features. "Eravin?"

"I said, *forget it.*"

When she didn't say anything more, the tension fell from his shoulders. They flew in silence for a while.

He needed to say something. The soft drone of the hover usually wasn't loud, but at that moment, it was deafening. It wasn't her fault she'd been unknowingly caught up in Kase's wrongs. "How about we stop for the night? We've covered a lot of ground today."

"Is there another inn or somewhere we could stay?"

Kase twisted his neck from side to side, and a satisfying crack rang in the air. Yes, it would be good to stop for the night. He looked back once more to make sure nothing else had appeared on the horizon. "If I'm not mistaken, we should be coming up on another village soon. Not as big as the last one, but a few pilots always said Laurent was a good stopping place and that the food was delicious."

It was also too small to have a military presence.

"Sounds good to me. Means I don't have to cook anything."

Kase laughed, glad the ice had thawed. "I'm grateful."

"Hey!" Hallie punched him lightly on the arm. "I resent that. Besides, you're not a bad cook. You could do it yourself. Save us both the trouble."

Kase smirked. "Cooking takes too long."

Hallie's laugh was laced with bitterness. "So, you agree with me, then?"

"Sure." Kase snorted. "I only learned because Mother said I couldn't. Seems too much of a hassle to keep it up if I'm not trying to prove a point."

"Ah, so it was out of spite. I approve."

While he couldn't see her face, she must've been smirking. This was much better than talking about Eravin or his father or anything in Kyvena. He berated himself for the slip of the tongue—especially since he wasn't ever returning. He was leaving it all behind, and he'd never have to look at his father's too-straight mustache ever again.

Just as the last rays of sunlight winked out of existence, Kase landed the hover near the village of Laurent. After two nights of sleeping on the ground, he was grateful.

The village was rather small, and he was surprised Crew pilots even thought to stop here. It was a smattering of houses on the open plain, like someone had tossed too few marbles in the children's game of Chance. They also wouldn't have heard anything from Kyvena yet. At least he hoped.

The inn was easy enough to find, as it was the largest of the cottages. The Lazy Lark was choked in dead vines, but the windows shone with welcoming candlelight. This place was too far out of the way for electricity. He and Hallie stepped out of the crisp air and into a room warmed by a roaring fire.

The dining room was crowded with townsfolk. Mothers, fathers, and their children all laughed and chatted as they shared some sort of dark bread. Many dipped slices into a chunky soup.

"Is that beef stew?" Kase groaned.

Hallie peeked over the shoulder of a man at a nearby table. "Yes, but it looks like it has little dumplings in it. It smells heavenly."

"You must be deluded."

Hallie laughed as they wove their way to the bar at the back. Someone had killed several wild boars and hung their taxidermized heads from the odd mix of dark and light wood-paneled walls. The whole room seemed like a mistake, as if whoever had constructed the building had done so in stages, each more haphazard than the last.

Reaching the equally mismatched wooden bar, Kase pulled a few coins out of his money pouch. He nodded to the barkeep, a man who looked to be about Harlan's age but without the severe lines around his eyes. "Good evening. We're in need of two rooms for the night, and supper."

Even if I'd rather starve.

The man set down the rag he used to wipe the counter. "Certainly. That'll be a silver fiver each."

Each? "Surely, I misheard you. Did you say a silver fiver for each room? They don't charge nearly half that in Kyvena."

The man shrugged, his gray bangs falling into his eyes. "Take it or leave it, but we have to make a living out here. Besides, we provide entertainment worth every bit."

Kase looked around for musicians or something of that sort but found none. He ground his teeth as Hallie stepped up, slapping a silver piece on the counter. "Thank you, sir. We'll take the rooms. And pray, what *is* this entertainment?"

"Hallie, he's ripping us off."

She glared him into silence. Kase forced himself to take a deep breath as he stuffed his coppers back into his pouch and fished out his own sum, sliding the coin across the ridged wooden counter. "Our rooms?"

The proprietor smiled as he reached below and held out two keys. "Rooms Three and Four are available. Second floor. As for the entertainment, put your things away and come on down for supper. You won't be disappointed! It's a Laurent specialty!"

Kase snatched the keys from the man and spun on his heel, his pack bouncing against his back. Hallie's footsteps pattered behind him.

"Kase," she hissed, catching up to him. "You paid more than that the other night at the Crown Haven."

"That was different." Kase handed her a room key. All he wanted was a roof over his head and a decent bed, but he preferred both to be affordable. He didn't know how many more village inns they'd be able to swing if they had to pay so much for a single room. His mother had only sent a small pouch with his pack.

"He can't help it," Hallie said as they wound their way up the stairs to the second floor. "This village might not get as much traffic. Besides, aren't you made of money or something?"

Kase halted, and Hallie ran into his back with an *oof*. He turned his head slightly. "We're on the run and can only afford so much. I'm going to need something to live on until I find a...find a..."

Stars, can I not keep my mouth shut?

"What do you mean by *something to live on?*"

Kase started walking again. "Nothing. Forget I said anything."

"No. Stop. Tell me what's going on. I still think it's strange you agreed to this trip when you were so adamantly against it before."

Kase pushed the key into the lock of Room Three and twisted. It opened with a satisfying click. He stuffed the key in his pocket. Hand on the knob, he spoke without looking back at Hallie. "All that matters right now is that you find your family."

"What're you planning?"

"Nothing."

"*Stop being a stars-idiot.*"

Kase started to twist the knob when Hallie's hand covered his, stopping him. Her voice was soft.

"What's going on in that head of yours? You can tell me."

The memory of the night following Zeke's death rose unbidden in his mind. He saw her earnest eyes sparkling with tears, her dirt-streaked hand clenching his, her silky hair falling out of her braid, his own anguished words as he broke.

Zeke made a choice. I couldn't have stopped it.

Zeke made a choice. I couldn't have stopped it.

Zeke made a choice...

The mantra was one he repeated often. It helped, and maybe one day he'd believe it. He cleared his throat. "I'll meet you downstairs in a few minutes."

Hallie waited a beat, her eyes searching his before she gave his hand a light squeeze. She didn't say anything as she moved past him and closed her own door behind her.

AS KASE DESCENDED INTO THE inn's small dining room, he pushed his melancholy thoughts to the back of his mind. He didn't need distractions. Thinking about what might have been would only cloud his judgment. His sole duty was to get Hallie safely to the Pass. That was it. Then he could figure out the rest.

At first, he only heard muffled murmurings as he

approached the first-floor landing on the stairs; but as soon as he entered the room, a wave of sound crashed into him. Peals of laughter echoed off the dark-beamed ceiling, and mugs of ale sloshed onto fists as men and women alike toasted to good health and the upcoming spring planting.

Kase found Hallie dipping bread into her soup, letting it sit for a few seconds before taking a bite. She'd already ordered him a bowl, so he trudged over and fell into the chair.

"So, how does it compare to yours?" Kase asked as he inspected the contents. Soggy bits of beef and carrots floated in a red pool, but so did what looked like small, round lumps of uncooked bread.

Hallie shrugged. "Better. I ordered you an ale. Hope that's okay. Promise me you'll only have one, though."

"I *hate* beef stew." Kase took up the nearby spoon. He plunged it into the liquid and took a small taste. Still horrible. He tried one of the dumpling things, and although the dough tasted much like the broth, Kase didn't hate it. The bite melted on his tongue. "Okay, these are passable."

Hallie laughed and took an impossibly dainty bite of her own soup, her lips perching on the spoon's edge. "Maybe you can make me a dumpling soup when we return home."

Except after she's in Stoneset, I'm gone.

They spent the rest of the meal eating quietly, Kase selecting only the good parts. Once the barmaid had cleared their table, a tall man dressed in simple trousers and a green vest strode in from the back, the neck of a fiddle clutched in his fist.

As soon as the other patrons spotted him, they leapt up and pushed their tables and chairs out of the way, making a space in the center of the room.

"What are they—oh! This must be the entertainment!" Hallie said, excitement lacing her words like glaze on a pastry.

The fiddler set up near the bar and pulled his bow across a few strings, the notes hanging in the air like the calm before a storm. Then, he broke into a song Kase recognized as one that was popular in Kyvena. The other patrons clapped a little before coupling off and forming two lines down the center of the room, men on one side, women on the other.

"Come on, Kase," Hallie said, the grin showing all her teeth, the canine on the right just slightly crooked. "Let's dance!"

Kase crossed his arms and settled further into his chair. "I don't dance."

"I'm rolling my eyes at you." Hallie sat on the edge of her seat as the dance began, the couples meeting in the middle and clapping to the beat.

Kase grunted in response, too tired to think of anything witty to say back. It's not like he hated dancing, and he wasn't so terrible at it. But the last time he'd danced like this had been at a ball with his sister. While he knew Hallie wasn't aware of that, he didn't feel like explaining it to her. Especially after the difficult last few weeks.

Kase burrowed deeper into the recesses of his chair.

Three songs into his set, the fiddler took a second to rest his arms and grab a drink. In that time, a man about Jove's age with too-yellow hair strutted over and bowed to Hallie.

"Wanna be my partner for this next one? Rob always plays a jig at this point." His grin was cocksure and blinding. Hallie giggled a little before shooting Kase a look that said, 'Look at all you're missing.'

Kase scowled as she took the man's hand. Her voice was like the pealing of a bell with a broken clapper in Kase's ears. She traipsed off and started the steps to the fiddle's long beginning notes.

Who was that guy, anyway? What made him think he could waltz right up to someone he didn't know and expect her to accept him? Only cocky *helviters* who were desperate to find a wife would do something like that. And Hallie was new. He probably thought he could flash his stupid grin at her, and she would fall into his arms.

Hallie wouldn't fall for that. She could see through that type of act.

But why had she said yes?

Kase flagged down the barmaid and asked for another ale. *Take that, Hallie.* In the meantime, he glared at stupid Cornhead Man clasping Hallie's waist as he lifted her up in the air. Her auburn hair was fire in the candlelight.

Kase snatched his new mug of ale from the barmaid and threw it back in three gulps, slamming it onto the table. "Another."

Jealousy was a terrible feeling. Kase knew that's what roiled in his stomach. He couldn't help it, and he hated the sensation. That only made his mood worse.

The barmaid raised a brow. "You sure? Rollis doesn't make his ale light like those weak-blasted *mimmirs* in the capital." He glared at her, and she shrugged her shoulders. "Suit yourself."

As she went back to the bar, Kase spotted Hallie as the dance ended. She laughed at whatever Cornhead said, and Kase's stomach twisted into a knot. If that blasted *dulkop* laid another finger on her, he'd knock him into next Tuesday.

With a small smile, Hallie held up a hand for him to give her a moment, and as she wove past the pushed-aside chairs and tables, Cornhead's eyes bore into Kase's. A challenge.

Cornhead turned away first. Kase smirked.

Hallie's breaths came out in little huffs as she took a seat. "You sure you don't want to join?"

The barmaid returned with Kase's next drink, and he snatched it from her once more, the condensation on the outside cooling the burning skin of his palm. He glanced back at Hallie's ugly dance partner. "You shouldn't be dancing with strange men."

"Stefan isn't some strange man."

"You met him five minutes ago."

"He's a farmer's second son who's saving enough money to move to Kyvena. It's called getting to know people."

Kase chugged a bit of his ale, but he needed to stop soon if he wanted to fly straight in the morning without a blistering headache. "We're not here to flirt with anyone."

"How many ales have you had?" Her voice trilled, exasperation bleeding into it. "And I'm *not* flirting!"

"Like stars you aren't. Did you not hear that blasted giggle of yours when he asked you to dance?"

"Oh, for moons-sake."

"You know what, if you think you and Cornhead are so perfect, why don't you stay here, and I'll fly off to the Pass without you."

Hallie snatched his mug as he was about to take another swig. Ale sloshed onto the table. "Stop being a blasted stars-idiot. If all you're going to do is sit here and pout, do everyone a favor and go to bed already."

ALLI EARNEST

Kase stood so fast, his chair toppled behind him. "Do what you want. I'm leaving at first light whether you're there or not."

He brushed past her, his gait slightly wobbly from the alcohol, but he gritted his teeth and marched toward the stairs. The barmaid had been correct. The ale was indeed stronger than what taverns served back home.

If Hallie wanted to be stupid, fine. Kase was tired anyway. At the door to his room, it took him three tries to stuff the key into the lock. Whether that was because of his anger or the drink clouding his head, he didn't know nor care.

He slammed the door and locked it behind him. Without removing his clothes or even his boots, he fell into the rickety bed and lay face-down.

He'd deal with it all tomorrow.

CHAPTER 17

READY TO FLY

Hallie

HALLIE ALMOST CALLED KASE'S BLUFF about leaving her in the village if she didn't show at first light, but alas, she beat him to the dining room by two minutes, according to the dusty mechanical clock on the wall. He didn't even glance at her as he trudged past, and she followed silently behind.

Three silent hours into the dawn, she peeked over at him through her lashes. He'd shoved his goggles into his curls, messing them even further. His jaw was firm as his eyes narrowed at the road before him, his hands clasping the steering control as if he were afraid it would slip from his fingers at any moment. The sun clawed its way above the distant horizon, and its golden rays outlined Kase's profile.

Her hand ached to draw, yet each time she thought about sketching, her stomach churned.

She didn't even know if her healed hand would work properly if she tried to coax fine strokes out of her pencil. What if she couldn't ever draw again?

But Kase's silhouette called to her.

Ignoring a slight queasy feeling, she dug in her satchel and pulled out the sketching supplies she'd purchased upon her return to Kyvena and hadn't touched since.

Holding the pencil wasn't the torture she figured it would be, if a little unbalanced from the missing little finger. A wave of relief flooded over her. Her queasiness abated.

In between stolen glances, Hallie sketched a rough outline. The lines were sloppy and wayward. The feeling of relief faded. Had she lost her touch? She lifted the pencil. Messy progress was some progress. It wasn't terrible for the first time in months, she supposed.

A bolt of blue light flashed in her memory, along with the lancing pain in her hand. Ebba's scream. She squeezed her eyes shut.

Just breathe. I'll try again soon.

Kase, for his part, didn't move—nor did he acknowledge her.

Good stars, was he still angry with her for dancing with the farmer last night? Hallie had already forgotten his name, and she didn't even care. It had been a fun diversion from all her pent-up stress, and Kase couldn't bring himself to enjoy a little bit of that?

Well, he is Kase.

What more could she expect out of him? He probably kicked small kittens to work off stress.

But that little voice inside her head told her she was being ridiculous. *He* was sacrificing all sorts of things so she could find out if her family was okay.

She was being ungrateful.

For moons-sake, what did she do all day? Stare out the window and nap? Make sure they didn't completely devour their food reserves? She was useless.

She tucked her sketching supplies away and adjusted her safety straps so they didn't dig into her shoulders. "Listen. While I don't see what's so wrong about a little fun, I'm willing to forgive you for being a complete *dulkop* if you do something for me."

Kase grunted.

"Talkative today, I see," Hallie answered in her most pleasant voice. It usually worked wonders in times such as these.

But Kase was as stubborn as the mountains they sped toward.

"You're being ridiculous." She tapped her fingers along the arm of her chair. The *rata-tat* clicking didn't relieve her frustration.

A hundred and three nail clicks later, he sighed. "I have a headache."

"That's because you drank *three* pints of ale last night."

"Two and a half."

Hallie stopped clicking her nails and clenched the arms of her chair, hoping to dispel her anger into them rather than into her words. "How does that make it any better?"

Kase still didn't look at her as he gripped the steering control even tighter in his fists. "What if Cornhead had been some sort of pervert?"

"*Cornhead?* Are you five?"

"I could've come up with worse."

Hallie sighed. "Gracious day."

"He deserved it."

"If he'd have tried anything, he'd have regretted it." Her cheeks heated at the thought, but she knew how to take care of herself, and she didn't have the time or the patience to analyze Kase's fickle emotions. Stars, he was like a blasted girl sometimes. "Besides, you don't get to decide who I spend my time with."

Kase's blue eyes found hers for a moment, and they softened under her relentless glare. He shifted and looked back at the road. "You're right," he sighed. "I have a lot on my mind, and I reacted badly. Sorry. What is it you want me to do? Allow you to finish off the last of the jam?"

"While I wouldn't hate that, I actually..." Hallie cleared her throat. "Well, I'm interested in learning to fly this...contraption."

"I thought you were afraid of heights?"

Hallie shrugged. "This hover doesn't get too far off the ground, and I'm curious."

Kase pushed a button on his control panel and twisted a knob. A small light flickered above the steering control as the craft sped up a little. "All right. We'll start tonight when we stop."

"Thank you."

Inspecting her fingernails, she tried to come up with something else to say. Anything else. But she had a speck of dirt stuck under her nail she couldn't quite reach. After a few more unsuccessful attempts to dislodge it, she glanced at Kase once more.

"So…um…" She traced her fingertips along the smooth metal of the panel beside her. "I brought *Frankenstein* with me."

Kase's head jerked toward her, and he winced. Hallie hid her smirk. Must've cricked it.

Rubbing his neck, Kase narrowed his eyes before turning back to the road. "And?"

"Well, if you'd like, I could read a little. I'm a master at voice impressions, if you recall."

"I think Ebba was just being nice."

Hallie dug in the pack behind her, fishing out the leather-bound book. "Suit yourself."

Kase pushed another button. "I guess I could listen if you didn't talk so loud, but you have to swear not to butcher Dr. Frankenstein's voice."

Hallie grinned as she opened the book and flipped to the front page, the parchment crackling. "I wouldn't dream of it."

"I'd never forgive you, you know."

Hallie cleared her throat. "Friends, Romans, Countrymen, lend me your ears—"

"That's *Julius Caesar.*"

"Just testing you. And besides, the Ides of March is next week."

"And he deserved what he got. Now, if you want to read, read. Otherwise, allow me to fly in peace." Kase pulled the goggles off his head and tucked them under his seat. "Headache, remember?"

Hallie closed the book, holding a finger between the pages to keep her place. "How about I read tonight after flying lessons? Would that be better?"

"Is this really my penance for trying to protect you from Cornhead?"

Hallie rolled her eyes. "Yes. I won't accept anything less."

"Then tonight is good. We'll stop early."

Hallie beamed. "Fine, you're forgiven."

They rode until sunset in companionable silence. For once, Hallie didn't feel the need to spout off whatever came to mind to fill it. Sitting and observing the countryside was just as nice. It was a strange and almost forgotten feeling, being at peace.

HALLIE BANKED THE CAMPFIRE WHILE Kase finished the last bite of bread and jam, the light from the flames tracing the curve of his clean-shaven jaw.

"I thought you were growing out a beard," she remarked as she dusted her hands before taking a seat next to him.

Kase ran a hand over his cheeks and grimaced. "I didn't know how long we'd be gone, and I'd rather not have a knee-length beard by the time I return you to Kyvena."

"I kind of liked it." She tucked away the bit about returning *her* to Kyvena for later analysis.

Kase snorted. "Why's that?"

Thank the stars he'd dropped his surly demeanor from earlier in the day. Hallie stretched out her arms, her back popping slightly. "You looked more mature. It helped your image."

Kase twisted the lid back onto the jam jar and studied her. She squirmed underneath his inspection. He smiled, his eyes crinkling in the corners. "You thought I looked dashing, didn't you?"

Her face burned, and it wasn't from being so close to the fire. "No, no, it's not that."

Kase stood with his hands on his hips, thrusting his chest out. "I mean, I can't blame you. Most people describe me as devilishly handsome. It's a curse, but I bear it nobly."

She threw the wadded cloth she'd wrapped the bread in at him. It floated harmlessly to his feet. *Stupid prat.*

Kase picked it up and crushed it in his fist. "*I know.* It's rather unfair, but what can I say?"

Even though her cheeks burned, she rolled her eyes. "Maybe, but then you open your mouth."

"I resent that."

A laugh bubbled up from the pit of her stomach and exploded from her chest, even with her earlier embarrassment. Soon, Kase was laughing too as he threw the thin napkin into the fire. Hallie wiped a tear from her eye.

"You ready to fly?" Kase asked.

She smiled. His eyes were bright and alight with joy, which made her heart dance a little. Such a contrast from four days ago. "Sure."

Hopefully, he didn't hear the slight tremble in her voice.

He helped her onto the hover wing and into the cockpit. She stood to the side, unsure of what to do next. Kase climbed up beside her.

"Hals, you have to sit in the chair to learn."

"I know that."

"Then what're you waiting for?"

"You're going to do this? Teach me how to fly?"

Kase settled into Hallie's usual seat. "Sure. Not only am I devilishly handsome, but I'm also the best stars-blasted pilot in the Crews."

Hallie shook her head, but she lowered herself into the chair. The steering control looked like the smaller version of a motorcoach wheel, its brown leather stretched tightly over the edges. She smoothed her hand over it, and her fingertips traced a few fractures in the aging material. There were so many buttons and switches around her to memorize.

Kase cleared his throat. "So, what do you do first?"

"Aren't you supposed to teach me?" Hallie squinted at him in the dim firelight.

Kase ran a hand through his hair. "What seems logical?"

Hallie racked her brain for anything that might help. She tried to remember how Kase started it up that morning. A button to her left flashed weakly. "Oh! You need to start it! Using...um, this button?"

She pointed to the flashing one she'd spotted.

The corner of Kase's lips quirked. "Wrong."

Hallie ran her fingers over the steering control again and inspected the array before her. How was she to know which one to push? Hadn't he also flipped a switch somewhere? "Um, you need to flip that orange switch."

Kase sighed. "Wrong again."

Hallie threw up her hands and let out a huff. "Then tell me, Master Pilot. Please impart your immeasurable wisdom upon your humble servant."

Kase's grin mocked her as she sat puzzled by the conundrum he'd set for her. After letting her squirm for a minute and mutter curses under her breath, he tapped the top right corner of her seat. "The most important thing you learn in flight school is safety. First, strap in. Of course, that's after you've checked the hover for issues, but let's pretend I already did."

"But you said..."

He held up a finger. "Do you want to learn or not?"

"*Fine.* I buckle up." She narrowed her eyes as she grabbed for the straps on both sides and clicked them into place. "Now what?"

Kase strapped himself in, and Hallie's blood chilled. "You're not actually going to let me fly this thing right now."

He laughed, its pure peals drifting through the darkness around them. "Of course not, but it's better to be safe. I'm going to walk you through how to turn on the ship, but that's all you'll do tonight."

His instructions on which buttons and switches would make the hover come to life were brusque in his clipped Kyvena accent, but Hallie listened hard. She would not mess this up. One thing was for certain; she was grateful she didn't do this day in and day out. She'd have surely blown up the hover by the time he finished explaining.

"That's it. You'd then push the pedal to move forward, but obviously, don't do that. We'll work on that next lesson." He unclipped his safety straps and turned to face her. "Now, point to what you would do first and walk me through it."

Sweat beaded at Hallie's hairline even in the night's subtle chill. Now, which was it? The black button or the black switch to her right?

"Any day now," Kase taunted.

"That isn't helping."

Kase chuckled softly as Hallie thought. *The black button?* "I think I hit...this one!"

Without thinking, she pushed it.

"Hallie! Don't—"

Too late. Instead of an engine humming to life, a different sound drifted through the air, coming from the seat behind her. It was light, and little staticky. *Music.* A violinist pulled his bow gracefully across the strings, creating a melody. It went to a particular dance she'd begged Ellis to teach her when she'd come to the city.

"Why is your ship—how is your ship—" Hallie stumbled, unbuckling her straps and twisting around in the seat.

Kase reached across and hit the button, his other hand leaning heavily on her arm rest. "It's nothing. Just something I rigged to make training a little more fun."

"What is it?"

Kase fell back into his seat. "An electric gramophone. It plays the one song, but it's—well, it's one of my favorites—stop laughing!"

Hallie couldn't help it. The gentle notes were better suited to a love scene from a play rather than the cocksure, surly pilot Kase was. "I wasn't expecting that."

Kase crossed his arms, his lips drawing into a scowl. "If you'd listened and walked me through what you were about to do, you would have never figured out my secret."

Hallie's grin deepened as she pushed the button once more.

"Hey!" Kase said, already reaching across.

"Not so fast." She pushed his hand back. "Finish off the dance with me, and I won't tell a soul how frilly your favorite song is."

Kase narrowed his eyes, which only made Hallie's grin widen further. The violin picked up in tempo as another musician added a light countermelody. Finally, Kase huffed. "It isn't fair I don't know anything cringeworthy about you to hold over your head."

"That's because I'm perfect."

Kase scoffed.

Hallie stood and swung her leg over the side of the cockpit. "Come on, you owe me anyway."

"What?"

"After last night." She hopped down and brushed off the front of her trousers.

"I thought flying was my penance," Kase grumbled as he

187

landed on the ground beside her.

The notes wove together and swirled around them as Hallie took Kase's hand in hers and placed the other on her waist. Her heart skipped a little. "It was, but that doesn't mean you don't owe me."

"For what?"

"Shall I list them for you?"

Kase shook his head, but he didn't say anything else as he gripped her hand and stepped to the beat, leading her through the dance with light feet. Hallie concentrated on the steps as she followed him around in a figure eight near the fire, their shadows flickering in the grass and dirt as they swayed. Kase let go of her waist as she spun out, their fingers intertwined, and she returned to him, his hand finding her waist once more.

"It's a little strange dancing without the other couples to cut in and do their part," Kase said, his soft smile catching her off guard.

"Well, if you'd simply danced with me last night, then maybe I wouldn't be forcing you to do this."

"You're impossible."

"More like incorrigible, but that's personal preference."

He snorted as he spun her once more, his fingers feather-light on the small of her back. With another turn around and a step-through, the final notes drifted into the air and hung heavily in the silence.

Kase's breath came out in little huffs as each exhale drew diamonds in the air above his lips. Hallie's heart raced. *From the dance. Nothing else.* Kase stared at her for a moment too long before he spoke, "Hold still."

He clambered up on the wing of the hover, and after a moment, the song started over. Hallie laughed. "Again?"

Kase's eyes sparkled in the light from the campfire as he took her in his arms. They danced the entire song, their hearts and feet keeping in time with the music. Hallie's stomach tightened each time he spun and pulled her back to him. All too soon, the music faded in the air like the morning frost, and Hallie's breaths were more labored, mixing with Kase's.

Her eyes found the ties on his cream linen shirt. Something told her not to look up. He was too close, and Hallie's heart beat like a drum in her chest. "I think I'm a little dizzy."

She peeked up at last. His blue eyes were like the stars floating in the endless dark sea above them, and if she let herself, she would drown in the depths. A strange fire sparked in her chest and rose, the flames moving through her veins and out through her fingers, her toes. She breathed deeply. His scent of wood smoke and leather overtook her senses.

Niels.

She stumbled. That small little voice doused the fire in her blood, soaking the emotions from the dance in its syllables and half-formed thoughts.

Niels. Blond hair and brown eyes shining in the light from a long-forgotten fire, his chapped lips a whisper on hers.

Hallie shut her eyes tight. *"No."*

Kase put a tentative hand under her chin, and she looked up. His calloused fingers were like electricity against her skin. His furrowed brow cast a shadow over his eyes. The memory of their near kiss in the temple corridor burned in her mind. She'd wanted to kiss him then, but why did it feel so terribly wrong now?

"Are you all right?" he whispered.

She stepped back, his hand falling away. She tried to inject confidence in her next words. "I just—maybe all the spinning got to me."

His eyes never left hers. "Maybe we should—"

Hallie turned away, his gaze boring in the back of her head. *What's happening to me? Why do I feel like this? Why now?* "We need to rest. Especially you, since you'll be flying tomorrow."

Hallie breathed deeply to control the shaking in her hands. She busied herself with adjusting her sleeping roll and climbed in. "I can take first watch."

"Are you sure you're feeling okay?"

The thick cloth of the bedroll bunched up around her hips as she sat with her knees pulled to her chest. "I'm fine. Promise."

Kase climbed into his own. "Hallie. I'm sorry. I didn't mean to..."

She shook her head. "No, don't apologize. Just...go to sleep, all right?"

"But..."

"I'll wake you in a few hours." Hallie tried to put the most reassuring smile on her face, but it probably looked as pained as it felt.

He stared at her for several tense heartbeats before he pulled the bedroll snug around his tall frame. "Goodnight, then."

"Night."

When Kase's breaths were soft and slow a few minutes later, Hallie analyzed what had happened. Or nearly happened. In her heart, she wanted to kiss him, and she nearly had. It'd happened before on their mission last fall—more than once. But this time, Niels waited at the end of the road.

Niels. That voice. The specter of what he once was haunted the cobwebbed corners of her memories, and she didn't know if he'd ever leave...because once she'd arrived in Stoneset, he'd be there waiting. Waiting for her.

She wiped the lone tear tracing a tried-and-true path down her cheek.

CHAPTER 18

IF THAT'S NOT LOVE

Jove

SITTING ON THE SIDE OF the bed, Jove cradled the newborn baby boy in his arms. His and Clara's baby. Their son. Holy stars, Jove was a father.

He and Clara couldn't do more than stare at the life they'd created. The baby was Clara's twin with his pink-tinged sepia skin, dark curls, and perfectly sculpted mouth, yet his eyes were a brilliant sky-blue. A small chance, yet those eyes were Jove's.

His son's.

Jove had been too young to remember his siblings being born. He had vague recollections of holding a pink, squirming bundle after Ana's birth, but he couldn't recall any more details. However, this one he'd remember until his dying day. Clara had been so incredibly strong throughout the night. Finally, around three o'clock in the morning, a baby boy was born.

Hearing the baby's first cries after worrying and panicking that it was too early, after coaching Clara through something he barely understood, he'd wept. His son's first breaths on Yalvara were so full of life. So unlike Jove's last few months.

He stroked the baby's curls with a careful finger. Jove was so afraid he might shatter. The boy grunted as he worked a tiny hand from his wrappings and tucked it into his mouth. "He's perfect."

Clara kissed Jove's shoulder, rubbing her thumb across his upper arm and snuggling close. "I think we should name him Samuel Lee."

Jove tore his eyes from the bundle in his hands and looked down at his wife. "Samuel Lee?"

"Mmhmm," Clara traced their son's perfect little nose. He squirmed a bit in response, grunting softly. "Firstborn sons are named Samuel in my family. It dates back to the Landing, with General McKenzie. And Lee...after Zeke."

With the mention of his brother, Jove felt a pull to find something to drown out the pain flaring in his chest.

Clara squeezed his arm. "You have to let go of your guilt, of your anger, eventually. Zeke will live on in our son." Clara raised her head up, taking his chin in her hand. She brushed his lips with her thumb before giving him a gentle kiss. "Lean on me. We'll get through this together."

Jove's eyes burned once more as he stared into the dark depths of her eyes. He'd gotten lost in them too many times to count—in their earnestness, their kindness. "I love you."

"And I, you."

He and Clara didn't speak for a while after that, caught in the bliss that was the long eyelashes dusting little Samuel's cheeks, his soft noises as he fell into a deeper sleep. The weight on Jove's shoulders only intensified. He was responsible for this life. He would die to protect it.

Before long, Clara's eyes also drifted shut. Jove let her sleep. She deserved a rest after what she'd done. Jove shifted himself on the bed, giving her room, and adjusted Samuel a little as his arm had begun to fall asleep.

A faint knock came from the door as his mother peeked inside. She wore a dressing gown, her dark braid glittering in the muted light from Secondmoon streaming through the window. She held a gas lantern in her hand. "May we come in?"

"We?"

A second later, his father slipped in behind her. He still

wore his uniform. Jove's grip on his son tightened with each step Harlan took toward them. The room was dim, the only light coming from the window, but even Jove could see the odd cast to his father's eyes. They weren't hard or spiteful. He simply looked tired. His mother trailed behind, setting the lantern on the floor as they stopped before the bed.

"May I?" his father asked quietly so as not to wake the sleeping Clara.

Jove slowly extricated himself from the loose covers, all while holding his son steady. He faced his father. He wasn't ready to hand him off to the monster before him, but he tilted the bundle enough to give him a glimpse.

"His name is Samuel, Samuel...Lee," Jove choked out. His mother sucked in a breath.

With a shaking hand, Harlan reached out and touched Samuel's curls. "A strong name."

After another moment, Harlan took his hand back, smoothing his mustache and clearing his throat. "We need to speak."

Jove held Samuel tighter, looking down at his slumbering wife before turning back to his father. "Can't it wait?"

The tiredness returned to Harlan's eyes. "I'm afraid not. I'm sorry."

His words were calm and remorseful. Jove didn't like it. It scared him more than anything else his father could have said. Did it have to do with the missive sent earlier that evening? Where had his father been this entire time? Had he just returned home?

Jove laid Samuel in the bassinet his mother had found in storage, a relic from a forgotten childhood. She stepped forward. "I'll watch him."

Harlan shook his head. "No, you need to hear this, too."

Jove and his mother exchanged glances before she followed her husband into the hallway. Jove fished Zeke's military pin from his pocket.

Ezekiel Lee Shackley. He rubbed his thumb across his brother's name.

Courage. Selflessness. Love. That was who Zeke had been.

Jove tucked the pin into the side of the bassinet.

He joined his parents in the corridor. It was dark save for

the lantern his mother held. She led the way on the short trek to his father's study.

Jove's eyes ached from lack of sleep, the sensation bombarding him as soon as his newborn son was out of sight. He yawned and took a seat in one of the leather wingback chairs before the dark grate.

He eyed the teacup and saucer on the desk and briefly wondered if his father had ordered tea this early in the morning. It would be like him to wake the maid just so he could have a hot pot of tea before the sun rose.

His mother set the lantern on the hearth, taking the seat next to him. Harlan remained standing, pulling a folded bit of parchment out of his military jacket's inner pocket.

"Do either of you know where Kase is?" His father's voice was low and without emotion.

Jove rubbed his brow. He didn't care where his brother was. He only wanted to be back in the room with his family—not argue about whatever Kase had done this time. His mother answered, her voice shaking slightly. "I haven't seen him...since the Rubikan dinner."

"Jove?"

Jove hid his face in his hands, trying to forget the blurry memories the Rubikan dinner evoked and the painful conversation with his wife the morning after. He needed a drink, or a smoke. Or both.

His words were distorted by his hands. "Why does it matter?"

Harlan's voice dropped a degree, his old vitriol bubbling to the surface. "Because of this."

Jove looked up to find he held out the missive from earlier. He sent a glance his mother's way, unsure if she needed to know the truth. He didn't know what it would do to her.

Jove took the parchment from the Stradat Lord Kapitan's hands and inspected the words again, pretending it was the first time he'd read them. Where had he seen that handwriting? "Lord Stephensen said something about a disturbance in the city."

His mother tilted her head. "Disturbance? Harlan, what's going on? What does this have to do with Kase?"

Harlan stared at Jove hard before turning to his wife. "The

Watch is handling it. Now, where is my son?"

"Something happened. Something you're keeping from me." Her hands clenched the arms of her chair. "I will not be lied to any longer."

"I will not be disrespected in my own household."

"Then tell me the truth." Les' voice shook with unshed tears. "I'm sick of it. I know about your affairs. I know what you've done to my children. I will not put up with it any longer."

Jove looked at her, his mouth agape. "You knew?"

"Not until the Rubikan dinner." Her voice was small. She wiped tears from her eyes, still looking at her husband. "I defended you, loved you, and this is how you repay me? Did you ever love us, love me, at all?"

Silence.

It was like any other argument, the calm before the storm. No one spoke. Harlan didn't answer his wife. Les didn't push her husband. Harlan merely gripped the edge of his desk, the muscles in his jaw working overtime. His other hand flinched as if itching to strike. Harlan had never hit his wife to Jove's knowledge, but Jove was merely their son, and a terrible one by his father's standard.

Jove thought back to the sleeping infant tucked in the bassinet down the corridor. How could anyone be so horrendous? So debased to terrorize their own children? He let the missive fall from his fingers.

Jove's voice dropped low. "I'm done."

He marched toward the door, ready to walk out on the Shackley name forever, but his father's next words stopped him in his tracks.

"I need to know where Kase is...because if we don't find him soon, he may very well be killed."

White hot fear shot through Jove's fingers, up his arms, and into his heart, his previous anger forgotten. "What?"

Harlan turned his back to his wife and son. "I did everything I could to cover up what that blasted stars-idiot had done. He started that fire, and I made sure he didn't hang for it. I risked everything." His fingers curled into fists. "*Everything.* If that's not love, then I don't know what is. Now the city is in an uproar because the secret is out."

Whether Harlan's voice shook with anger, regret, or fear, Jove didn't know. All he could focus on were the words.

His mother fell to her knees. "No, no—Harlan, stop lying to me! How could my Kase...how could he...*Ana*..."

The only sounds in the room were her sobs. Jove stood frozen, staring at the scene before him. His father's straight back as he faced away from his family, his mother shaking on the floor.

"He wouldn't have run, wouldn't have been barely aware of what in the blazes he was doing, if you hadn't beat him nearly senseless." Jove's voice echoed off the bookshelves. "You would've killed him if I hadn't stepped in."

"You *don't* run away from your responsibilities," Harlan spun around, spit flying from his mouth. "I had no choice but to teach him a lesson. Little good that did." Harlan breathed heavily as if he'd run a race. "He killed Ana with that fire. Then Zeke on that mission. And here I am trying to clean up his mistakes again."

Jove saw red. He launched himself across the room and pummeled his father's jaw. Harlan stumbled, falling. Something in Jove's still healing knuckles cracked. His mother screamed.

His hand was on fire. It felt as if he'd punched the wall again. Except no landscape Clara painted could cover the Shackley family's sins.

Jove cradled his injured hand to his chest, blinking back tears and panting as he looked down on his father. Harlan spat to the side, his eyes a little unfocused. Jove hadn't realized he'd hit his father that hard. His heartbeat picked up.

Oh stars. How could I...no...no...

Jove nearly tripped over his own feet as he backed away. He turned to sprint out the door, only to find Thoreau on the other side. The butler was unfazed by the sight before him. He merely nodded, his candle holder bobbing with the motion. "A runner is here for the Stradat Lord Kapitan. It's urgent."

Jove, in a daze, moved out of the way as a boy dressed in the uniform of a military messenger strode in. Harlan had picked himself off the floor, his eyes returning to their normal hard glaze as he examined the boy. The messenger bowed deeply, holding out an envelope. "Urgent missive from the airfields, Stradat Lord Kapitan."

Harlan snatched it from his fingers, ripping open the parchment as the boy retreated into the hallway to await an answer. Thoreau shut the door behind them, leaving Jove and his parents inside. His mother hadn't moved from the floor, her wet face trying to decipher her husband's as he read the missive. With each passing second, the line of his mouth hardened until he ripped the parchment to shreds and kicked the gas lantern into the empty hearth, where it shattered. Glass mixed with oil littered the green carpet.

His mother leapt back, but bits of oil dotted the hem of her dressing gown as Harlan took the forgotten teacup from his desk and hurled it at the bookshelves, where it exploded into a thousand tiny pieces. The saucer followed.

"Harlan!" his mother screamed.

Jove stared. At least he wasn't taking his anger out on anyone else. "What did it say?"

Harlan's look would've killed him if it had the power to do so, his face partially lit by the early morning light peeking through the windows. It made his face appear red, the shadowy places even more pronounced, the swelling in his jaw growing. "Kase. Stole a hover. Tampered with the others. He's gone. I have no choice but to put a warrant out for his arrest." He shoved over the chair Jove had been sitting in earlier. It thumped against the carpet below. He grabbed his chest, panting heavily. "That's if someone else hasn't caught him first."

Then, as if his anger had been the only thing holding him up, he collapsed to the floor. His mother stumbled over, careful to avoid shards of lantern glass. She held his face between her hands. "Harlan. Harlan, wake up."

He didn't respond. Jove whipped open the door with his good hand. "Call a medic!"

Thoreau, who had been standing down the corridor with the runner, nodded, sending the boy off. Jove reentered the study, still cradling his hand, but picking his way over to his unconscious father and near-hysterical mother.

He knelt. His father's pulse beat faintly against Jove's sweaty fingers. "He's alive."

His mother rocked back and forth; her palms pressed into her eyes. Jove stared sightlessly forward. His hand throbbed. He stood, striding over to the desk, and rummaged through the drawers until he found a bottle of whiskey. He tugged out the cork and tipped the bottle back, taking a swig.

He gasped as it scorched his throat, but he felt secure in knowing numbness was on its way. He took another drink.

"Les? Jove?" His father's voice was barely a whisper. His mother gasped and placed her hands on his chest.

"What hurts?" she asked, her hands checking various spots for anything tender. He flinched when her fingers ran across his swollen jaw. His father clumsily grabbed her hands, stilling them.

"What...happened?"

Jove didn't let go of the whiskey bottle as he leaned against the desk. He swirled the dark liquid before taking another sip.

Harlan pulled himself to a sitting position with his wife's help. His hands shook. "Maybe you shouldn't get so worked up. Looks like it's bad for your health," Jove said.

Enough time had passed for Jove to start feeling the effects of the alcohol thrumming through his veins. He swallowed another mouthful before corking the bottle and slamming it on the desk.

The medic arrived shortly, Thoreau following behind. That's when Jove took his leave.

He needed to forget the world for a little while, to forget who his father was, to forget Kase, to forget all the wrongs in his own past. As he carefully slipped in beside his slumbering wife, he prayed she didn't wake to smell the alcohol on his breath.

CHAPTER 19

SOLLIE CAP

Hallie

TWO MORE DAYS PASSED WITHOUT the luxury of staying at an inn. Hallie regretted saving a few silver fivers by purchasing a cheaper bedroll in Kyvena. Every rock and root made permanent indentures in her back, she was sure. She was also certain the dark circles under her eyes had gotten worse.

"I don't think I've gotten such good sleep since...well, I don't even know the last time," Kase said, stretching and popping his back. "Who knew sleeping out in the open like this could be so restful?"

Blasted dulkop.

"Rub it in, why don't you?" Hallie grumbled, rubbing the sore spot on her neck. It felt like someone had struck it with a dull knife for at least an hour straight. Though that might've been from the fact she hadn't slept hardly at all.

Neither of them had brought up the dance from a few nights before, but they had finally fallen back into a regular rhythm and comfortable banter.

"That means you get to make breakfast," Hallie added.

"We're safer off with that, anyway."

"You won't let that joke die, will you?"

Kase laughed and rolled up his bedding. "We're almost out of that jam, though. Could you not have grabbed bigger jars?"

Hallie snatched up her crumpled ribbon and tied off her braid before twisting it up into a messy lady's bun. "I didn't know how much to buy because I wasn't sure how long it would take us."

Kase tossed their bedrolls and his pack into the cockpit. He rummaged around while Hallie kicked dirt on the glowing embers of their campfire.

She asked, "How much farther until we get to the Pass?"

Kase pulled out their last loaf of bread and tore off two chunks, handing one to her. He split his into two smaller pieces. "Less than a day? According to the map, there's a good-sized town before we reach it. I assume that's where you could hire a trapper. I would go in with you...but...somewhere like that is bound to have a sizable military presence, and I'm certain the Stradat Lord Kapitan has put out an arrest warrant."

"Because you ran off with me?"

"Exactly."

From her pack, Hallie fished out the near-empty jar of jam and stuck her bread in, scooping some out. She sighed as she put it in her mouth. The taste never got old. If it were socially acceptable, she might eat it straight from the jar with a spoon. It was nearly as good as her mother's.

Soon, she might very well be stuffing her face with that jam. She hoped so.

"Did you stick your bread in and...Hallie! That's our last jar!" Kase said, taking it from her hands.

"Hey!"

Kase stuck a piece of his own bread in and swiped out a glob. "I won't let you take the last bits without a fight."

Hallie snatched the bite from his fingers before it made it to his mouth and stuffed it into hers. Her words were garbled with the food as she teased, "You gotta be quicker than that, Master Pilot."

Kase held the jar protectively to his chest, stuffing another bite of bread inside and mopping the last bit of jam. He shoved it into his mouth before she got a chance to spirit it away again.

Hallie laughed. After Kase swallowed his bite, he joined in as he closed the lid back on the empty jar and threw it in her pack. "You owe me."

"When we get back to Kyvena, I'll make sure you get an entire jar to yourself."

Kase's smile didn't quite reach his eyes. He glanced up at the clouds. "If the weather holds, we should reach Nar in a few hours. I'll drop you close as I can without drawing attention."

He headed back to the hover, the supply bag on his back.

Her mind flashed back to when Kase had drunkenly told her she'd hate him if she knew what he'd done. And his insistence she not say anything to Ellis. She kicked more dirt over their dying fire for good measure and followed him up into the cockpit.

It wasn't until they'd been flying for an hour with only idle chit chat that Hallie found the courage to ask. "Kase, why are you scared of returning to Kyvena?"

No answer, just a grunt.

"Is it because you'll be punished for leaving without permission? What's the penalty for that?"

"I told you, it's complicated."

"But maybe I can help."

"*Hallie.*" Kase ran a hand through his hair. "I don't want to talk about it."

She played with the edge of her blouse sleeve. The hem was patterned like spring roses. She'd made the lace herself, but her mother had sewn the stitches attaching it to the cuffs. She fingered the identical fringe at her neckline before looking over at Kase. "I promise I won't hate you."

"Blast!" Kase whipped his head around and pummeled a button on the dash as he spun back around.

"What?" Hallie glanced back.

Farmland had given way to hills the closer they got to the mountains, and they'd only met two horse-drawn carriages and a motorcoach headed toward Kyvena the past few days. However, there on the horizon was something else. It was traveling too fast, growing by the second.

Before she could confirm with Kase that it was in fact a

hover, something golden and glittering in the light shot toward them.

Kase cursed and hit something else on the dash. He jerked the steering control. Their hover veered to the right as the sparkling light shot past them. Hallie clung to her safety straps. "Kase, what is going on?"

"Pulse. Disables the electricity."

"But why—"

His next jerk of the steering control preceded another pulse flashing by. "Me."

"What happens if they take us in? Do I also get arrested? Oh, stars, I can't get arrested. They won't let me back into the University if I have a record!"

Kase's jaw was clenched, the cords in his neck taut as he twisted a knob to his right. "Hold on!"

The force of their sudden speed pressed her back against the seat. Kase held a lever with his left hand and pulled on the steering control with his right. Hallie gasped as the hover rose sharply, and before she realized what was happening, she was upside down, looking down at the now too-close hover. They had done a loop. Over the other hover.

She screamed. Her stomach flew into her chest. Bile rose in her throat.

So high.

As quickly as they'd backflipped over the other hover, Kase righted the ship, the hover components screaming in her ears. They didn't bottom out, but Kase's face was redder than her hair. Sweat like rain leaked down his face. He grasped for a lever sticking out of the floor, maneuvering it, following the enemy hover's path before clutching the trigger on top. Two golden blasts shot out from their ship and hit the other square on.

The ship fell out of the air ten feet and skidded to a stop, sparks and smoke exploding from the vehicle. Kase released the trigger lever and spun the steering component to the left, their ship following too fast. Hallie screamed again as she held onto the armrests for dear life.

"Sorry." Kase was breathing hard. "It was the only thing I could think of."

Her stomach roiled like the sea in a hurricane. "Is he dead?"

He shook his head. "We need to get out of here before someone in Nar sends a hover out to investigate."

They left the road and the still-smoking hover behind.

KASE PARKED THE HOVER BEHIND a large outcropping of boulders. The smoke from the other hover still stained the sky—even miles away.

"I guess I'll go into town, then? It's that way?" Hallie voice shook as Kase helped her out of the hover.

Her legs nearly gave out once she hit the ground. Kase caught her, his hands careful on her upper arms. He let go quickly.

"Thank you," she said, her voice small and unsure. Stars, they'd attacked a government official. She straightened her satchel and played with the cloak tie at her neck. "I know that could have been worse, but...well, I guess...Kase, what's wrong?"

He hadn't looked up the entire time. He hadn't said anything at all while trying to hide the hover. Perhaps he'd known the other pilot.

He climbed up into his hover and grabbed her pack. "You're not going in alone."

"I'll be fine."

Surely, he wasn't serious. He'd spent all that time explaining why he couldn't. He'd be arrested. He would still leave her at the end of it all.

That didn't prevent the little glimmer of warmth from sparking in her chest.

"They've caught up with us, and that pilot will let the soldiers in Nar know what happened. They might arrest you, too." He threw the pack at her feet before turning back and rummaging around some more.

"I can talk my way out of anything." Hallie threw her pack over her shoulder. Her cloak got caught up in the strap. She teased it out. "All I need are some extra supplies and a trapper."

Kase pulled out a green jacket and matching cap and hopped down to the ground. They looked familiar, and when he slung the jacket on, the sigil of a tree inside a sun flashed in the sunlight. A military uniform.

"And you don't think wearing that will make you stand out?"

"On the contrary, I should blend right in." Kase dusted his shoulders. Spreading out his arms, he made a small turn. "Don't I look dignified as a soldier?"

"I'd much rather you be a pilot."

Kase tugged a soldier's hat on. "Let's pray no one looks too closely at the nametag. I'm not sure..." He peeked down at the embroidered name on the breast pocket. "...Private Yolen would appreciate his uniform being used this way."

"Private Yolen?"

Kase strapped on his electropistol. "Stars-idiot should be kicked out if he's easily robbed like that."

"Kase..."

He nodded toward her satchel and pack. "Got everything you need? You're not coming back here."

His words echoed in her ears. He was right. She looked back at the hover. In the late afternoon light, the ship reminded her of another one lost and forgotten in a forest thousands of miles away.

The crash of the *Eudora Jayde* hadn't been so long ago, yet it seemed so far. The large airship had been a regular visitor in her nightmares these last few months, and looking at Kase's standard hover now, she wished she could forgive the *Eudora* for all the pain it had caused. For Ebba. For Zeke.

But like her inability to sketch, she had a sneaking suspicion she wouldn't be able to work past those feelings for stars knew how long. Hopefully, discovering more about her past by talking with her parents would help. She didn't know how, but it was something she could do—something to occupy her mind.

"Let's go." Kase stuffed his pilot's goggles in his pack, tugged it onto his shoulders, and headed for the dark splotch on the horizon that was Nar. With one last look, she grabbed her own and followed.

Though Nar was only two miles away, it felt like ages. With each step, Hallie's heart only beat faster. Smoke still floated lazily from the ruined hover. She prayed that whoever had been flying it was okay—even if they didn't seem to have any qualms about shooting her and Kase down.

Just find a trapper to take me through the Pass. Then I can be on my way.

She looked ahead at Kase's back. He wasn't coming with her, but he wasn't going back to Kyvena from what she gathered. Unless he planned on turning himself in, which would've been stupid considering what they'd done.

Her stomach flipped again at the memory of the risky flying. *Risky flying...that was an understatement.*

Instead of wandering along a road, they trudged through the barren wheat fields dressing the surrounding hills. A part of her wished she could be there when they harvested the crop. It would be dreamlike to run through these fields with the mountains in the background. Peaceful, even.

Hallie stretched out her arms as she walked. "Nar is the old Yalven word for 'pointed.' Makes sense as this city is at the foot of the Pass."

"So Narden means...?" Kase turned slightly. The afternoon sunlight traced his features. He looked almost angelic.

Hallie wiped sweat from her brow. While the nights were still crisp, by midday, the sun's rays draped heavily on her shoulders and back. She should've stowed her cloak away before hiking into the city. "Pointed Teeth. Not that brilliant, if you ask me, but there you have it."

"Makes sense." Kase cracked his neck and kicked a stray pebble. "But I would've come up with something much better. Pity they didn't ask me."

Hallie gave a humorless laugh. "What would you have named them, oh wise one?"

"Ithacan Mountains."

"If you're going to go with a classics theme, maybe something like Achilles Peaks? There's only the Narden Pass through them, which makes it the Achilles Heel of the Nardens."

"Probably the thought process when naming Fort Achilles?" Kase laughed. "Or what about something else from First Earth? I always liked the name Himalayas. The old texts say—"

"That they housed First Earth's tallest mountain, Mount—"

"Everest. Shame the sun blew it all up."

"Agreed," Hallie said with an even bigger smile. It was refreshing to have someone who understood almost exactly what she was thinking. Someone on her level. "At the University, I found an account of Sir Edmund Hillary, the first—"

"Man to climb it without dying? Yep. That's a good one. Mother donated it to the University years ago." Kase smiled. "I thought I was the only one who cared to read it. I'm impressed."

Hallie couldn't help the blush rising in her cheeks, but it competed with the soft fluttering in her stomach. "Seems like I'm not the only classics enthusiast. Petra comes close, but she just reads what's required for class."

"I think I would've liked University."

Hallie remembered what Ellis had told her, about how he'd dropped out after his sister's death. "Ellis told me you didn't finish school..."

Her words and his deadened look killed any camaraderie they'd had moments before, and she chewed on the inside of her cheek, the blush now burning like fire. "Forget I said anything."

Kase worked his jaw as he faced forward once more. "Where should we check first? A tavern? I'm not too familiar with trappers."

"Yeah." Hallie willed the embarrassment to fade faster. "I'd say we try one. Maybe the inn. They usually stay close to the Pass during winter. I hope I have enough money. A trip in the late spring snows isn't easy. Wish we could take a hover, though."

"Hovers don't do well in extreme cold. Something about the metal. Uncle Ezekiel was working on fixing that when...well, when he died."

"Were you close with him?"

Kase shrugged. "Father was the one who gave the orders for his and my cousins' executions."

Hallie had again stuck her foot directly into her mouth. Blessed stars. "Oh."

His cousins were also killed? Had they been traitors as well? She didn't dare ask.

The silence was thick as the snow awaiting her in the Pass as they entered the city outskirts. She vaguely remembered riding through in the horse-drawn carriage nearly four years earlier. She hadn't paid too much attention, as everything following Jack's death had been a blur.

Shops and cottages grew on either side of the lazy lane. Each building climbed higher than the last. Cheery travelers and townsfolk bid each other hello with a simple wave and a smile. A few children with dirt-streaked faces chased a stray sheep across the street and into an alleyway. A lone orange-and-white striped cat perched in the bakery window. Its narrowed eyes inspected each passerby, and it meowed at the sheep and children who ran back out of the alleyway. Kase slowed to walk beside Hallie.

"*Lara Lane Peaton*! What did I say about running in the streets?" Someone called.

Hallie looked up to find a motherly-looking woman with tight corkscrew curls peeking out from under her kerchief. She tucked a square paper-wrapped parcel underneath her arm and strode toward one of the sheep-chasing children. The girl, who looked to be about ten, had frozen mid-stride, her skirts still swishing about her ankles. She was too young to wear a lady's' bun, but she'd tied her hair in a single braid down her back. Tiny curls clung to the girl's face. She breathed quickly.

"Mama, please!" She wiped sweat off her brow. "Mr. Cadden said he'd give out a copper to whoever caught his sheep."

"Well Mr. Cadden should catch his own livestock. Young ladies such as yourself do not run willy-nilly where those blasted death ships could run you right over." She grabbed her daughter's hand and tugged her along. A cry erupted from one of the vendors on the side of the road as the sheep plowed past, knocking over bolts of fabric.

The girl threw her head back and sighed. "How many times must I tell you, Mama? The hovers *fly!*"

The rest of their conversation was lost in the chatter and noise of the crowd. A group of men wearing overalls cornered the sheep, tossing a lasso over its neck. The animal lowered its head in defeat.

Hallie smiled at it all. It felt like home. A home she barely remembered.

"You're happy the sheep got caught?" Kase asked, tugging

down his cap as a soldier appeared on the corner. He spoke with the overall-wearing men.

Hallie nodded to where the mother now dusted off her daughter's skirts. "I can't tell you how many dresses I muddied growing up. It didn't help that Jack was the same with his trousers. Mama finally got fed up and made us do the mending and washing."

At that moment the girl looked up and met Hallie's eyes. Hallie gave her a wink and a smile. The girl tilted her head but waved back.

"Sounds terrible," Kase said as they entered the market square proper. "Whenever I messed up anything, we simply sent the butler or maid out for a new one."

Hallie rolled her eyes. "Must've been nice."

"It was." Kase gestured to a building across the square. It was built in the same style as the others: brown brick with a red roof and crooked chimney. The sign above read *Ye Olde Raven Tavern*. The large black bird painted on the wood wore spectacles. "Should we try there first?"

Hallie led the way over. With each step, the bird never seemed to take its bespectacled eyes off them. A little creepy, but that wasn't the worst part. A message board of sorts full of wanted posters hung outside the door, and in the center was one whose portrait held someone Hallie knew. If it'd been in color, the curls would've been brown and eyes blue as sapphire.

Kase stopped, too. He inspected it for a moment before scoffing. "They got my jaw all wrong. And my nose? It's not as short as that."

Hallie whipped her head around. "What in the blazes do you think you're doing? Are you trying to get caught?"

"Still should get my nose right."

"My stars, I'll sketch your portrait later with a nose as long as your forearm if you shut up." Hallie turned away from the board and laid a hand on the door. She looked back at Kase. He flipped the collar of his uniform up and tugged at his cap before pushing past her. First, he wanted to avoid the city altogether, and now he wanted to flirt with death.

"Elf-skinned harpy," Hallie muttered under her breath.

Kase paused, one foot inside the establishment, his hand still on the handle. "If you're going to insult me with

Shakespeare, choose a good one. Like 'thou hast no more brain than I have in mine elbows.'"

"No one reads *Troilus and Cressida* anymore. Except for you."

Kase smiled and entered the tavern, his boots clicking smartly on the stone floor. Hallie's heart skipped a beat at his look, his disregard for his own safety forgotten in a moment, and she took a second to compose herself before she followed.

She needed to figure out how to say goodbye. She assumed she'd return to the capital once her parents had answered her questions, but with the military out to capture Kase...she didn't want to entertain the possibility that she'd lose him forever.

That was a funny feeling. She'd almost lost Kase after Ben stabbed him, but that was different. She'd been through a rather stressful ordeal, and the only hold to her sanity, Kase, had nearly died. She hadn't liked the idea of losing him forever then, but in the adrenaline of the moment, it felt all the more powerful.

This time was different. They weren't on a death-defying adventure. They weren't in any imminent danger of being stabbed by an ancient magical being that had taken over their friend's body.

No, this time, if Kase left, it would be because he chose to. Hallie didn't like the gnawing sensation in her gut at the thought of never seeing him again but knowing he was somewhere out there living his life, marrying some beautiful girl, and starting a family of his own.

She gritted her teeth.

She was being ridiculous. This was how it had to be. Besides, hadn't Niels been on her mind lately? She had enough to deal with going back to Stoneset without worrying about Kase.

As Hallie stepped into the tavern, the musty scent of decaying parchment enveloped her. Her eyes adjusted to the sudden change in light, and she gasped. Gas lanterns hung from the beamed ceiling, the light illuminating the bookshelves lining the walls of the room. She looked up to see glimmering spiderwebs draped in the rafters, which somehow made the space cozier.

At this time of day, the sights and sounds of the tavern

filled her with warmth. Each table was full to bursting with people of all sorts. Some were traders, judging by their fur caps and electropistols slung in straps across their shoulders. A few of the traders were women. One table in particular held two who sat knitting scarves and gossiping away. Hallie caught a bit of their conversation as she passed.

"John's no longer ferrying people across the Pass, what with that mess with Cerulene going on. Said it was worth the less money to do his hunting on this side of the Nardens," The younger woman with spindly fingers said as she looped yarn the color of the sun around her needles.

The other scoffed. "I think that's all a bunch of hogwash. We hadn't heard anything all winter. Besides, you know John's only jealous of Ham Gallagher making eyes at you."

Both women giggled, and Hallie continued on to the bar. Kase had already hailed the barkeep, whose black mustache contrasted with his pale skin. The women's words rang in her ears. They hadn't heard anything all winter.

The telegram's cryptic words rang in her ears.

Come home. Need to talk.

If she couldn't find someone to guide her through the Pass, would she be brave enough to trek it alone? Stoneset had its own set of caves through the mountains she could use, but she didn't know where they came out on this side. She, Jack, and Niels had never found out, even though they'd traversed the tunnels for hours as children. They were supposed to be used in emergencies only as the caves were unstable.

That, she knew all too well.

If she couldn't hire a trapper, could she find the cave entrance? She chewed her lip as she leaned on the wooden bar top.

"Yarrow should be able to point you in the right direction, I believe," the barkeep said, answering Kase's inquiry. He poured a tall brown drink into a wooden tankard, which Kase grasped by the handle and took a long gulp.

Hallie distracted herself by finding a crack in the wooden bar. It would not do well to point out that consuming alcohol at that time was a stupid idea.

He set it down and turned to Hallie. "You want anything?"

She shook her head. "So, Yarrow? Who is he?"

"Trapper." The barkeep wiped down the top where Kase's drink had sloshed onto it when he'd grabbed it. "He might be the only one still taking anyone over. Corner booth. Never orders more than my darkest ale."

Hallie gave him a smile. "Thank you."

"It's Edgar, and you let me know if you want a sip of anything, pretty lady."

Kase slammed his tankard down, more drink spilling onto the bar. "Let's go talk to him, Hals."

He brushed past her, heading over to where Edgar had indicated. Hallie hesitated a moment. She peeked back at the barkeep, who stared too hard at Kase. The back of her neck prickled.

Nothing is wrong. We're newcomers.

The trapper was dressed in a cap with flaps over the ears and a large coat and cloak combo about his shoulders. The weapons propped beside him on the bench weren't electropistols, or anything someone would have used since the advent of electricity. One was a simple wooden bow complete with a quiver full of blue-feathered arrows. The other was a long-barreled rifle, a bayonet attached to the end. If Hallie hadn't known any better, she'd have thought she'd been flung back in time...or into a story of the Landing. His pack beside him had frayed to near bits in some places. Somehow, it looked craggier than the trapper himself.

None of it would be helpful if he ran into Cerls with their cannon guns.

The man looked up at Kase and Hallie from beneath his hat, his long lashes brushing the edges of bushy black eyebrows. He wore a thick scarf bundled around his neck even in the warmth of the tavern. His skin was the color of his clothing—gray—odd in the golden light from the gas lanterns above. His eyes, though, were his most startling feature. They were bluer than the sky on a clear spring day. And with those lashes, Hallie could almost forget the sickly pallor or the crevices webbing out from the corners of his eyes and lips.

They also looked eerily familiar, though she was certain she'd never met the man before.

"I don't do whatever you're selling." The man's voice matched his general appearance—ragged and unused.

Hallie sat down across from the trapper. "We're not here to sell you anything, Mr. Yarrow."

Kase leaned over the table. "You'll be taking us through the Pass."

"What he means to say," Hallie said through gritted teeth, "is that we heard you can take me to Stoneset. It's urgent."

"Us. We'd both be going."

Hallie looked up at Kase, strands of her hair tickling her eyebrows as they rose. She turned her gaze back to the trapper. "Both of us. And quickly."

The bead of warmth from earlier returned and swelled.

She wouldn't have to say goodbye...yet. She fought to keep the smile from surfacing. It wouldn't help their negotiations.

He's coming with me.

The man's piercing blue stare made her stomach squirm. "It's dangerous this time of year, even if Cerulene wasn't sniffing around."

Kase leaned in further, his nose only a few inches from the man's. Yarrow didn't flinch. Kase's voice was low. "Listen, we'll pay you handsomely. Will you do it?"

"You don't get to demand anything, city slicker," Yarrow grunted. "I'll do it for fifteen gold tenners each."

Hallie sucked in a breath too fast and coughed. "I think that might be a little too handsome."

"That's my price." Yarrow sat back, his arms crossed. His fur cap tipped forward, casting a shadow over his eyes. They still seemed to glow in the dim light.

"Ten each." Kase slid into the booth next to Hallie. Sparks flew where his upper arm met hers. She didn't want to move away, but her face grew warmer and warmer with each second her arm stayed in close contact with his. She shuffled a little, her leg bumping his.

Another spark.

Blast it.

The trapper leaned across the table, his cap falling further into his eyes. He slid it back into place and sniffed. "Fifteen gold tenners."

Hallie clasped her fingers in her lap, trying not to think about Kase's proximity and what that meant. She needed to focus on the task at hand. "Except you're not making much soaking up space in this tavern, Mr. Yarrow. We'll pay you well, but fifteen gold tenners each isn't reasonable. I'm from Stoneset. I know what the average rate is—ten."

"Except I'm your only hope through, Miss..."

"Walker. Hallie Walker."

Yarrow sat back, rubbing his face with gnarled hands.

Kase pulled out his money pouch. "Look, here's ten gold tenners up front." He stacked the coins neatly on the table, the light glancing off them. The trapper looked at them hungrily with those ice-colored eyes. Kase continued, "We'll pay you ten more and a little extra at the end... depending on your service."

Yarrow stared at the money, at Kase, at Hallie. He lingered too long on her. Hallie fought the urge to squirm underneath his inspection.

Kase took off his hat and ruffled his curls. Yarrow eyed it.

The old man turned thoughtful. "Throw in the *sollie* cap."

"*Sollie*?" Kase asked, holding up the cap. "You mean this?"

"Certainly. Throw in the cap, and I'll take you over for thirteen each."

After a second's hesitation, Kase threw it in. "Fine."

Hallie's heart thumped in her throat as Yarrow scrutinized the gold. He bit each piece before stuffing them into his coat pocket. He took Kase's soldier cap and stuffed it in his threadbare pack. "Then you have a deal, slicker boy. I'll meet you here at first light. If you ain't there, that's on you."

Kase breathed sharply out his nose.

"Thank you," Hallie said, holding out her hand. She didn't need Kase losing his temper here.

The man reached out with a knobby hand and shook it. He didn't let go. "You're welcome...Miss Walker, was it?"

"Yes."

The man grunted before finally releasing her hand.

Kase stood up quickly. "Okay then. We need to stock up on supplies if we're to leave tomorrow morning." He stalked off toward the front door.

"Thank you again." Hallie gave the trapper a weak smile before sliding out of the booth herself and following Kase.

CHAPTER 20

GOOD RIDDANCE

Hallie

ELECTRIC BULBS HUNG FROM THE mercantile ceiling at regular intervals, casting odd shadows between the shelves. Kase and Hallie were only two of many customers meandering through the wares. If they had time, Hallie would love to peruse each row, but alas, staying in town too long might attract unwanted attention.

Hallie knew they would be staying in trapper huts along the Pass, but she didn't think her current sleeping roll would cut it. Her payment clinked among others as the cashier dropped the coins in the till. Kase slid a handful of bronzers across the stained and polished counter. He held up a thick wool cap with flaps on the ears, more gloves, and a crinkled bag of caramels.

Hallie raised her brow. "Planning on sharing? You ate all mine last time."

"Depends on if you're nice to me or not."

Hallie rolled her eyes. The cashier stared at Kase a little too long, his brown eyes narrowed. "You, young sir, look familiar.

Have you been through here before?"

Hallie tried not to look at the wanted poster hanging behind the man or the fact Kase wasn't wearing the stolen soldier cap. Even with the shorter nose and incorrect jawline, it still looked like Kase. Hallie gave the man a grin, hoping it placated him. "Sorry, this is our first time through. We appreciate your help."

Kase stuffed the gloves and caramels in his bag and tugged on the wool cap. "Let's go."

Following him out of the shop, Hallie tried not to focus on the store owner's gaze burning the back of her neck. She caught up with Kase, catching the sleeve of his stolen uniform. "I think the wool cap might make you stand out more..."

She stopped talking as they passed a group of soldiers talking with the barkeep from Ye Olde Raven. Hallie's mouth went dry, her tongue more like sandpaper on the roof of her mouth. It was just a coincidence. He was probably friends with them. Or he wanted extra security at night. Cerulene *was* on everyone's minds.

Kase didn't stop, nor did he respond. He kept walking, his head down and cap low. Hallie hoped the shake in her hands wasn't noticeable as she fell in stride with him. "Kase..."

"We lay low. Can't risk going to the hover."

"But—"

A low baritone interrupted her. "You there, stop and turn around."

"Kase..." Hallie's whisper came out strained.

"Yes, that's him. That's Shackley!" Another voice joined the first. "Kase, it's me, Ike!"

Kase didn't turn, only grabbed Hallie's hand, and broke into a run. She gasped as her legs instantly protested, her thighs burning against the sudden strain and the weight of the pack she carried. They sprinted through the city, the alleyways and side streets, shouts and the thrumming of military-style boots chasing behind.

"Kase!" Hallie's lungs burned, and his name came out like a desperate prayer. She had never enjoyed sports, preferring the sweet delicacies that were First Earth classics and the scratching of pencil on parchment.

She and Kase tumbled out of an alleyway onto the main

thoroughfare only to stumble over the sheep that had been running amuck earlier. Hallie screamed as she fell to the ground, Kase beside her.

Fingers like pincers grasped Hallie's arms and hauled her up. Her pack slid from her shoulders, causing her to tumble off balance, but the pincer grip held her steady. The man who held her relieved her of her pack.

"You're under arrest, Kase Shackley." The voice was gruff, the same baritone from earlier. "The High Council has given orders to detain you."

Hallie didn't dare glance at Kase. She squeezed her eyes shut instead, hoping this was a mistake, praying they would let them go. But she'd seen the smoke from the hover. She'd been right beside Kase when he'd shot it down.

"And who are you?"

The words were directed at Hallie. She opened her eyes, but she couldn't move her lips. Couldn't coerce her voice into pushing out the words. The pulsing of her heart nearly overwhelmed her. Would she be detained? An image of being chained to the stone wall of a leaky dungeon formed in her mind. She shook her head.

Kase answered instead, his breathing labored. "She's no one."

He was trying to help her, she knew, but the words still cut deep. They burned in her chest.

"Yet she's clearly traveling with you," the voice said.

Hallie finally recovered enough courage to peek over at Kase. He stood without his pack, his arms pulled behind his back, his new cap askew. The soldier holding him had a few medals tacked to his shoulder. Someone important. Only two stripes, though. Kase was tall, but the man keeping his arms pinned not only had his height, but the girth Kase lacked. His full beard clung to the edge of his jaw and appeared blond in the afternoon light.

Kase stared forward, not glancing at Hallie nor at the winded man who'd appeared, soot staining his pale, angular face. "They should've known better than to try and catch you in a hover, Kase, even if it was one of them fancier ones. They should've sent Bradley, but of course, I got—"

"I'd suggest you keep your mouth shut, Pilot Henry."

"And I told you, you can call me Ike."

The soldier whose badge Hallie could finally read once Kase had shifted—Captain Maltby—glared, and Ike went silent. Hallie took in his leather pilot's jacket. He must've been the one flying the hover Kase shot down. He didn't seem to mind. Hallie didn't know whether to take heart in that or not.

Captain Maltby turned to Hallie. "Again, you're traveling with Shackley here, so we'll need to take you in for questioning."

Kase pulled against his captor. "She's innocent. I picked her up in Laurent. Said she needed a ride to Nar."

The man's light brow rose. "Is that so? Then, you are?"

Before she could answer, Yarrow the trapper stepped out of the alleyway. The late afternoon was warmer than it should've been this close to the Nardens, but he still wore his immense coat, fur cap, and scarf. His ice blue eyes found Hallie. "She's my client, Miss Barbary, right?"

Hallie was trying to figure out how the trapper had forgotten her name when she finally caught a glare from Kase. She stumbled through her words like molasses. "Yes, Barbary. I'm Hallie Barbary. I'm hoping to visit my parents on the other side of the Nardens. I didn't realize..." she chanced a quick look at Kase, who in turn had looked away, "...I didn't realize the military was after him. I expect my gold back, you beslubbering boar-pig."

Not her best Shakespearean insult, but it was the best she could conjure at such a moment. Kase nearly ruined the effect when a ghost of a smile spirited across his features. Thankfully, the trapper distracted the soldiers who looked at Hallie with suspicion alighting in their eyes.

Yarrow crossed his arms. "Yes, now, you'll be taking his sorry slicker hide in for questioning but allow the lady to go free."

Neither Captain Maltby nor the hover pilot had taken their eyes off Hallie, but after a terse nod from the captain, whoever had been holding her captive released her and returned her pack. Slinging it onto her back, she toppled over.

This time, the trapper caught her by the upper arm. He quickly let go, and Hallie straightened. She tugged on her cloak where it was choking her and nodded. The soldiers dragged

Kase up the main street, but before he disappeared around the corner, he looked back at Hallie.

His sapphire gaze met hers. Her heart gave a painful thump. Then, he was gone in a swirl of dust from the road and a wistful glance.

She turned to the trapper. "Why? Why did you save me?"

The man threw a copper over to the same girl from earlier—the one who'd been scolded by her mother for chasing the sheep. She smiled, holding the coin close to her chest, and scampered off. Yarrow nodded and turned back to Hallie. "You're Hallie Walker."

"Sure, but I'm no one important."

He took off the opposite way Kase had gone. With one last glance behind her, she hurried to catch up. She had to take twice as many steps as he did to stay abreast with him. "You could've taken the money and let me be dragged in for questioning. It would've been the easiest gold you'd ever made."

He continued to walk, ignoring her and the people who leapt out of his way. Hallie growled beneath her breath. Stupid men.

She caught up to him once more. "Traversing the Pass is dangerous this time of year."

He finally stopped but didn't look at her. He gazed toward the sky, which was now pregnant with dark, rumbling clouds. "I carried your letter through the Pass. Was paid a fine bit of gold to do it."

The eyes. She remembered them, but not the bear of the man before her. "I didn't hire you. I hired—"

"My brother, but I took over."

"Your brother?" The icy blue eyes and shock of night dark hair surfaced in her memories. It'd been nearly a month ago. Impressive both he and his brother not only made it through the Pass twice in that time frame, but Yarrow was willing to go again. Maybe he was worth the steep price he demanded. "Is he coming with us?"

"He's dead. Good riddance, too."

Hallie's stomach plummeted. "Oh."

No other words of condolence came to her mind. Of anyone, Hallie could relate to Yarrow the trapper. Except she cared that her brother had died. The bear of a man in front of her spoke with such callousness, as if the brother had been a wolf Yarrow sought to skin.

Had he killed his brother? As he slogged through the crowds of Nar, grief didn't bog him down, nor did guilt lace his stride. She'd hired him to take her through the Pass. Kase was in the military's custody.

"We're not leaving Kase." Hallie caught Yarrow's cloak. He turned.

People milled about like a current streaming around an island in the middle of a river. Yarrow smirked a little. "I've seen the wanted posters. Woulda turned him in myself if I didn't hate the system."

Hallie's heart gave a harsh thump as she let go of his cloak. "I'll pay you an extra five gold tenners if you help me."

Yarrow's visage turned thoughtful. "I'm listening."

"Great." Hallie gave him a tight smile and prayed she didn't go the same way as his brother when he discovered she didn't have the extra gold on her. His initial fee cleaned her out. That was a problem for future Hallie. "We'll need a distraction, the keys...oh stars...I need to think this through."

People passing gave her varying degrees of inquisitive looks. She didn't make eye contact with any of them. Yarrow coughed, then spoke, "They'll be keeping him at the holding cells near the airfields 'til he's ready for transport. Storm should hold 'em off for a bit."

He paused, rummaged in his pocket, and pulled out a chunk of lumpy jerky. He bit off a piece before stuffing the rest back in his jacket. He chewed with his mouth open. Hallie glanced to where a man selling rutabagas haggled with an elderly woman. She raised her cane in the air, and the vendor cowered. Hallie looked down at her feet as Yarrow continued. "Only problem'll be the hovers. Don't want those blasted contraptions scouring the mountainside—storm or not."

"What do you suggest?"

Yarrow looked around and beckoned for her to follow. She clutched her pack strap as she traversed after him—not in the direction Kase had gone. He turned down an alleyway, his cloak billowing out behind like the dark of the night. He didn't stop until they came to a doorway where a small boy sat, head in his hands. Yarrow dropped a copper at his feet. The coin bounced and rolled into the stoop.

"Make sure the *sollies* don't leave the city in one of their machines. And there's another copper awaitin' if ya do it right this time."

The boy with overly large brown eyes and unkempt hair scooped up the money and nodded. "Promise I won't let ya down this time."

The boy sprinted off, his smile practically glowing. With the sun setting soon, surely, the soldiers wouldn't risk flying a hover at night. Kase might have been wealthy and the Stradat Lord Kapitan's son, but he wasn't a danger to society. There wasn't a real need to get him back to Kyvena quickly. He'd only stolen a hover...that wasn't too bad, was it? And he was a Shackley. He wouldn't get into too much trouble, right? He'd been born into privilege.

Wait. Hadn't he said he went on the *Eudora* mission because he'd nearly killed someone? Blast. The more Hallie thought about it all, it got worse and worse. What would his father do to him when he got to the capital? The last time she'd seen the Stradat Lord Kapitan, he'd busted Kase's lip. And that had been because he'd brought Hallie to an estate dinner. Her stomach roiled.

"We have to get him out," Hallie said, maybe a little too loudly, the words echoing off the walls of the alleyway.

The trapper smoothed the lines around his mouth with a gnarled hand. "The lad will stall any transfer if he wants to eat tonight."

Hallie walked forward, hand playing with her bag straps. "Is there a place to stow my pack and satchel until after I break him out?" She needed to figure out a distraction and a way to neutralize the hovers. "Somewhere safe."

The trapper led her out of the alley and pointed up the main street to where the mountains loomed above them like sentries. The red-shingled cottages and shops ended, but the road continued up into the forest of fir trees. "Up there, about a mile or two into the woods, is a trapper's cabin. Old Ossie'll watch over them for ya." At Hallie's skeptical look, he shrugged. "No one much bothers him except me. And that's only 'cause I bring him moonshine. Never says no to hooch."

Hallie opened her mouth but didn't quite know what to

say. She closed it. She didn't like the idea of leaving the pack with some old man who drank too much. But did she have a choice? Not really. With the idea currently forming in her mind, having something extra to slow her down was not an option.

"Show me the hangar and the holding cells. I have a plan."

C H A P T E R 2 1

ALWAYS

Hallie

"BE GOOD TO ME, OKAY?" Hallie whispered to the airship as
she scrambled up the abandoned hover's wing. The brown
metal winked at her in the little sunlight peeking through the
angry clouds above. Like it trusted her. She climbed into the
cockpit, the rough metal seams scratching her palms.

Hallie was alone, a good two miles outside of Nar, and
about to do something incredibly stupid. She prayed Kase
forgave her.

Rumbling thunder echoed off the airship and through her
skull. Nothing ever went the way she intended. She, Kase, and
Yarrow would be running full speed into the Pass with a storm
on their heels. Or on top of them. And in the Pass, the rain
would become snow. That is, if Yarrow fulfilled his part of the
plan and got Kase out of the holding cells. He had the easier
task.

Gracious day.

Maybe the soldiers wouldn't come looking in the Pass. They would probably mock the frozen bodies they found later instead. She didn't know if that was better than the alternative.

Hallie brushed her sweaty, stinging hands on her trousers. She could almost feel Kase beside her as she pulled the glass closed and settled into the pilot's seat. The memory of their earlier escapade replayed in her mind. She shut her eyes tight as her stomach reenacted her reaction to the speed and subsequent air loop. Everything in her thumped along with her heart.

After last fall, how could she be afraid of anything? Well, false bravado would have to work for now. She waited until another roll of thunder shook the hover. Yarrow was waiting on her signal, though he wasn't entirely sure what that signal was.

He would figure it out fine.

Hallie opened her eyes and inspected the dash. What to do first...Kase's voice floated through her mind.

The most important thing you learn in flight school is safety. First, strap in. Of course, that's after you've checked the hover for issues, but let's pretend I already did.

A nervous chuckle tumbled from her lips. As if she'd know what an issue was on a hovership. And safety mattered little with what she was about to do, but she strapped in anyway. The thick material cut into her shoulders as she leaned forward, pressing the black button.

A string of soft violin notes met her ears. Kase's song.

The notes took the tension from her shoulders. She could do this. She allowed herself a breath before flipping the correct switch. The hum of the hover engines joined the ensemble. The odd symphony fortified her heart as she pressed the ship forward. She pushed the other lever at the same time to lift the craft off the rocky soil below.

"Whaa—"

Her hand went too far, and the airship sprang into the air, her stomach flying into her throat. She yanked the control toward her only for the ship's nose to rise sharply. She flew back against her seat as she screamed. She let go of the steering control and took her foot off the pedal. Tears bubbled up in the corners of her eyes as the ship righted itself, the hover components stabilizing the craft.

"Just a little bit at a time."

Shutting her eyes, she pressed the pedal with her big toe, inching it, really. The craft edged forward.

Just don't get too crazy.

Her hands held the steering control in a death grip as she puttered toward Nar. She would need to speed up soon if her plan was going to work, yet the thought of doing so made her want to vomit. She slipped one hand off the control to feel for the lever between her legs.

I can do this. Time it right.

As the smudge on the darkening horizon morphed into the cottages and shops of Nar, sweat beaded at Hallie's hairline. She pressed the pedal more, and the craft responded with a soft rumbling. She swallowed. Steering toward where she knew the other hovers waited, she sped up. She was only fifteen feet in the air, but that was enough.

She couldn't breathe. The air in the cockpit froze and burned at once. A brief image of Kase in that blasted gas mask flashed in her mind, but she didn't think this was what he'd meant. She couldn't remember which button would flash for that anyway.

The small airfield didn't have individual hangars, only one large structure that sat at the edge of the runway. She'd be a fool to miss such a target. People—pilots and soldiers—pointed at her and scrambled out of the way.

Her foot slammed the pedal until it smacked the floor, and she shrieked as she yanked the lever between her legs. Her head and neck flew forward as the force of ejection shot her straight into the air. Her safety straps dug into her shoulders as weight pressed onto her spine.

The whoosh of air in her ears was loud, but the screeching boom from below was deafening. A direct hit. She still hadn't opened her eyes. She couldn't. Her throat was too tight to keep screaming even as her upward momentum stopped, and she fell.

As suddenly as she'd been thrust into the air, the snapping of something shooting from the back of her seat made her eyes pop open. A parachute unfurled and caught the air with a pop. A large tug and her descent slowed. She looked down.

A mistake.

She stiffened as ice flowed in her veins. The ground was too far. Much too far. But she wasn't falling at the pace from earlier. The parachute was holding up. She peeked through her lashes at the airfield.

Orange, red, and yellow flames engulfed what was left of the hangar. People like the ants of a destroyed nest ran amuck. It looked as if they were organizing a water bucket brigade. Hallie nearly choked on the burning bile in her throat.

The ground was coming in fast, and before she knew it, the pilot's seat smacked the ground, the parachute fluttering over her. She didn't move. Eventually she remembered the rest of her plan.

She needed to get out of here before anyone arrested her. With shaking hands, she unbuckled herself, but a shout stopped her.

She didn't recognize the voice. That wouldn't matter.

"Take whoever that is into custody for questioning!"

Fear like fire raced up Hallie's spine as she untangled herself from the straps. Her hair spilled over her eyes. She needed a way out. She couldn't fight them. Any weapons she might have used were now melting in the flames. Not that it would've made a difference.

Think.

She reached the edge of the parachute as the material was ripped off her. The hangar was a hundred feet away, but the heat still warmed her face. The flames billowed from the top and side where the hover must have crashed. She looked away and dove into the arms of the soldier waiting there. He dropped his electropistol and caught her as she sobbed into his arms. That part wasn't acting. "Please, please help. I was kidnapped...and...and I..."

Her tears were coming so hard her words were mangled. The soldier pulled her to her feet. He held her at arm length. "Ma'am, I need you to calm down."

This man doesn't know women, does he?

She wiped streaming snot from her upper lip and glanced toward the fire. "He took me...I tried to fight him, but he...he..." she couldn't catch her breath. Each sob choked her. "Is he dead?"

The soldier looked toward the ruined hangar. "Someone

else was flying? Who?"

"Dunno...he was...tall..." Her hands shook as she hid her face in them. The man let go of her shoulders. She blubbered into her fingers. "Pa is going to be worried."

"We'll need to question you, Miss—"

What was the name the trapper had called her earlier? She couldn't recall it. She couldn't tell him her real name...stars. Her eyes found the gentle rolls of the hills, the nearest illuminated by the fire. "Hilly."

Hallie Hilly. Now that was terrible.

"Miss Hilly, please come with me. I'll take you down to the station."

"But Pa, he doesn't know—I was in the market, and—"

"I'll have the deputy send for him."

He held her elbow and steered her away, giving orders to others along the way, but Hallie was too entrenched in her own thoughts to pay close attention. She needed to lose him. She needed to get to the holding cells. She needed to get to the Pass.

As they entered the town proper, the first droplets fell onto Hallie's already wet face.

Kase

THE ARTISTRY OF THE HOLDING cells was a mystery to Kase. Why put the time and effort into creating pointed arch door frames if one was only going to use the rooms to detain criminals? The doors themselves were of solid wood with a grate at eye level. Someone had to cut it into that ridiculous shape, too. The walls were white and plain, the sliver of a window on the back wall too high to reach and too small to slide out of. The sleeping cot tucked underneath the window was clean. Really, the only terrible thing about it was the fact Kase could reach out and touch both walls with his arms outstretched. Well, that, and the rudimentary chamber pot underneath the cot. It wasn't made of porcelain, metal, or anything useful for bludgeoning unsuspecting guards. Instead, it was soft and slick, and lighter than his copy of *The Odyssey*.

The soldier who'd locked him in said the pot was only to

be used in emergencies. He'd be let out to relieve himself in the lavatory before he went to sleep and before they left in the morning. Thoughtful of them. Criminals like Kase didn't deserve such treatment. What would Harlan think if he knew petty thieves and tax evaders were being treated so well? Or was Kase receiving special treatment because of his last name?

A blessing and a curse.

The room grew darker as the storm rolled in with the night. Stupid of him to think he could get away with being in the city after shooting down Ike. The other pilot must've drawn the short straw if he was chosen to go after Kase. Blasted poor luck. And then with Kase's face plastered all over town?

Stars-idiot.

He couldn't help it. When they'd landed, the overwhelming feeling that he needed to go with Hallie hit him like a ton of bricks. The thought of saying goodbye to her for good...well, he hadn't wanted to do that yet.

Lot of good it did him. He would be heading back to Kyvena at dawn once the storm passed. He wouldn't get to say goodbye at all.

He massaged his temples. Hallie was safe. She'd be home soon. That was the most important part. Then he could forget about her and rot in Kyvena's prison for the rest of his life. Or maybe he would hang like Uncle Ezekiel. He wasn't sure which he preferred.

The posters hadn't said what Kase was wanted for, but he knew. If it wasn't desertion or theft, it was something to do with the fire. Neither boded well for him. Especially with a name like Shackley.

He sat heavily on the end of the cot. What was Hallie doing now? Had she found a place to stay for the night? He hoped she wasn't at the tavern dancing with someone like Cornhead from Laurent. She deserved better than a farm boy who made empty promises. Kase played with the ring around his finger. What would Ana have thought of her?

It was Kase's fault he'd never know the answer.

Thunder boomed in the distance as Kase fell back and stared at the nondescript ceiling. Where was Ana now? Had Zeke joined her? Were they in some aether realm looking down on Kase?

He didn't give much credit to a higher power. Clara did. She followed the Bible, one of the ancient texts that had survived the journey from First Earth and the millennium since. She'd tried to get Jove to read it, said something about living even after death. Kase didn't buy it, neither did Jove. Ninety-two people were dead because of the fire Kase started in Kyvena over three years prior. Why did some all-powerful deity allow his creations to feel pain and anguish and anger? Why did he allow someone like Zeke to die in such a horrible way?

He blinked away the image of his brother's death, of the blood pooling at his feet, of the metal door slamming in Kase's face.

Maybe Kase didn't deserve to be free, to be happy. Kase didn't deserve to have a virtuous god to care for him. Zeke and Ana were dead. He hadn't been able to save either of them. Hallie was better off without him. That way she could live happily away from the grief and turmoil that was Kase's life.

Kase dreaded the look on his father's face when he arrived back in the capital. The son who couldn't do anything right. Harlan wouldn't be able to pull any strings to get Kase free this time.

Another rather loud rumble of thunder interrupted his thoughts. It was so loud that it shook his cell. He sat up as the screams started. "What in the moons?"

Kase climbed onto his cot as the soldiers stationed at the detention cells spoke in rapid tones. He couldn't quite make out what they were saying, but whatever it was, it wasn't about the storm.

He still wasn't tall enough to see out the thin window, even standing on the cot. Grasping the edges of the sill, he pulled himself up. His forearms screamed with effort, and his boots slid while trying to gain traction on the wall. He grunted, but slowly raised himself enough to peek over the lip and see outside.

The view wasn't much, just of the next building over, but above the roof, an orange glow glimmered in the storm-darkened sky.

He squeezed his eyes shut and let himself drop back to the cot. Shouts came from down the corridor. A fire. Blast. His hands shook as he stumbled over to the door. He pressed his ear to it and caught bits and pieces of conversation.

"Airfields...Captain Maltby...send word to Achilles and to Colonel..."

A few doors slammed, more shouting. Kase stood on the tips of his toes to see out the door grate, but that didn't help one bit. He was too far from the commotion. Although distant, shouts and screams still filled the air.

A new voice joined the fray—except this one came from the corridor.

"If you're here, slicker boy, wave out that little grate on your door."

The rusty and haggard voice was familiar. *Slicker boy...*

Kase waved fingers out the grate. Why the trapper was there, Kase didn't know, but whatever he had in store had to be better than heading to Kyvena at first light.

Within seconds, the trapper's face was even with his. Shocks, Kase hadn't realized the man was so tall.

"Get back. We don't want any busted noggins."

Kase did what he was told, and the door opened. A small boy about the age of eight stood in the doorway with a gap-toothed grin and ring of keys in his grimy fingers. Kase frowned. "What—how—"

The trapper grabbed Kase's arm and towed him out into the corridor. The young boy shut the door behind them and locked it. "Could I have my extra copper now?"

Yarrow burrowed into his jacket and tossed a copper piece into the boy's waiting hands. "Put those keys back and get."

The boy scampered off, and Yarrow grabbed Kase by the collar and dragged him down the corridor. Kase tried to wriggle away, his stolen military jacket choking him a little until the trapper released him. "What in the blazes is going on?"

Yarrow looked back. "I didn't realize prisoners of the state were ungrateful for a rescue."

"No, not that." Kase waved his hands. "Why you?"

Yarrow shrugged and trudged down the hall. "Your girl is paying me extra."

"My girl?" Kase's face lit like the fire currently burning somewhere in the city. He ran to catch up. "Where's Hallie?"

They made it out of the corridor to the lobby. Both

soldiers who'd been there when the Captain and Ike had left him here were strewn like rag dolls on the floor behind the desk.

"What—"

"Your girl paid me well," Yarrow said with a wink. "I'm a man of my word where money's concerned."

The gap-toothed boy from earlier was just reattaching the ring of keys to one of the unconscious guard's trousers when the front door opened. Cold, wet air blew through and ruffled Kase's curls.

"Please, I promise I'll come back. I just need to—"

That voice. Kase looked up.

Hallie was soaked to the bone. Her disarrayed red hair clung to her face, and water dripped into the collar of her jacket and cloak. Shocks, rain like that would slow them down. He focused on the person with her. His drenched uniform with the Jaydian symbol on the right breast told him he was a soldier, but not one Kase recognized. He held Hallie's upper arm in a tight grip.

"I already told you, Miss. We'll call your father to the station and..." the soldier met Kase's eyes. "Hey! What are you..."

Hallie looked up and sagged into the soldier's grip, her lips forming a relieved sigh. The soldier released her, his hand going to the electropistol at his side. The little boy was quicker. He kicked the soldier in the shins as Kase tackled him. Hallie screamed, and the small boy ran out the open door.

Kase pinned the man's wrist to the floor and grabbed the electropistol holstered at the soldier's waist. The man's other arm launched at Kase, scratching his neck.

Kase's fingers found the grip of the weapon and tugged it out. With a mighty swing, Kase whipped the soldier in the temple with the pistol barrel. The soldier went limp, his head knocking against the stone. The hand that had been trying to claw Kase's face fell away. Blood oozed from the cut on his temple and stained the end of the pistol grip. Kase's fingers lost all feeling. The electropistol clattered to the floor.

"I didn't—I didn't mean—oh, shocks."

Hallie bent down and felt the man's neck, careful of the blood trickling down his face. She waited a minute before looking up at Kase. Her face was as white as snow. "He'll survive.

I think."

Kase stumbled off the soldier. What if he didn't? What if Kase had dealt the man a delayed killing blow? He hadn't meant to. He hadn't been thinking clearly. All he knew was that if he didn't subdue the soldier, Kase would've been on the floor writhing in pain from an electrobolt.

He tried to stand, but his legs weren't working correctly. The stone floor bit into his hands and knees as he fell to them. His breathing quickened. Pounding in his heart turned into crushing pain. He clawed helplessly at his chest. His mouth was bone dry. Burning bile churned in his stomach.

Zeke. His blood. Deep red and slick. Pooled on the ground. His shout. The slamming of the metal door.

"Kase," Hallie whispered, her cold hand cupping his cheek. The room spun. "We have to go. Now. Before someone comes."

"Can't." He choked out the word. Sweat beaded on his forehead though the room was cold.

Ana's blistered and bubbling skin. Her tattered sweater. The smell of burned hair.

The numbness of his fingers traveled through his hands, his wrists, his forearms. It begged for his heart.

"Focus on breathing." Hallie squatted beside him, but he barely saw her. His vision had narrowed to a point. All he could see was the blood dripping from the soldier's temple, down his cheek, and onto the floor. Hallie's hands were ice as she gripped both sides of his face. "Slow and steady. In and out."

"These blokes behind the desk will wake soon." Yarrow's rough voice didn't help.

Hallie's right hand twitched. "He's having a panic attack, Mr. Yarrow."

"Then he'd best stop panicking soon."

"You've clearly never had one before," Hallie muttered. Her hands fell to Kase's. They were slick with a mixture of sweat and blood. "Listen to me, Kase. No one else. Breathe with me. In through your nose..." She took in a deep breath, "...and out through your mouth."

Kase obeyed, the freezing air burning in his lungs.

Hallie's voice was soft. "Good. Now reach out with your mind. Feel the stone beneath your hands and knees. Ground yourself."

The stone was cold. It was hard. It was rough. Immovable. The tightness in his chest that had been painful before loosened slightly. His lungs expanded. Contracted.

Hallie's hands left his. "Continue to breathe."

A few more seconds and the nausea faded. Kase opened his eyes. Hallie's freckles stood out painfully on her cheeks. Her golden eyes were soft, her smile relieved.

Yarrow trudged over and threw Kase's pack beside him. Kase took another deep breath and, with Hallie's help, stood. He rummaged through the pack and grabbed his own electropistol, stowing it in the back of his waistband. He could do this. They needed to get out of there.

He tossed the pack on his shoulders. "I'm okay."

His legs were a little shaky as they exited the holding cells, but he walked without assistance. Yarrow led them through the city. It was practically a ghost town with the storm and whatever had caused that orange glow. Nobody to see them escape. The first thing to go right.

His heart still beat too fast. The cold rain mixed with the sweat coating his skin. Holy shocks. He shivered.

What happened? A panic attack? It'd felt like what he'd experienced last autumn after the hover crash, except a thousand times worse.

How had Hallie known how to calm him down? He looked back at her. She was focused on their surroundings, eyes alert for anyone who might stop them from leaving the city. Over her head, the orange glow still raged. The rain hadn't dampened whatever fire had started.

He whipped his head back around. The image of the bleeding soldier materialized in his mind, and the tightness in his chest returned. He stopped.

A hand found his, and Hallie appeared on his left. She gave his hand a squeeze. Water dripped off her chin. Light from the gas streetlamps made her pale skin shine. "You can do this."

He didn't let go of her hand as they ran after Yarrow.

They followed him through alleyways and the market square, where the raven on the inn's sign watched him with black eyes. Rain slid down sodden awnings and pooled in between the cobblestones. Water splashed onto Kase's boots. Yarrow took them down another street, and the final cottage at the edge of Nar loomed ahead. After that was nothing but trees. *Almost there.*

"Halt!"

The shout was guttural and nearly drowned out by a crack of thunder. Kase looked back to see soldiers. Three of them. The one in the lead was the same captain from earlier. The captain unsheathed his electropistol and took aim.

Hallie yelled as she tackled Kase. They fell. His shoulder slammed into the wet cobblestones, his pack keeping him from slamming his head as well.

"Ow," Hallie whimpered as she slid off him. He rolled to his stomach. The bolt zipped above them as another answered. Kase looked up. Yarrow stood with his too-large coat billowing in the storm's wind, his hands before him clasping a pistol with blood on the grip. He dodged to the side and fired again.

Kase yanked Hallie up with him, and they ran past Yarrow, who hit one of the soldiers with a bolt.

The screams would haunt Kase's dreams. Getting hit with a bolt while soaked with rain might kill the man.

It would've been you if Hallie hadn't pushed you out of the way.

They made it into the trees, the rain letting up as the fir branches shielded them from the storm. Yarrow's labored breathing followed them. Hallie's mirrored his, scattered and shallow, but they couldn't stop now. He didn't know where they were going, exactly, but he knew they needed to lose their tails. Quickly. Before his lungs gave out.

He followed Hallie through the trees, and soon they stumbled upon a small cabin. Light flickered in the dirt-encrusted windows, and smoke puttered from the chimney — even in the rain. Warmth. Hallie pounded on the door, and after a few tense seconds, it opened to reveal a withered old man with a gap-toothed grin.

OSSIE LERMOTH WAS A RETIRED trapper who only allowed Hallie to store her effects in his cabin with the promise of moonshine from Yarrow. None of that made Kase feel any better, but he needed to get out of his wet clothing. Not that he would admit it out loud, but the soaked fabric had chafed in certain places. He hoped he'd hid his winces as they'd run through the woods.

However, if they were leaving soon, the rain pouring outside would only drench whatever he changed into. Kase shrugged off his stolen jacket and set it in front of the fire—though far enough away to not catch flame. Stupid thing wasn't like his leather pilot's jacket, as the shirt underneath was plastered to his skin. He peeled that off as well. Mother hadn't packed his pilot's jacket, and while Kase loved the feel and power the leather gave him, he hadn't fancied a run-in with his father to retrieve it. It wouldn't have ended well for either of them.

The fire's heat warmed his bare skin. It drove away any lingering effects from the earlier panic attack. Some of the worry and fear melted from his shoulders. If he didn't look at the flames, he would be fine.

"Good stars, you don't have to strip here," Hallie grumbled. Kase peeked over his shoulder. Her face was redder than her hair. She turned away, shivering. Goosebumps ran up Kase's back and down his arms. From the rain, of course.

Finding a mostly dry shirt from his pack, Kase pulled it on. He'd deal with the discomfort his trousers created for a while longer, until he could have a little bit of privacy—even if his legs were screaming with frustration. Kase ignored it and dug out his crumpled trainee pilot's jacket. An envelope fluttered to the floor.

His mother's writing graced the outside, the 'K' having an extra flourish. He hadn't read it yet. He didn't know if he'd ever be able to, knowing he wouldn't ever see her again. His heart gave a painful throb, the goosebumps vanishing.

Stuffing the envelope back in, he held up his trainee pilot's jacket to Hallie. "You can wear this if you don't want to change."

"It's all right. I have something else in there, but I can wait." She glanced back and nodded to her own pack. Her cloak dripped onto the wooden slats. The water rolled down toward the front door and disappeared into the bear rug stretched before the fire.

With a dim gas lantern on a leaning end table, Yarrow and Ossie continued to murmur in the corner, the latter eating soup that he hadn't offered to anyone else. Kase dropped clumsily to the floor, his muscles sore from their sprint, with his back to the fire as Hallie slipped off her cloak, leaving it in a sodden heap on the floor. She scooted next to him and encircled her knees, pressing her face into them. Her teeth chattered.

Kase put his trainee jacket around her shoulders.

"I don't need it." She pulled it tighter around her shoulders without looking up. "But thank you."

"You're welcome." Kase brushed soaked dead foliage from his boots. "Care to tell me what happened?"

Hallie pulled the jacket higher, burying her head further. "You don't want to know."

"Hallie...tell me."

"No."

"Why not?"

Yarrow laughed from the corner and took a puff from his newly lit pipe. He coughed as smoke spilled from his lips. "Blasted thing." He coughed some more before handing the pipe to the other trapper, who tamped the tobacco and set it next to the gas lantern. Yarrow continued, "She done exploded the airfield hangar. Didn't see it myself, but that's what some *sollie* ran by shouting. Figured that was my signal to get your sorry bum outta that cell. Your girl got some intestinal fortitude."

Kase cricked his neck turning to look at Hallie. He rubbed the smarting muscle. "What in the blazes did you *do*?"

"I put your flying lesson to good use?" Her words were muffled.

"Hallie..."

"I might have...possibly...or most definitely...um...well, I crashed your hover into the hangar."

"You crashed my—Hallie!" Kase's mouth fell open so fast, his jaw popped. "What made you think that was a good idea?"

"It was either that or have hovers on our tail when I broke you out!" She peeked up over the collar of the jacket.

Holy blasting stars. She's crazy. Absolutely crazy.

Except a part of him couldn't deny the seed of pride taking root. They'd rot together in a cell if the Jaydian military got ahold of them any time soon. Without hovers, the soldiers would be much slower chasing them through the Pass. He

REALMS OF WRATH & RUIN

shook his head. "And how did you manage to escape?"

She hid her eyes once more. "Ejected just before I hit."

"My hover?"

"Probably a hunk of melted metal."

Kase closed his eyes and chuckled. She'd faced her fear to save him. "You're a stars-idiot, but I'm honored you committed a felony for me."

There wasn't anything they could do about it now except make it into the Pass and pray that no one connected Hallie to the crime. It was more likely they'd blame Kase--somehow.

Wouldn't hurt to add to his running list of crimes if he wasn't there to suffer for them, right?

Pounding on the door interrupted his thoughts. Not with knuckles. Something much harder. Like the butt of an electropistol or the hilt of a military-issued sword. "Open up in the name of the Stradat Lord Kapitan!"

Hallie's head popped up as Kase lurched to his feet. Yarrow stumbled over to the bear rug and wrenched it aside, revealing a door beneath. It was flush with the wooden floor. He hooked a finger into a hole in the wood and lifted. Kase grabbed Hallie's hand and his sodden jacket before climbing down the ladder into the hole, not stopping to question it. All he knew was that whatever awaited them in the dark below was better than anything in Kyvena.

Especially since Hallie had blown up the blasted hover hangar. Shocks and bolts.

Hallie followed, and Yarrow threw down their packs before climbing down himself. They fell at Kase's feet, nearly bludgeoning Hallie's head, but she moved at just the right moment.

The last thing Kase saw before Ossie closed the door and covered it with the rug was Hallie's too-pale face.

He dropped his jacket and pulled her to him. She clung to his shirt, her breathing irregular. Her wet clothes bled onto his.

So much for changing into a dry shirt.

"Kase..." she whispered. He shook his head. He couldn't see much in the dim light slipping through the narrow spaces between boards where the rug ended. His body was rigid with anticipation and Hallie's lithe form tucked up against him. He was tall, but the top of her head was even with his mouth—

something that was rather distracting.

"I will kick this door in if you do not—" the soldier shouted, but the door creaked open.

Ossie coughed. "By the moons, ya don't need to bust my door in. It cost me a pretty copper, I'll have ya know. I'd shined it up somethin' fierce for weeks."

"We're looking for three people. Two men. One woman. All wanted by the military," the soldier responded as he entered. His boots clicked loudly on the wooden slats. "I heard voices."

Kase reached to where he still had his electropistol stowed in the back of his trousers. The memory of blood leaking from the soldier's temple flashed in his mind, but he shoved it away. If the choice was limited to shoot or be captured, well, he might have to get used to the feeling.

Hallie tensed against his chest.

Focus.

"Ah," Ossie chuckled. "That's just me and ol' Gus, my feline. It's almost like he's human, ya know? There was one time when he was little bitty, and I swear he told me he wanted his belly rubbed, and sure enough, he did, blasted stars!"

Feline? Kase hadn't seen a cat. If there had been, Kase would've had a runny nose. He was rather allergic to them.

"Except I can see every corner of this room, and there is no cat in sight. However..." The soldier's voice was hard. The bear rug dampened his footsteps as he strode further into the cabin. Shuffling followed. Ossie.

"Oh, Gus is always here. See? He's a squattin' there in the corner!"

Was he mad?

The soldier wasn't buying it either. "This cloak. Drenched. Like it's been out in the rain recently."

Hallie gasped. Kase slapped a hand to her mouth. *Blast.*

"No, no," Ossie laughed too hard. He stomped his foot along with each chuckle. "Oh mountain blazes, that's mine! I left it poor out on the stoop to dry from last evenin', and would you know, it started stormin' before I got to brung it in. Gus told me to set it there. Said he would fix it up for me tonight."

Hallie's lips were warm and soft against his palm. He removed it and wiped his hand on his damp trousers. The tingling didn't stop.

Something plopped to the floor. Probably the cloak. The soldier sighed. "You'll be coming to the station for questioning, Ossie Lermoth. Yes, we know who you are."

"You serious?"

"As the stars." Kase could hear the edge to the soldier's voice. If the unhinged trapper didn't follow orders...Kase knew all too well what they were capable of.

"Gus will have to make do then, won't he? Until morning? I can't be aways too long."

"I assure you, your...cat...will be fine. If your story checks out, we'll return you at first light."

"I'll come along as long as you don't hurt Gus."

"On my honor as a soldier in the Jaydian military."

No other words were exchanged, only footsteps, the sizzling of dying fire, and the slamming of the door filtered through the floorboards. Light between the cracks dimmed.

Kase, Hallie, and Yarrow waited with bated breath for who knew how long. Kase's legs ached. Without the fire at his back, the chill settled in once more. Hallie shivered. Kase pulled her closer, but it didn't help.

Finally, Yarrow spoke up. "I think we're in the clear. Let's get a few hours' sleep, and then we'll head out before they get back."

His boots thumped on the ladder as he climbed, and flickering light shone through the hold as he opened the trap door. Kase followed.

Yarrow grabbed the gas lantern and handed it to Kase. "You both stay down there. Use the furs to keep warm. Just don't drink that moonshine. Ossie would have my head if ya did."

Kase's fingers gripped the lantern's handle. It was rough with age and slightly greasy. Hallie popped her head out of the hole. She had pulled her arms through the sleeves of his jacket. She shook her head. "The soldiers are looking for you, too. We should leave now."

Kase strode over and handed her the lantern. "If we leave now, we'll run into patrols. It'll be easier to wait until we've had some rest and the initial search is over."

She looked between Kase, Yarrow, and the trapdoor. Kase didn't fancy sleeping in a pit, but as they'd seen earlier, the soldier hadn't known it was there.

She sighed. "All right, but don't be all heroic and sacrifice yourself, Mr. Yarrow. I still need you to get me through the Pass."

"Of course, Miss Walker." He went to the windows and pulled the filthy curtains closed before grabbing an iron poker and stoking the dying fire. "I'll do my best if they come looking."

Kase nodded. "Good night, then. We'll leave before dawn."

He followed Hallie down into the hole. Yarrow closed the door behind him. Now that a lantern lit the space, they could see it was rather small. To each side were shelves of dusty bottles holding opaque liquid. Moonshine. Past those were several pelts of various types hanging from the ceiling.

At least they'd be warm.

After creating two rather cushy pallets, he and Hallie settled in. The chill from earlier had abated thanks to the furs, but Kase still felt uneasy. So many terrible things had happened that day, things he'd surely be paying for later. At least he'd kept Hallie safe.

That is, until he'd gotten himself arrested. And then she'd saved him, at great personal sacrifice. Kase had very few people in his life who cared enough about him to do that. Warmth and a little bit of trepidation settled in his chest.

He looked over as Hallie turned the gas lantern down, the cellar melting into near darkness.

...yet you paraded that girl *in front of the most important people on Yalvara tonight. What a* blasting *disgrace.*

His father had never been more wrong, assuming Hallie was something beneath the Shackleys and Jaydian high society. Kase hoped she found what she needed in Stoneset and then settled down with someone who didn't have such a bloody history—someone who could take care of her without glancing over his shoulder for ghosts in the shadows.

He swallowed the lump that had formed in his throat and whispered, "Thank you."

For several seconds, only silence answered back before finally, a rustling of fur met his ears. He could just make her out in the dull light filtering in through the cracks above. Her hair, still damp, clung to her right cheek. Even in the near darkness, her golden eyes shone bright. Hallie Walker was beautiful. How Kase could have ever thought he'd despised her was a mystery now. What a fool the Kase of last autumn had been.

Hallie smiled. "Always."

"Goodnight, Hals."

"'Night."

It was warm, and Hallie had saved him from certain death, and they were safe for now. Regardless, Kase fell into a fitful sleep.

CHAPTER 22

BEGRUDGING LOYALTY

Jove

JOVE HADN'T SLEPT IN DAYS. It wasn't just because he had a newborn, although waking with every cry, and to check if Samuel was still breathing, was surely contributing. The fight with his parents still haunted him. Jove worked so hard to keep his temper in check. He was too much like Harlan in that regard, and although it was perhaps justified, he'd lost control. *He'd hit his father.*

Jove's fist still ached. He figured it was fractured...a just punishment for resorting to violence. He'd kept it wrapped the last few days, which helped the physical pain a little. Better than what Harlan was facing.

There was something else that bothered him. Kase had fled the capital, and the city wanted blood. Jove and Clara had been sequestered in Shackley Manor ever since the birth because of it. The most violent rioting was happening outside the inner wall. Even though Jove and Clara's townhouse was in the circle of the upper city, security at the manor would be much tighter.

Just bearing the Shackley name made them a target.

Clara's mother hadn't been able to get into Kyvena because of the turmoil. Those wishing to enter the capital were required to have proper paperwork, and even then, only on official government business. The birth of one's grandchild wasn't considered such, even if Jove's own mother had pleaded otherwise with the city guards.

The gate to the upper city had also been closed. His father and High Guardswoman Heddie Koppen had been forced to pull soldiers and Watchmen from nearby towns to man it all. The people wanted to see the Stradat Lord Kapitan hang, Kase with him.

It was a week after the fight that Jove was summoned to the Jayde Center.

He'd left Clara and Samuel with kisses on their foreheads and a promise to return as soon as business for the day was over, yet he hadn't told them what was happening. He'd expressly warned his mother not to say anything to his wife. There was no need to stress the already sleep-deprived Clara.

She didn't need to know quite yet that Harlan was facing the High Council on charges of high treason. The trial would last nearly a week, though Jove was only needed for testimony the first day.

He wouldn't be attending the others. This one day was enough.

Jove's wife had always been reasonable, believing the best in people. If she'd known ahead of time what was happening that day, she might have pointed out that Harlan should get the chance to make penance, that he should be forgiven.

Jove disagreed.

He tugged at his tie as he rode to the Jayde Center, tapping his foot to an erratic beat. Harlan would expect his son to defend him— that's what Shackleys did. They protected each other and their reputations with everything they had.

But Jove and his father thought differently on how one went about that.

As he rode through the upper city, Jove took note of the combination of soldiers and Watch patrolmen at every corner. No one expected unrest from the Jaydian elite safe in their manors behind the upper gate. But the lower classes weren't the only ones who'd lost loved ones during the fire of the year 4497. The still absent Owen Christie, for example, had lost his entire family save for his wife.

It was only a matter of time. The wealthy class was merely waiting to hear the details of the day before deciding how they would react.

The chauffeur, Avery, pulled the motorcoach around the outside of McKenzie Square, stopping in front of the stairs to the Jayde Center. Jove took several deep, fortifying breaths as the soldiers stationed outside came to the door, opening it for him. Sliding out of the coach, Jove stood, straightening his jacket and setting the bowler hat atop his head. Soldiers flanked him on each side as he climbed the stairs. After showing his identification papers to those at the door, he entered the Jayde Center and headed for the chamber where his father and the High Council awaited.

The courtroom held benches along the outer walls and a dais in the center. Harlan sat straight-backed in one of the chairs before the dais. He was all alone. The Stradats—Loffler and Sarson—along with Heddie Koppen and several members of the City Council, sat in the benches along the dark-stained paneled walls.

Armed soldiers guided Jove to a seat next to Heddie, who gave him a tight nod. Her demeanor mirrored the others assembled. Once Jove was seated, sweat dripped down his face. It wasn't hot in the room. He slipped the bowler off his head and set it on his knee. He stared hard at his father, who in turn focused squarely on the floor in front of him.

According to the medic, Harlan had experienced a minor heart attack the night Kase ran. He'd been prescribed bed rest, but considering his current situation, Jove doubted his father's heart was any better off than it had been. If anything, the chance of him having another over the course of the day was high.

When the mechanical clock showed nine, Stradat Sarson rose from her chair. "Today, we, the remaining members of the Jaydian High Council, bring before you Stradat Lord Kapitan Harlan Shackley. He is thereby accused of the high crimes of the obstruction of justice, an intent to conspiracy, and betraying the oath of office. Senior Hover Pilot Kase Shackley, though not present, is thereby accused of obstruction of justice, intent to conspiracy, reckless arson, and involuntary manslaughter. A warrant has been issued for his arrest. Today, we will begin the proceedings regarding the Stradat Lord Kapitan."

Jove bent over, his head in his hands. The bandaging on his right knuckles scratched at his face, but he didn't care. All he could do was stare blankly at the marble beneath his feet. He barely listened to the rest of Sarson's remarks, the context for today's case. Jove knew it all. He prayed that he would get through the day without losing what little he'd eaten for breakfast.

"The Council recognizes Mr. Ellis Carrington of Kyvena." Sarson's voice rang throughout the still chamber.

Jove's head shot up as the doors to the chamber opened. A young man with blond hair walked in, his head held high. Jove recognized him as one of Kase's friends from school. He didn't know him well, only that he came from a wealthy family.

Ellis strode forward, guards flanking him, and took a seat on the opposite side of the dais from Jove's father. He was sworn under oath by the clerk by placing a hand over his heart.

Sarson shuffled the parchment in front of her and eyed the witness. Jove could see through her calm mask; she was thrilled with the prospect of the Stradat Lord Kapitan being convicted. Beside her, Loffler looked positively bored. His drooping eyes were closed, and every few seconds, his mustache billowed with an unseen wind. He'd fallen asleep. Figured.

Sarson continued, fingering her scar as she spoke, "State your full name for the record and your relationships with the defendants."

Ellis smoothed his pant legs as if trying to dry off sweaty palms. He looked at the various members of the Jaydian government seated in the benches surrounding him. "My name is Ellis William Carrington. I attended upper school with Kase Shackley."

Jove picked at his nails. He didn't understand why someone friendly with Kase would be in here testifying against him and the Stradat Lord Kapitan. Sarson and the judiciary members of the City Council would have done their research appropriately.

"And what information do you have regarding the fire of October 11, 4497?" Sarson asked, tapping her finger on her parchment.

Ellis Carrington looked directly at Sarson. Each word he spoke echoed off the chamber walls. "Kase Shackley confessed to starting the fire and using his father's position as Lord Kapitan to cover up his crime."

"And when did this confession come?"

"On March 3, 4501. In Estelle's Tavern, in the lower city. We met up for dinner after he finished flight training for the day."

Jove resisted the urge to hide his face in his hands. *Kase, you blasted stars-idiot.*

Sarson wrote something on the parchment in front of her before asking, "And what was his confession exactly?"

Ellis rubbed his pant legs again. Harlan still stared at the floor. Ellis' voice quivered slightly at his next words. "He said he set fire to a cottage in the lower city. He'd been smoking and wanted to see...wanted to see what..." Ellis pinched the bridge of his nose, emotion bleeding into his next words. "...wanted to see what would happen if he lit the roof on fire. He said he did it because he knew his father could get him off."

No. The word bubbled up from Jove's gut, and he leapt out of his chair. "Objection!"

The entire room focused on Jove, including his father. Harlan didn't give any indication of his thoughts, but Jove felt the heat of his stare regardless. Sarson was the only one who hadn't turned to stare at him. Her voice was deadly calm when she retorted, "Denied. The Council will allow your testimony after Mr. Ellis Carrington's concludes. Until that time, please hold your tongue, Lord Shackley."

Jove opened his mouth to say something else, but Heddie yanked him back down into his seat. She didn't look at him, only gripped his sleeve. Jove ground his teeth but nodded. "Thank you, Stradat Sarson."

Heddie let go, and Sarson continued. "And what did you do with this information?"

"I was...scared. I didn't know what to do because Kase is my friend. He—he trusted me. But I knew what he did was wrong.

So, on March 4th, I went to the nearest Watch station and told them what I knew."

"And you told no one else?"

"Correct, Madame Stradat."

Sarson raised an eyebrow. The motion tugged on the scar that ran from her ear to the right corner of her lips. "Yet the capital city is in an uproar. The gates in the outer wall as well as the upper city are closed, manned by soldiers and Watch agents. They all want the Stradat Lord Kapitan and his son to hang. The rioting didn't begin until the night of March 4th. Who else did you tell?"

Ellis swallowed visibly. "No—no one, Madame Stradat. I swear!"

Stradat Sarson steepled her fingers in front of her. She took a moment, pressing them to her lips, before sitting back. "So how did the information leak to the public?"

"I—I don't know. Maybe someone overheard in the tavern." Ellis had gone pale. He looked sickly in the electric light from the chandelier above. "I told Sergeant Powers at the Nile Street Precinct station."

Sarson leaned forward on her elbows. "You're under oath, Mr. Carrington. I'll give you one last chance. How did the information leak to the public?"

Ellis shook his head fitfully. "I don't know. I swear on—on Tovo's name! Please, you have to believe me!"

"Except the exact, correct details have leaked to the public. If someone had overheard, the story would have been distorted with missing details...and yet, every other witness we have questioned has the same story."

"Maybe Sergeant Powers—"

"All government agents are under strict orders to report to their uppers. Leaking any information is considered a betrayal of their oaths and punished severely."

Ellis' mouth opened and closed, but no sound came out.

At that moment, Jove thought back to the missive, the one the Stradat Lord Kapitan had received the night of Samuel's birth, of Kase's flight. Did the familiar handwriting belong to Ellis? Nevertheless, it didn't help the young man. In fact, it made him look worse.

Sarson sat back and waved to the guards near the door.

"Your testimony is complete. Privates Yasley and Greene, please escort Mr. Carrington to the holding cells. We'll question him further at a different time."

Ellis shot up from his seat as the soldiers reached him. "You can't hold me against my will."

"On the contrary. Privates, please."

Ellis attempted to throw off the men, but he was quickly restrained. His protests only stopped once the doors closed behind him. Shock radiated throughout Jove's body. He'd been in this chamber many times, seen the exact thing happen more often than he could count, yet this was different. This was about his family.

Dread filled Jove's stomach like lead. Ellis Carrington knew something he refused to say, and Stradat Sarson had called him out on it. The man would be facing perjury charges and possibly inciting a riot, if Jove remembered his Jaydian criminal law correctly.

But was Ellis Carrington acting on his own accord, oblivious to the repercussions of coming forward? Or was there someone else pulling the strings, and Ellis was simply caught up in their tangled web?

It all came back to the missive. One World knew. Ellis had to be part of the group. Did whoever commanded the group send in the young man knowing he'd be caught out? The shock rolled like ocean waves through his body. *Holy stars.*

And if Ellis was dabbling in rebellion, what other wealthy elites had joined or contributed funds to the cause?

Jove scanned the room. So many faces. So much money. If it could be Ellis Carrington, it could be anyone. His heartbeat was like a dagger stabbing against his ribs.

It could be Kase. Except, why would he run?

Jove was so engrossed in his thoughts that he didn't hear his name being called until Heddie needled him with her elbow. Jove blinked and rubbed his arm. Stradat Sarson was looking straight at him. "Lord Jove Shackley, the Council calls on you for testimony."

His heart rate shot through the roof as he stood. Heddie caught him before he fell. She gave him a questioning look, but he shook his head. "Yes, Madame Stradat."

Stars, Jove's hands were clammy as he made his way to the

chair Ellis had vacated. His eyes burned from lack of sleep. His legs felt like rubber.

Breathe. You've done this before.

Just not at the expense of sending his father and brother to the gallows.

Tell the truth.

Sarson rearranged her parchment pages once more before the clerk came forward, stopping before Jove, one hand across his heart. Jove copied his posture and repeated the words that bound him to truth and the law of Jayde.

"I swear to tell the truth in its entirety. I understand I shall be held accountable to the full extent of Jaydian law should I distort or omit the truth."

His hand shook as he removed it from his heart and sat back down. Stradat Loffler still snoozed in his chair. Stars, the commotion with Ellis Carrington hadn't woken him either. His mustache still rustled with each breath, so he wasn't dead.

Stradat Sarson laced her fingers together, her eyes boring into Jove's. "State your full name for the record and your relationships with the defendants."

Jove willed his heart to slow as he took another deep breath. He forced his fingers to release their grip on the arms of his chair. "My name is Jove Harlan Shackley. I'm the eldest son of the Stradat Lord Kapitan. Kase is my brother."

His voice was level and strong. He worked hard not to show the turmoil in his heart. It felt odd to say simply "brother" when for so long he'd been Jove's youngest one. Now, there was only Kase.

Sarson continued, "Would you say your family ties impede your judgment in the situation at hand?"

Blasted woman. "By situation at hand, do you refer to the fire of October 11, 4497, in which I lost my youngest sister? Or are you referencing the events detailed by Mr. Ellis Carrington? My family ties pose no impediment to either."

A few people shifted uneasily, but Jove's focus was on the scarred Stradat. She showed no reaction to his words, only answered his question. "Let us begin with Ellis Carrington's testimony of events. Were you aware of your brother's whereabouts the night of March 3, 4501?"

"No."

"Why?"

Jove ran his tongue across his teeth. He'd been dealing with the residual effects of consuming too much alcohol the previous night and had no clue where Kase had been. "My brother does not live with me, nor am I his keeper."

"And did your brother tell you about his confession in the tavern?"

"No." She continued to use the word *brother*, as if she were trying to rub salt in the wound that he no longer had more than one.

"When did you last see your brother?"

Jove closed his eyes for a second. Peppering him with rapid fire questions was her way of getting him to slip up. He leaned forward, his elbows on his knees. "The night of March 2, 4501, at the state dinner celebrating the Rubikan alliance."

Sarson wrote something down. A few whispers of those assembled met his ears, but the Stradat looked back at Jove. "So, you cannot confirm or deny your brother confessed his crime to Ellis Carrington on the night of March 3, 4501?"

"I cannot confirm or deny where my brother was on March 3, 4501."

"And how would you describe your relationship with your father?"

Jove blinked. All eyes were on him. His palms were slick, but he didn't dry them. Body language was how Sarson had caught Ellis Carrington in a possible lie; Jove had seen her use the tactics before. He looked her square in the eye. "We have our differences."

"Differences?"

Jove sat back, crossing his right ankle over his left knee, projecting confidence he didn't feel. "Respectfully, all you need to know is that Harlan Shackley and I rarely see eye to eye."

"Except it could make every difference in the world for you."

Jove shook his head. "It doesn't."

"Then, pray, how should the Council know your family relations aren't impeding your testimony or judgment of the events being examined today?"

Jove planted both feet on the ground, his hands on the arms of his chair. "Because my duty is to my country and its citizens first."

The memory of his son floated to the top of his mind, of Clara singing him to sleep the previous evening. *You can do this.*

Sarson set her pen down, lacing her fingers together. "Then tell us in detail what you were doing the night of October 11, 4497."

Jove's stomach hardened. He knew this question was coming. That didn't mean he was prepared for it. He took a deep breath. "At the time, I was a Watch Captain of the upper quarter. I was finishing my shift when my brother...Zeke Shackley..."

"Your deceased brother?"

Jove clenched his jaw. He would not lose it here. "Yes."

"Please continue."

Blasted helviter.

He smoothed a hand across his stubble to quell his nerves. Sweat left a cold trail across his cheek. He sat up straighter. "Zeke sent me a missive stating that Kase and Ana were planning on running away. He'd received a note from our sister, Ana. He asked if I could go to the manor and stop Kase. He would try and find Ana."

Jove closed his eyes again. They burned.

Zeke hadn't found her in time.

"Why would they want to run away?"

Jove hesitated. Did it matter? "My father."

Murmurs broke out in the room. Stradat Sarson waited a minute for the conversation to die down before pinning Jove with her stare. "How so?"

Jove refused to look at Harlan. "Kase wanted to attend University after he finished upper school that coming spring, but our father wouldn't allow it. He believed Kase would benefit from the discipline the military offered. For Ana, she was betrothed against her wishes to Lord Morgan's son." He swallowed. "I found Kase and my father at the manor. They were arguing. It turned...it turned violent."

"Violent how?"

Jove's hands shook. His breathing grew heavier. A phantom pain spread across his forearm where his father had fractured it by shoving him against the desk. Jove had jumped in to save Kase. All Jove had seen in that moment was the little boy, his

250

brother, asking to be like Jove one day. Kase coming to Jove when he'd hurt himself falling out of the tree because their current governess frowned upon such horseplay.

"Lord Shackley, please answer the question."

Jove shivered, still looking at the floor in front of him. "I...I..." He took a shaking breath and tilted his head up to meet Stradat Sarson's gaze. "Kase suffered a broken rib, a fractured eye socket. I stepped in. Kase ran. My father...my father...had beaten my brother..."

Gasps and shouts erupted across the room. The lights flickered. Stradat Loffler woke with a great snort before falling back asleep once more. Stradat Sarson had to raise her voice to regain control.

Jove choked as the words, the secrets, tumbled from his lips in front of every major player in Kyvena. He was a weak and terrified little boy once more—not one of the most powerful bureaucrats in all of Jayde. "Kase ran as far as he could until he couldn't. A stray cigarette started the fire. It was an accident."

Stradat Sarson's words were quiet, as if she cared. "And were you aware of your father's dealings behind the scenes to keep Kase from being punished by the Council?"

Harlan met his eyes. They weren't cold, only void of emotion. Jove didn't know which was better. He looked back at Stradat Sarson. Her scar seemed to mock him, already knowing the answer he'd give. "Yes."

"You violated your own oath of office by allowing your father to lie to the High and City Councils?"

Jove hadn't realized he'd started crying, the tears falling down his cheeks and onto the collar of his jacket. He thought of Clara, of Samuel. Of how he hated his father with every fiber of his being. He clamped his hands on his knees, doing anything to stem the emotions pouring out of him. "I do not regret protecting Kase. He did nothing deserving of this. It was an accident—an accident that killed our sister and so many others. He's paid dearly for his sins.

"However, I accept my role in this. But I will not make excuses for the Stradat Lord Kapitan. He doesn't deserve my begrudging loyalty any longer."

Sweat and tears dripped to the floor of the dais as Jove

leaned forward.

He was done. He couldn't do anything more. He'd told the truth.

"Thank you, Lord Shackley. You may take your seat," Sarson said, her voice quiet.

With legs of lead, Jove stood and walked back to his seat, falling onto the bench beside Heddie. The absolute silence of the chamber clamored in his ears. He'd done what was asked of him. He'd done his best to save Kase, but it wasn't going to be enough. He pressed the heels of his hands to his eyes until he saw amorphous shapes.

With his confession, he'd probably be called in later to face his own charges.

Stradat Sarson cleared her throat and tapped her papers together. "The Council will reconvene tomorrow morning at nine to hear further evidence."

She banged her gavel.

They led his father away, the soldiers he'd trained flanking him. The chamber buzzed with questions, accusations, and rumors. It wasn't until someone laid a hand on Jove's shoulder that he finally looked up.

Heddie Koppen stood above him, her gray hair refusing to stay in a proper lady's bun. Her spectacles were tucked into the outer pocket of her Watch uniform. "Let's get you home."

He followed her out of the chamber and into the afternoon sun.

CHAPTER 23

A GLUTTON FOR PUNISHMENT

Kase

THE ONLY SOUNDS FOR HOURS had been the crunching of snow beneath their boots and Yarrow's labored breathing. Kase's muscles already ached from the ordeal the previous day, and the hike into the Nardens only made it worse. He'd been there before, last autumn, but he'd been in a hover without freezing rain pelting his face. His boots kept out most of the rain and snow, but his socks hadn't fully dried from the night before. The tingling on his left heel had morphed into stinging. A blister.

To say Kase was miserable was an understatement.

He'd lost track of time. The sky grew darker as the road rose even more, weaving back and forth like a snake. The cobblestone was miles behind them now, replaced by rocky dirt, and tall, overarching trees crowded both sides. The evergreen branches above cracked under the weight of ice. Above the trees, rocky spires towered like menacing guards, piercing the murky sky.

The snow fell faster and began to gust when Yarrow paused, looking back. He'd fashioned a fallen limb into a walking stick soon after they'd left Ossie's cabin. He leaned against it, his nose a berry pink and eyes sparkling like the ice lining his thick coat. Kase shivered and willed the ache in his fingers to disappear.

Yarrow gestured to the sky with his free hand. "Should probably stop for the night."

Kase folded his arms, ducking his face behind his collar. He wished he'd bought a thick scarf in Nar. At least he had his wool cap.

"Where?" Hallie asked, her teeth chattering. Kase barely heard her over the wind picking up. "We can't weather a blizzard out here under a tree."

"We're out a mile from a hut."

Kase's voice shook. "Hut?"

Hallie looked back at him. She had pulled the hood of her new fur-lined cloak up around her face. It'd dried out decently in front of Ossie's fire the night before. The dark material and the cold made her skin appear even paler. "Yarrow knows the Pass and where the trappers' huts are. Niels' brother had one on the other side, closer to Stoneset."

"Niels?"

Something like pain flashed in Hallie's eyes.

Kase didn't like the twisted feeling in his gut when Hallie looked away. What wasn't she telling him?

Yarrow coughed. "The lass is right. I'm worth every copper."

"We paid you in gold," Kase said, tearing his gaze from Hallie.

"That you did." With that, Yarrow was off.

Hallie followed, still refusing to look at Kase. He chewed the inside of his cheek as he walked. Why should he care so much about a passing comment? Hallie had had a life before Kase ever came into the picture. He had his own past he wanted to hide. In fact, it was his sole reason for leaving Kyvena; Hallie needing a hover ride was merely a convenient excuse. Besides, it wasn't as if there was anything more than friendship between him and Hallie. She didn't owe him an explanation.

Then why couldn't he stop thinking about it?

After a good way in silence, Hallie slowed to walk beside him. She tugged her cloak closer around her shoulders. "People used to visit Stoneset just for the mountains. Sometimes, they'd stop on their way to Fort Achilles for a day or so. It's rather beautiful, despite the fact my eyelashes have turned to ice."

Kase pulled his cap down further as a large clump of snow landed on Hallie's pack. "I don't think I'd mind living up in the mountains if I could bring all my books with me. I'd live in a little cabin with no one to bother me."

"All by yourself?" Hallie's soft laugh was barely audible over the wind as she shook the snow off. "Living in the city has so many more perks."

"Like people blocking up every blasting street?"

Hallie ignored him. "For one, Kyvena has the best food. And two, there's so much more to do...like going to the theaters. Growing up, my brother, Niels, and I entertained inn guests with our own little plays. Not nearly as grand."

"Niels is a friend?"

She looked down at her boots as they lagged behind Yarrow. "He was Jack's best friend. And...well..."

"And what?"

It was the way she'd said his name. Like it was some sort of secret. She was facing away from him, examining the dark hollows between the tree trunks as they passed.

Kase cleared his throat. "So, you used to put on plays for the inn's guests? Did you make people's ears bleed with your stars-awful voices?"

Hallie hit him lightly on the arm, knocking off a bit of snow and ice. *Good. Back to normal.* "Yes, we did, but Jack always took the best parts. Blasted *dulkop*. I always wanted to be Odysseus, but alas, he refused to give up the role."

"He sounds a little like Jove," Kase said with a small laugh.

Hallie was silent for a moment too long. "I miss him."

"Sorry, I didn't mean to bring it all up."

Hallie shook her head. "I'm fine most of the time, but then, all of a sudden..."

"Yeah, I know what you mean. " Kase understood that feeling all too well. It was one of the things that bound him and Hallie together. He was glad of that, terrible as it sounded, though he would've traded it to get Ana and Zeke back in a heartbeat, and he knew she would do the same for her brother.

Without warning, the wind picked up, whipping the cap off Kase's head. He lunged for it, barely catching it by a flap, but another gust nearly knocked him over. "What in the blazes—"

Yarrow stumbled toward them. "We're almost there, but the blizzard ain't waitin'!" He held out his free hand to Hallie. "Hold on tight!"

Hallie grasped it and turned to Kase. Her gloved fingers were clumsy in Kase's as he grabbed her other hand. What had been uncomfortable weather seconds before was a raging storm now. He ducked his head further into his jacket, the other hand pressing his hat down.

Relief flooded Kase's body, bringing a little bit of warmth to his frozen extremities, as they reached a dark structure peeking out between drifts of snow. The hut. Kase could barely stand straight as Yarrow tried the door. It didn't budge. He beat it with his stick, which broke. "Blast it! The lock's frozen solid."

Even over the wind stinging his ears, Kase heard the fear lacing his voice. He shook his head. "Let me try."

He let go of Hallie's hand and stumbled forward. The handle was indeed frozen. He peeked at the frame. It opened inward. *Luck at last.*

He handed over his pack to Hallie. "Stand back."

Yarrow moved to stand beside Hallie as Kase squared up in front of the door. He picked up his foot and placed it beside the handle where the locking mechanism should be. *Okay, here we go.*

He stepped back, trying to ignore the ache in his bones. He had to be sure to not kick the handle, and a twisted or broken ankle would spell disaster. Yarrow would leave him behind.

Steeling himself, his eyes narrowed in concentration, Kase drove his heel into the door with as much force as he could muster.

Crash.

The door flew open, exposing a shadowy interior.

Yarrow harrumphed and strode forward. "Not too bad. Come on."

Kase took his pack from Hallie, and they scurried in. He closed the door behind them, but it wouldn't stay completely shut. *That's what I get for kicking it in, I guess.*

He set his pack in front of it. Hallie and Yarrow added theirs to the pile.

"You happen to bring a lantern, city slicker?" Yarrow asked.

Kase could barely see. There was only one dirty window, and the darkening skies blocked most of the dying sunlight. He squinted at the outlines that were Hallie and Yarrow. "No, but I do have..." he rummaged in his pack. When his hand felt the cool metal of the electropistol, he pulled it out and lit up the muzzle with sparks, pointing it away from the others, "...this. It'll work until we get a fire going."

Hallie's face flickered with shadows as she edged closer. "Just don't pull the trigger."

Kase rolled his eyes, but handed it to her, muzzle pointed down. "I'm not an idiot."

Yarrow laughed. Kase bit back a retort. He owed the man his life for breaking him out of the holding cells.

Hallie took the pistol and turned, using the sparks to search the cabin. Kase dug out the second pistol and inspected the other side. There was a small bed, but Kase thought it might fall apart just looking at it. He also tripped over a small stack of firewood.

"Found some bread. More mold than bread," Hallie grunted from her side.

Yarrow lowered himself onto the bed. "I don't eat mold."

Ignoring him, Kase picked up a few of the logs he'd tripped on. "These should last us until morning."

Hallie came up beside him and nodded. "Put them in the grate there, and I'll grab the flint."

"My task for the day is done," Yarrow said, easing himself onto the bed, scarf still wrapped around his neck. "When you make food, I'll eat it. Otherwise, don't bother me."

"Whatever." Kase mumbled. *Blasted old man.*

Kase shivered as he trudged over to the fireplace. It was like his bones had turned to ice. His fingers were numb and shook as he laid the wood in what he thought was a good formation. It resembled a pyramid, each piece stacked like a brick.

A second or two later, a cloak fell around his shoulders. He looked up to see the outline of Hallie's face in the poor light. He smiled. "Thanks."

She inspected the wood. "What are you doing?"

"Stacking the wood."

Yarrow snored in response.

Hallie bent down, shaking her head, and took the log from his hands. "The fire has to breathe a little. I thought fire-building would be standard practice for military training."

"Well, as pilot training was a bit of a joke..." Kase said, sitting back and pulling the borrowed cloak around him. "...I never learned how to build a proper fire."

One of the reasons.

Hallie rearranged the stack into a cone structure, the tops of the logs meeting at the top. She grabbed the flint from her pack and turned to Kase. "If I remember correctly, you didn't start any of the fires on our mission last fall either."

"Don't know how."

"I guess you've had servants to light them for you?"

"Your point?"

"Nothing. Will you hold the electropistol, then? I would rather light this paper I found in the cabinet, not my cloak."

Kase grabbed the pistol from her and held it where she could see. Once she had a spark catch and smoke, she leaned down further and blew. Kase uncocked the electropistol. When the flames finally began to consume a larger piece of wood, Hallie sat back and dusted off her hands. "We'll need to add more as the night goes. Whoever's on watch can handle that." She looked over at the still snoring Yarrow. "My guess is it'll be one of us."

"I don't think anyone's stupid enough to be out in this storm. Or in the Pass, for that matter." Kase set the pistol beside his pack.

Hallie shrugged. "Only us, then."

"Ha, right."

"How about some dinner? Didn't you say you picked up some sort of meat before you got arrested?"

After the fire was hot enough, Hallie roasted little sausages with a frying-pan like spit she'd found in the cabinets. They ate that with a glob of cheese. They tried to wake Yarrow as requested, but he cursed Kase and turned over. A few links were saved only at Hallie's request; Kase wanted to throw them at the old trapper.

Finishing his portion, Kase leaned back on his hands, the fire warming his back. "Looks like you're getting better at cooking."

Hallie rolled her eyes and wiped her fingers on her trousers. "It was a team effort, I'd say."

Kase laughed. "I wish we could eat more, but I know we need to be prepared in case it takes us longer to get out of here."

"Yeah," Hallie said softly, her arms sliding around her knees and hugging them to her chest.

Kase fiddled with the edge of his jacket for a moment. "Care to tell me what we're doing out here?"

Hallie's eyes looked almost like molten gold in the firelight. "Seeing if my parents are okay isn't good enough?"

"That's not what I meant," Kase muttered.

The howling wind and rattling door drowned out Kase's sigh. Fine, if she didn't want to talk, she didn't want to talk. He turned toward the fire. Kase needed to escape the city, but he still didn't understand Hallie's motivations. Checking on her parents made sense, but there was something else she didn't want to tell him.

They sat in silence, ignoring the wind and snow pelting the window. The fire crackled happily in its grate, and Kase watched the shadows flickering on the front wall of the little hut. How could something so incredibly destructive also be so comforting? What was that saying? Too much of a good thing?

"I'm going to sleep." Hallie moved and grabbed her bedroll from her pack.

Kase jumped. The flames had teased him into a trance, and all he could see were those tongues climbing higher and higher over the rooftops of lower Kyvena. He shook his head. "Too bad Yarrow took the only bed. I'd have let you have it."

"I didn't think you had such good manners, Lord Pilot."

"Very funny, Miss Walker." Kase stood and stretched, his cloak falling to the side. "I couldn't sleep in good conscience with you on the floor, but as our esteemed guide has taken it, we're stuck down here."

Hallie spread out her roll, her head nearest the fire, and climbed in. Kase pulled his out and settled a few feet away, using the cloak as a pillow. Hallie said, "Six months ago, you would've taken the bed without any hesitation. Kicked Yarrow out of it, too."

Kase laughed. It felt nice. "I was such a *dulkop*, sorry...are you sure you want to sleep down here?"

She shook her head. "I'm fine."

"What if we push him off the bed and both sleep in it?"

Even in the dim firelight, Kase could see the red blush spreading over her cheeks, and he chuckled. Hallie scowled. "Goodnight."

"Come on, I was teasing."

In response, Hallie pulled the top part of the sleeping roll over her head. Kase heaved an annoyed sigh and tucked his own over his shoulder. He faced Yarrow's slumbering form.

Can't take a joke, for moons-sake.

After a while, the blizzard died down to a whisper. Even so, his mind wouldn't let him rest, choosing to replay his worst memories. He saw Zeke's chest jerk again and again, heard Eravin's words as he laid out the plan to blackmail Kase and take Hallie, felt the soldier go limp after he hit him in the head with the pistol.

"Kase?"

He rolled over. Hallie's eyes were visible over the lip of the cloak she'd laid on top of her bedroll. He hadn't even heard her move to grab it. "Yeah?"

"I'm sorry. About all this."

Kase pushed himself up on his left elbow. "I don't think you can take credit for the blizzard."

Hallie pulled herself up, the cloak pooling at her waist, and turned to face him. "No, I mean, for dragging you out here. Maybe it was stupid. Especially now my face will be joining yours on a wanted poster."

"You didn't force me to do anything." Kase yawned and rubbed a hand over his eyes. "In fact, my drunken memories tell me I practically begged you."

"Still, though. Thank you."

"You're welcome."

Then he remembered what else he'd grabbed in Nar. He got up and rummaged through his pack until his fingers found the rough edges of the paper sack.

Hallie leaned forward. "What is that?"

Kase fished out a wrapped caramel chew and tossed it to her.

She caught it with deft fingers and grinned. "I'd forgotten you'd bought these."

"I thought another reckless journey called for some caramels."

Hallie unwrapped hers and popped it into her mouth with a soft groan. "Agreed."

Kase took one for himself and threw it up in the air. With an adept movement, he caught it and chewed. The buttery-sugary goodness spread across his tongue like wildfire. Hallie laughed. "Bravo! You've practiced."

Kase swallowed and chuckled. "Obviously." He set the bag in the middle, and they both had another. "You sure you won't tell me the other reason we're out here?"

Hallie sucked her teeth and played with the candy wrapper, the crinkling competing with the crackling fire. "The caramels were a way to butter me up?"

"Possibly. But they're also simply delicious."

Hallie's eyes were hard as she stared at him. She broke eye contact first, looking down at her fingers and biting her lip. "You've risked a lot to get me here."

Kase stayed silent. He didn't want to break the small bit of trust he'd just earned.

"I'd always wondered about the Yalvs, ever since the Stoneset schoolmistress brought them up," Hallie said. "When Jack died, and I got to go to the University, I couldn't pass up the opportunity to study them. The more I learned, the more curious I became."

She looked back at the fire, her voice soft. "And then after I opened the door, I had to ask Pa. I had to know."

"What do you mean *opened the door*?"

She fiddled with a wrapper. "Do you not remember? How I...used my own blood to open the door to the Gate chamber?"

The memory flashed in his mind. He'd remembered some of it the night of the estate dinner when the Rubikan ambassador had commented on Hallie's eyes. "I can only remember bits and pieces. But I wish you'd stop beating around the bush. Just tell me, already. It hurts my head to think too hard."

Hallie looked like she wanted to stick in a quip by the way her eyes brightened, but she caught herself and shook her head. "My blood opened the door because...I'm...well, I'm Yalven."

Yarrow grunted in his sleep. Hallie and Kase jumped. When the trapper didn't stir any more, only breathed deeply, Kase turned back to her. "*What?*"

Hallie was Yalven? *Holy moons.*

He wracked his brain again. "How? You don't look anything...anything like...blast it. Your eyes. That's why the Rubikan...oh, shocks."

"Yes."

"And why didn't you mention this little nugget earlier? Like the time the Yalvs captured us and tied us up? Don't you think your supposed lineage would've helped there?"

Hallie crushed a wrapper in her hand. "I didn't know for sure. I'd found a Yalven portrait tucked away in our inn's attic years ago, and when I asked Papa about it, he forbade me from snooping. I didn't listen, but I couldn't find anything else other than a locked chest. Even Jack couldn't jimmy it open."

"You saw a portrait...and that means you're Yalven? I thought you were some sort of scholar."

Hallie stood, her sleeping roll falling away, and paced in the small space before the fire crackling in the hearth. "The woman in the picture looked like Saldr, like the Lord Elder, like every other Yalv we met in Myrrai."

"But that wouldn't necessarily mean you're Yalven."

"We needed to get into the chamber. I acted on instinct and hoped for the best."

Kase ran both hands through his hair and cradled his head in them. "And why does this matter now?"

"It matters because...because...well, I just, I think that portrait is more than someone my great-grandmother painted, which is the story Papa told me. What if she was someone I'm related to? So yes, I do want to know if my parents are okay, but...I need to know about...the other stuff, too."

"Okay, so you're Yalven. Again, why does it matter?"

"I have to know."

What in the stars was she going on about? Kase rubbed his eyes. "Why? I don't care if you're Yalven or a blasted dragon."

Hallie stopped her pacing and sat. She pulled her knees to

her chest. The fire lit one side of her face. "I need to know what I am, *who I am*. Because I don't know anymore. Ever since the mission to Myrrai, I feel like I'm living some sort of lie."

A pang throbbed in Kase's chest. He knew exactly what she felt. Their first meeting in that dusty bookshop replayed in his head. How could he not have known then that the girl who'd insulted him with a line from *Romeo and Juliet* would be so much like himself? Why had he taken so long to realize that? He reached across the short distance and grabbed her hand, slipping a caramel inside. He didn't let go.

"You're Hallie Walker," Kase whispered, giving her hand a soft squeeze, "Intelligent, spirited, and stubborn as the stars. None of the rest matters."

Hallie's eyes were wet as she looked at him, and Kase's chest lurched again. *Stars, this girl.*

"Thank you." Hallie pulled her hand from his and wiped her eyes. She unwrapped the caramel. "Your turn. Why'd you come if you thought it was pointless at first?"

Kase ran a hand through his hair. "It didn't matter whether I stayed in Kyvena or not. Either way, I'd be in deep trouble."

"Is that why you keep alluding to the fact you aren't returning?"

Kase tossed the empty candy wrappers into the fire. They popped and fizzled as they caught, though not so easily as a thatched cottage roof. "There was this thing...it's a long story, and one I'm not ready to tell yet. I left because...I don't want to drag my family into it. Well, Jove and my mother, that is. This way, it takes the pressure off them. I had no choice but to leave the city."

Hallie leaned in and took his hand. She didn't say anything, just held it, the heat from the flames mixing with the feeling of her fingers laced in his. She looked up into his eyes. "Thank you."

"Yeah...and I guess...I guess I couldn't pass up an adventure even if the last one ended badly." Kase smiled, his heart in his throat. "Maybe I'm a glutton for punishment."

Hallie's laugh was pure and simple as she took her hand away. "You and me both." She paused, looking back at the fire. "We should get some sleep. Yarrow can't be the only one awake enough to traverse the Pass in the morning."

Kase nodded as she scrunched herself back down into her sleeping roll. He followed suit, pulling the material tight around him. After a while, Hallie's breaths were slow and deep. Kase's own eyelids grew heavy, and before sleep claimed him, Hallie's eyes danced into his mind.

They look like honey...I like honey.

CHAPTER 24

YOU'RE GONNA SINK

Hallie

AFTER TWO DAYS OF TREKKING through the Pass and staying in cabins only Yarrow could find—the last one being hidden behind a rather large outcropping—Hallie was grateful they'd picked up more clothing in Nar. The extra gloves and socks worked wonders, but as the third day wore on, snow fell once more. The sky didn't look as dark as it had with the blizzard, but if they didn't find another hut, they might as well dig themselves an icy grave. Snowpacks overhead watched their every move.

As long as they moved quickly and avoided doing anything to dislodge the latter, they should survive the Pass. Maybe.

Thankfully, they began their descent as the tree line grew closer. Under the safety of the trees, walking might be a little easier the further they went. If she remembered correctly, they should be within a day or so from Stoneset.

"Mr. Yarrow?" His name became several syllables with the trembling in her shoulders. He turned, his cheeks bright red with the cold. "Are we close to stopping for the night?"

Kase stood beside her, his own body quivering from the cold. His fur cap was frosted with flakes. "If I don't sit by a fire soon, I'm going to be turning into one of those blasted ice sculptures."

Hallie shook her head, nose running. She swiped at it with her wet gloves, leaving a scratchy feeling on her upper lip. "This was a horrible idea, wasn't it?"

Yarrow leaned on his broken stick. "I never said it was easy. We have quite a ways until we stop."

"Could we rest under the trees?"

Kase gestured with his hands to Yarrow's pack. "We have a little bit of firewood."

The trapper spit into the snow. "A fire that will blow out with the wind and—"

Blue fire zinged through the air and nailed the trapper's shoulder. Hallie screamed as Kase dove for her. The snow cushioned them, but Kase was blasted heavy.

Blue fire. Cerls. They were here, but how?

Stars. Stoneset.

Kase held her as more bullets flew above them. He rolled off and fumbled through his pockets for his electropistol.

Hallie grabbed it from the back of his trousers and shoved it into his hands. "Shoot!"

He fired blindly in the direction the bullets came from. Hallie scrambled to her feet. If she could get to the tree line, she could find her own electropistol tucked away in her pack and help.

She stumbled toward the trees, not looking back. Kase followed, firing twice over his shoulder. Once they made it to cover, he turned. Two people were up on rocky ledges, hidden behind outcroppings. Hallie dropped her pack and rummaged through it. Kase kept firing. A shout followed as Kase ducked behind a tree.

"Get up!" He jerked her up as a trio of fiery blue bullets hit her pack. The thing exploded. Hallie clung to Kase. Even through his many layers, she felt the pounding in his heart. It mirrored hers.

Kase released her and leaned out from behind the tree, firing his electropistol three times in rapid succession as blue fire arched above them. They ducked as a branch fell directly on her pack.

"Got him!" Kase breathed as he stepped out from behind the tree. Hallie fell beside her destroyed pack. Her extra clothing, their food...all blasted to shreds. She had a few things tucked away in her satchel, but how was *Frankenstein* and the telegram her parents sent going to help?

Kase stumbled over to Yarrow, who hadn't moved. His blood coated the snow. *No.*

Kase looked back at her. "He's alive, but—"

He grunted as he lifted the large man up. Yarrow groaned. "Leave me, slicker. It's what I deserve."

Hallie ducked under the trapper's other arm. "It'll be all right. We've got you."

Another whizzing sound erupted from the direction of the Cerls. Hallie caught the blue light in the corner of her eye as it hit Kase's leg. He screamed as he fell, electropistol flying from his hand and Yarrow toppling with him. Hallie hit the ground, scrambling for the weapon. Her hands were stiff with the cold, but she grasped the pistol and fired in the direction the bullet had come from. Had there been another Cerl in the trees? *Oh, stars. Oh, stars.*

Yarrow pulled himself up and yanked the weapon from her grip. Red blood gushed from his shoulder. His breathing was shallow and labored, but he fired in the direction of the Cerls. "Take him, lass. I'll lead them off."

"But—"

"Go!"

Kase sucked in a breath as Hallie grabbed his arm and hauled him up as best she could. He leaned heavily on her as they made for the trees. A natural with a pistol, Yarrow fired relentlessly at the ledges, limping toward where blue fire answered his taunts. His right arm dangled, blood dripping onto the snow with each step.

Hallie turned away. She didn't want to see Yarrow die.

Kase moaned once they'd reached cover. "I don't think I can make it much further."

"We're too far from Stoneset." Hallie's eyes stung as tears leapt to them. "I don't think—oh, blasted stars—don't you go dying on me now!"

He grimaced. "Didn't say I was dying."

She looked behind them at the trail of speckled blood on the disturbed snow. "Let me see your leg."

He winced as she sat him down underneath the boughs of a nearby tree. The small area was mostly clear of snow. He loosened his boot and lifted the hem of his pants. "Grazed me. Still hurts like a demon."

Blood leaked from his calf, not gushing but enough to be a problem. She eased his pack off his back and rifled through it for something to use as a bandage. "We need to get help before it gets infected." She found a sock, wadded it up, and pressed it to the wound. The gash wasn't too deep. "Hold this. I'm going to go look for Yarrow."

Kase grabbed her arm, preventing her from rising. "He'll find us if he's alive, but if not...I don't want you out there if the Cerls are still hunting."

"Except the blood trail you left will lead anyone right to us."

"Then we'd better find a stars-blasted good hiding place." Grimacing, he stretched the sock and tied it around his calf with gloved fingers. Hallie helped him lace his boot. Kase grunted as he used the tree to help himself stand. "Let's get out of here."

Hallie bit her lip to keep herself from saying something that would only make the situation worse. She wanted to help Yarrow, but she was powerless. He'd sacrificed himself just to save them.

Just like Zeke. And Ebba.

"Vask Initru!"

Hallie head snapped around, and she froze. A man appeared from behind a rock, an enormous weapon on his shoulder. A cannon. Like the one that had destroyed the forest near the *Eudora Jayde*.

"No, no, no." Hallie tugged on Kase's pack, making him wobble.

He caught himself on her shoulder and cursed as he followed her line of sight. Ethereal blue smoke leaked from the cannon's barrel, the plume growing. Hallie and Kase staggered away. They couldn't outrun that cannon.

Hallie could only cling to Kase as the resounding boom pierced the frigid air.

The entire mountain shook. Hallie stumbled, Kase with her. She caught herself on a nearby tree.

A rumble, low at first, but gradually increasing in volume.

She looked up at the mountainside.

The cannon fire had hit the snowpack. Snow slid from the cliff face.

The Cerl hadn't hit her and Kase for a reason. He'd meant to start an avalanche.

"CLIMB!"

Kase didn't question her. He grabbed a jutting branch from the nearest trunk and scrambled up, hissing in pain. The rumbling grew louder as Hallie followed.

Stars. Stars.

Blood smeared against the tree where Kase's leg brushed against it. Hallie didn't care. Growing up in the mountains had taught her many things—first, don't play too close to the mountainside; second, if you're caught in an avalanche, it's too late.

Climbing a tree might mean their deaths, but it was the only thing she could think of in that moment. Her father's voice rang in her ears as the snow grew louder.

Try to stay on top, but you're gonna sink. Create breathing room and pray someone finds you soon.

The snow barreled into their tree. It shook and swayed. Hallie lost her grip. She scrambled for purchase. Kase yelled something, but she couldn't hear it as the snow caught her ankle and ripped her from the tree.

Swim toward the source.

Her arms flailed. The snow was icy hot against the exposed skin of her face and neck. The roaring in her ears drowned out anything and everything until she slowed to a stop, her arms flung in front of her face.

It was dark and too quiet, a contrast from when she couldn't hear herself think moments before.

She had little time before the snow solidified. She took the deepest, largest breath she'd ever breathed and held it. She had yet to open her eyes. Cold seeped into her very being. She clawed at the surface above her, praying she wasn't the wrong way up.

Seconds ticked by as her fingers grew weaker. Had she

come all this way, blown up a hover hanger, and survived most of the Pass only to die here in the snow? She took small, shallow breaths as nausea crept into her stomach. What if no one ever found her? What would Kase think? Was he even alive? Would her blue body thaw out with the spring?

The seconds ticked by. Tears trailed down her cheek like icy rivulets. Had Jack felt like this in the seconds before he died? He'd been buried by stone instead of snow. It'd been quick. Hallie would suffocate slowly.

She let out a sob.

"Hallie!"

The voice was faint and muffled, but she heard it. Her heart skipped. *Kase.*

She knew enough not to shout yet, only pawed at the snow above her. It was getting more and more difficult to do so, like trying to break through rock. Her numb fingers were soaked in the gloves, but she nearly cried when her fingers met the open air. She prayed it wasn't some random air pocket—that it was indeed the outside.

She opened her eyes at last. Light filtered in around her extended arm. "Here! I'm here!"

"Hallie!"

She waved her hand, creating a slightly larger hole. "Kase!"

The light darkened above her. Kase's breathless voice answered. "I'll dig you out. Hold on."

Scraping and chipping followed while she waited. She took breaths of fresh air streaming in through the hole, more tears cascading down her frozen face. She'd survived, gotten incredibly lucky to be that close to the surface after being pulled out of the tree. Her limbs started quaking.

"It's okay," Kase said, still hacking away at the snow above her. "I'm getting you out. Yell if I'm about to carve up your face."

It took a few more minutes, but at last, Kase's face came into view, snow falling onto her cheeks as he cleared it away. He threw the machete he was using as a shovel aside and reached in to grab her other hand, tugging her out.

At last, he brought her to the surface and crushed her in a hug.

She clung to him, her body still quivering with cold and

shock. He held her tighter. "You're safe."

A few more moments and the shaking in her limbs faded, leaving her skin bitterly cold. Kase pressed her closer to his side, worry pulling at his face. "We need to get you warm and find a place for the night."

He helped her stand, though he wobbled himself. Blood soaked the leg of his trousers and the snow he'd knelt on. She wrapped her arms up in his, and they held each other, stumbling off, trying not to fall into the packed snow from the avalanche.

"Think the Cerls got caught in that?" Hallie asked, her teeth chattering. Ice settled in her bones. Kase slid his arm around her shoulders, pulled her closer.

"Not sure."

"Yarrow?"

He pressed his lips in a firm line, clearly worried but not about to respond.

They wound their way through the trees, each one a giant, throwing shadows over the forest floor that shaded them from the sun. They kept close to the mountainside until she spotted a dark crevice nestled into the base of the mountain.

"There!"

Kase hobbled toward it. The cave stood out against the snow, and if aftershocks swept through, it might get buried. They had little choice, though. Kase's breath labored as they walked, his limp worsening with each step. Hallie's body shook under the snow permeating her clothes.

The cave stretched wide and tall, with a sturdy overhang near the mouth. Rock walls ushered them in, cold and brutal, but clean. Nothing had made its nest here.

Hallie nearly cried with relief. It would work for the night. She helped Kase inside and eased him to the cold ground, listening to him sigh in relief as the weight lifted off his injured leg. Without his meager body heat, she shivered even more violently.

He slipped his pack off, digging through it. He tugged out a shirt, trousers, socks, and his trainee pilot's jacket, throwing them in a slightly-less-wet heap at Hallie's feet. "You can wear these. Otherwise, you'll catch your death."

She gathered up the clothing with quaking fingers. The

wind stayed outside the cavern, relieving some of the bitterness she felt. It was a miracle she hadn't succumbed to hypothermia yet. She held Kase's clothes close to her chest and peered around looking for somewhere private to change. But with its intimacy and the waning light, nothing in the cavern presented itself as appropriate.

Kase pushed himself along the cavern floor, inching toward the mouth. "I'll sit at the edge of the cave and keep watch. You change."

Hallie smiled, a little warmth entering her heart. "Thanks."

His clothes engulfed her. The shirt sleeves flopped comically past her fingertips, and with the shirt tucked into the waistband, it fell to mid-thigh. She used her sodden maiden belt to keep the trousers from falling and frowned at her icy toes wiggling freely about his socks, but with the exploded remnants of her pack buried beneath the avalanche, she didn't have a choice. She laid out her wet clothes and hoped they wouldn't turn to solid ice before she could wear them again. While Kase's shirt was nice and dry, it wasn't her favorite lace.

What were they going to do now? They'd freeze to death without a fire, yet they couldn't risk one if the Cerls were in the Pass. Hallie hated to think about why they were there in the first place. If they'd slipped past Achilles' defense...or worse, they'd defeated the forces at Achilles...

No, they were probably a rogue band. Stoneset had been raided several times when she was growing up. That was the risk of living on the border. They were worrisome, but not as devastating as an avalanche or sub-zero temperatures. The natural elements threatened them more than a pack of bandits—especially without a fire.

All the legends she'd heard as a child replayed in her head: hikers going missing, found buried beneath the snow weeks later, or the blacksmith's daughter losing six toes to frostbite after trying to run away in the dead of winter. Hallie's breathing sped up. "Kase...what are we..."

He kept his eyes to the woods, watching for signs of life, but his gloved fingers bit into his wrist. "The cave will protect us from the wind and snow. We'll be fine." He paused. "You changed?"

"Yes."

He turned around and chuckled. "You've looked better."

Her teeth chattered as she stuffed her feet back into her boots. "Well, if only you weren't quite so tall, then maybe I wouldn't look so...what did you call yourself earlier...dashing?"

Kase's laughter echoed against the cavern walls, and Hallie's joined him. Everything would be all right. Kase scooted himself out of the opening and up against the wall with a grimace. "You'd look beautiful no matter what you wore."

Hallie's face caught flame. "Thank—thank you."

With trembling fingers, she fished out the cheese Kase had in his pack and gave him half. She joined him leaning against a drier part of the cave, trying not to think of his nearness, his compliment, and the thousand things that could make things worse. Stupid really. They'd weathered two of the worst.

Her cheese was a little stiff from the cold, but she choked it down. As they finished their meager dinner, the light outside faded to black night. No sign of the Cerls or Yarrow. It was a bittersweet feeling. Yarrow might have been rather crotchety, but he didn't deserve to die.

Soon, small fractals of Firstmoon's light stretched onto the newly fallen snow and into the entrance of the cave.

"Might as well try to sleep, I guess," Kase said, nodding to his pack. "Do you mind taking first watch?"

She agreed immediately, watching the blood drying on the leg of his pants. Kase needed sleep. He was a stars-idiot who refused to admit when he needed help after all, and if she entrusted him to wake her if something happened to his leg, well, she had a suspicion he might just die instead.

She laid out his bedroll and helped him into it. She grabbed his extra cloak and used it as a cushion as she sat a few feet away. It didn't help much. The cold seeped through, and she was sure if she didn't warm up soon, she'd end up freezing to death. What were the symptoms of hypothermia again? Slurred speech? Shivering? She couldn't recall the others. Jack had been the one fascinated with that sort of thing.

Clenching her teeth as Kase shifted in his bedroll, she tried to remember days in the summer sun back in Stoneset and winter nights in front of the inn's fireplace. Anything warm. Maybe she could trick her brain into believing it was hot inside the dark cave.

She shivered harder, her teeth chattering. Despite her best efforts, all she could think about was the snow piling on top of her, the ice seeping into her clothes as she waited for rescue.

After what must've been a half hour if not longer, she finally spoke up. Her jaw ached from the constant chattering. "Kase? Could I light a fire?"

He rolled over to face her. "I'm cold, too, but lighting a fire now would be the worst thing we could do."

Hallie gritted her teeth as another chill ravaging her body. "I'm going to get hypothermia or lose all my toes like the blacksmith's daughter...and I—"

"Hallie," Kase said, pushing the blanket down so he could speak clearly, "you're not thinking straight. Breathe. You don't want to speed up your heart in times like this. I remember a little from pilot training."

She forced herself to breathe deeply. "Anything else?"

Kase looked away. "Well, I know the best way to warm up is to trap the body heat, so we could...um, well, you could..."

Hallie's cheeks blazed with heat. At least that warmed her for a second. "I'm not so far gone I think I need skin-to-skin contact!"

She caught sight of Kase's red face in a sliver of moonlight. "*That's not what I meant.* I only meant we could share this bedroll, and it's best to wear as many clothes as you can. Unless, well, unless you are going to—"

"But it's not proper!"

With a grimace, Kase rolled back over. "Then freeze to death in silence, please."

Stupid prat.

Hallie sat there shivering still, the uneven bits of the cave floor digging into her bones. She twisted and adjusted herself, hoping to find a better position, but it was no use. The stories of people freezing to death in the mountains came back to her.

She sat up. "*Fine.* But if you can't keep your hands to yourself, I'll kick your wound."

Kase snorted. "I believe it." He sat up and undid the ties along the side.

Hallie gathered the extra cloak and tucked it around her. After she'd helped Kase scoot over without jostling his leg too much, she took a deep breath and crawled in beside him, her back to his. He tied up the other side of the bag.

As he settled back in, he bumped her shoulder, and she tensed. She couldn't believe she was this close to him. He'd commented earlier about how she shouldn't let her heart rate get up, and this wasn't helping. At all. And all this after he'd said she was beautiful no matter what she wore. Holy stars. She squirmed a little, trying to get comfortable, flinching a little every time she rubbed up against his back or his leg. Each little touch was like icy fire.

Why did I think this was a good idea? Have I lost my mind? Was that one of the symptoms of freezing to death?

The image of the hiker's body, blue and frosted with ice like a macabre cake, bloomed in her mind.

"Great shocks, will you stop moving?" Kase growled, his voice muffled. "I promise to leave you alone, on my word as a gentle—"

Hallie elbowed him in the back.

He cursed. "What was that for?"

"Shut up, will you?"

"*Women...*"

"I heard that."

Kase didn't respond, but the muscles in his back relaxed a little. Hallie sat there, her shivers slowly dissipating as their shared warmth created a small cocoon around them. He knew his stuff. She had to give him credit for that.

"Goodnight, Master Pilot." She smiled at his soft, annoyed sound.

"You're not going to sleep, are you?"

"No, I'll wake you in a few hours." After several minutes, she finally relaxed all the way. It was so much warmer, and she wiggled her thawing toes. "And thank you."

Her voice was a whisper, so she wasn't sure he'd heard it, but after a few seconds, his chest rumbled with a low laugh. "Goodnight, Hals."

HALLIE WOKE WITH THE FIRST rays of sunlight peeking through the opening of the cave. She hadn't frozen to death—a near miracle. They needed to get moving soon if they were to make it to the end of the Pass by sundown.

If they were lucky, they could take the forest road and sleep at her father's inn tonight. The idea of sleeping in a real bed was almost enough to quell the anxiety of seeing her parents and Niels again. Granted, it'd be slow going with Kase's leg.

Air met her back.

At some point while she'd slept, Kase had extricated himself from the bedroll. She must have been extraordinarily tired not to wake as he did so. He leaned against the cave wall, weight off his injured calf and holding his electropistol loosely.

Hallie sat up. The cave floor was chilly even through her gloves. "How're you feeling?"

Kase shrugged and pushed himself off the wall, limping to his bag. "Sore, but I can put a little more weight on it today."

"Good." She looked away, down at the mud-streaked blankets. "You don't think Yarrow is alive?"

"No."

"But how do you know?" Hallie picked at a loose string. "Maybe he's out there looking for us."

Kase found the rest of the food Hallie had buried underneath his other effects the previous evening. He pulled out the wrapped cheese—probably too cold to eat now. "Not with the way the Cerl bullet hit him. He'd have bled out by now if he avoided the avalanche. I'm sorry."

Hallie blinked away the moisture in her eyes. Yarrow hadn't been the best traveling companion. He'd been ill-tempered. He'd been greedy.

But he'd helped rescue Kase. He'd taken the bullet for them.

Kase's muttered curse followed a soft tinkling against the rocky floor. A ring rolled toward her. She picked it up when it stopped next to her. It was thin and dainty, made of what looked like Zuprium with its bronze sheen. The edges were shaped into tiny vines leading to a trio of roses. Small diamonds dotted the band at regular intervals. Kase held his hand out. "Blasted thing is too loose because of the cold. Shouldn't have taken off my gloves."

"Why are you wearing a ring to begin with?" Hallie asked,

setting it in his outstretched hand. "You secretly engaged or something?"

Kase slipped it onto his pinky finger and replaced his gloves. "It was Ana's. I've never come close to marrying anyone, much to my mother's dismay."

Hallie pulled herself to her feet and packed away the bedroll. "You're lucky."

"If by *lucky* you mean having your mother question your every motive as to why you haven't found some girl to chain yourself to until death do you part, then, sure, I'm blasted lucky."

Hallie attached the roll to Kase's pack and grabbed the cheese he'd left out. She broke it into two halves. It wasn't much, and one half was much larger than the other because her fingers tingled from the cold. "That's not what I meant."

"Then what did you mean?" Kase limped over, taking the smaller bit of cheese.

His face was above hers, his eyes shadowed in the dim light. She turned away from him. What could she say to that? She didn't like thinking of those awful memories. Why did she have to open her mouth? Why couldn't she ever just shut up? "Nothing. We need to go."

"Hallie..."

Her boots echoed off the stone wall with each step. "I shouldn't have said anything. Sorry."

Kase closed his pack and slung it onto his shoulders. He followed her into the snowy dawn. "Tell me."

Hallie pulled the hood of her cloak up. "I want to find my parents, want to make sure they're all right, but there's a reason I haven't visited since I arrived in Kyvena. Not on holidays or breaks. I didn't want to face them...and...and Niels."

"Niels?"

Hallie hoped the shadow of her hood hid her warming cheeks. They walked for a few minutes in silence. With whatever was budding between her and Kase, she didn't want to ruin it by talking about her past, but...Kase deserved to know. He'd come this far with her, been arrested, thrown into a jail cell, shot by Cerls, and nearly killed in an avalanche. If she couldn't trust him, she couldn't trust anyone.

She paused, focusing on single snowflake fluttering from

the sky above to join its brethren below.

Kase's boots paused beside hers. She spoke to her toes. "Niels and I were…sweethearts."

Kase didn't move, didn't seem to breathe. But now that Hallie's secret was out, she couldn't stop.

"But Jack died. And I found a life I love at the University. I haven't been home, barely written, because…because…I can't. Not after Jack. Not after I've discovered what truly makes me happy. Yet I feel guilty, because if he hadn't died, I might never have realized how unhappy I was. And now that I know, I can't go back to that life."

Tears left burning cold trails on her cheeks. She swiped at them.

"The only person who has any control over how you feel is you." His voice was soft, a whisper. "Besides, maybe it was a stroke of luck you ended up in Kyvena, but I'm sure glad you did."

She looked up at him through her tears. He stared back, a soft, solemn expression on his face. He'd only looked at her this way once, so genuine and open. It'd been that night in the trapper's cabin with the caramels.

She was Hallie Walker, intelligent, spirited, and stubborn as the stars.

A bubble formed in her chest. "Thank you."

Kase glanced away for a second, as if trying to process exactly what he wanted to say next. "Do you still have feelings for…Niels?"

The name was still like a gut punch. She'd never closed off that part of her life—only hid it beneath books and charcoal pencils in Kyvena. She picked at the hem of the trainee pilot's jacket she wore. "He's part of the past I'd rather forget."

After a beat, Kase squeezed her shoulder. "Thank you for telling me."

He turned her toward him fully, his gloved hands cradling her upper arms. She gazed into his too-blue eyes. The curve of his jaw was lined with stubble again. He leaned forward until his cold lips met her forehead. It was brief, but it was enough to set her heart aflutter. "I promise, everything will be okay."

"When did you become such an optimist?" Her words came out jumbled.

He smiled, and her knees wobbled for a moment despite the memories so fresh in her mind. "Just now, I guess."

The feeling wasn't new. She'd nearly kissed him that night they danced by the fire. She was falling for him, but that was dangerous—dangerous because she didn't know what awaited her in Stoneset. She didn't know where he was going afterward. Likely, she'd never see him again, and her already-shattered heart couldn't survive another breaking.

He searched her eyes for a moment before stepping back, hands falling to his sides. She looked away, off where Stoneset lay.

"Glad to hear it." She tucked her feelings away, shoving them down deep until she could sort them out. She started off. "We don't want to spend another night in the cold, do we?"

Around midday, they stopped for only a few minutes to take a swig of the insulated canteen they'd brought along—not that it gave them much to drink. Kase gave Hallie a frozen caramel to suck on. The sugar was nice, but not as good as if she were able to chew it. She wished she could say something other than *thank you*, but anything she said now seemed awkward and forced. She'd laid her soul bare, and he hadn't scolded her for it. He hadn't scoffed. He'd understood.

She didn't want to shatter that new *whatever it was* with meaningless words, lest he take it all back. It also didn't help that Hallie's stomach ached from the lack of what little food they had brought with them. It felt like ages since they'd stopped in Laurent and had a full meal. It was almost impossible not to dream of what awaited her in Stoneset. Winter vegetable stew. Toast that crunched in her teeth. Juicy, tender roasted lamb. The dread that had filled her stomach before now gave way to ravenous hunger.

She might have to face her past at the end of this road, but at least she'd be well fed.

When the sun drooped toward the horizon hours later, they stumbled across the first sign they were nearing the edge of the pass. Without thinking, she grabbed Kase's arm and pointed at a smudge on the horizon.

Kase squinted in the distance. "Military outpost?"

"The one closest to Stoneset." Hallie shook out her hands and feet, trying to bring more warmth to them. "They allow boys from the village to visit. Those interested in joining up, that is. Jack went once and returned, saying he regretted it." Hallie laughed at the memory of his dejected face. "Said he didn't fancy having someone yell at him because he didn't make his bed properly."

Kase leaned on his good leg. "And you? You never thought about joining the military?"

"I want to open a school one day."

"I remember you telling Mother that."

"Wanted to do it ever since I moved to Kyvena."

They walked for a little bit in silence before Kase said, "And what about before? Did you not want to do that when you lived in Stoneset?"

Hallie stopped, biting her lip. It was a casual question, and one that was expected, but it still caught her off guard. Kase turned. "What?"

She didn't look up at him as she trudged ahead. "Jack wanted to be a healer, and as the firstborn by a mere three minutes, the savings were his for the taking. The only life left for me was to marry, though I'd inherit the inn."

"That's not fair."

"It's not a bad thing. I've grown up since then. I still want to marry, but I also want to follow my dreams."

Kase didn't say anything as they continued to trudge toward the outpost. Hallie refused to look at him. Had she misread him? Oh, stars, did he think she was hinting at the fact that she wanted to marry *him*? That hadn't been her intention at all. She'd merely been honest.

But that didn't mean she necessarily wanted that with Kase...though that possibility wasn't as egregious as it had been last autumn.

Except he was leaving once she was in Stoneset. It couldn't happen, and he probably thought her one of those social climbers who preyed upon rich men.

Hallie chewed on the inside of her cheek before speaking, "That is, if I find someone willing to put up with my incessant need to devour literature and my penchant for the smell of dusty tomes."

Kase chuckled, "I understand the feeling."

Well, that was cryptic.

As they approached the outpost, Hallie let the conversation drop and looked for signs of habitation, but no smoke billowed from a chimney, no one patrolled the outer perimeter. Had they stopped using this one?

The tower itself was built more like a sturdy lighthouse. It climbed until the roof reached a point where a weathered Jaydian flag flew, a tree within a sun on a green field. The frayed ends flapped sharply in the wind whistling in from the mountains. Hallie gestured toward the trees where she knew another path lay. "I haven't seen anyone, but I think we should take the forest road to Stoneset. I assume the soldiers in Nar have alerted their counterparts here about us?"

"Probably."

She led him to the edge of the woods where a slim, but worn, path lay. As a girl, she'd visited the outpost once, but it was only because she and Jack had stolen away up the mountain path to play. Jack had told her the tower was a witch's lair, and the men patrolling were the minions she sent to find humans for her ritual sacrifice to retain eternal youth. They'd only been nine years old at the time, so Hallie believed every word, as Jack had just read a folktale about that very subject. It seemed plausible with the vines crawling up the brickwork and the point at the top piercing the summer sky.

Niels had found them and ruined the whole thing by pointing out the guards wore uniforms with the Jaydian emblem on their breast. Jack had still fought with him, claiming it was all a ruse, when a patrol found them and marched the trio back to the village. Mama's lips had turned white when the men told her where Jack and Hallie had been playing. Hallie had been cross with the soldiers for ratting them out, but how were they to know that Mama had set her and Jack to weeding the back garden?

A little over three miles away, Niels waited. Would she be married to him with a babe in her stomach by now, if things had gone differently? Would she be tending her father's inn?

Had the Cerls attacked and destroyed everything? Was Niels even there? Or had he fought until his last breath before help could arrive?

She didn't think she wanted to know, and she didn't deserve to. She'd run away, hadn't she?

With that thought in mind, she led Kase into the dark, her waking thoughts filled with memories of warm nights by a raging fire playing Stars & Blasts, wearied miners with Zuprium-dusted faces, and two mischievous boys who'd allowed her to join their adventures.

CHAPTER 25

STARS-BLASTED KINGDOM

Kase

THE FOREST WAS SILENT. SNOW and the coming evening had sent the birds to their homes. Kase's eyes adjusted to the darkness of the surrounding trees, which created a premature night. The trail they followed was nothing more than a path of dampened snow weaving around white-mantled boulders. Bald patches of rock broke the snowy surface like the heads of kings presiding over their wooded kingdom.

The trail was littered with footprints, though none of them human—mostly cloven hooves and something with paws. Kase ran his fingers along his electropistol grip. His leg ached, and he'd nearly tripped twice on the forest path. Walking so far on an injury the day after receiving said injury was the worst thing he could do for it, but Kase wasn't a medic. Zeke had been.

What would his brother have said? What would he have done? Knowing Zeke, he would have spouted off some sort of encouragement while still warning Kase of all the things that could possibly go wrong. All which Kase would have simply ignored.

Kase blinked away the stinging in his eyes.

He pulled the electropistol from his trousers and lit up the muzzle to see by, but it would also do well in a fight if needed—whether soldier or clawed beast. Now was not the time to dwell on his past.

He hoped soldiers didn't wait at the end of this road. Avoiding the outpost altogether had been a good idea, and if they entered the village at night, then maybe they could sneak in without many problems.

He thought about how, once Hallie was finished in Stoneset, she'd go home to Kyvena. Without him.

He'd lost Ana, Zeke, and Ben...even Eravin. How much more could his heart take?

Now his mother and Jove joined that list, though not in the same way. He'd never see them again if everything went according to his plan. Eravin's words rang in his ears as if he was right there next to him, their syllables cutting to his very core. He worked his jaw as he focused on Hallie's back.

When they reached the edge of the trees, Hallie stopped, holding up a hand. "Wait."

Kase adjusted his pack and took in the view. Stoneset sprawled before them in the moonlight. Houses—more like rustic cottages from a First Earthen fairytale, with their painted upper floors and thatched roofs—dotted the mountainside. Darkened streetlamps lined the lane that wove out of sight and into the village proper. The only illumination was the moonlight above on newly fallen, undisturbed snow. No one had cleared the paths through the labyrinth of homes and shops. It reminded Kase of a perfectly iced cake at the bakery near his old upper school.

Hallie glanced back at Kase. "I don't understand."

"How late is it?" He shifted his weight to his good leg. Shocks, he needed to rest.

She stumbled down the slope before Kase could stop her. *Guess I won't have to worry about being turned in to the military here. Terrible security.*

They entered the town. The ground floors of the buildings were constructed of stone, and more unlit lanterns draped above doorway arches. He followed Hallie through the winding streets until they found themselves facing a large building with empty flower boxes hung beneath the ground-floor window. There was a wooden placard over the door.

Walker's Rest.

"Is this it?" Kase asked. This place looked like it hadn't been inhabited in quite some time—save for the dim light emanating from within. It stood three stories tall, the stone chimney breaking up the front facade and stretching to the starry sky above. Dry, wispy vines with curled leaves snaked up its side. Kase thought he recognized the pastoral scene depicted in the stained glass of the front window.

"Papa never goes to bed this early." Hallie put her hand on the door handle.

"Hals, we don't even know what time it is."

Hallie's hand tightened on the door as she looked back. "Keep watch out here, will you?"

"Are you sure you don't want me to come in with you?"

"I'm sure." She stared at the handle. Kase shifted his feet, the unease growing in the pit of his stomach. She finally shook her head. "I'll be a moment."

He stepped up beside her and grabbed her arm, pulling her into a hug. She hesitated a moment before burrowing her head into his shoulder and snaking her arms around him. Kase's heart beat too hard. Her mountain air scent didn't stand out here now that they were in the Nardens, but it calmed his nerves, nonetheless. He took a deep breath before stepping back and handing her his electropistol. "Just in case."

"But what about you?"

"I have an extra."

She nodded once and entered the building.

He remembered when Ana had passed, how he couldn't bear to even walk by her room at the Manor. Must be a similar feeling for Hallie. He didn't think he'd want anyone intruding on his own grief.

Shocks, they were quite the sorry pair.

The small mountain town was as silent as the forest they'd just trekked through. Patches of wearied and cracked cobblestones peeked through the footprints Kase and Hallie had left behind. Something was wrong. Maybe since the attack on

Achilles, Stoneset was under a strict curfew, but the snow sat undisturbed, and the sky was clear. It hadn't snowed for hours.

If Kase looked closer at the houses, patches of repaired stone and boarded windows caught his attention. The cold feeling of dread pooled in his stomach. Kase whipped his head the other way just as something moved around the corner two buildings away.

Blood pumping, heart pounding, he fished out the extra electropistol and set down his pack. With one last peek at the inn, assuring himself Hallie was fine if she was inside the building, he tiptoed toward the lip of the alley. He glanced up and down the road once more before stepping into it, electropistol cocked. The sparks from the tip danced in the shadows. Nothing.

The end of the alley ran to the next street, shadowy alcoves lining the lane. But no one waited. The buildings were too close together for snowfall. No footprints.

I'm on edge and weak from hunger, so I imagined whatever that was. The town is empty, for better or for worse.

He was about to turn and head back toward the inn when the cool edge of a knife bit the skin of his throat.

Kase froze, gripping the electropistol so hard he was sure it would leave permanent indentures in his palm.

"Turn that weapon off if you know what's good for you," a deep voice growled behind him.

Blistering shocks.

Kase's hand shook as he held the pistol tightly. The knife at his throat pressed deeper, and the voice grew more forceful. "I said turn it off, or I'll slit your throat."

With his mouth going completely dry, he uncocked it. If the man gave him an opening, he could use the small hand-fighting techniques he knew, but any move he made now would slit his throat. *Try not to panic.* He had to pretend he was in a hover. Easy, right?

"Much better," the voice said again. "Now, drop it."

"Who are you?" Kase managed to gasp.

The knife dug into his skin even more, and Kase gritted his teeth against the pain, blood trickling over the edge of the blade and dripping onto his cloak. "I don't have any money—"

A scream interrupted his words. Kase used the distraction

and brought the heel of his boot down hard on where he estimated his attacker's toes to be. He winced against the sharp pain lancing through his leg at the motion.

The grunt and clatter of the knife on the cobblestones were the answer he needed. He spun with his elbow up, catching the man in the jaw, knocking him into the side of the building. Kase grabbed the man's arm before he could react and twisted, bringing it around to his back, pushing his face into the stone wall with his other hand. The man went limp.

Another scream split the air. *Hallie.*

He shoved his own attacker and ran for the alley opening. His blasted leg slowed him down, and his neck ached from where the knife had bit into his skin, but he barely felt it. Nothing compared to the pure, unadulterated terror coursing through him. He turned the corner.

Two men dressed in dark uniforms pulled a struggling Hallie by her arms, pinning them behind her back as they covered her nose and mouth with a handkerchief. She went limp. The shorter of the two threw her on his partner's horse before swinging onto his own.

"NO!"

Kase sprinted after the men. He slipped in the snowy patches and didn't care if anyone else lurked in the shadows, nor about his own attacker. All he could see was the auburn braid waving in the winter wind as the men galloped away.

Without warning, Kase's leg gave out. He barely caught himself and saved his nose from a sure break. He rolled, scrambling, trying to get to his feet. His leg refused to cooperate.

"Please..." he cried, reaching with useless fingers.

His vision blurred as the horses disappeared from his sight. *No. I can't lose you. Not like this.*

He crawled, his fingernails digging into ice and the cracks between cobblestones underneath. His calf throbbed as he tried to climb to his feet once more, only to fall from the pain.

"Guess you're not a blasted Cerl, then." The voice was the same as earlier, though the gravelly tones were muddled with what sounded like a swollen lip.

Kase's heart pounded in his chest as he grasped a loose stone and flipped over, ready to launch his pathetic attack, but the man held up his hands. "I don't mean you any harm."

"Except you nearly killed me not even five minutes ago," Kase growled, still holding the stone. The rough edges bit into his fingers.

The man was tall and rather muscular through his arms and shoulders, the sleeves of his jacket almost too tight. His bottom lip was swollen, and blood trickled out the side of his mouth and onto his tanned face. The man shook his head, the blond hair catching in the moonlight. "Can never be too careful. Besides, we should scat before the others come hunting."

Kase still didn't lower his stone. "Scat?"

"Means get outta here." The man's dark eyes were steady on Kase's. "Listen. I didn't mean to scare you, but if you'd been in my position, you would've done the same."

He reached into the back of his trousers and pulled out Kase's electropistol. With careful precision, he set the weapon onto the cobblestones and took several steps back. "See? You're armed. Now, I'm sorry about your neck."

Kase dropped the rock and grabbed his electropistol. He scooted into a position where he could pull himself up, but as soon as he put pressure on his leg, white fire shot through it into his hip, and he collapsed. His pistol clattered to the ground. "My leg. I injured it."

The man cautiously stepped forward. "I can help with that."

Kase cursed.

"I can take you to someone who can fix you up."

Jaw clenched, Kase climbed to his knees, trying to keep weight off his injury. He didn't have time for this. He didn't have any *blasting* time.

Taking a deep breath, he stood on his left leg, his good leg, and almost toppled over, but a strong hand caught his arm and helped him stand. "It's the least I can do."

Kase tugged his arm out of the man's grip and almost fell again, but the man caught him once more, slinging his arm over his shoulder. Kase took a deep steadying breath. "I have to go after those men."

"They're Cerls."

Those uniforms. They were soldiers. The ones who'd attacked them in the Pass had been wearing something similar.

Had the avalanche not killed the rest of them? Hallie and Kase had been spared, so it wasn't out of the question. Kase shook his head. "Achilles said they beat them back."

The man's laugh was low and rumbling, yet it lacked any mirth. "I don't know what lie they tell where you come from, but those *helviters* never left."

Kase halted his hobbling and stared at the man's busted face. "What do you mean? Where are the soldiers from Achilles?"

"The fort held out until about mid-January. We were grateful because it took the focus off us here." The man shook his head. "In the end, it didn't matter. Let me formally welcome you to New Cerulene, the newest colony in King Filip's stars-blasted kingdom."

PART III: RUIN

CHAPTER 26

NOT HOW IT WORKS

Kase

HALLIE'S SATCHEL SWUNG LIKE A pendulum at Kase's waist, reminding him of what he'd lost with each staggering step toward a cottage at the edge of town. What were they doing to her? Grotesque images flooded his mind, each angering him more than the last. He would make them rue the day they were born if they hurt a single hair on her head.

He needed to do something about his attacker-turned-ally. And heal his leg. And figure out where in the stars they'd taken Hallie in the first place.

Once inside the cottage, the man led him through to the kitchen. Kase leaned on the overturned table, watching him fiddle with the knothole in one of the floorboards.

"You're not sticking me in a hole. Already been there, done that."

"This ain't no hole, not really." His mountain accent was strong. It was difficult for Kase to understand some of the words, especially with his busted lip. "Got a shorter tunnel through one of the older mines, but no sense risking our lives making it that far."

He pulled on the knothole, and a trapdoor sprung open. The darkness below reflected Kase's mood. The man continued, "Before I take you further, I'm gonna need to know exactly who you are. I know you're not a Cerl, but if you mean us harm, you won't make it outta here alive."

Except you just told me how to get to your base. Real smart, mountain man.

Kase spoke through his teeth, "You nearly killed me earlier."

"I'd say you plum near knocked all my teeth out banging my face against that wall, but I guess I can't blame you for it." The man fingered his swollen lip.

Kase grimaced. He knew how that felt. "You first."

"Fine, if it'll make you feel better." He held out his hand. "Name's Niels Metzinger. Grew up here in Stoneset."

Niels? Surely, it isn't...

Kase hesitated slightly, but he clasped the man's hand and gave it a firm shake. "Kase Carrington. From Kyvena."

Like moons he'd use his real last name. There was no telling what this Niels would do if he found out who he truly was. Who his father was. He'd use him as leverage or something with the Cerls. Kase would have if it meant getting Hallie back.

"Nice alliteration. Your parents must be poets."

And that was the most terrible joke I've ever heard. This can't be Hallie's...old sweetheart. She wouldn't have stood for that.

"My mother." Kase gave what he hoped was a trusting smile. "Her nose is always in a book, so I was doomed from the beginning."

Niels' laugh was short and more like a wheeze. "Sounds like an old friend of mine. Now, Kase Carrington, how about we get that leg of yours fixed up? Stowe might not have been trained at the fancy University or anything, but he does work wonders. He's been helping the town medic out for years, and good thing since Graham died in the attack, may his soul rest among the stars."

With Niels' help, Kase climbed into the hole. The blond followed and shut the trapdoor behind him. After a minute of scuffles, Niels lit a gas lantern, the light melting away a portion of the bitter darkness. Arm around the taller man's shoulders, Kase limped along the dank passageway. It wasn't cramped, but the roots and other dirt clumps hanging from the ceiling made it feel that way. It also reminded him of Eravin's meeting chamber.

Blasted man. Blasted everything. If none of that had happened, Hallie wouldn't be a Cerl captive now.

"So, did Kyvena send you to investigate or something?"

Kase winced as he accidentally hit his ankle on the side of the tunnel. "The person I was with, the one they took, she needed a ride here. But our hover broke down in the Pass."

A slight lie. It wasn't worth going through the entire explanation with what Hallie did in Nar nor what had happened to Yarrow in the Pass.

"And you still made it here on foot?"

Kase placed a hand against the dirt wall to steady himself. The weight of Hallie's satchel was throwing him off slightly. "Barely."

Niels' whistle echoed slightly in the darkness. "Then what in the moons did you come out here for?"

Kase was silent. Even if he did say he was from Stoneset, trusting this Niels with Hallie's secret was another thing entirely. Simply thinking of her made his calf throb even more. A lump formed in his throat.

The man didn't push him further on the topic, and they walked the tunnel in silence with only the occasional worm to hear their shuffling footsteps. After roughly an hour of walking by Kase's estimation, they finally arrived at a rotting wooden door.

Niels made sure Kase had a good grip on the wall before he ducked out from under his arm. He beat a series of knocks on the door before grabbing the handle and turning back to Kase. "Welcome to Stoneset. It's not as pretty as the town we left, but we make do."

The cavern was enormous. Patched and worn tents and what appeared to be Stoneset's entire population filled the space. Gas lanterns glowed overhead, brighter than Kase expected after the dark tunnel. Niels led him through the strange forest of stalactites and stalagmites, casting unusual shadows on the inhabitants.

An elderly woman with unbound curly hair washed laundry in a small basin to his left. A man a few years older than

Kase heaved a crate of measly looking potatoes onto a ramshackle table. A trio of children with mud-streaked faces nearly bowled Kase over. Niels saved him with a tight grasp on his arm and firmly chastised them, but the discipline was followed by a grin and ruffling of one boy's dust-ridden hair. The boy obviously admired Niels by the way his own smile streaked across his face.

Soon, they came to a place where moonlight streamed in through a large opening in the cave. A few people sat around a fire, talking and eating. One woman knitted and gossiped with another. The view beyond caught Kase's attention and nearly made him forget his aching leg.

What he saw distantly reminded him of Myrrai. The mountains reached so high, their peaks were lost in the clouds, but the lower peaks and steep inclines created a barrier to the right and above him. To his left, he looked out onto a valley of evergreen trees and rolling hills. The full moon hung above them all.

In the distance, maybe a few miles out, there were ruins. Cottages stood in disrepair, roofs caved in, entire structures in piles of rubble.

"And that's why we have these caverns," Niels said. He pointed to the ruins. "Cerls destroyed Ravenhelm nearly fifty years ago."

Kase blinked. That name sounded familiar, but he couldn't quite place where he'd heard it. Maybe a book? Or maybe he'd heard about the attack in school?

"Massacred nearly everyone there. All I know is some kids survived because they hid in the mines. And legend says one boy took out the Cerl commander with a well-placed crossbow shot. I dunno if I believe that."

Kase stared hard at the ruins. Something about that tickled the back of his mind. He *must* have studied it in school. It would have been required in Jaydian history classes. "Beautiful view, though."

"True. Ruins or not, this is one of the best views in Stoneset," Niels said, tugging on his arm. "Maybe if the blasted Cerls leave, I can show you the other from one of the old mine entrances. That one will take your breath away."

Kase shook his head. "I don't think I believe you." His leg

gave a rather painful throb, and he winced. "You said something about a medic?"

"Stowe's over this way."

Niels led Kase away from the opening. Kase hobbled along, still held up by the stronger man. Shocks, this was frustrating. If his leg hadn't given out, maybe he would've been able to...been able to stop those men. He felt so useless.

After passing another firepit with an equally beautiful view, Niels stopped. A bald man, who looked to be in his mid-fifties based on the amount of gray in his russet goatee, ground herbs at a makeshift table of salvaged wood sitting on ale barrels. He was about as tall as Kase, but he had a little pudge around the waist. The man grinned at the two of them and set aside the pestle he'd been using.

"You find another stray, Niels?" The man's voice would've been perfect for a storyteller with its deep tones. That is if his accent hadn't been so blasted thick. "Gracious day. What happened to that lip?"

Niels fingered the offending wound. "I'll survive."

The older man shook his head. "Well, take this poultice, will you?" He grabbed a small packet from several piled up in the corner of his table. "It'll help with the pain."

"I'm fine, really." Niels didn't take the poultice but helped Kase sit on a craggy stone outside the man's tent. The canvas had been patched in a few places. "This is Kase Carrington from Kyvena, but I'm not sure if he's a stray yet. Doesn't like to talk much."

Kase pointed to Niels. "He said you could fix my leg?"

"I'll leave you to it, Stowe." Niels nodded. "I've gotta take my report to Guy."

"And that lip? You'll see me if it gets worse?" Stowe asked.

"I'll be *fine.*"

The man shook his head and chuckled. "Stubborn."

Niels left with a soft, lopsided grin. Stowe wiped his hands on his apron. His eyes were a golden-brown and spoke of something deeper, something sadder, something Kase felt like he knew all too well. The man fetched an old apple crate and took a seat. Kase paused, and his heart hammered in his chest. Those eyes.

Like honey on toast.

"Looks like you busted it something fierce judging by the state of your trousers." The man grinned again as he sat before Kase. A wave of shock mixed with adrenaline hit him. He *knew* that smile. "If you take off your boot and roll up the pant leg, I'll take a look. Care to tell me how you hurt it? And your neck? That don't look too pleasant neither."

Kase blinked. He had to be related to Hallie. Her father? After a second of staring too long, Kase undid the laces of his boot and slid it off with a grimace. "Got hit by one of those Cerulene weapons. Patrol ambushed me. Lucky it was just my leg. It was feeling better until I tried to run, and then...well..." No use in explaining *every* detail. Kase rolled up his trouser leg. The old sock stuck to his skin. He held back a wince as he removed it. "The neck was a...misunderstanding."

"Neck's an easy fix. Made some salve this morning for cuts. Keeps out the rot." Stowe's fingers were cold on Kase's bare skin. The wound was an angry red, but no streaks fanned from it. Yet. "Those blasted Cerls. You're lucky. This'll need some salve, too."

"I wouldn't call myself lucky."

The man snorted. "What brings you out here? Didn't think anyone cared about us border folk."

"You're Hallie's father, aren't you?" The question spilled out before he could stop it.

The man's head shot up, his golden gaze meeting Kase's. "You know my girl?"

Kase swallowed. Should he tell the man his daughter was missing? That she'd been kidnapped only an hour or two before? No. Not yet. Not before he fixed Kase's leg—because if he was one of those over-protective types, he might break it instead. Kase might've if he'd been in Hallie's father's place. "Yeah, I...we're...acquaintances."

The man shook his head, a warm smile ghosting across his features. "She's not someone you could easily forget, even if you met her in passing. I swear she got that tongue from her mama." Stowe cleared his throat. "How's she doing? Haven't heard from her in a while, but with everything going on, it's to be expected."

"She's...worried. She sent letters."

He snorted. "You sure we're talking about Hallie Walker?

Only received three letters since she left us for Kyvena." He pressed the outside of Kase's wound again, causing him to wince. He nodded. "Should be okay to walk on it in a day or two, long as the salve works its magic. Bless the rocky moons it isn't deep."

Would Hallie make it two days? Could he afford to wait that long? "Thank you."

The man stood and fetched a small pot from his tent. "Slather on a thin layer three times a day. And make sure you don't get any dirt in that wound. Like I said, you're quite lucky, son." Stowe held out the pot.

Kase took it and set it aside before looking up. "After we heard about the Cerls attacking Achilles, Hallie didn't know what to believe when you didn't send letters back."

"Blasted Cerls probably intercepted the messengers."

Kase should tell him about Hallie. It was the honorable thing to do. Except the words wouldn't form as Stowe spread a thin layer of the clear goop onto Kase's leg. The pain lessened slightly. Some of the tension bled out of Kase's shoulders, but he couldn't fully relax. There was something awry here. Stowe didn't mention the telegram at all.

Stowe stuck out a hand and helped Kase to his feet. "Let's get you well, and then maybe we can have you help us out here. No one but you has been able to get through the Pass. Anyone else we've sent hasn't returned...including my wife."

"What?" Kase hobbled along with his help to the nearest fire pit. "You've sent word to Kyvena?"

"My wife is as hard-headed as my daughter and said she could make it through the cave network and get to Kyvena herself. We don't trust that blasted new tele...tele...whatever technology after the attack. 'Course, I would've gone with her except I'm the only thing closest to a medic Stoneset's got. A stars-blasted Cerl killed our other one..." He trailed off, probably because he noticed Kase's wide-eyed stare. "What is it?"

Kase shook his head. Everything was coming together in his head, though he still didn't quite know *how*. He fell gracelessly onto a log set up by the firepit, barely saving his leg from hitting the cave floor. "Kyvena knows nothing. Everyone believes Achilles took care of the problem."

Stowe's eyes narrowed. "What do you mean?"

"I'm a...hover pilot." Stowe may have been Hallie's father, but trusting him with who Kase really was... "I know things...and we've heard nothing about this."

"I need to go talk to the others." Stowe ran a hand down his face. "Try not to move too much."

With that, he was off, and Kase was left feeling more lost than he had in quite a while.

KASE APPRECIATED THE WARMTH OF the fire against his chilled bones. The salve had relieved much of his pain, yet the skin was still puffed up. Thankfully, it hadn't turned weird colors, which would have spelled disaster. And that would've been worse for Hallie.

"Now that we have you all patched up for the moment, and a hot meal is on its way and you'll be staying in my extra tent, care to share why you and your friend were in Stoneset?" a voice asked from behind him.

Kase tore his gaze away from the flames before him to look at Niels. He must have put something on his lip in the last hour or two, because the swelling had faded. The only evidence Kase had slammed his face into a wall was a small cut to the right of his mouth. Kase put a hand to his neck and felt the crust of dried blood. It'd stopped aching, at least.

He looked back at the fire. "First, tell me why communications aren't working. We've received word in Kyvena that all is well, and everything is encoded correctly."

"That's because the Cerls planned for this. Don't know for how long, but they did." Niels' laugh was sardonic. He found a seat on a log on the other side of the fire. "Our guess is some of the soldiers at the Fort turned traitor. Not nearly enough troops arrived to help our small contingent stationed in Stoneset. Said the Fort was overrun, but without Kyvena's help, we were doomed. The Cerls know their ground troops are no match for our hovers, so they had to think of something. My guess is they're planning something big. Bigger than taking land away from Jayde."

"Yeah, they want Zuprium." *And to do something with*

whatever that Gate thing is in Myrrai.

Niels' faint eyebrows disappeared into the blond bangs hanging over his forehead. "Zuprium? I haven't seen anyone near the mines on my scouting trips."

Kase shifted, moving his leg further from the fire. The heat wouldn't help with the swelling. "I know they want it. It's why they attacked in the first place."

That was Jove's theory, at least; but now, Kase didn't know. There had to be more.

"But don't they have their own mines? Have they run out?"

"Don't know." Kase shrugged. "All I know is that Jayde was worried about the mines being compromised, and they've been in talks with the Yalvs..."

Kase shut his mouth. Because he remembered Ebba and Zeke. Even Skibs. They'd died to prevent this from happening. And now, Hallie might as well join their number. He clenched his jaw against the emotion threatening to spill.

"What do they want it for? Hovers?"

Kase shrugged. "Probably."

Niels played with a small stick, breaking it into pieces and tossing each into the fire. A small spark erupted with each one. "I see. Then why kidnap citizens? Why not kill us or march on to the capital? And what did you mean, *talks with the Yalvs*? I thought they were all dead or something."

Kase shook his head and adjusted his leg again, moonlight and firelight warring on the wound, making it look even more ghastly. It wasn't bleeding, but a mix of fresh congealed blood, salve, and day-old scabs made Kase's stomach turn. He looked out at the night sky, avoiding Niels' gaze. "I'm not allowed to say more, but Hallie and I were working with one of the Yalvs, well, until we came out here."

"Did you say...*Hallie?*"

Kase looked over to the man's wild eyes and cringed. *Blast.* "She's from Stoneset, you probably know her."

"Hallie...Hallie Walker?"

"Yes."

Niels dropped the last of his stick. "You said *we* came out here?"

"Yes." Kase stared at the ground, trying to keep his frustration and temper at bay.

"And the Cerls...they had someone...oh, stars. Oh, *stars*. Those blasted *helviters* kidnapped *Hallie?*"

"Yes." Kase could barely get the word out. Shame nearly drowned him. It was his fault. He should've been right there with her. He should've saved her. Now everyone, including Hallie's father, would hate him, punish him for his failure.

A strangled sound came from Niels' direction. Kase looked up. All the blood had drained from the man's face, leaving it whiter than the mountain snowcaps. "We were...we were good friends. Her brother and I, too, but I haven't...I haven't seen her since she left. For Kyvena."

Kase didn't know what to say. Jealousy once again reared its ugly head, and his jaw ached from clenching it. "She received a telegram from her parents and wanted to make sure they were okay, but now..."

Kase swallowed hard. Niels spoke up, "Zelda, Hallie's Ma, went to Kyvena herself, but no one sent a telegram."

Kase could hear his own heartbeat. It thumped in his ears, his fingers, his toes. It pumped blood throughout his body, yet he couldn't feel anything other than the thumping. It was like he'd been enveloped in cotton and stuffed in a barrel.

He and Hallie had come out here for nothing.

Then who had sent the telegram?

"That blasted General Correa took the townsfolk who hadn't made it to the mines in time. We've tried busting them out, but our last two attempts failed. Miserably. We can't spare any more men." Niels' words were choked. "And if he has Hallie..."

"They're holding them prisoner?" Kase asked, his voice growing strained. "Why not just kill them?"

"Hope."

Kase shook his head. Hallie was with them. Hallie was there now. Hallie could be dead. "Where were they taking them? Achilles?"

Niels nodded.

Kase's face drained of warmth. He dug his nails deep into his palms. "And do you know where they might be keeping prisoners if they haven't killed them?"

Another nod.

"Then let's plan. If we work together—"

Niels ran a hand across his face. "But the last two missions..." he paused at Kase's intense stare. He took a deep breath and looked back toward where the group of men, including Hallie's father, were still in deep discussion. "I don't know if I can convince the others. No matter if it is Hal."

Kase didn't miss the casual use of the nickname. Something in his stomach hardened. Stupid, considering where he and Hallie were at present. He closed his eyes for a second and took a few calming breaths. Thinking with his head would be the way he got her out. He could do this. In fact, he already had the seed of an idea. An incredibly stupid idea, but sometimes the craziest ones worked best.

He tried to make his voice as calm as he could. "We have to try, with or without their help. I will not leave her there to...to..." He coughed into his hand, hoping Niels didn't hear the crack in his voice. He looked Niels in the eye. "Now, tell me. Where exactly in the fort would they be holding prisoners?"

Hallie

HALLIE'S HEAD POUNDED AND HER heart hammered in her chest as she blinked, her eyes opening to utter darkness. It was almost like the time she'd awoken after the crash on the *Eudora Jayde* after the monstrous storm. This time, however, her entire body ached like she'd been beaten to a pulp.

The last thing she remembered was entering the inn. Anything beyond that was a complete and total mystery. Where was Kase? He'd been waiting outside keeping watch. Had she fallen down the stairs or something? That would explain why she hurt so badly. She remembered how slippery those stairs were, especially when they were wet. Jack had taken a tumble down them when they were eight years old. Knocked out one of his teeth, too.

Was she in the attic? The kitchen? The slight chill of the air and the dripping echo made her feel as if she were in the cave with Kase, and for a moment she reveled in the memory of his warm back pressed up against hers. But there was no warmth here. Only pain.

She flung her hand out to grasp his, to make sure he was still there right beside her, but her fingers grasped at nothing, only slime-covered stone. "Kase?"

No one responded.

Hallie pushed herself up to her elbows, swiping at the hair falling into her face. Her braid had come loose.

"Where am I?" Her voice was like dry sawdust. She coughed.

Water. She needed water.

She twisted her head with a wince, taking in the environment. The other corner of the small room was awash with Firstmoon light trickling in through the barred window too far above her head. She sat on a torn and rotting strip of cloth, scratchy hay underneath.

Not trusting herself to stand on weak limbs, she crawled toward the door. Her loose trousers scraped a little against the stone floor, almost echoing in the stillness. The door itself wasn't much; just bars spaced wide enough to let a small animal through. She thought of the dungeons she'd read about in those old fairy tales about princesses, princes, and dragons.

How in the blazes had she gotten there? She shivered and pulled Kase's overly large shirt tightly around her. Something had happened to her jacket and cloak.

And where was Kase? Why was she in a prison cell? Her throat ached with thirst. Her stomach rumbled.

"Hello?" a whispered voice called out in the near darkness of the corridor. The only light to see by was what came through the door at the far end and the window in her cell. She couldn't see anything in front of her except a solid stone wall.

"Hello? Is anyone there?" the voice called again. Hallie clenched the bars. The metal was even colder than the cavern floor.

Her heart beat quickly as her hands slipped a little. "My name's Hallie Walker. Who are—"

An anguished sob cut her off. "*Hallie? Is that really you?*"

That voice. Hallie *knew* that voice. That voice had been her entire inspiration for going off to the University. Its owner had gifted her a copy of *The Odyssey* right before she'd gotten into that carriage nearly three years prior. "Mistress Jules?"

Hallie put a hand over her mouth. Her former school

mistress let out another cry, and the rattling bars echoed a little off the stone walls. The sound came from nearby, but Hallie couldn't quite pinpoint where.

"Oh, sweet girl." Her schoolmistress' voice cracked. "You're supposed to be in the capital."

Hallie shut her eyes and breathed in and out through her nose to calm her nerves. She didn't know where she was or why she was even there, but the thought that someone else was here with her made her want to cry. Whether out of pain or joy, she didn't know. "I needed to check on Mama and Papa. I got a telegram, but then we got to Stoneset, and the last thing I remember was going into the inn. We didn't see anyone in town, and—"

"That's because they're dead."

Hallie blinked. "But...the telegram."

The silence that followed weighed on her like a too-thick blanket.

Hallie's heartbeat sped up. "Tell me what's going on."

"We're at Achilles."

Hallie's stomach fell right out onto the floor. "What do you mean?"

"They killed my Blaine," Mistress Jules gasped. "Like so many of the other men who tried to resist. Achilles held out for only so long, but they were no match for the Cerl forces. We didn't know why we were being held here at first. Why they didn't just kill us."

"*We?*"

"It doesn't matter anymore. I'm the only one left in this part of the dungeon. Not sure about...about the others."

"Mistress Jules," Hallie whispered, "what about the...mountain cavern? Do you think anyone made it there? Are you sure Master Blaine isn't with them? And my parents?"

"I don't know, but I wouldn't hold out hope."

Hallie sat back, looking down at her hands. She could see them in the faint light. Her stomach roiled with emotions and her thoughts. If she hadn't been so stars-bent on coming out here, she'd be tucked safely away in her bed in Kyvena. Kase would still be—

Kase.

Her head shot up. "There was a—a man with me. He's tall

with stars-awful messy curls. Is he here? Did they bring him in with me?"

"You were the only one."

Tears welled up once more in Hallie's eyes at the scenes blossoming in her head. Kase dead on the mountainside, a sword stuck through his heart. Kase's body jerking as a Cerl bullet hit him again. Kase blue and freezing, frosted in ice.

He wouldn't have given up without a fight. He wouldn't allow himself to end in such a way. He's out there somewhere.

"I'm sorry, Hallie."

Hallie covered her face with her hands. "If he's not here with me, that means he's still out there. There's no way he'd die that easily. He'll come for me. I know it."

If she could only believe the words that tumbled from her shaking lips.

"Try to rest if you can. They'll want to...to talk with you tomorrow, I think." Mistress Jules' voice grew fainter, like it was floating away on a lazy breeze. "But prepare your heart for the worst. If the young man you speak of isn't here..."

She didn't finish her sentence.

But he can't leave me here. Not after everything we've survived together. That's not how this works.

But it didn't truly matter because she was here, and Kase might very well be dead. Her parents, too.

There was no one to comfort her as she cried herself to sleep.

CHAPTER 27

IN THE DAWN

Jove

JOVE ITCHED TO ADD SOME of his father's whiskey to his regular morning coffee, but a row with Clara wasn't worth it. She was already on edge with the lack of sleep and her mother not able to enter the capital. A camp had been set up for those awaiting entrance, whenever that would be. With the riots still raging in the lower city, he doubted anyone would be allowed inside any time soon—not until the verdict officially passed down from the High Council in two days' time.

Jove hadn't gone back to hear the rest of the trial, which had ended the day before.

The bitter liquid cascaded across Jove's tongue as he took a sip. Its bite woke him only a fraction. The servants had opened the drapes in the dining hall, allowing the sunlight of the new day to cascade in. It filled the room, evaporating the shadows and glittering off the sword hanging above the mantle. It had been in the Shackley family for eons, but it only reminded him of his father. Jove fingered the scar on his palm.

He set down his coffee with a quiet *thunk.* The newspaper watched him from the corner of his eye. Wary of what sordid trial details it might entail, he grasped the front page, its dusty-feeling paper crinkling as he did so. He flicked it open and took another sip of coffee. His father's military portrait winked at him in the corner of the second page. Jove's eyes scanned it. Harlan didn't smile. His mustache was still perfectly groomed. His medals and ribbons stood in straight lines across the right breast.

Then Jove noticed the headline.

Shackley Secrets: A Tale of Abuse, Adultery, and Artifice

He choked. The scalding liquid burned the back of his throat and stung his nose. He coughed violently.

"Lord Shackley, are you all right?" one of the servants asked from his station near the door.

Jove regained control of his lungs, setting his mug down and waving him off. "Fine."

Shackley Secrets: A Tale of Abuse, Adultery, and Artifice

With great power comes great responsibility. The words of the ancient First Earth author Stan Lee have come to Jaydians' minds these last few days. We put faith in our leaders to use their power for the good of all, yet many times, they fall abysmally short. Such is the case with the Stradat Lord Kapitan Harlan Shackley.

Rising to fame for his efforts during the Great War, Shackley could do no wrong. We even cheered when he executed his own brother-in-law in the name of patriotism. Ezekiel Fairchild, his wife's brother, sold state secrets to Cerulene. Harlan was the hero for standing up for what was right. He was brave. He put the country before his own pride.

But it was all a lie.

Sources close to the family say the ties within the Shackley clan are strained—especially considering the recent mysterious passing of Harlan's second son, Lieutenant Colonel Zeke Shackley. Whispers of infidelity and physical abuse have begun circulating throughout the populace.

Of course, we should have known that something was amiss when Ana Shackley, youngest and only daughter of Harlan and Celeste, ran away and was killed in the fire of 4497. Why would a seventeen-year-

*old girl with the world at her fingertips want to leave? What's more—
we now know his own son, Kase Shackley, started the fire to kill his
abusive father. But the obvious grief on the Shackleys' faces at the
Burning was enough to douse suspicions that anything untoward was
afoot.*

But Camelot was sure to fall, and along with it, King Arthur.

*The beginning of this story doesn't even start with the fire or the
Great War. No, as we can exclusively reveal here at the Daily Jaydian,
it began long before, in a village on the other side of the Nardens...*

The door to the dining room opened. Jove shoved the
newspaper under his leg as his mother entered. She wore the
same dressing gown from the fight nearly a week before. Her
curls were in a tangled braid. Dark circles graced the space
below her eyes. For once, she looked close to her age of fifty-
five.

Shuffling over to the table, she fell into the seat nearest
Jove and poured herself a steaming cup of tea. She simply
stared into the liquid, not caring to drink it. Jove shifted in his
seat, unsure of what to say. His father deserved what awaited
him. The verdict would be passed down. The city was crying for
blood. Hit pieces like the one he'd been reading would only
increase in number.

Jove took a sip of his coffee and blanched. Lukewarm. He
signaled for one of the footmen to bring him another. His
mother's voice was hoarse as she broke the silence: "What did
the paper say?"

Jove's ears burned, but he didn't retrieve the article.
"Nothing good."

"Of course." She picked up her tea only to set it back on the
saucer with a quiet clink. "Because there's no such thing as lack
of decorum when it comes to parading good peoples' names
through the mud."

"Mother..."

Fiddling with the handle, she twisted the cup in a
nonchalant manner. "Our private affairs shouldn't be fodder for
the papers."

"In our position, our lives have never been our own."

She set her face into her hands. "This wasn't how it was
supposed to end. It's not what we planned. Harlan always said

we'd retire to the countryside when...except...except..." Her shoulders shook. "All our hopes, our dreams...gone. Every time I finally find my feet, I'm knocked down once more."

Jove leaned forward, squeezing her forearm lightly. He didn't need to say anything. He understood.

He let his hand drop when the maid brought in his new coffee. He took a sip as his mother continued to cry. He didn't know what his father had promised her. He didn't care.

His mother sat up, drying her eyes with the cloth napkin. "I'm sorry. It's just that—everything has been difficult to digest. With Zeke, with Kase...Ana...my brother...and now with your father..."

They sat in silence. Jove drank his coffee even though he still wished it contained something to numb the myriad of thoughts running through his head. Quiet tears leaked from his mother's eyes as she played with the teacup before her.

Jove never liked to remember the time before Uncle Ezekiel's execution, for it only reminded him of the effervescent man who looked too much like Kase with his wayward curls and blue eyes. Remembering the man only brought back memories of playing cricket in the courtyard with his older cousins.

Would Jove's fate be the same? Would Samuel grow up without a father? The little coffee left in his cup quivered as Jove set it down once more. He couldn't swallow past the lump in his throat.

Soon, the door opened to the butler, Thoreau. He bowed to them both. "I apologize for interrupting your meal, but I have two guests waiting to see you, Lord Shackley."

Jove paused in taking his next sip. "Who?"

"The Head Guardswoman and the Yalven emissary."

Jove set his cup down. "Show them in, please."

With another short bow, Thoreau left the room. His mother stood, using the table for support. "I'll fetch something for Clara. She'll need a break soon." She left her untouched tea and headed for the kitchen.

Thoreau soon returned with Heddie. Jove rose from the table and invited her to sit. "Please help yourself."

"Lord Saldr said he'd wait outside until we finished, but he has to speak with both of us." Heddie poured herself a cup of tea. Jove laced his fingers around his coffee, leaning forward on his elbows. Heddie added a sugar cube and a dash of cream before taking a sip. She set it aside and fixed him with a stare. "I need you back."

Jove stared at the pristine white tablecloth before him. "All I'd be is an exhibit like the ones in the City Menagerie."

Heddie grabbed a muffin from the plate in front of her and bit off a chunk. Probably to keep herself from giving him a tongue lashing. She chewed it slowly, then swallowed. "They only care about your father. Besides, you have me to thank for saving your—" She coughed and took another bite of the muffin. "Listen, you've been through a lot, but there was a reason you were appointed High Guardsman."

Jove scoffed. "Except I quit after two months."

"I'm aware." She dug in her bag and pulled out a roll of parchment. She slid it across the table. The rough edge scratched Jove's knuckles. He didn't grab it, only shook his head.

"I can't, Heddie. I'm sorry."

"This is from Cerulene, the one you were working on the other day. I'd break it myself if the city wasn't about to blow. That is, if I had a partner."

He grabbed the parchment, tempted to crush it, but he set it aside. "Fine."

"Thank you." Heddie sipped her tea once more before pushing herself to her feet. "Send a missive when you've cracked it." She walked to the door and opened it. "We're ready for you, Lord Saldr."

He entered like a specter. His too-pale skin was a terrible contrast to his jet-black hair tied in a braid over his shoulder. Many of the other Yalvs in the city had begun dressing in typical Jaydian attire, but not Saldr. He still wore his long white robes with their embroidered hem. He'd added a cloak for warmth, but Jove didn't think it was adequate. As Saldr glided to the open seat Jove's mother had left, for a moment, the man seemed to flicker.

Jove blinked. *Stars, I'm tired.*

Saldr lowered himself into the seat, perching on the edge like a bird about to take flight. "Thank you both for seeing me."

Heddie finished off her muffin, dusting the crumbs off her

fingers. "What can we do for you, Lord Saldr?"

"Are we in a place where no one else can overhear?" Saldr looked around the room, noting the two footmen awaiting instructions near the door.

Jove narrowed his eyes, but he gestured for the servants to leave the room. They bowed and closed the door behind them. Jove leaned forward, his elbows on the table. "Is everything all right?"

The Yalv clasped his hands before him. Tightly. The man was trying to squeeze the life out of his fingers. Stars, was he about to confess?

"Have a muffin. The cinnamon ones are stars-fantastic." Heddie set one on her saucer and slid it over.

The man gave a small smile but didn't touch the pastry. He looked at Jove. "Miss Walker hasn't returned any of my urgent missives. None of my people in the lower city have been able to locate her."

Heddie took a sip of her tea. "I doubt she's in the thick of the riots. She doesn't live near the upper gate, and she's a good girl."

"It is not that." Saldr shook his head. "It is a matter of life and death that I find her, but with your help, maybe we can together."

The man's face was tight, his skin rather pale, like he was about to be sick.

Jove ran a hand through his short-cropped hair. An idea entered his mind. If he could find Miss Walker, she might be able to tell them where Kase had gone. They were certainly close if his brother had brought her to that estate dinner, not to mention how he hounded Jove to push her papers through.

"And why do you feel this is a matter of life and death?" Jove said, inspecting Saldr's face. "Like Head Guardswoman Koppen said, I doubt Miss Walker is in any real danger. Anyone who knows of her involvement with my family only believes her to be a passing fling my brother used to annoy my father. And those people are locked in the upper city with us."

Saldr's entire body flickered. Just for a fraction of a second.

Heddie gasped, dropping her teacup. The remaining liquid speckled her uniform and the white tablecloth. Jove stared, his mouth opening and closing. "What in the blazes—I thought I was seeing things—but you just—how did you do that?"

Both Hallie and Kase had assured the High Council the Yalvs had done nothing to breach the treaty. But that was the only explanation for what had happened.

Saldr didn't move. He breathed deeply and made eye contact with both him and Heddie before speaking. "I was sent here for two purposes. The first was to enter the alliance."

"Yet," Heddie said, dabbing her Watch uniform with a cloth napkin, "you expect us to trust you would hold to that? You just demonstrated you still have power...unless the Shackleys serve spiked tea for breakfast."

Saldr held up his hand. His long, spindly fingers were nearly double the length of his palm. His hand shook. "The second was for my people. My ancestors kept your treaty in the beginning, allowing the Essence wielders to die out, though one who possesses the power of our god may live centuries. However, Toro will not be manipulated by his creation. The Essence wielders who passed were reborn." He clasped his hands together once more. "Some Essence powers were reborn into our kindred in Myrrai, but others were not."

Heddie froze as she refilled her teacup. A bit overflowed, and she hastily dabbed it with a cloth before replacing the pot.

Cerulene had at least one Essence. That explained one part. Jove shifted in his chair; the repercussions of what the man was saying could be disastrous. If the Essences were truly unleashed onto the world with Cerulene in control of them, Jayde didn't stand a chance in all the stars of surviving this war. "Then why did you come here? Do you believe we have Essences?"

"My people have been searching for the remaining two for centuries. One came to our doorstep last autumn, fighting alongside the Cerls, who were already in possession of two due to the rebirth. The other...the other I have reason to believe is here in the city."

Neither Jove nor Heddie moved. They didn't even breathe. If what the Yalv was saying was true, Jayde truly was in terrible danger. Not only did the Cerls possess three Essences, but a rogue fourth was running around the capital. Heddie was first to regain her senses. "You said something about Miss Walker...you don't think she's a..."

Holy moons.

Saldr hesitated, but then shook his head. "As someone who is Called, I will not inherit an Essence power. I can wield Vasa…"

"Vasa?" Jove asked.

In response, Saldr took Les' forgotten teacup and dumped the contents onto the table. Before Jove could protest, the Yalv stuck his hand in a pouch hanging at his waist. Jove had figured it to be a money pouch, but alas, the man brought forth glittering bronze dust. He smeared it onto the growing tea stain, the dust and tea collecting on his fingers. He then pressed them to the spill, mumbling words under his breath in a singsong voice.

After a few seconds, the tea glowed. Another second and the stain had disappeared. One more, and the tea was back in the teacup.

Heddie again dropped her own drink. The fine porcelain slipped from her grip, spewing hot tea on her uniform and the tablecloth once more. This time, she didn't catch the cup. It fell and shattered onto the cold floor below.

Jove's chin dropped so hard, his jaw popped. "What?"

"A gift from Toro that allows us to manipulate time, though we are limited with its uses." Saldr tucked away his pouch. "However, the use of Vasa isn't my only purpose as Called. My other holy duty is to discover those who have the potential to be Chosen."

Heddie hadn't bothered to clean herself up this time. She leaned forward on the table. "Speak plainly, Lord Saldr, because you're not making a lick of sense."

"Chosen and Called are merely designations among my kind. Called are those who protect the Gate in various capacities. My late brother, Rodr, was gifted with the ability to track creatures who escaped the Gate during the Dawn, such as the dragonar. My specific gifts are as I described. Chosen are those who will take on the power of an Essence—that is, if the current wielder of the Essence doesn't die before they pass it on. Otherwise, the Essence power will be reborn into someone of Yalven blood. Again, this is what occurred with the Treaty."

Jove's head ached from lack of sleep and the words the man spewed. He'd seen what could only be described as magic. Yet… "So, Miss Walker…?"

Saldr nodded, the fear in his eyes palpable. "She may not

be aware of who she is, but—but she is of Yalven descent. Only someone such as I can hear the blood singing, and hers was a mighty chorus. I fear she will be found by the Essence wielder I seek, but she won't be ready to take the power, which could...which could mean death. If one fails in the transfer of power, I fear to think of the repercussions not only to Miss Walker, but to the world at large."

Jove pressed the heels of his hands into his eyes. The information was merely another stone to add to his ever-growing burden.

Heddie's voice was hesitant, "And the Essence? It manipulates time?"

"All Essence powers are facets of time. To go into the history would take a lifetime to explain, but in short, each Essence power is a sliver of our god, Toro, shattered in the Dawn—the beginning of time on Yalvara, during the legendary battle with Jagamot, the great evil of our lore. The Essence wielder I believe is here is one of the most powerful barring the Lord Elder, though with him potentially not surviving the attack on Myrrai..." His voice wobbled. "The reason I came to you both is because I trust you will do everything in your power to find Miss Walker."

"Still not a clue as to what you're talking about, but I get that it's dangerous." Jove's head spun, but he nodded. He would do what he could. "And the Essence wielder in Kyvena? You don't have a location?"

"I believe he or she is in the upper city, but I will continue to search." Saldr rose from the table, bowing to each of them. "You have my thanks. May the stars not fall when morning breaks."

And then he took his leave. All Jove and Heddie could do was stare after him as the door swung shut.

CHAPTER 2 8

THE ONLY TIME IT TRULY MATTERED

Hallie

HALLIE HAD ALWAYS WONDERED WHAT it would be like if she'd ever gone back home. She'd show up on her parents' doorstep with bags in tow, hoping for a bite of her father's best roasted lamb and her mother's mazelberry jam on toast. After taking her fill, she'd visit Mistress Jules and talk to her about all the books she'd read at University and how ancient cultures weren't too different from their own. After that, she'd visit the bakery, then the marketplace.

But the picture she'd blissfully painted was far from the reality she would've found even if the Cerls hadn't attacked. Because for all her bravado and assurances that it wasn't true, Hallie had run away. She'd fled from her problems, her life, her family. She knew that now.

Jack's death hadn't been Niels' fault. It'd been hers.

But now, *now*, she wouldn't ever get the chance to make it

right. Instead, she choked on the breakfast scraps guards left outside the dungeon cell bars. While the bread wasn't moldy, it certainly wasn't fresh, nor was it enough to feed the family of spindly-legged spiders who shared her cell. She'd discovered a small cistern of water that smelled slightly of algae over in the corner. Between the bread and water, Hallie didn't know if she had the strength or mental capacity to come up with an escape plan.

After the guards left, Mistress Jules explained in her disembodied voice, "They bring down bread in the morning, cheese for the midday meal, and jerky at night. Though if you please them, you're rewarded."

"Please them?" Hallie's stomach roiled.

"Whatever they ask you to do, do it. Keep fighting."

"I don't understand."

"They're looking for something."

"Looking for what?" Hallie picked at a pebble on the floor.

"The Yalvs, but all we know is that they disappeared."

Hallie hesitated. "But why?"

"Don't know. But for some reason, I'm still here."

Hallie's stomach clenched. "I thought you said they weren't trying to kill us. You said so last night."

"I also said I'm the only one left," she said in a whisper, and then went silent. The minutes passed like sap seeping out of a maple tree. "What else would they do with them?"

Hallie tried to keep her breathing even as she thought about what all the soldiers would do to them if they knew who Hallie was. The stories of the monstrosities she'd heard about the Cerls replayed in her mind, as well as the time Kase and Ben had met one in the forest. She remembered the sheared-off faces in the mountain temple chambers.

There would be more nightmares when she fell asleep.

Before Hallie could voice her thoughts and fears, the door opened once more. This time, the soldiers tramping down the stairs smiled at her like she was a prized horse at the fair. Hallie's fingernails bit into her palms.

The one in front, a man with a short nose and the tell-tale diamond tattoo on his neck, grinned as he stopped in front of her cell, the bars obscuring part of his face. "I apologize for the way you were brought in. The men have been punished accordingly, but they await further pain if they've hurt you in any way."

Hallie didn't like the way his eyes glittered with emotion, but it was difficult to tell whether it boded her well or ill. She didn't move; she couldn't move. Her body was still incredibly stiff and didn't want to budge from its position on the cold stone floor, but that didn't matter. The man gestured to one of his companions, who unlocked the door and promptly lifted her from the floor with careful hands, as if she were the hand-me-down fine china her mother kept in the cupboard for special occasions. His delicate handling was at odds with his frown and the firm planes of his face.

Mistress Jules didn't say anything as the man carried Hallie in his muscled arms up the steps and into the corridor above. The first man strode beside them, a scowl marring his otherwise handsome features. His eyes were black, though they sparkled in their depths, overshadowed by his furrowed brow.

These people had kidnapped her, but now they were treating her as if she were a doll to be set upon a shelf. It was a strange turn of events, and she didn't trust it.

"What's going on? Why am I here?" She might as well try and get some answers from them while she could.

Neither spoke for a moment. Finally, their leader's gruff voice echoed off the stone walls. "General Correa will decide what happens to you."

She didn't know much about him, but something about the way the man said the name made her involuntarily shiver. All she knew was that Correa controlled most of Cerulene's armed forces, but she'd only learned that through gossip in the few months she'd been back in Kyvena. Why did someone so important want to deal with a simple girl like herself?

Unless he knew she was Yalven.

She chewed on the inside of her cheek.

The rest of the way was spent in silence. She ran through the options in her head. Could she somehow get out of the situation? Fighting these men wasn't viable. Even if her strength were at its height, it wouldn't be a match for the biceps carrying her as if she weighed no more than a roll of parchment.

Could she trick them? Pretend to pass out? Roll out of the man's arms? She might outrun them, but she didn't know what the situation was elsewhere. Did guards patrol the corridors? Yes, a pair appeared from around a corner and passed by with a subtle whiff of sweat and smoke. Even then, could she make it to the main road without being spotted or running into anyone else? Possibly. But she'd never visited the fort before, so the layout was a mystery to her. She would have to wait until she had a better sense of the corridors. Maybe Mistress Jules knew something, and they could make it out alive. Maybe.

Her heartbeat was painful in her chest as she plotted, but each idea was more ridiculous or dangerous than the last. And there was no way she could do this on her own. Especially if they didn't feed her properly. She'd be helpless within a week.

Before she was ready, the men stopped in front of a plain oak door. The leader knocked on it, and the door opened from within. The brute set Hallie down and gestured her further into the room.

The door slammed behind her. She spun, but the guards had left her alone. She turned back to the room itself.

It must've been the office of a high official before the Cerls had taken over. The bookshelves lining the far walls overflowed with various tomes; several had pages sticking out the tops. The desk in the middle took up most of the space. A sprawling map covered it, the edges of the worn parchment curling slightly. Hallie thought it was of Jayde, but someone had placed blue markers in various places across the surface. She tilted her head, curious to see what they meant. Before she could take three steps forward, another door to the right opened and snapped shut. Hallie jumped back.

The man who entered was abnormally tall like the Yalvs, though his skin wasn't nearly as pale. His smile told Hallie he was expecting her. His eyes were a light brown, like the softest loam in the fields where the Metzingers' crops grew. Or used to grow. The Metzingers were probably all dead.

"Welcome to Achilles, frontier of the Cerulene Empire."

Hallie gritted her teeth. She wouldn't give this man the satisfaction of an answer if she could help it.

The man strode toward her with the elegance of a mountain lion planning on his next meal. A single earring graced his right ear. It was merely a stud, but it looked like Zuprium. He stopped short of where she stood, arms spread before him. "Ah, aren't we a quiet one now? I hope you saw how well we're treating you. I ordered those men not to harm you. Most guests aren't treated so lightly."

"*Guests?*" Hallie gasped incredulously. "Guests are invited, not kidnapped!"

So much for keeping quiet.

The man shrugged, crossing his arms over his handsome military jacket. It was the deep blue of the night sky before the sun disappeared. Several accolades spilled across it in the form of medals and pins. "Kidnapped...invited against your will? Does the difference matter?"

Hallie's blood boiled underneath her skin. "You invaded my country and killed my friends, yet you expect me to have this conversation as if we were discussing lace patterns? I want to know why I'm here."

The man rubbed his smooth chin and considered her for a moment before speaking again, revealing too-straight teeth. "Let's start over, shall we? My name is General Correa of Sol Adrid. May I ask whom I have the pleasure of speaking with?"

Hallie's nostrils flared. She couldn't figure out what his ploy was. Why hadn't he beaten her like kidnappers did in stories? Not that she minded being left alone and relatively unharmed, but she couldn't make sense of the man's calm demeanor. He appeared to be in his early thirties and reminded her strongly of Jove Shackley with the earnest stare.

Maybe if she played along, she'd figure some way out of this debacle. "My name is Hallie."

General Correa grinned, his teeth catching in the soft sunlight streaming in through the window. He met her eyes. Hallie suppressed a shiver.

"A pleasure to meet you, Hallie. Do you have a surname as well?"

Hallie didn't blink. "Hilly. My name is Hallie Hilly."

His eyebrows rose nearly to his widow's peak hairline. "Hilly, you say? Intriguing. Now, Miss *Hilly*, we are pleased you have joined us. I will call the guards back to escort you to the bath and have you put on clean clothes shortly, but before I do, allow me to give you a little bit of advice."

Hallie swallowed as he leaned forward, invading her space, but she refused to back away. She would not show fear.

His breath rustled the bit of hair beside her ear as he whispered, "I would suggest you refrain from lying in the future. It's better for the both of us, wouldn't you agree?"

She bit her lip to keep herself from flinching at his words. He stepped back and held out his hand to shake. Instead, she simply stared at it, confused by the gesture.

"Let's try once more. What is your surname?"

She shook her head. "I told you, it's Hilly."

He grasped her wrist, and a shock rent up her arm like lightning. She screamed at the white-hot energy lancing through his fingers. She screamed so loudly she didn't think she'd ever use her voice again, but when he removed his hand, the pain left as suddenly as it had come. Her knees gave way, and she fell to the floor, sobs fumbling on her trembling lips, tears spilling down her dirty cheeks.

"Let's try it once more. What is your surname?"

Hallie's only reply was to whimper. Her entire body throbbed. She'd never been struck by lightning before, but she knew how it felt at that moment. Her breaths came out in sobs as she tried to calm herself. Her fingers felt like they'd taken a pot off the stove without a mitten.

The man sighed. "Hopefully you now understand that when I ask a question, I expect the truthful answer. It's the only way you'll make something of yourself here. Now, tell me. What is your surname?"

Hallie's gasps were heavy still, but she choked out, "W-Walker. My name is Hallie Walker."

The tears still burned on her face, but the pain in her fingers had dulled slightly. She focused on getting her breathing under control. She was weak. She'd given in so easily at the first sign of pain. Shame filled her chest and crawled up her neck.

"See? Now was that so difficult? Worth all that trouble? Of course not." His too-shiny boots came into view, but she didn't look up. "You're wondering how I knew you'd told a falsehood? It's simple, really. *Quite* simple. It's not that you gave anything away with your demeanor. No, you looked me straight in the eye while the lie rolled off your tongue. You didn't fidget. Your voice didn't catch or stutter over the syllables. You're better at the skill than many of your fellow Jaydians, the sorry lot."

He squatted in front of her. His fingers found her chin, and she flinched, but the pain didn't come. Instead, he lifted her head until she met his eyes. Their light brown color no longer reminded her of crop fields. Instead, all she saw was pain and lightning and more pain. Her jaw quivered as he smiled. "No, I knew because you *are* our guest. I did indeed invite you here."

Taking his hand from her chin, he reached into the inner pocket of his stiff jacket and pulled out a folded parchment. The edge was slightly worn, but Hallie's stomach plummeted when she caught sight of the writing across the front. Messy and cramped, the Es too loopy. Her writing.

Stowe and Zelda Walker

Walker's Rest Inn, Stoneset

No. How had this man, this General Correa—

No, this can't be happening.

Hallie's mouth gaped, but she shut it quickly as fear colder than the snow she'd journeyed through the past week filled her from her head to her toes. If he had those letters...

She snatched them from his hand and clutched them to her chest. "Where did you get these?"

Her voice came out as a choked whisper; any defiance or courage she might have faked earlier had evaporated at the sight of her letters. Had her parents even received them? Or had he stolen them. And...and...

Stoneset was empty. The inn had been empty. And then she'd woken up in the dungeon.

Correa stood, and his boots disappeared behind the desk with the map spread atop it. His voice betrayed his glee even if he tried to hide it. "That one was from the hands of a traitor. Of course, my man attacked him without realizing what a gift he'd stumbled upon."

Hallie stayed silent, only tightening her grip on the parchment in her grasp. Yarrow's brother. He'd been killed by Cerls.

Tapping a pencil on the desk, Correa continued, "After that, all it took was a simple telegram, and you came right to me. It was a risk, yes, but I liked my chances."

Tears burned the corners of Hallie's eyes. Her throat constricted, silencing anything she might say, though all that echoed in her head were the man's cruel words. Her parents had never received her letters. Was her father alive? Her mother? All the telegram had said was that she needed to come home. It hadn't bothered Hallie that the missive was short. Sending something like that took money that her parents couldn't afford to lose, but now that she knew this...

Correa's boots came back into view. "This has been a lovely chat, and as a reward for telling me the truth at last, I will allow your gracious guards to escort you to the bathing chamber where a maid will look after you."

"My parents, where...where are they?" she gasped, trying to keep her panic at bay—and failing.

He squatted down to her level once more, yet she still refused to look him in the eye. The blinding memory of the pain was nearly too much with him so close, followed shortly by the knowledge that her parents were probably dead, killed by the man crouching in front of her. She wanted to curl up in a ball right there and pretend this was all some terrible, terrible dream she was having while freezing to death under an avalanche of snow.

Maybe it was a hallucination after all. She'd wake up from this nightmare, and Kase would be sound asleep beside her.

Please, for all that is good and holy and...and...stars, please let me wake up.

General Correa's breath was warm as he leaned forward to whisper in her ear again, his words falling like stones. "I will see you again soon, *Miss Walker.*"

She recoiled at the hands towing her off the floor, and she slumped against them, her letter fluttering to the floor. As the guards from earlier carried her out, she turned once, catching sight of General Correa's wolfish grin.

Kase

RECOVERY TO THE POINT OF doing more than simply limping to Stowe's to fetch more salve took Kase nearly two days. He'd never felt so helpless. Sure, he'd broken his arm once, and had been relegated to staying inside all day every day for weeks, but that'd been years ago when he and Ana had slid down the banister at Grieg's Theater. And at the time, Hallie hadn't been in the hands of the Cerls.

However, he and Niels made use of the healing time. Turned out the man wasn't so terrible when he didn't have a knife at Kase's throat. While he'd grown up in a backwater town raising crops and sheep, he'd found a way to read the classics. That shouldn't have surprised Kase so much, as Hallie had come from Stoneset as well, but it did. Niels had also been on scouting missions to Fort Achilles to see if he could figure out a weakness. He had yet to find anything helpful.

Kase, on the other hand, was the son of the Stradat Lord Kapitan. That had to count for something. If anyone could figure out how to break into the fort, it should be him. Not that Niels knew who he truly was.

"There's but two gates in the walls," Niels said, pointing at the small diagram he'd drawn in the dirt before the fire. "This one is used for supplies only. If we're gonna find a way in, it will be through there."

"But how heavily is it guarded? If they're smart, they won't let anyone in they don't recognize or who doesn't have proper identification."

Niels rubbed the blond stubble along his slender jaw. "True, but the main gate is out of the question. It's manned night and day with soldiers with those blue fire pistols and cannon things. Those are the only ones that are visible, too."

Kase tapped his fingers on his bent knee, his injured leg stretched out before him as he sat up against the log supporting his back. "If the back gate is only manned by a few men, I can take them, but it would also help if we had some sort of distraction. I don't know what yet, but something to keep them on their toes. The problem is getting around to that gate. We'd have no cover."

"Right," Niels said, drawing another line from the triangles he'd used to indicate the tree line. "If we were to go up into the Pass and circle around, we might be able to make it work. Except we risk of running into patrols that way."

"Yeah, like we did."

"Your leg?"

Kase nodded. He thought hard. How could they make this work? Niels vaguely knew where they might be keeping prisoners, but he couldn't be certain. Only a handful of men who'd survived the initial attack hid in the mountain cavern, none of whom knew the full layout of the structure. Anyone who had known was dead.

They needed more information. It wouldn't do well to use all their tricks getting inside only to be captured once they did. Kase ground his teeth. "Our only option might be a Trojan Horse."

He thought it would be, but he'd hoped for a miracle. No such luck.

Niels looked up, his stick scratching a line through his sketch of the wall. "How'd you figure that?"

Kase swallowed. "It's something they won't be expecting."

"But we already decided disguising ourselves wouldn't work."

Kase pushed himself heavily to his feet. The stiffness in his leg was nearly gone. He walked to the edge of the cave lip and crossed his arms. The sun set on the horizon, its golden rays highlighting the clouds above it. The ruins of Ravenhelm watched him from where he stood.

He knew exactly what could get him inside the fort. It would be a gamble, but getting out when the time was right was the missing piece.

"You mentioned something the other day about explosives. How many could you get your hands on?" Kase said, still facing away.

"We'd have to filch them from Stoneset, but it could be done. Some flash bombs. Even then, it won't be enough to bring down the wall. And don't forget those blasted cannon guns."

Kase shook his head and turned slightly. "No, that's not what I meant. We need enough to cause a panic. Somehow, we need to plant them in certain areas and have them go off at specific times. That way, it causes confusion. Yes, a few of them would need to be lobbed at the gates. Both of them, because I don't know which one I'll be able to make it to with Hallie in tow."

"With Hallie..." Niels' words were mumbled. "What do you mean? If we're outside..."

Kase turned away from the sunset, the fire warming his face. "I told you we needed a Trojan Horse."

"I don't think I'd call the bombs that."

Kase shook his head. "Let them capture me first. That way, I could figure out where Hallie and any others are being kept. Your knowledge is only a guess."

Though I don't plan on getting the others out if it costs me Hallie.

Niels shook his head, his blond hair flopping back and forth. "I can't let you do that in good conscience. Especially with your leg. Besides, they might decide to string you up along the outside of the wall. They did that...with, um...with one of the commanders."

Kase closed his eyes against the roiling in his stomach. It was a very real possibility, but for the first time in his life, he was thankful for who he was. It might be the only time it truly mattered. "I doubt they will...at first."

Niels threw his stick into the fire, the sparks leaping into the air. "You'd risk it? You don't know them like we do, what blasted horrors they commit."

"I know *exactly* what they're capable of, and I also know what they want. Partly. I'm the only one who could go in there and come out alive."

"I don't understand."

Kase rubbed a hand through his curls. He wished Hallie was there to talk him out of his harebrained plan that might very well end up being his demise. Not that it mattered. He was never going to see his mother and Jove again anyway. Hallie was the only...she was the only...well, he didn't know what she was. Not quite. But it was up to him to do something about saving her; the remnant of Stoneset had wasted months because they didn't have the ace up their sleeve. Kase did.

"Trust me. Now, let's figure out the rest of it. I'd say give me two days inside. They'll probably...well, I'll probably be indisposed for some of it," Kase said through a lump in his throat. "But after that, I'm sure I'll be able to figure out something. I'll get them out through one of the gates as long as you've done your job on the outside. Go back up the Pass and around. You'll have to recruit a few helpers as well. Anyone with impeccable aim."

I'm coming, Hallie. I promise, I'll get you home.

CHAPTER 29

NOT GOOD ENOUGH

Hallie

THREE DAYS AFTER HER ARRIVAL at Achilles, Hallie still sat in the dungeon healing from the brief exchange with Correa. The only good to come out of it was that they'd supplied her with clean clothes—new trousers and an overlarge tunic shirt belted at the waist. She felt positively medieval in it, but she didn't mind. If she closed her eyes, she might be one of the dashing heroes of old instead of a prisoner in a too-large tunic. However, these clothes were clean, as was her hair and skin. Her stomach was full of a small meal sans mold.

But none of that helped keep her mind off the fact Kase and her parents were dead and rotting on the mountainside somewhere. For three nights she cried herself to sleep, vowing to survive, to work even harder, to find a way out. No amount of imagination or positive thinking would chase away the tears.

She'd almost come up with a way to escape. Each day, she was taken to a bathing room where a maid waited. She then received a small but fresh breakfast of fruit and toast. She hadn't seen Correa since his office, yet she indeed felt like a guest—just one kept locked in a dungeon cell.

Tracking their progress through the corridors each day, Hallie memorized the pattern of turns and guard rotations. She took note of the doors and approximate locations of windows. She'd even befriended her guards. The handsome, dark-eyed leader was named Caesar, and the man with the muscles, Ajax. Hallie told them she loved their names, as they were redolent of ancient Greece and Rome.

Since Cerls were descendants of those who'd fled another First Earth-like planet centuries before Hallie's ancestors arrived, they didn't understand the reference, but they no longer scowled at her. It was progress. She hoped they wouldn't suffer too much when she eventually escaped.

On the fourth morning, Caesar and Ajax retrieved her as usual, but they didn't take her down the same passages as before. Her heart sped up as she turned her head this way and that. The corridors were much the same with their tan brick and craggy edges. Lanterns hung at regular intervals, creating shadows. The air smelled damp, like forgotten laundry left in a basket.

"Are we not headed for the bathing chamber?" she asked Caesar. His dark eyes didn't sparkle this morning. Upon their first meeting, she'd figured that look had been there because he was to ravage her or torture her in some other way, but it seemed as if he always wore it in his eyes. Yet, the fact that it wasn't there this morning...

She turned to Ajax, his muscles rippling beneath his deep blue uniform. His beard showed signs of age with salt peppered in with the brown. Most of his grays were gathered around his ears, but his strength hadn't waned with his growing older. He was also a man of few words.

"Master Ajax, why are we not going to the dining room?"

Ajax's beard rustled slightly as he shook his head. Hallie sighed. No matter, she would take advantage of this and use it to flesh out her mental map.

The new corridor was long and windowless. Gas lamps hung from the ceiling. It seemed Achilles was devoid of electricity. The damp smell now mixed with that of earth and dust and a little bit of smoke.

If she could figure out a way to break the lamps and release the liquid inside…she would need a spark. But where would that leave her? The stone wouldn't burn.

What if she created a river of flames along the corridor? Would that prevent the Cerls from getting through? Could she use that to her advantage? She tucked the information away in the back of her mind. She'd talk with Mistress Jules when she returned and see what she made of it.

At the end of the corridor, they turned once more and took a doorway to the right, which led to a spiraling stair down into the depths of the fort. Strange. She'd thought the dungeon was the lowest point, but whoever had designed this structure was a genius. Or mad.

The dark floor and walls held mismatched stones, and dirt and roots trickled through cracks. The stairs were uneven, as if the ground beneath had shifted over time. There were several sudden drops. Ajax caught her before she took a tumble on one of those.

As they journeyed deeper, chill pricked her exposed skin and raced up her arms. Her tunic was thin and didn't offer much protection from the elements. She'd learned that each night as she tucked herself up against the corner of her cell for warmth before saying goodnight to the spider family who hadn't abandoned her yet—but it wasn't as if they were in the Pass. This air was different. It seeped into Hallie's bones the further they trekked, twisting and turning with only the lantern Caesar carried to prevent them from stumbling.

At long last, they came to an arched wooden door at the bottom, and Caesar rapped lightly on it. A velvety voice answered, and Caesar opened it. Ajax, his graying beard aquiver, pushed her inside with a light hand and shut the door behind her.

A sense of déjà vu made Hallie's heart beat erratically, even though this room was nothing like the light and airy office floors above them. It was more akin to Dr. Frankenstein's laboratory.

Jars full of liquids and other substances lined the shelves on the walls. Gas lanterns lit up the space and hung from the ceiling, yet they weren't enough to light the room completely.

She wished they weren't lit. She wished she were in complete darkness.

Because if she were, she'd be unable to see the man on the table before her.

His hair was dark as midnight, his skin white as snow. The long tail once well-groomed and menacing was mangy and matted. His eyes were no longer ageless, attempting to delve deep into her psyche. They were closed as if he merely slept.

The Lord Elder.

Hallie gasped and darted forward, only to be stopped by *that* voice. The one she heard in her most recent nightmares. The one that caused pain.

"Miss Walker, glad you could join us this morning. I hope my soldiers and staff have helped you regain your strength these past few days."

Hallie froze. She tensed her muscles, ready for the electricity to spark through her veins and burn her from the inside out...but it didn't come. Not yet.

Soft footsteps sounded behind her. She hadn't seen him when she'd entered the underground chamber. The Yalv spread across the table like a lab specimen had distracted her. General Correa had probably planned it that way.

She flinched when his hand found her shoulder, but nothing issued from his touch. No pain. She took a shuddering breath in and pushed it out with a slight rattle of her lungs.

"No need to fear. As long as you tell the truth."

Hallie felt like she might puke all over the floor or the prone body of the Lord Elder before her. Her fingers shook first, but the tremors made their way up through her hand, her arms, until her entire body quaked. "He's dead, isn't he?"

She'd left him in Myrrai all those months ago. How had he come to be here, of all places? Saldr thought he'd died defending the city.

The soft chuckle from Correa's lips was at odds with the icy undertone that chilled Hallie to her core. "Not quite yet, my dear. Not quite yet, thank Fate. His death would doom us all."

"Then why am I here now?" Her voice sounded more confident than she felt, and she was grateful the quiver was contained only to her extremities at present.

Correa placed both hands on her shoulders and squeezed.

She couldn't help the flinch at his touch. No electricity still. Thank the stars. But what did he want from her?

"Your lineage. I didn't quite believe how lucky we had gotten, but when Fate speaks, who am I to question her?"

Hallie knew many Cerls worshipped Fate, a goddess who they believed controlled people's lives. Hallie didn't think it feasible, but she didn't point that out. "My family's lived in Stoneset for ages. I don't see how that's of any value to you."

Correa smirked, his teeth peeking out beneath his upper lip. "Telling the truth? Excellent. You're learning, aren't you? Pity your great-grandmother never revealed the extent of it."

Hallie's heart pounded painfully in her chest, and against her better judgment, words spilled from her mouth—she'd never been able to stop herself, anyway. "I don't understand."

Her words were a desperate plea. She shouldn't trust this man, but he might very well have the answers she sought on this reckless journey. At least she could die knowing a version of the truth.

Her mother had always told Hallie her curiosity would be the death of her one day. Her mother was a prophet.

Correa continued, "You, my girl, are the key to all of this. Your great-grandmother ran away, but we found her. In you. She was a selfish woman, making you pay for her numerous sins."

Hallie recalled the attic portrait she'd found so long ago. She remembered her father's words that it was simply a painting of a stranger. But what if...what if...

Phantom pain radiated through her. She'd been brought here to this room with the near cadaver in front of her. To do what? To die?

Correa's breath smelled of garlic, and the scent turned her stomach as she closed her eyes tightly. "But why?"

"Through your bloodline and that of others, we will release the power from the Gate to defeat Jagamot."

Jagamot. From the prophecies. Oh, how she wished she knew more.

"But what if—" she gasped. "I don't understand. I'm not who you think I am. I don't know what you're—"

"Navara, your great-grandmother, grew too scared, too reluctant to follow through with her gifts. She could have brought about a world of peace. Of one united world."

Navara. Where had she heard that name before?

Correa grabbed Hallie's arm, and white-hot pain lanced through the limb and up into the rest of her body. She screamed, and he released her after a second. "We have the power to change the world. You, Miss Walker, will take the Essence power of the Lord Elder, your great-great grandfather, and save us all."

Hallie's eyes widened even in the aftermath of pain. Her twice-great grandfather? She looked at the man and his unwrinkled face. How could he be so old? How could she have not known they were related when they'd met last fall? Shouldn't she have had some sort of feeling about it? Correa had to be lying, but that thought alone couldn't stop the fear flowing through her veins. "*I don't understand.*"

"You will take his Essence power. Thanks to Filip, he's stayed alive this long despite his injuries," he pointed to the Lord Elder. If she looked hard enough, she could see the faint imprints of scars lancing the man's chest. He'd been burned, but with whatever *Filip* had done, they were almost faint memories on the Lord Elder's skin. Correa clasped his hands behind his back and looked deeply into Hallie's eyes. "As he was unable to pass his power on when his time came, it's not at its height. Add in the fact he's nearly dead, well, we are at an impasse."

"How do I know you're telling the truth?" Hallie was ashamed of the wobbling in her voice, but she didn't want to face the pain again. She didn't want to feel his fingers on her skin.

He walked around the table and grabbed her wrist. She flinched, but the lightning didn't come. Instead, he placed her hand on the Lord Elder's icy forehead.

Correa let go of her wrist. "Only by mutual consent must the power be transferred. Convince him."

Hallie snatched her hand away, the deadly chill of the Lord Elder's skin lingering on her fingertips. "But he's nearly dead. He's so cold. How can I—" Correa stepped toward her, and she slapped her hand back on the Lord Elder's forehead. "You have the wrong person. I'm not Yalven. I'm from Stoneset."

Correa sighed and dug into his pocket, holding up a mangled object. "This belongs to you, doesn't it?"

It was small, smaller than Correa's hand. The brown sheen was evident even in the dim light of the underground room. He strode over and grabbed Hallie's free hand, setting the item in her palm. Warmth radiated from it. Like magic. She felt it in her soul.

Someone had tried to destroy the object, as evidenced by the shattered glass and melted bits of metal. Hallie's heart hammered. The cover. It was difficult to tell what the image carved there had been, but if she concentrated on the tiny, untouched section, she could just make out the tip of a slanted, yet thin, pointed roof.

Jack's pocket watch.

Hallie's hand shook and her lips wobbled. "How..."

It'd been left in the ruins. She thought she'd never see it again. Tears bubbled to the surface as she clutched the timepiece in her hand.

Correa continued, not seeing or caring about the effect his words had on her, "Yes, you thought it was a simple family heirloom, didn't you? At times, Essence wielders use relics crafted from Zuprium to focus and control their power." He fingered the earring in his right lobe and stared down at the Lord Elder. "The timepiece is as such. It belonged to the Lord Elder, who gifted it to his daughter, the Chosen of Time, only for her to run away and never return."

Hallie's heart pounded in her ears. "I still don't—"

"Some Essence powers can only be passed down in a familial line unless rebirth occurs. The most powerful ones, that is. And in the quest to find Navara's descendants, that dead trapper and this timepiece led me to you." Hands pressed on the table, Correa bent over the Lord Elder's body. "Now, inject the Essence, communicate with the Lord Elder. If you fail, my own powers are ready to inflict pain."

His eyes turned dark as Hallie's breathing hitched. She kept her left hand on the Lord Elder's forehead, while her right clenched the ruined pocket watch. The revelations in Correa's words barraged her thoughts.

She was indeed Yalven. The Lord Elder was her great-great grandfather, who lay cold and unresponsive on the table before her. How was she supposed to communicate with him?

Hallie closed her eyes, tears leaking through her lashes.

Blood ran down her hand where the sharp edges of Jack's destroyed pocket watch dug into her palm. The Lord Elder's skin was the same temperature as the snow in the Narden Pass.

"My patience is wearing thin, Miss Walker."

Her thoughts were too frazzled. She couldn't concentrate. Her great-grandmother had run away from this for stars knew what reason. Kase was dead, bleeding out in the streets of Stoneset or succumbing to his previous injury. Hallie would never know what became of her parents. Mistress Jules would be alone in the cell block tonight if she didn't succeed.

Her breaths came faster and faster until all she could hear were the screams she didn't realize were hers. All she could feel was the lightning underneath her skin that threatened to come if she wasn't successful.

"Not good enough," came Correa's cold voice as his fingers touched her arm.

And then she knew no more.

CHAPTER 30

BY THE MOONS

Kase

IN A FEW SHORT HOURS, Kase would be with Hallie. The afternoon sun shone brightly in the cavern, casting shadows along the cavern walls as people milled about. A group of middle-aged women washed shirts a few tents over. Children with dirt-streaked faces chased a cat around some of the larger rock formations. A man with a hastily trimmed beard slung a bow on his back, readying himself for a hunting trip. The people of Stoneset went about their lives as if nothing had happened. Kase didn't think he could do it. He didn't think he could live his life expecting any moment to be found out.

Yet, that was his plan after Hallie was safe.

She would finally be going back to Kyvena, and Kase would be...somewhere. Hiding. Hoping he could live out the rest of his miserable life in relative peace.

Kase dug through his pack looking for anything that might help him, but all he had were extra clothes, his pilot goggles, a near-empty money pouch, and a crumpled envelope.

He picked up the envelope. The flourished 'K' mocked him. His mother's letter.

He hesitated. Did he want to read whatever guilt she'd imbued into the words? He sat down on the log next to the fire, ignoring the people eating their dinner on the other side. The tanner, a man who went nowhere without his patched and fraying cap atop his graying hair, looked too interested in what Kase held. Kase turned away and stared at the envelope.

He hadn't said goodbye. He hadn't wanted to face the disappointment and hurt in her eyes.

Yet, she'd written this letter, intending for him to read it.

He fingered the flap sealed with the Shackley crest. With his impending death on the morrow, it wouldn't hurt to read it.

He popped the seal and tugged out the parchment.

My dear Kase,

I'm not going to wax poetic here. It's not the time nor the place. All I want for you to know is that I understand. I know why you must go. My only wish is for you to be happy, to be safe, to be loved. You'll always have a home here with me.

Mother

He blinked away the budding tears burning the corners of his eyes. She'd never see him again, no matter what happened over the next few days. Would her words have changed if she'd known? Would she care that he was doing something incredibly reckless that could lead to consequences for those he loved in Kyvena?

Was this all worth it?

In his mind, he watched Hallie fall limp as the soldiers kidnapped her, slinging her over the horse. It was like the avalanche all over again, except this time, he would have to do more than simply dig her out from the snow.

His mother would understand. Probably more than anyone.

"Leaving, son?"

Kase stuffed the letter in his pocket. Stowe stood before him, salve in his hands.

Hallie's father held it out. "It's time for me to check your leg. Niels says you're heading out?"

Pulling up his trouser leg, Kase sat on the log. His wound had scabbed over nicely, the edges blending into new skin. Stowe bent down and inspected it, dabbing salve where it looked like the scab had pulled away. Kase grunted when he pushed a tender spot. "There's someone who needs me."

Stowe sat back, replacing the lid on the small jar and standing. "It's nice to be needed. Gives you purpose."

Kase carefully pulled down his trouser leg. The letter in his pocket crackled as he did so.

My only wish is for you to be happy, to be safe, to be loved.

He cleared his throat, not looking at Stowe. "Thank you. For taking care of my leg."

"Of course. I'll whip up another jar to take with you."

Kase pushed himself to his feet. He was taller than Stowe, but not by much. He put a hand on his shoulder. "Wait. There's something I need to talk to you about."

Looking into the man's near-golden eyes made his palms start sweating. How would he react to what Kase had to say? Would he hit him? Kick his still healing leg? Kase clenched his jaw.

In the man's eyes, he saw Hallie. He saw her warmth, her kind spirit. Kase knew what he needed to do.

"In private." Kase's hand slid off his shoulder.

The man gave him a questioning look, but he nodded, leading Kase back to his tent. Kase took a seat on the same rock he'd used when Niels had first brought him here. It'd only been a few days, yet it felt like a lifetime.

Stowe took a seat across from him, crossing one leg over the other. Kase leaned forward, forearms on his knees. Deep breath in. "I haven't been completely honest with you."

Stowe said nothing.

"Maybe it was selfish of me, but I didn't know how to say it, especially because I didn't know you." Kase picked at his fingers. "I'm sorry for that."

Hallie's father leaned forward. Kase met his eyes as the older man spoke. "We all have our secrets, son. I didn't expect you to relay your entire life to me for fixing up your leg. In fact, I don't expect anything in return."

Kase shook his head. "It's not that. It's more complicated, and I'm trying to figure out how to tell you this...and I can't tell you everything because it might jeopardize what I'm about to do, and you have to swear you'll allow me to go through with it. Because it's the only way to save her."

"Her?"

Kase wiped sweaty hands on his trousers. It was time to come clean. He knew it. But the words were like tar in his mouth. "Hallie's a prisoner at Achilles."

Stowe's face lost all color. "*What?*"

"We came out here to find you because you sent her a telegram—"

"I didn't send a telegram."

Kase blinked. Niels had been right. "Then who did?"

"Don't know." Stowe stood, Kase following. He grabbed the older man's shoulder as he took a step. The man turned. "I need to get her out of there."

"You can't."

Stowe threw off Kase's hand. "By the moons, I will."

Waving his hands, Kase blocked his path. "You'll die trying."

"I can't sit here and do nothing." Water pooled in the older man's eyes. "She's there because of me. Because I never told her about the journals. If I had, then maybe...maybe...oh, stars...the Cerls know. My little lark..."

Kase settled both hands on Stowe's shoulders. He looked him directly in the eyes. "I swear on the stars-blasted gods that I'll get her out of there. I might be the only one who can."

Stowe stared at him long and hard, as if dissecting him bit by bit with his gaze. "Who is she to you?"

Kase dropped his hands, stepping back. His stomach squirmed. "A friend."

"A friend."

"Yes."

Stowe rubbed his bald head. "You're a terrible liar, son."

Kase turned away, looking off toward the rest of the cavern. Several villagers sat around the dozen or so campfires, laughing, talking, not knowing the turmoil in Kase's heart. He didn't know how to answer Hallie's father because he didn't know himself. "All I know is that I'm not about to lose her now."

Stowe was silent.

Kase played with Ana's ring, twisting it on his finger. A reminder of all that he'd already lost. "You have no reason to trust me, but that's all you can do now. If you want to help, talk to Niels when he returns tonight. We have a plan."

Kase grabbed his pack. Before he could take a step, Stowe spoke up. "Bring her home."

"I will. I promise."

C H A P T E R 3 1

TO BE A GENTLEMAN

Kase

KASE HADN'T EXPECTED ACHILLES TO look like a castle
fortress out of legend. It wasn't a work of art like the Yalven
palace in Myrrai, but its towers and turrets had their own
beauty. The white stone wall surrounding the structure gleamed
in the late afternoon light and soared higher than Kase thought
necessary, towering over the nearby evergreen trees. No
wonder the people of Stoneset hadn't been able to make
progress.

The fortress itself was carved into the mountainside and
rose above the wall. How *had* the Cerls conquered it? By siege?
Why hadn't anyone in Kyvena been informed? Yes, Niels said
the communications had been compromised, but someone
should have escaped. The fort was surely equipped with hidden
escape routes into the mountains.

Niels' words came back to him then, answering his
unspoken question—the survivors of Stoneset believed

someone had betrayed them.

Kase wished he could contact Jove, even if it might very well end in the gallows for Kase. But it was no use thinking about all that now. His mission was to get inside and break Hallie out, even if it cost him his life.

On this side of the Narden Pass, the weather had finally turned a little. Flurries drifted by, losing their power in the thawing winter wind. A subtle scent of woodsmoke hovered in the air—probably from the fort's furnaces. Kase no longer needed to wear an additional cloak. All he was equipped with now were fingerless gloves, stained trousers, and his filched soldier's jacket. Didn't matter, really, because strolling in stark naked would've been enough to get him inside the military fortress.

Niels knelt beside him as they peeked out from behind the massive trees at the edge of the forest. The man had memorized the patrol routes. Kase felt like they could've become good friends, one of the very few he had. Better than Eravin or Skibs, but he couldn't make attachments now. It would only end in fire and tears if it followed the current trend. Kase's connections, his family ties, were the reason General Correa might string his body from that blasted too-white wall.

Niels adjusted his brown cap and turned to Kase. "You're being a stars-blasted idiot if you think they'll take you right in without filling your chest with those fiery bullets."

Kase closed his eyes. His nerves were frayed, and while he'd never admit it out loud, he was absolutely terrified of what might possibly happen...but he didn't have a choice. "We need someone on the inside for our plan to work properly, and I have the best chance of getting in there. Now, let's go over the specifics."

"Fine," Niels said with a sigh, looking back at the fort. "You have until dusk on the second day to find her and figure out how to make it to the smaller gate. At that time, the boys and I will be blowing as many holes in that wall as we can. And probably die in the process."

"Not if you're careful."

Niels' gave him a deadpan look. "I'm trying to be a realist."

"Which doesn't help with morale." Kase straightened. He raked a hand down his jacket, his fingers tumbling over the double rows of buttons, and tugged at the sleeves. He'd tried to clean it as much as he could, but a few stains would have to do. "You get back to the cavern and prepare for the assault. I'll see you in two days."

Before Kase could step out of the protection of the trees and make his way to the gate, Niels snatched his sleeve. "At least tell me why you have it in your head you can make a difference, that they won't shoot you right where you stand."

Kase gritted his teeth, ready to scold him, when he stopped. The man's brown eyes were earnest, pleading. He thought he was about to lose Kase.

He cared.

Kase chewed the inside of his cheek. While their acquaintance had started out with a slice to the neck and busted lip, the man before him had done nothing wrong. He'd helped him traverse the underground tunnel to the Stoneset villagers. He'd made sure Stowe looked after Kase's leg. He'd be putting his life on the line in two days. After a moment more, Kase relented, his shoulders falling as he turned back to the man. It wouldn't matter soon. "My name isn't Kase Carrington."

"What?" Niels grabbed Kase's lapels. "*You lied?* So help me, if you—"

Kase untangled the man's fingers and pushed him away. "My name is Kase Shackley, I'm the best stars-blasted pilot in the Crews and youngest son of the Stradat Lord Kapitan. You nearly slit my throat in that alley four days ago and allowed those *helviters* to kidnap Hallie. Trusting you with the truth could have cost me everything."

Niels' jaw went slack as he stepped back.

Kase plowed on. "I know my name will get me into that fort because Correa is a smart man. He took over this side of the Nardens without my father any the wiser. Correa won't dare execute someone he can make use of."

"Kase—wait, you don't have to...look, I'm sorry, I—"

Kase shook his head. "Be ready. Two days."

Niels' face was pale. "You'd do that for her?"

Kase's heart thumped in his ears, but he nodded. "I would."

After a moment, Niels nodded, and with only slight hesitation, he held out his hand. Kase took it and gave it a firm shake. Niels looked him straight in the eye. "Be safe."

Kase bowed his head. "I will...and thank you. For everything."

And with that, he turned and marched off through the trees and into the open, his hands raised.

I'm coming, Hals.

AS KASE HAD PREDICTED, ONCE he announced who he was and proved his words with the identification papers in his jacket pocket, the men at the larger gate took him into the fortress. The room in which Kase now sat, unarmed and flanked by two beefy men—one with a graying beard and hawkish features— was what his father's military office had looked like back in Kyvena. Military records filled the shelves, and a map covered the desk.

Kase took note of the blue markers below. They were spread all over Jayde, and while Kase wasn't sure what they were intended to represent, he still memorized their locations in case they came in handy later. His father, even with all his faults, had trained him well. Maybe Kase would've made a good spy if he'd stayed in Kyvena and joined One World. The irony.

He took controlled breaths. The clock on the wall ticked with each passing second. Too much time.

The room was silent and smelled of sterility—of alcohol and lemon. Kase crossed his arms to hide the slight tremble in his fingers.

At last, the arched door in the far-right corner opened with a resounding screech. The man who he assumed was Correa strolled in like a noble entering a lavish dinner party. His chest was held out and his shoulders thrust back in authority. He was at least a head taller than Kase. His hair was black, and his eyes were as sharp as a soldier's spare blade. His navy uniform was pressed with nary a wrinkle, and the shiny buttons reflected the last rays of sunset streaming through the window. Kase's own buttons at their cleanest dulled in comparison.

Correa dismissed the guards with a wave of his hand.

"So," the man said once the door had closed with a sharp snap, his voice like the slithering of snakes, "am I to understand the Stradat Lord Kapitan's son has willingly given himself up to our cause? While I know Jaydians aren't the brightest, as we were able to maneuver our way into this position with relative ease, I didn't think the esteemed Harlan Shackley's spawn would be so stupid."

Kase clenched his jaw against the insults. It was expected, and he'd heard worse. From his own father. Once he was certain he had his emotions under control, Kase spoke. "If your spies knew anything, anything at all, you'd understand my motive for turning myself over."

Correa's laugh was like cracked bells in a dusty church tower. "If you're so confident, would you care to explain, then?"

"I'm here because I *hate* my father."

Kase didn't even have to lie.

"Really? And why do you expect me to believe that?"

"I've come to give you information in exchange for the release of one of your prisoners."

"Interesting." The man's eyebrows, already too high, rose even further. They made his skin look incredibly tight across his features, like a barely clothed skull. "And which prisoner do you believe we have in our possession? Why would it matter to you?"

Kase fisted his hands. He wanted to see Hallie. He needed to figure out how to get her out if this didn't work. Calming himself by focusing on the bookshelves, he took another breath before looking Correa square in the eyes. "Hallie Walker. If you release Hallie Walker, I will tell you what I know. Eravin Gray in Kyvena sent me to seek you out."

Using Eravin's name here was a gamble. A complete gamble, but it was one he was willing to take.

"Ah, yes. Seems he would think it wise to recruit someone of your station."

"Then you're agreeing?"

Correa bent slightly at the waist, his eyes boring into Kase's. His grin grew, revealing too-straight teeth. Before he said anything, he traced a single finger down Kase's scruffy cheek, a sting of electricity following in its wake.

Kase flinched, and Correa's smile grew. "You prove to be an interesting specimen, and I believe you'll do well for what I have in mind."

"What do you mean?"

"Our relationship, Master Kase Shackley, son of the Stradat Lord Kapitan, will continue, for I have use for you yet." He snapped his fingers, and in a moment, the door opened once more. The guards had returned. "Allow our esteemed guest to take up residence with the other for now."

"But what about our agreement?" Kase gripped the sides of his chair. The wooden corners bit into his palms.

Correa shook his head. "I need to think on it. In the meantime, please be our *guest.*"

The guards grabbed Kase's arms and towed him out of the room before he could respond. He struggled, but it was half-hearted. He should have expected something like this.

Down the corridors they went, and through so many passages, Kase lost track of exactly how many turns they took. It was as if they were trying to confuse him, which was to be expected. At last, they led him down a steep staircase, the grime on the walls growing thick on the bricks as they descended. At the end stood a door with iron bars covering the window at the top. They pushed him through it and then over to a cell, the bars on the door stretching from the craggy ceiling to the equally craggy floor. After unlocking it, they shoved Kase in and slammed the door behind him.

Kase nearly fell over from the push, but he regained his footing easily. He spun back toward the bars and clenched them in his fists. The guards left through the door, shutting it behind them, leaving him in near darkness.

Blast.

Kase's fingers slid down the bars, his fingertips catching on the rough metal. *Blast. Blast. Blast.*

Before he could plan anything else or even inspect his new environment more fully, someone gasped behind him, and Kase turned. The room was cold and dark, and the rapidly fading sunlight coming through the impossibly tiny window did nothing to remedy this. The cell was about a quarter of the size of his bedchamber at the Manor, but it was the woman stumbling toward him who caught his eye.

In the time he'd spent with her these last few weeks, he hadn't noticed how sunken her cheeks had become. The sight lit a fire in the pit of his stomach.

It was his fault. The *helviters* would've never taken her if he'd only been there to protect her.

That didn't stop him from meeting her halfway, nor did it stop her fingers tangling in the lapels of his soldier's jacket. Her golden eyes were jewels filled with unshed tears.

"Kase?" she choked.

"Yes."

She leaned into his chest, her quiet sobs wracking her entire body. The corners of his own eyes prickled as he wrapped his arms around her thin frame and breathed in her scent. He squeezed her tightly, leaning his cheek against her hair.

Holy shocks.

He'd found her. She was alive.

After another moment, Hallie pulled back, wiping her face with the edge of her sleeve. Kase didn't let her out of the circle of his arms even as she whispered, "Sorry about your jacket."

His hand shook as he cupped her chilled cheek, using his thumb to wipe another runaway tear. Three sleepless nights worrying about her led to this at last. He hadn't realized how much he missed her until that moment. They were both prisoners yet holding her in his arms had never felt more right. Hallie leaned into his touch, her watery smile flickering in the dim light of the dungeon cell.

"You know I don't care a *stars-blasted* bit about this jacket." His voice was thick, and he coughed a little to cover the emotion threading through each word.

Her laugh was pure, echoing in the small chamber. He pulled her in close again, holding her even tighter than before. Her arms snaked around his waist.

They stood there wrapped in each other until someone else coughed. He whipped his head around.

"Sorry...to interrupt," came the voice once more, "but the guards should be bringing dinner soon...and it might be best..."

Hallie sprang back, and Kase stood straight. Hallie's voice was strong once more as she said, "What do you mean, Mistress Jules?"

"Don't give them a reason to use him against you," the woman warned.

Kase untangled his arm from Hallie's and glanced at her

before speaking to the empty wall in front of them. The woman must be in the adjacent cell. Were there more? "Thank you. My name is Kase Shackley of Kyvena."

The woman's voice was faint. "Jules Tucker. I'm Hallie's former schoolmistress."

"The one who gave her *The Odyssey?*"

"Of course. She and her brother were my best students." It sounded as if the words were a chore, quiet and wispy as if the woman was wasting away.

Footsteps echoed on the other side of the main door. Hallie pulled Kase to the far wall and sank down against it. With their backs pressed up against the grimy stone and Hallie's hand grasped tightly in his, they waited.

In a moment, the door opened, and a soldier threw a few scraps of jerky near the bars before giving some to Mistress Jules next door.

When the soldiers left, Hallie gathered the food, giving Kase half.

They didn't say anything for a while as they chewed the tough jerky. It was only enough for a snack, but Kase made sure Hallie got the bigger pieces. Once he'd finished his share, he gripped her hand even harder.

That moment in Stoneset, when she was thrown onto the back of a horse like a rag doll, he thought he would never see her alive again. And now she was here. Right here with him. And they were going to get out of here in two days. They just needed a plan.

Kase rubbed his thumb across one of her knuckles. "Will the guards be back?"

"Not until morning."

"Good." Kase tangled his other hand in his hair, thinking. "What do guard rotations look like in here?"

"Soldiers patrol the corridor regularly. I think there might be others trapped down here with us, but I never see them. Mistress Jules thinks she's the only one left." Hallie looked away, her jaw working on a piece of jerky.

"Maybe they're holding soldiers that refused to surrender," Kase mumbled to himself. That could be helpful. Or not. There wasn't any way he could guarantee their safety. He wanted to help all the people trapped, but Hallie was his priority.

"Why?" Hallie whispered, shifting her weight, not letting go of his hand. Even imprisoned, he couldn't help the fluttering in his chest at the feeling of her skin on his. Six months ago, he would've never thought he'd be sitting here, holding her hand, happy he was here with her. He thought of their time in the cave, sleeping back-to-back, their muscles tensed.

How far they'd come. Shame that it took this long for him to realize—to realize—

No. Not the time. Kase had other things to think about if they were going to get out of here alive.

"Not everyone from Stoneset died in the attack," he whispered.

Hallie tore her hand from his and turned her body full toward him. "What?"

Kase glanced at the bars. No matter if Hallie said the guards weren't stationed outside; he wouldn't risk the lives of those hidden in the cavern. "Not so loud."

Hallie shut her mouth, and Kase continued, his voice as soft as he possibly could make it, "A friend of yours is going to cause a bit of a distraction two days from now. That doesn't give us a whole lot of time, so you need to tell me what you know, if anything, so we can come up with something to get us all out of here."

"Who? Who is it?"

She and Niels had been sweethearts. Hallie might no longer have feelings for him, but Kase had seen the look on Niels' face when Kase asserted he would do anything in his power to save her. Hallie's eyes pleaded with him in the near darkness.

Kase was being petty, so he took a deep breath. "Niels."

"He's alive?" Hallie's face crumpled slightly.

Kase chewed the inside of his lip to keep from spouting words he'd regret. It strained him a little, and something squeezed in his chest. "Along with several of the others. They're holed up in the mountain cavern."

"My mother? Is Mama there, too?" Hallie wiped her eyes. "And Papa?"

"Yes. Your father fixed up my leg, but your mother...well, I'm sure she's fine, but..."

"But what?" Hallie grabbed his hand again. "Is she hurt?"

He shook his head. "No, she's just...well, she traveled through the caves to the other side of the Nardens. She's on her way to Kyvena."

"Why?"

"To let someone know what's going on here." Kase shifted a little against the stone wall. "They've sent others through the Pass, but my guess is that the Cerls killed them like they tried to do to us before that avalanche."

Hallie was quiet for several minutes before speaking up again. "You said something about breaking out of here?"

"Niels and others are planning a distraction." Kase drew his index finger along a crack in the stone floor. "Tell me what you know about this place. We have to come up with some way out of this dungeon before he strikes the day after tomorrow."

Kase should've known Hallie would already be putting together an escape plan—she, who'd been chosen above other well-versed scholars at the University to go on a mission to the Yalven continent, Tasava. Of course, she'd already made a mental map of the locations they'd escorted her to on a daily basis as well as noted any potential exits and patrols. In true Hallie fashion, she'd even been working on the guards—the two men who'd delivered Kase to the dungeon room.

"I'd rather not hurt them if possible," she said, tucking her chin to her knees as she wrapped her arms around her legs.

"They don't deserve your pity."

The small bit of Firstmoon peeking into the room laced Hallie's face in pale light as she shook her head. "They aren't cruel and have had plenty of chances to...to...to lay a hand on me, but they've treated me with respect. I don't think they agree with what's going on."

"But they're Cerls."

"Not all Cerls are like Correa."

Kase rubbed his eyes. "All right. We'll *try* not to hurt them, but that's all I can guarantee."

"Thank you."

They fell into a comfortable silence—as comfortable as it could get in their situation. Kase's stomach rumbled a little, but he ignored it. He could go hungry for a while yet.

Hallie's shoulders shook as she leaned against him. He looked down at her, fearing she'd started crying again. "Hals?"

She turned, her teeth chattering. "Gets a little cold sometimes."

He studied her clothing—a thin tunic and too-loose trousers tucked into her worn boots. The clothing wasn't ragged, but it wouldn't hold up in the dungeons even if spring had started showing itself in the light of day.

Leaning forward, he unbuttoned his jacket and shucked it off. He held it out to her.

She put up her hands. "No. I'm okay."

"Why do we always fight over me giving you a jacket?"

"But what if you get cold?"

"Again, this is me trying to be a gentleman."

Hallie snorted. "Fine, fine. But if you start shivering, I'm handing it right back."

She pushed her arms through the sleeves with Kase's help. The coat swallowed her frame whole, but she stopped shivering as she pulled it tight around her shoulders. He brushed a bit of dirt from the sleeve.

Something skittered over his other hand, light as a kiss. He jumped, snatching it off the stone floor, and knocked into Hallie, who groaned. "Stars, what'd you do that for? You nearly bloodied my nose!"

Kase stared at the spot where his hand had been, but it was impossible to see anything now that Firstmoon had set an hour ago. Secondmoon would be rising any minute. "Thought I felt something."

Hallie settled herself back against the wall, his jacket scraping a little against the stone. "A big something or little something?"

Kase tilted his head, though he couldn't see her expression in the dark. "Probably a spider."

"Did it feel extra hairy?"

"What?"

"The legs. Did the legs feel hairy to you?"

Secondmoon's golden light finally peeked through the window, but it wasn't bright enough for Kase to tell any of her features apart. "Does it matter?"

Hallie shifted, her shoulder bumping into his. "Well, if it was hairy, then it was Jacob. He's a particularly large spider who lives in my cell, but he tends to be more skittish than his twelve

sons. I've been having particular trouble telling Simeon and Joseph apart, but then there's also Judah who I accidentally called Jacob yesterday."

"What in the blazes have they been putting in your jerky?"

"The twelve sons of Jacob in First Earth's Biblical text..." she paused and looked up at him. He could see her eyes now, and he quickly wiped the gob smacked look off his face. "Mistress Jules sleeps a lot, and I didn't have anyone to talk to, and thirteen spiders live in the far corner of my cell. Jacob and his twelve sons were perfect names for them all."

Kase couldn't help the grin breaking on his face. "So, you've befriended the spiders?"

"Is that a problem?"

"Not at all. Make sure to tell them I'm a friend. I'd rather not end up with my blood sucked dry."

"They don't suck blood, you *dulkop*."

Kase laughed, and soon Hallie joined in. He relaxed back against the wall, though he made sure to check whether he was about to squash one of Hallie's cellmates.

After discussing more possibilities for their escape, Hallie and Kase fell silent again, and before long, Hallie laid her head against his shoulder. Kase's heart thumped in his chest, and his breathing sped up a little, but instead of freezing or fretting over what to do with his hands, he let it happen, pulling her closer and tucking her head beneath his chin.

She didn't protest, simply snuggled deeper into his embrace. He held onto her, and before he drifted off himself, he whispered into her hair, "I promise, I'll get you home."

Her answer was so soft, he barely heard it, but he just caught her words as his eyelids drooped. "Thank you for coming back for me."

"Always."

CHAPTER 32

THROUGH THE MUD

Jove

THE COURT CHAMBER ITSELF HADN'T changed one bit in the eight days since Jove told the world that not only was his father abusive, but also that he'd had a hand in covering up the real reason behind the Kyvena fire. The same stone benches ran along the outside of the room. His father still sat alone on the raised dais in the center.

However, the number of people in the room had doubled.

For one, his mother sat stiffly beside him, her face drawn and eyes never leaving her husband. Jove held her hand tightly in his. It was small, bony, and chilled. He felt the heavy absence of his siblings as he stared at his father, who awaited the Council's judgment. Heddie sat on his other side.

Others of the government and the city were also present including both Anderson and Saldr. Several reporters sat closest to the door, notebooks ready to record the verdict Stradat Sarson would read at any moment. What heinous lies would they print in tomorrow's paper? How much further could they drag the Shackley name through the mud?

Probably not far enough.

Jove barely registered Stradat Sarson calling the hushed murmurs to attention. He'd not noticed the dull noise until there was a lack of it. She stood, her scar contrasting with her pale skin. "The Council has reached a decision as to your fate, Harlan Shackley. Will the defendant please rise."

Jove squeezed his mother's hand as his father stood. He wore a simple tunic and trousers. His boots were the standard military issue, but that was the only article of clothing that remained of what Harlan had once been.

Sarson stood as well, her fingers pressing into the podium in front of her. "Harlan Hale Shackley, you have been accused of obstruction of justice, an intent to conspiracy, and betraying the oath of office. We have heard the witnesses speak to those accounts. Do you have any last words for the Council and those assembled here?"

His father clasped his hands behind his back, standing tall and proud. "I did everything in my power to protect this country, to protect my family. I do not regret my actions."

The room burst into a buzz, the reporters' pens flying across their notebooks. The rapping of Sarson's gavel rang as she called everything to order once more. "Then allow me to read the verdict and the ruling thereof. On all accounts that you have been accused, you have confessed to your guilt. Therefore, the penalty of such crimes is death. You will hang at first light."

Jove's mother hid her face in her hands as the noise erupted once more. Jove pulled his mother into a hug as the guards led his father from the room. She shook, and Jove held her tighter. It was the only thing keeping him together at that moment. Heddie squeezed his shoulder.

The end had come—and with it, more death.

CHAPTER 33

A COPY OF HOMER'S ILIAD

Hallie

WITH PUFFY EYES, HALLIE WOKE with the first rays of sunlight, wrapped in Kase's jacket. They were both slumped against the wall, Kase's cheek pressed against the top of her head, his arm loosely around her waist.

She'd smiled last night for the first time in days. And she couldn't help the grin spreading across her face at that moment, either. She shouldn't, because he was trapped—with no guarantee their vague plan would work—but *he was with her.* That was all that mattered.

She snuggled further into his chest, her heart fluttering pleasantly at being so close to him. It helped keep reality at bay.

She'd come out here in search of her parents, only to be kidnapped by Correa. She'd probably die here without ever seeing them again. Kase and Niels' plan would take more luck than they could afford.

It was funny how much she'd changed after believing Kase was dead. When the guards had shoved him in the room the previous evening, Hallie hadn't believed her eyes at first; as soon as she caught sight of those messy curls, she'd lost all her careful composure and control. All she knew was that she had to be near him, feel him, to make sure she wasn't hallucinating from all the pain she'd gone through the last few days.

But no, he was real. He was there in the dungeon room with her. He'd come back for *her*. Like he had when the *Eudora Jayde* had plummeted toward the ground. She should have never doubted him.

The creaking of unoiled door hinges snapped her out of her reverie. Kase groaned and straightened, the noise waking him. "What—where—"

"It's breakfast time," Hallie whispered, untangling herself and looking up at him. His eyes were bleary with sleep as he rubbed his neck.

"Remind me never to sleep at that angle again."

"Both of you are to come with me," a gruff voice above them announced.

Hallie looked up to see Caesar outside their cell, his eyes dull. Hallie's heart skipped painfully. *No.*

"Why? Correa only needs me." She scrambled up, nearly tripping over her feet.

Caesar shook his head. "I just follow orders. He said you are both expected."

Kase used the wall behind him to rise to his feet. "I'll go."

"No." Hallie shook her head so hard it throbbed. Nothing Correa wanted with Kase would be good. She refused to let him suffer, and she didn't know what he'd do if Correa used his lightning on her—which he surely would. "No, Kase, you stay here."

"Correa requests both of you," Caesar said firmly, waving to Ajax standing near the door. "Feed the other prisoner, and then help me." The other man trudged by and laid bread at the opening of the next cell.

Kase's hand on her shoulder was reassuring as he squeezed it lightly. He bent down to her ear. "Go along with it."

Taking off Kase's jacket, she set it on the floor. "All right, Caesar."

Hallie peeked over at Mistress Jules' untouched bread as she and Kase left the dungeon. At least she didn't have to go through this. If she were left alone, then maybe it would be worth it. Hallie could believe in that and hope it brought her peace eventually. Her limbs shook with each step they took toward the underground lab.

Kase tried to grab her hand, but she tugged it away with a shake of her head. She wouldn't give them any hint as to what he was to her. Because he was more than she'd realized. And if they knew...if Correa knew...she would do almost anything—throw herself off Achilles' highest tower, destroy Jayde, sell her soul to Cerlulene's devil king—to keep Kase safe.

That absolutely terrified her.

The room hadn't changed since the first day. The jars of liquid and whatever disgusting things they held still lined the walls. The Lord Elder's body was still on the table. Death was better than anything else Hallie imagined he'd gone through the past few months.

Kase gasped, but she couldn't find her voice to answer his unspoken question...because Correa waited, his brown eyes alight with joy. Kase pushed past her, grabbing the Lord Elder's sallow hand.

"What did you do to him? Why is he like this?" Kase's voice echoed in the stone chamber. Hallie winced; she put a hand to her abdomen to stop the sick feeling.

Correa's voice was laced with mirth as he answered Kase, "He's still alive."

Hallie refused to look at Kase; if she did, she'd lose all the composure she'd pieced back together like a shattered vase.

Correa continued, "Now, as to the why, well, it's a good thing you joined us today, Master Shackley."

Hallie squeezed her eyes shut. *Don't let him see how Kase affects you.*

"What do you mean?"

Don't provoke him.

"Leave him alone," Hallie hissed, and she immediately regretted it. She hadn't meant for it to slip out. "I'm the one you want, Correa. Kase has nothing to do with it."

The laughter rang in her ears. "*Kase,* is it?"

Hallie sucked in a shaking breath at her mistake. *Stupid.*

She looked up, her nostrils flaring and trying to keep the emotions at bay. "You know I'm the only one who can do this."

"What's going on?" Kase moved away from the Lord Elder, falling back to Hallie.

"You think I brought him here to replace you? Miss Walker, I thought you were smarter than that. Navara would be disappointed she had such a dullard of a great-granddaughter."

"Don't you dare—" Kase lunged for the Cerl general, fist pulled back.

Hallie shouted a warning, but she wasn't quick enough. Correa laughed as he caught Kase's punch and squeezed.

Tears sprang unbidden to Hallie's eyes as Kase's screams tore through the air. He stood frozen, his fist in Correa's hand. Hallie shut her eyes tight. Her knees blazed with pain as they smacked the stone floor. "STOP! STOP IT!"

Kase's screams cut off as suddenly as they'd started. Hallie covered her face with her hands. Correa's voice was as gentle as a summer breeze. "And this is precisely why I asked Master Shackley to join us today. I know all about your little reunion. Could've guessed it would happen. Especially as this poor excuse of a lover begged me to trade his life for yours yesterday. I needed to know if you cared for him...and, well, I don't think I could've played my cards better than this."

Kase had fallen to the floor, and his words came out in labored breaths. "You—you—blasted—"

"You brought it upon yourself, I'm afraid."

Hallie pushed herself to her feet, her knees still throbbing. "Leave him alone."

Correa tucked his hands behind his back. "Leave him alone? After that little display, I think not, but I could be persuaded to make a deal with you...if you'd be so obliged."

He stalked closer. Bending to her eye level, he placed a finger on her cheek, tracing it down to her chin. Her breathing picked up, but she didn't flinch. "What deal?"

"Get your filthy hands off her!" Kase shouted from the floor, but his body still hadn't recovered from his first taste of lightning.

Correa didn't move his finger. "Perform for me, and I'll spare him."

"I've been at this for two days, and you still haven't—" she stopped when Correa pulled Kase into a chair and tied his arms behind his back. He struggled, but in his weakened state, it was useless.

"Haven't what, child?"

Tears blurred her vision. "How do I do this? Please, just tell me."

"Find the Essence in the void."

Hallie's breaths were painful. That was all he'd ever given her. Maybe she should try...she didn't know. She knew she had to. "Leave Kase alone."

Correa's teeth flashed as Hallie pulled back and looked resolutely away from Kase, who tugged at his new restraints. The wooden chair screeched across the stone as he fought to reach her. She didn't want to see the betrayal in his gaze.

"Hallie, don't...whatever it is, I'm not worth it!"

She shook her head and approached the Lord Elder's body. Placing her hand upon his forehead, she closed her eyes.

"Hallie—stop—don't!"

She shut out the world around her and concentrated. Emptied her mind. She needed to find the Lord Elder somewhere in the void, grasp the power, and tug it out bit by bit. But how she was supposed to do that, she didn't know. All she knew was that if she failed, Kase would suffer. She would suffer. They all would suffer. The Lord Elder would stay in his state, unable to move, but was that better than being pulled out of his body and thrust into Hallie's?

Her mind grasped at nothing.

She opened her eyes. "I don't understand what you mean by—"

Kase's renewed screams cut through her words. He jerked and thrashed against his restraints as Hallie choked on the tears flooding her eyes. "Please—please, stop! Just tell me what to do! I'll do it!"

Kase's breaths were labored and thick with sobs as Correa removed his fingers from his cheek. He turned. "You must empty your mind. You must convince him to give up his power."

Hallie shook her head viciously, wiping her eyes with the palms of her hands. "I don't sense anything...don't see anything!"

Kase's voice was faint. "Hal—Hallie ...don't worry...don't do..."

"Try again. If you fail, Master Shackley will pay for your ineptitude."

Hallie turned her gaze back to the table. She moved to the side and placed her hand over the Lord Elder's heart instead. She shut her eyes.

Please. Please. Please, Lord Elder. Help me. I don't think I can take much more of this.

She kept pleading as she searched in her mind, in her consciousness, as she reached out through the emptiness for anything she could grasp onto. The memory of Kase's raw and bloody screams tried to interrupt her concentration, but she pushed it as far back as she could.

Please, I'm begging you. I'll do anything. I can't let them hurt Kase anymore. Please.

She was about to pull back when a presence filled her like a wave of heat in the midst of winter.

Child, why are you here?

Hallie gritted her teeth to contain her shock, terrified if she moved, she would break the connection.

The voice was familiar to her. The cadence hadn't changed a bit since she'd last spoken to him all those months ago. The Lord Elder.

I need you to help me by allowing me to take...to take your power.

The answering roar was enough to throw her back into the dank cell. Hallie's eyes snapped open as she gasped for air.

But it wasn't enough; Kase's screams rang in her ears once more. She'd nearly had it and failed. She shut her eyes and plunged again. She found the Lord Elder much easier this time.

I have to. If I don't, he'll kill everyone. He'll destroy the world as we know it, but if you help me, maybe we can stop him. It's the only way.

Silence.

Thrown back out to Kase's screams once more. She dove back in.

Please, Lord Elder. I'm begging you. I don't have a choice.

Silence.

Without any other options coming to mind, she tried a different tactic.

Your daughter, Navara. Do you remember her?

There wasn't a reply, but Hallie felt the warmth tug at her

senses. He was listening. She grasped at that little progress and continued.

She...she was my great-grandmother. I came to find more about her because I used my own blood that night on the door to the Gate's chamber. I didn't realize what it meant then, and I still don't understand, but I'm...I'm your descendant, too. If you help me, maybe we can figure out how to...how to free you. I need you to trust me. Please. I don't want anyone else to die.

The presence warmed her like a hug from a loved one.

You don't know what you ask of me. You don't know what power you will draw upon yourself. My power is painful. You won't be able to contain it.

Hallie shook her head, but then realized he couldn't see that in this weird in-between world.

If you're as powerful as you say, you can help me. If I don't do this, Correa will kill...will kill Kase. He'll kill my parents and Mistress Jules. He'll kill the Stoneset survivors. Please.

And if my power burns through you. What then?

Then it burns through me. I have to try. Together, we can find a way to harness it.

Child...

Tears coursed down Hallie's face, the chill of the dungeon room making them like fire on her cheeks. *I can't let them torture anyone else for my sake. I can't take it anymore. Please.*

All right.

And then her world exploded.

HALLIE'S SKIN STILL BURNED WHEN Caesar and Ajax carried both her and Kase back to their cell. His screams still echoed in her mind. They joined the incessant dripping in one of the adjacent cells. She didn't know how much more she could take.

How naïve of her to think nothing could've been worse than feeling that pain herself. She had been wrong. So horribly wrong.

The Lord Elder's Essence, his power, lingered at the back of her mind, deep within her consciousness, but the heat explosion had burned itself out. The Lord Elder held back all he could—the heat radiating off her skin at present being the only evidence. It was as if she had a weight pressing on a part of her brain, but that was all it was. In all, she didn't feel much different than when she'd entered the lab that morning.

With more care than she'd expected, Caesar set her down near the cistern of water. Ajax half carried Kase, and the guard allowed him to regain his dignity by stumbling on his own the rest of the way to Hallie, who caught him and lowered him to the ground.

She swallowed and turned toward the men. "Thank you."

Her voice was a whisper, but it was all she could manage. Caesar hesitated, but in the end, he bowed. They then turned and left, the click of the lock echoing against the unforgiving stone. Hallie took a shaky breath. She didn't know how late it was. Had they missed dinner? Kase needed food, something to help him regain his strength.

"Mistress Jules?"

No answer. She looked at Kase, and he pushed himself to a sitting position against the wall, his sweaty face lined with pain.

"Mistress Jules?"

Silence.

"No...no...no..."

Hallie stumbled toward the door, grasping the bars. "Mistress Jules? Are you there?"

Nothing. Pain and sorrow clawed at her chest. *No.* "Kase, she's...she's gone. They've taken her somewhere."

She turned back to him, a single tear rolling down her clammy cheek. Kase's eyes were dark in the shadowed light from Firstmoon coming through the window. She fell to her knees and crawled the rest of the way back to him. "I can't believe she's...I can't believe they..."

Kase reached out, and like someone drowning in a vengeful sea, Hallie fell to the floor, fumbling for his hand, grasping it, not letting go. It was too cold. She put it to her burning forehead, tears falling freely onto the stiff material of her loose trousers. "Kase..."

But all she could do was cry. She was gone. Mistress Jules was gone. Why keep her alive this long, if all Correa was going to do was kill her in the end? Was it a game? Or had she simply wasted away, too overcome with grief at losing everyone she'd loved?

Hallie wrapped her arms around her knees, the ruined timepiece in her pocket digging into her thigh, and pressed her face into the scratchy cloth of her trousers. Kase kept a hand on her back while she cried.

After a while, she helped Kase drink some of the algae-tinged water, but most of it ended up on his shirt. His body was still weak as he laid his head on her shoulder. He didn't say a word, hadn't said anything since they'd returned. Had he lost his voice through all the screaming? Had Correa's power damaged more than she'd thought?

It's all my fault.

They sat there for so long, Hallie nearly drifted off into her old nightmares. Her eyelids had fluttered shut when Kase spoke, his voice rough and dry.

"I started the fire. The one that burned the lower city over three years ago."

"What?" Her voice was tight as she tried to comprehend the words. If he noticed her tense muscles, he ignored them. He hadn't moved his head from her shoulder.

"My father and I argued," Kase whispered, his voice thick. "He knew I intended to run away. Not sure how he did. Ana and I had planned it all. She'd already snuck out of the Manor and was going to find the boy she loved, Owen Christie's grandson, and convince him to join us."

Hallie's mind spun. What was he talking about?

"Father caught me, and one thing led to another. I lost my temper. Shouted obscenities at him. Called him foul, vulgar names. I knew exactly what it took to make him lose control."

Kase's breath rattled with emotion, but Hallie only brought a hand to her lips. She remembered the words he and his father had slung at each other the night of the estate dinner. She remembered the slap, the busted lip.

She'd known it was worse. She'd felt it in her bones, but hearing this now...hearing more about...

Her breathing hitched. Kase didn't stop.

"He might have killed me if Jove hadn't...if Jove hadn't..." Kase's face crumpled, and he pulled up the neck of his shirt to cover his eyes.

"You don't have to tell me," Hallie choked from behind her

fingers, pure shock coursing through her blood. She didn't want it to be true. That this boy, this man, had suffered so much in his life. Shame flooded her cheeks when she thought of her own treatment of him. He might've been rude to her on occasion, but she shouldn't have acted the way she did, said the things she'd said.

"Jove stepped in, took the hardest blows...for me...I ran after that, broken rib, fractured eye socket and all. I ran as far as I could, but my lungs wouldn't let me go much further than the lower city. Too painful. Hid myself in some back alley with a pack of stolen cigarettes and a handful of matches. Breathing hurt like stars, and the smoke soothed it all away. But I was careless. I wasn't thinking straight, and before I knew it, the cottage I'd hidden behind caught fire."

Hallie sucked in a breath. Pieces of the puzzle fit themselves in the gaping spaces. Kase refusing to start the campfire now made sense.

"The blaze was out of control before I could do anything, and soon, nearly the entire city was up in flames. That's how...that's how Ana died. I found her right as she ran into the burning house to save Jasper. I killed them. I killed her lover. I killed stars know how many people because I was blasted—" His own anguish cut him off.

Hallie swallowed hard. "You didn't mean to."

"No one knew what I'd done. My father covered it up, but Eravin knew. He'd always known. His mother died in the fire. He used it as blackmail to get me to turn traitor before you and I came out here. If I didn't join One World, he'd spill to the city who'd burned their neighbors, their friends, their loved ones."

"I don't understand."

A sliver of moonlight painted a stripe across Kase's tearstained face. Hallie closed her eyes as Kase continued, "Father has no qualms about executing family. My uncle, my mother's brother, sold hover secrets to the Cerls, and when I was eight, he went to the gallows. His sons got the firing squad. A small mercy. If I return to Kyvena, I'll face hanging. I didn't have a choice but to run."

"Why—why are you telling me this now?" Hallie barely got the words out. Her throat was clogged with too much emotion.

Kase's eyes opened, and he sat up, his face wrenching in

pain. He brushed off Hallie's offer of help, taking several deep breaths before facing her. The moonlight outlined his form yet shadowed his face. "Because you deserve to know the truth. If I hadn't been so terrified of my father, maybe this wouldn't have happened. If I'd owned up to my actions, taken responsibility, we might not be here now. If I'd done what Eravin said, you'd be safe."

"Kase..." she choked. "You could've escaped. You could have stolen away into Tev Rubika or anywhere else. Instead, you gave yourself up to Correa. Why? Why not save yourself?"

Kase's eyes shone out of the shadows as he cupped her too-cold cheek. Hallie sucked in a breath at his touch. His voice was but a whisper. "Not once have I been able to save the people I wanted to. Not Ana, not Zeke, not even myself. But...but I could sure as stars save *you*."

She blinked furiously, but the tears spilled over anyway, splashing onto her cheeks, onto his fingers. Never in her life had she felt so conflicted. Confusion warred within her with his confession, with his choice to rescue her rather than run away. She felt so...so incredibly...

I love him.

The feeling burned in her mind like the flames he'd described minutes earlier, and it caught her off-guard. Instead of announcing itself at the front door, it'd crept up on her like a thief in the night.

But she knew it to be true.

She'd known it ever since he'd woken after Ben pierced him with that sword. She'd loved him when he'd given her the caramel that night in the trapper's hut, when he'd told her he didn't care who she was, only that she was Hallie Walker. She'd even loved him that evening so long ago when he'd strolled into the bookshop after hours, pilot's goggles and all, demanding a copy of Homer's *Iliad*.

Hallie found the rough stubble on his cheeks, and without stopping to analyze her actions, she pressed her lips to his.

He froze a moment before his fingers trailed from her cheek and twisted themselves in her hair. She kissed him deeply, ignoring the pain aching in her bones, and he his.

He pulled her closer. His lips tasted summertime sweet and salty from their shared tears. Something like fire and ice, sunshine and rain, something wild and untamed sparked in her blood, and she couldn't get enough of him. His fingers tightened at the small of her back, and his other hand caressed her cheek as he smiled against her mouth.

She'd thought she'd loved Niels, and if Jack had never died in that mine, she would have kept on believing that. But whatever that had been was but a single drop in the ocean crashing through her the very moment Kase's lips found hers once more. Her fingers tangled themselves in the messy curls she adored, their silky texture tickling her fingertips.

He pulled back slightly, his breaths coming in soft pants. He leaned his forehead against hers, and his hand drifted down to her neck. Just above the laces of her tunic, his thumbnail traced a pattern on her collarbone, making her weary, aching heart dance. "Hals, I...I..."

Her breath mixed with his as she looked into his eyes and found her own feelings reflected in their depths. A tear escaped her hold. He wiped it with his thumb, but it wasn't born out of fear or sorrow. It wasn't anything other than pure joy, something she hadn't believed possible.

"Thank you." Her voice came out raspy and low, but Kase smiled.

His voice echoed hers. "For the kiss?"

She looked away, heat creeping up her neck. "For saving me."

He was silent for a moment, as if contemplating the words she didn't say. She hoped he knew what it meant to her. When Jack had died, she didn't think she'd ever discover someone who would care enough to find the part of herself she'd hidden away—the woman who yearned to be loved for who she was, past, present, and future.

The cracks in her soul had finally begun to heal thanks to the pompous pilot who'd barged in with his crooked smile, messy hair, and soft heart.

"Always." His warm lips caressed her temple as he spoke, bringing her back to the present.

As she snuggled closer, tucking herself into his side, Hallie couldn't keep the small smile from her face. It never left even as she fell into a dreamless sleep.

CHAPTER 34

ESSENCE OF TIME

Kase

KASE'S BONES ACHED FROM THE lightning coursing through his body the previous day. His muscles didn't want to move, nor did his eyelids want to open, but that, in particular, was because the dream he'd found himself in didn't involve screaming. It didn't involve him reaching out for Zeke's hand as a pool of blood swallowed his brother. For the first time in a long time, his unconscious mind hadn't tortured him with his mistakes.

Instead, he and Hallie ran through a field of golden grain, hand in hand, the Nardens a serene backdrop. She laughed when he pulled her close, the breeze sweeping her unbound hair off her shoulders, her eyes alight with mischief and something else he couldn't quite name.

A single drop of icy water splashed onto his face. He blinked. He wasn't in a field of dreams any longer. His reality was that of a dank and cold dungeon.

Instead of holding his hand, Hallie sat up, knees pulled to her chest, face pressed against them.

"Hals?"

She looked up. Red rimmed her eyes, and her skin dripped with sweat, even though Kase himself shivered from the chilly air. Her voice was soft as she said, "Couldn't sleep."

"I know my kisses are good," Kase said, running a hand through his hair, "but I don't think they're worth losing sleep over."

Her laugh was too forced and shook as she wiped sweat from her brow. Kase grabbed her hand and pulled her closer to him, but he dropped it almost immediately.

"You're burning with fever!" Grunting in pain, he scrambled to his knees and cupped water in his hands from the cistern and unceremoniously poured it on top of her head.

"Kase!" she squealed and shivered hard. "That's not helping. At all."

Kase stopped in the process of grabbing another handful. "You need a medic."

He suddenly wished he'd gone into the medical field because he didn't know what diseases leaky dungeons and the consumption of algae-tinged water could cause. Nothing good.

Hallie shook her head vigorously, grabbing it as she did so. "No, no, no. It's not that. I think it's the Lord Elder. I can...I can feel him deep down inside me somewhere. Like he's on the other side of a fogged-up window. I think he's been holding back the heat since yesterday, but now...now he's losing grip or something. I can't talk with him. He can't hear me. I don't know what to do."

The whole idea of the Lord Elder being inside Hallie's head made him uneasy, but Kase didn't have time to worry about it. He put a hand to her forehead. It burned. "We'll figure it out."

She laid her head against his shoulder, and he laced his fingers through hers. Ana's ring glinted up at him even in the poor lighting.

He squeezed tighter and placed a chaste kiss on her sweaty, soaked hair. "I promise."

The rest of the morning passed in relative silence, and her breathing became easier the longer they stayed together. The heat receded from her body, and Kase was grateful for the small reprieve. He still couldn't fathom that she'd taken in whatever was left of the Lord Elder...for him.

So he wouldn't be in pain.

He clenched his jaw as he remembered Correa's electric touch. It had felt like Skibs had stabbed him with that sword all over again. The thought of possibly having to relive it once more that day made his stomach roil. He didn't know if he could take it.

But the memory of Hallie's lips on his, of her fingers tangled in his hair, made his heart thump in his chest and brought a sad grin to his face. Of course, he would find it—whatever the feeling was—when he was imprisoned in a dungeon. He looked down at their hands again.

If she got out of here alive, it would all be worth it. If he needed to, he would die to make that happen.

Hallie

THE HEAT IN HALLIE'S BODY subsided with rest and her hand tucked into Kase's. She hadn't been able to contact the Lord Elder the entire time, and that worried Hallie. Her head ached, and she wondered if it was a manifestation of him holding back his power. The world was bleary as she opened her eyes to the dungeon cell.

She blinked, and everything came into clearer focus, though it fuzzed in and out. She put a hand to her head.

"How're you feeling?" asked a soft voice above her.

Hallie looked into Kase's haggard face. His skin had a new pale undertone, and his eyes were slightly bloodshot, as if he'd not slept in days. His curls were tangled.

At least she could take the memory of their kisses with her when she died; she wouldn't last long with the Lord Elder's power. She felt it in her bones; she felt the heat. He'd been correct. Her body couldn't handle it.

A tear slipped down her cheek, and Kase wiped it away. "Talk to me."

She shook her head, too tired and too overcome with the knowledge of her fate to say anything. She simply burrowed herself into his chest.

I need to enjoy the hours I have left.

Kase slid his arms around her, and he laid his cheek against the top of her head. Though she was at the end, she'd never felt so safe.

But like every other time she'd finally found a place to belong, a place to finally become part of, something dashed it to pieces.

The door to the cells clanked open and boots clacked upon the stone. In seconds, Caesar and Ajax stood outside the cell door, the former unlocking it. Hallie sprang out of Kase's arms and stumbled to her feet.

Caesar's voice was less gruff as he said, "You're to come with us." He looked back toward the other door before he opened the cell. With a nod from Ajax, Caesar's eyes betrayed pity. "I'm sorry."

Kase used the wall to help him stand, but he did it without her help. His strength must've been returning. That gave Hallie hope. If they were going to break out of this place, he'd need to be able to walk. Hallie would have enough trouble getting herself to the window on the second floor. This was it. And then Hallie would die somewhere up in the mountains where there was no one else to hurt.

She hadn't told Kase that last part. The burning in her head had grown in the last few minutes alone.

Please, Lord Elder. Just a little while longer.

No response.

"Where are you taking us?" Kase growled, still holding onto the wall. He let go of it, faltered a little, but before Hallie could put out a hand to steady him, he gained control of his body and stood tall. Stubborn prat. "Correa's done enough."

Again, the pitying look. This time from both Caesar and Ajax. Caesar spoke up, "We only follow the orders."

Kase crossed his arms. "And if we refuse?"

Ajax shook his head, but Caesar was the one who answered. "Then we all pay the price."

"It's okay." Hallie put a hand on Kase's arm. "We'll be all right."

The lie was acid on her tongue, but she said it all the same.

With both their guards being a little sympathetic, it might

be easier to give them the slip. She wondered how late it was, and if the distraction was about to start; but nothing in Kase's eyes told her the answer. Nothing about his demeanor gave her a clue as to what they would do if they couldn't work themselves out of this knot. All she knew was she couldn't subject Kase to the lightning again...except she didn't know if they had a choice. If they didn't go with the guards, Correa might come down and make them. Hallie would rather it be on her own terms instead.

She turned back to Caesar and Ajax. "What happened to Mistress Jules? Is she still..."

The look on Ajax's face said it all.

She blinked and buried the emotion within. Now was not the time to lose her head. She had to keep it together, though everything around her was falling apart.

Caesar waved his hand toward the door. "Please, don't make this any harder on yourselves."

With one last deep breath, Hallie slipped on Kase's jacket and grabbed his hand. His fingers latched onto hers and held them tight. He gave her strength even though his steps faltered. She kept him upright as they followed Ajax up the stairs and through the corridors.

Kase squeezed her hand once they reached the second floor near the planned escape route, but of course, with a guard behind and before them and two sets of patrol teams going opposite ways, it would be a long shot. She gave him a subtle shake of her head, and he nodded back. Kase was too weak to do anything to take out the soldiers. They'd have to wait for Niels' distraction, which would hopefully come soon. Even then, they might not make it out.

Her body's temperature rose another notch. She should've left the jacket behind.

Lord Elder. I don't know what else to do.

No response. No feelings of comfort. Nothing.

Ajax led them to a set of arched doors that looked to be older than Achilles itself. Chariots and horses adorned them, calling back to an epic battle Hallie wished she could read about. Ajax opened the doors with both hands, pushing them inward into a cavernous room with a ceiling high as the dining room at Shackley Manor. The arched beams met in the middle, making it cathedral-esque. At the front of the room stood a dais, and upon it, a long table lined with people. Many were dressed in military uniforms, their various achievements flashing on their shoulders and breasts.

Kase gasped, dropping her hand, as he stared at the end of the table where a few soldiers were stationed. They stood behind the final seat to the left. In the chair sat a man Hallie never thought she'd see again. He wasn't wearing his fur hat, which gave her a clear view of his too-blue eyes framed by impossibly long lashes. His winter coat and scarf were also missing.

Yarrow.

The last time she'd seen him had been with his blood dripping onto pale snow, his face determined as he fired relentlessly at the Cerls in the Pass.

Once he noticed Hallie and Kase's gazes, he looked down at the table. Hallie's heart pounded in her chest.

"Mr. Yarrow," she rasped, her throat tightening.

The trapper didn't listen, didn't make a move toward them. He only turned to speak with a soldier behind him, revealing the interlaced trio of diamonds tattooed on his neck in blue ink.

Cerl soldier.

She itched to grab Kase's hand again, if only to make sure she wasn't stuck in a nightmare, but Correa's eyes were on her. Any other words she might have said died on her tongue.

Yarrow wasn't only working with their enemies. He *was* one.

Holy blasting stars.

Hallie didn't like the grin spreading across Correa's pale face in her peripheral as she continued to stare at the trapper. Heat pulsing in time with her heartbeat, she tore her eyes away, focusing on the steps before her. She needed to appear strong. She didn't know how much longer she could hold it all in, not with the pressure and the revelation of Yarrow sitting there among Jayde's enemies.

At any moment, she would combust.

Reaching the center of the room, they stopped, Caesar and Ajax holding onto Kase and Hallie's shoulders to keep them in place. Correa stepped forward, and Hallie looked away from Yarrow, who still refused to make eye contact. Whether from shame or hatred, she didn't know.

With each step Correa took, Hallie wished she could step back, but Ajax's hand held her firm. Could he feel the heat radiating off her skin?

Lord Elder, please.

Correa stopped in front of them and turned to the awaiting dignitaries and leaders. Many of them wore the same uniform as Correa, but there were a few who were not military. A porcelain-skinned woman sat near the center of the table. She twisted the tail of her thick navy braid and leaned on her other hand, gazing up at the man beside her.

The man she watched was young, maybe a few years older than Hallie. He was wide of shoulder and looked like he'd much rather be watching a groggon match than sitting here privy to Hallie's fate. Light from the single-tiered, unembellished candle chandelier hanging above caught in each swish of sparkling white wine as he swirled his glass. He was the only one with a drink. A golden circlet crowned his blond hair, which fell around his face before ending in a simple knot at the nape of his neck. His mouth was quirked as if he were about to laugh, but it was his eyes that held Hallie fast. They were bright gold, even more so than his hair.

Yalv.

But who was he? Somehow, he seemed...familiar, like a half-remembered dream. Had she met him in Myrrai?

"Our esteemed guests," Correa started as he came to stand beside Hallie. She tried not to flinch away as he laid a hand on her shoulder. She bit her lip to keep from crying out, though no electric shock ripped through her body. "We welcome you. Before our demonstration here today, His Royal Majesty, King Filip will—"

Yarrow stood. Even without his jacket, he was a mammoth of a man. The soldiers behind him grabbed his shoulders, forcing him back to his seat, hands on the pistols at their sides. Yarrow didn't sit. Instead, he glared at Correa. "I don't give a blasted crap about your demonstration. Ya got the girl."

What? Anger fueled the flame already kindling under her skin.

"Of course, Mr. Barbary. You did well bringing us Miss Walker, and as we agreed, you will receive your reward.

However, your brother wasn't nearly as *agreeable* as you are."
Correa's hand left her shoulder as he stepped toward the bear of
a man. "Like you, he knew the consequences, yet he chose to be
difficult, and you, more than anyone, know that Cerulene
cannot survive on disobedience."

Yarrow roared, leaping across the table with agility Hallie
would never have guessed he possessed. Several of the others
stood; some drew weapons and pointed at the unhinged
trapper. Correa merely grabbed Yarrow's face with both hands,
sparks leaping from his fingers. Yarrow dropped like a stone,
howling.

Kase grabbed Hallie's hand. She squeezed back, hard
enough to make her own fingers ache. Their guards didn't stop
them.

"Most deserters never get the chance to right their wrongs."
Correa dusted his hands and waved at the others to seat
themselves once more. "Pity you wasted yours, Mr. Barbary.
Being as it is, this is an excellent segue into our first event. Your
Majesty, if you will."

He paused. Hallie glanced up from where she'd been
focusing on the twitching Yarrow to find everyone staring at the
handsome blond man, who only smiled and took another sip of
his drink.

That man was King Filip? The same one who starved his
people so he could live lavishly in his castle in Sol Adrid?

He was Yalven? Or was Hallie mistaken?

This is worse than I imagined.

Hallie glanced at Kase in her peripheral vision, but he
hadn't reacted. In fact, he looked bored. His eyes watched
another corner of the room like he didn't care a bit. The only
indication of his true feelings was the slight shaking of his hand
as she clutched his fingers.

Even in the Gate chamber when they faced Ben, Kase had
been confident. Now, with the unknown torture surely awaiting
them...what would they do to the son of the Stradat Lord
Kapitan? Kase was basically a prince. He was someone
important. Someone Cerulene could use.

Hallie's breaths grew shallow and faster. She had to get him
out of here. But how? How could she do anything when Correa
stood feet away in all his power? In their weakened state, they

couldn't handle Caesar and Ajax either —much less everyone else in this room. Hallie's throat was closing as she tried to swallow the vile, bitter taste in her mouth. Her eyes scanned the room for anything, anything at all, they could use.

But all she saw was the long, thin window directly behind the king's chair, the sun setting on the horizon. They were too high. She and Kase would never survive that even if they could make it through the opening.

As the king set his glass aside and pushed himself to his feet, the tension in the room rose even more. Yarrow's twitches morphed into sobs as Filip walked around the table. He stopped in front of the sniveling trapper.

Tears slid down Hallie's cheeks. Kase's shaking grew more prominent. She squeezed his hand until her own was numb.

"My love," Filip said, looking back at the table. His voice was silky and deep, like the ocean, immense and unmoving. "Your focus."

The woman with the braid rose from her seat. Her draped purple skirts swished as she joined the king. She took his offered hand, and they each held out the other above Yarrow. Without a word, sunlight enveloped the quaking man. The trapper screamed so loudly, Hallie felt as if something inside her was breaking. It echoed in the chamber, its pitch magnified a thousand times with the stone walls and high ceiling. Hallie clenched her teeth against the pain in her heart.

Then, there was silence.

The light faded, and King Filip and the woman lowered their hands. The glow from Yarrow might have been gone, but now, the woman's chest, where her heart lay, emitted a faint light. She covered it with her hand, a grimace on her face. The king led her back around the table and to their seats. Correa gestured for the guards to remove the immobile body.

Because that's all Yarrow was. A shell. His limbs no longer twitched. His chest refused to rise and fall.

He was dead.

Hallie couldn't move. She couldn't even breathe. She stared at the spot where Yarrow had lain before the king of Cerulene and the woman sucked the life from the trapper's body.

Correa's voice held an undercurrent of mirth as he spoke

next. "Fate has blessed His Royal Majesty with this gift, the Essence of Souls...for if she'd chosen to turn her eye from our plight, Jagamot might reign. But alas, Fate is kind."

He turned, looking directly at Hallie. Nausea reared its ugly head. She oscillated from hot to cold and back again. Correa gripped her shoulder, touting her forward, her numb hand slipping from Kase's. "She has brought us the key."

Darkness warred with light at the edges of her vision.

"You, Hallie Walker, Essence of Time, will save us all. With four of the five Essences prepared, we are closer to fulfilling the prophecies, to uniting the wayward nations of Yalvara, and finally defeating Jagamot once and for all. With Miss Walker, we are one step closer, with only the Essence of Spark to bring under our banner."

She looked back at Kase, who was nearly white as the snow outside. Even then, his glare was icy. He no longer shook. Instead, his gaze was directed at King Filip. It was like he was piecing something together, but the answer kept leaping out of his reach.

"We've tried the diplomatic option with Jayde," Correa continued, his grip still tight on her shoulder, though she was past feeling pain as heat raged within her. "We warned them with the assassination of one of their Stradats, but they refused to yield. Therefore, we will force them under our wing for their own good."

He let Hallie's shoulder go and walked past her to put a hand on Kase's. He didn't flinch. "Which is one reason I've invited this particular guest to today's demonstration. Council, please welcome Kase Shackley, son of Jayde's Stradat Lord Kapitan."

Hallie closed her eyes. Her lids burned. Her fingers burned. Everything burned. The linen material of her tunic stuck to her shaking body underneath Kase's jacket.

Let this end.

"Then, please," King Filip said, picking up his glass once more, "quit this posturing so Fate knows you haven't wasted her gift. My brother should be carrying out the attack on the Jaydian capital as we speak."

Attack on Kyvena? Hallie's breaths sped up. *Petra, Ellis, Nole, and Mazie.*

Hallie looked up to find King Filip surveying her. He smiled. It made his face even more handsome, though it was a cruel, cold sort. He continued speaking as if she wasn't about to lose the little that she had in her stomach. "Besides, I think your guests tire of being the objects of our stares, Correa."

The woman who'd helped him murder Yarrow quirked her lips, but she was the only one who truly reacted to the king's statement. The glow had faded from her chest at last. Many of the other officials murmured at the words, but they quieted once Correa spoke. "Of course, Your Majesty. I only wanted to give context for our work. Our esteemed patronages have waited for this day nearly as long as we have."

Even in Hallie's feverish state, she heard the dissonance of his words. She peeked over at Kase, who glared, and then at Filip, who smiled, his interest radiating like a sunbeam.

Hallie's throat burned as she puked onto the floor, marring Correa's polished boots. Lightning burned through her as Correa slapped her across the face.

Her vision went dark as her knees slammed the stone floor. Kase's screams joined hers.

And then her vision returned. She knelt in her own vomit, Kase panting beside her. She couldn't even register what had happened until someone wrenched her up by the shoulder.

"Please," Ajax whispered in her ear as he helped her straighten. "Just do as he says."

Kase fought Caesar to get to Hallie, but he was no use after the torture; Hallie wasn't any better, the fire burning within her.

Hallie's breaths came out in sobs as Ajax held her up. Correa's smile faltered, but it'd been a slip so fast Hallie was unsure if she even saw it through her tears. He turned back to the assembled crowd. "The Essence of Time's power is beyond our imaginings, for it has the ability to manipulate time. Hallie Walker, heir to the Lord Elder, will demonstrate this by unwinding the Stradat Lord Kapitan's son. If she does not, he will suffer the deserter's same fate, a fate worse than death." He stared right into her eyes, but she could hardly see them. "Hallie, my dear girl, you will choose his death. My gift to you after causing you so much pain."

I'm begging you, Lord Elder. Please. Please, help me.

"No," she moaned, her breaths coming harder now as she

cried, wiping her mouth with her jacket sleeve. Yarrow screamed in her head, drowning out all coherent thought. "No, please. There must be another way. There must be some other way I can prove to you—"

The sting and force of Correa's second slap sent her keeling over into Kase. This one hadn't had the force of lightning behind it. Ajax hadn't been expecting it, but he righted her before she fell to the ground. Kase roared and launched himself at Correa only to be hauled back, his arms twisted behind him.

Correa turned to Caesar. "Bind Master Shackley's hands." Then he leaned toward Hallie, close enough to whisper in her ear. "His life isn't worth the millions who will die once Jagamot's darkness reigns. If you love him at all, kill him and save the world."

She didn't want the power. She didn't want to save the world. She wanted to die.

Correa stepped back as Caesar forced Kase to his knees. Hallie's tears came too hard and too fast. She couldn't control her breathing. The pain in her head climbed to a crescendo.

She couldn't hold on for much longer.

And then Kase looked up at her, his blue eyes clear and calm, so different than they had been only minutes before. Caesar bent down to check Kase's bindings, but he didn't fight. He didn't do anything but look up at Hallie.

He knew they'd lost. He'd given up.

If Hallie didn't kill him, King Filip would. What would break inside her at Kase's death scream?

Correa found her hands and guided them to Kase's face. His cheeks were wet. He hadn't been able to escape his fate; he would die no matter what he did, no matter what Hallie chose.

Death awaited them both.

His lips moved, but she couldn't hear his words. She shook her head, tears blinding her. Her fingers trembled on his skin. She couldn't do it. She couldn't kill him.

PLEASE, LORD ELDER.

The door to the room burst open, someone shouted something, but Hallie couldn't decipher the words. She could no longer contain the power within her. With everything she had left, she channeled her heat into Correa's hands on her wrists.

And then, the world burned.

CHAPTER 35

AT THE END OF ALL THINGS

Kase

KASE CURSED CORREA, YARROW, AND Harlan. He cursed himself.

How had he allowed those thrice-blasted Cerls to take Hallie away from him? Why had he wasted time arguing with her? What was his purpose, if all he was destined to do was die here in front of these people without any way to stop the oncoming storm?

And Kyvena. Being attacked. By Cerls.

He'd left his mother, Jove, and Clara, to keep them safe; it was all for naught.

What had he done in his life that helped anyone? He remembered Hallie's words from the night Zeke died; she'd said he'd saved her, and he'd tried to do so again. But neither led to a future of happiness. Neither ended with a solution to the sorry excuse his life was.

He kept his outward visage calm, though he raged inside. As much as he hated himself, he wanted even more to kill the man who stood before them like an actor on stage, preening and posturing to show off the monster he created. Though his monster was Hallie, her hair and tunic soaked with tears and sweat.

Kase's heart thumped painfully. He wanted to hold her so tightly he lost himself within her, but his mistakes made sure that would never happen. His time was up. He could run no longer.

He barely heard anything besides the pounding in his ears as he fought to control his emotions, which wavered like leaves in the wind. His captor bent to check Kase's bound wrists. He didn't want to die on his knees, but what was the use in fighting?

Correa took Hallie's hands and placed them on Kase's tear-streaked face. Her eyes flooded, and the dam burst. Her mouth opened in a silent, painful grimace.

I'm sorry, Hallie. I'm not going to get you home.

Her burning hands pressed into the sides of his face, shaking and slick with sweat. Correa held them in place. This was the end. He didn't know what she could do. He didn't know what Correa meant by unwinding him, or about Jagamot, or any of it. He didn't want to know. All he wanted was to die.

He looked up into Hallie's golden eyes that still shone like jewels through her tears. If only he could take her pain away...but he couldn't even manage his own.

"I love you."

At least he would die with the truth on his lips.

Hallie collapsed as Correa's hands exploded, lightning flashing in all directions. Kase fell backward, his anguished shrieks ricocheting around the cavernous space as the door burst open, revealing a guard. "Attack at the gate!" The man yelled.

Niels.

Then everything caught fire.

Shouting. Crashing. Heat.

Cool metal bit into his wrist before the rope fell away. His guard. He'd cut his bonds. Blood rushed into his hands and out the slice near his right wrist, but he ignored it, diving for Hallie as the world exploded around them.

A roar grew in the room. It sounded like the walls themselves were coming apart at the seams. Bodies pressed in around them, trying to escape, but Kase only held Hallie's limp body in his arms, his blood staining her tunic collar as one hand held her burning face. Ana's ring glowed with the flames climbing walls behind him.

"HALLIE!" he screamed. "HALLIE!"

She didn't answer. Kase didn't think. He scooped her into his arms and staggered toward the door. He took two steps and nearly fell over, his legs weak, when another pair of arms caught him.

Kase wrenched free, turning to see who stopped him, but it was one of his guards. The one who'd cut him loose. He mouthed something, but the crashing behind him and bodies pressing in drowned out his words.

The man grabbed Kase's dirty, too-stiff shirt and dragged him and Hallie from the room. Kase didn't look back as the arched ceiling fell and crashed with a resounding *boom*. He sprinted through the corridors, the walls shaking and creaking and about to collapse.

Had Niels found something stronger than the flash bombs? Holy blasting shocks. He was going to kill them all.

At another rumbling sound, the tall, muscular guard stumbled into Kase as the floor cracked into shards and tripped them both. Kase took the brunt of the impact as they barreled into a wall, cradling Hallie in his arms. He thanked the stars-blasted adrenaline pumping in his veins, but his shoulder flared with pain. The guard tugged him back the other way, and they sprinted, passing guards and soldiers and servants. No one cared what Kase was doing. He'd lost track of Correa and King Filip.

They passed the second-floor window that was to be Hallie and Kase's escape route, and Kase slid to a stop. "Guard! Through here! We don't have time!"

The guard skidded and nearly fell, but he whipped out a pistol from his holster. The barrel was jagged and frayed like the ones Kase had seen in Myrrai. Kase turned, shielding Hallie. "What're you doing?"

The guard fired at the window. The glass splintered into a thousand pieces like the light of shattered skies. It cut Kase's exposed skin, and he gritted his teeth against the stinging pain. At least Hallie was unscathed.

The guard kicked out the rest of the window as the fort gave another shuddering quake. Kase was going to kill Niels if they survived this. He peeked out the window. "Can you land that?"

They were only two stories from the ground, and hanging from his hands, the guard could probably make the leap without breaking his legs. The snow patches were dirty and sparse, a layer of dead grass oozing through the holes. This was the back of the fort closest to the smaller gate.

The guard climbed through the window. Kase watched him lower himself down and hang by his hands before letting go. *Thank the stars.*

Another rumble. Kase fell to his knees, Hallie nearly tumbling out of his arms, but he caught her before her head cracked against the floor. Fire ripped through the corridor to his right, impossibly eating away at the stone.

He froze.

The cigarette landed in a pile of filth as Kase lit another. Blood coated his fingers. His head pounded.

Kase couldn't escape the fire. It followed him. It would never grant him peace, even here at the end of all things.

The long drag of the next smoke only ended in a coughing fit. His lungs screamed. Throwing the cigarette behind him, he pulled out another and tried to light it, but the pain building in his head was too much. He couldn't concentrate. He couldn't control his fingers. The match and cigarette lit, but both slipped onto a patch of straw below.

Heat grew behind him. He didn't know where—

He blinked. His back. It burned with heat, and he turned to find the fire licking at the stones feet away from him. Hallie's hand grasped his as she struggled to sit up. "Kase! We have to..." Her words slurred.

Blood spurted from his mouth and trickled down his chin and into his tunic collar as he ran. He didn't have time to stop and cough. The city was on fire. He needed to find Ana. This was his chance to leave this place behind, but he sure as the moons wouldn't leave her.

The roof of the neighboring cottage collapsed in a shower of sparks. Screams rent the air as people fled the blaze. The Watch patrolmen tried in vain to pump well water up through hoses and douse the destruction. The streets ran with black water, but it wasn't enough.

He turned the corner and saw her.
"ANA!"
The firelight limned her blonde hair. Did she see him?
"ANA!" He stumbled closer. "ANA NO!"
She shook her head, tears and panic lacing her eyes, as she turned back to the building. Kase reached for her, but she leapt away from his grasp, darting into the carnage. He fell to his knees. He couldn't get up. Everything hurt.

His body burned. He screamed, and someone dragged him away from the heat. His body refused to move on its own. Muscled arms encircled his torso.

Ana stumbled from the door, her sweater in charred tatters, her skin red and raw. The cobblestones bit into Kase's knees as he caught her, only adding to the searing pain in his head, his chest, and his back.

"Ana, no, please..." She didn't move. He turned, looking for anyone. "HELP! PLEASE! I NEED A MEDIC!"

But the lane was empty.

Kase pulled his sister into his lap and hugged her tight, her blood staining his soiled trousers further. Tears seared his skin. His eyes burned from the flames mere feet away. Smoke clogged his lungs.

Then darkness came.

CHAPTER 36

SMOLDER INTO DUST

Jove

JOVE DUG OUT A SMOKE and his lighter as he and his mother rode through the upper city. The streets were too quiet. Only a few brave souls ventured out into the early evening, probably to drink themselves into denial that the world was changing too quickly for anyone to keep up. First, Cerulene had murdered Stradat Richter and his entire family, and now the Stradat Lord Kapitan would hang.

The city air smelled of smoke and revolution.

His mother looked up with bloodshot eyes as he lit the tip of the cigarette. Her demure black gown and matching cloak reflected Jove's mood. "Is there nothing we can do?"

He stuffed the lighter in his pocket and cracked the window using the crank in the door. He took a puff before he responded. "No."

"I don't know how much more I can take," she whispered. She took in a shaking breath. "I married your father because he promised me a better life, one of freedom from our station. And now, I'll have lost nearly everything that means anything to me at all."

Jove used the top of the window to knock ashes from his cigarette tip. They tumbled in the breeze as the motorcoach drove through the front gates of Shackley Manor. He didn't say anything as he helped his mother out. She walked to the door where Thoreau welcomed her inside. Jove didn't follow.

Instead, he strode toward the front gate, one hand in his pocket, the other tossing the last of the cigarette onto the cobblestones to smolder into dust. In his memories, the streets ran with blood and ash-laden water. Jove sniffed and fingered another cigarette. He meandered through the upper city, keeping far from the wall. He didn't want to hear the cheers when the wall guard announced that his father would be executed in less than twelve hours.

It was a miracle Jove wasn't to hang with him.

He found his way into a tavern not far from McKenzie Square. Only a few patrons sat inside, and Jove took the booth in the far corner. The wood was too hard, the room too silent. He ordered himself a tankard of ale and waited, staring at nothing, counting the seconds until he could get lost in the sweet numbness of alcohol.

His father's words still echoed in his head.

I did everything in my power to protect this country, to protect my family. I do not regret my actions.

It sounded so noble on the surface, until you looked deeper, until you knew the truth.

He took a long drink of ale once the barmaid delivered it to the table. His mother, his wife, and his son waited for his return home. Clara would be frustrated that he'd chosen to drink away his worries. She meant well, but she didn't understand. She couldn't understand. Raised in a lovely family where everyone was honest, where everyone was simply kind, Clara had never experienced the trauma Jove suffered.

He was thankful for that, but only one person could understand why he sat alone in a near empty tavern planning to drown himself in ale. Unfortunately, that person was a stars-blasted idiot of a brother.

Jove hated that he cared so much. He despised the white-hot pain in his chest when he thought of Kase, of his father, of Ana, of Zeke. How much more could he take?

He drank deeply from his tankard. The warring notes of sweet fruits and bitter hops clashed on his tongue.

Bliss.

The tavern door swung open as Jove sloshed more alcohol down his throat. Someone slid into his booth. The man was built like a politician and dressed to the nines. The scarlet color of his tailored frock coat brought out the warmer, rosy undertones to his umber skin—something Jove would only notice with alcohol beginning to flow in his veins.

"Figured I'd find you here," Anderson said, thrumming his fingers on the tabletop. He peeked into Jove's tankard. "And empty. Blazes, mate. You could out-drink a fish."

Jove waved at the barmaid, signaling for another. "You come to berate me? Be the father I never had?"

Anderson didn't say anything when Jove's next drink was delivered with a prompt *thunk*, amber liquid and foam sloshing over the side. Jove took a pull. Anderson waited until Jove had replaced the tankard onto the thick tabletop. Then he leaned forward, making sure Jove looked at him. "Your butler sent me to make sure you didn't end up in a ditch. I don't particularly enjoy being your keeper, but I owe you."

"For what?"

Anderson smiled. "You saved me from predation. Remember that vampire woman who masqueraded as the Silver Coast's head magistrate's daughter?"

Jove blinked, trying to think back. "That was years ago, and she wasn't a vampire."

"I don't know." Jove's friend leaned back, looking around conspiratorially. "She was too pale, even for a white woman. And I swear she had fangs. Noticed them when she ate her prime rib—rare."

"You sound like Kase." Jove shook his head. "And all I did was promise *him* my dessert if he spilled wine all down her dress."

Anderson stole Jove's tankard. After taking a long pull, he wiped his mouth with the back of his hand. "If you survive the night without getting rip-roaring drunk and challenging a disreputable character to a duel, then I've done my duty. It's thanks to you, and Kase, I'm marrying Miss Lieber instead of someone who can transform into a bat at will."

He slid the tankard back over, and Jove took it. "What's to say your betrothed doesn't feast on blood every night? You don't even know her."

The barmaid deposited another ale at the table without Jove asking. He pushed it toward his friend. Anderson didn't drink it. "She's as good a match as any." He traced the rim of the tankard. "Not all of us are lucky enough to have a Clara."

His wife's soft smile came to his mind. She was probably sleeping by this time, awaiting Samuel to wake once more so she could feed him. "I definitely don't deserve her."

"Self-deprecation isn't charming."

"I don't. Not after everything. She deserves to be with someone who—someone who isn't me." He took another drink, not bothering to wipe the foam from his lip. "She's good. I'm not. At all. Not after being raised by that monster."

Anderson looked around once more, sliding out of the booth. He slapped a few gold fivers on the table. "Let's get you home."

"No."

"Listen." Anderson put one hand on the table, the other on the bench behind Jove, and leaned in, his words coming out as a harsh whisper. "Too many people in this city want your head even if the High Council has cleared you. My job is to get you home in one piece so you can stay with your wife and son for a very long time on this stars-forsaken planet. You're not the only one who had a crappy childhood, so stop playing the martyr."

Jove looked up into his friend's dark eyes and saw the turmoil wrestling in their depths. Growing up in an overly privileged home was something many people didn't realize was a burden. Where power and influence abounded, a lack of love and attention followed. Lord Reuben had abused his son in a different way. "Why did you come?"

"Because your butler asked me to."

"Cut the crap and tell me the truth."

Anderson clenched his jaw, breathing deeply. He pulled back, looking off toward the front door. He took a moment before turning back to Jove. "Because I know what it's like to lose a father—particularly one you only wanted to care that you existed."

Jove could feel every beat of his sorry heart. Sliding out of the booth, he dug some change out of his pocket. He snatched Anderson's coins from the table and pressed them into his friend's chest. "Then let's go."

Jove stomped out of the tavern, his friend following close behind. Night had fallen, and with it, the temperature. He shivered in his coat, wishing he'd worn something thicker underneath instead of the thin linen shirt and vest. The streets were still empty. A faint chant came from the direction of the upper gate. Jove couldn't decipher the words. He could still taste the last swig of ale on his breath.

He walked in silence up to McKenzie Square and across it to the Jayde Center. The glass dome glowed with light from within. He made his way up the stairs. Anderson hadn't said a word in the time they'd left the tavern, but he seemed to know exactly what Jove planned to do, and he would stand by him.

Fishing out his identification papers, another roll of parchment fell. The intercepted Cerl missive he was supposed to break for Heddie.

He stuffed it back in the outer jacket pocket. That could wait. He flashed his other papers at the door guard. Anderson copied his movements, and both entered the building.

Once inside, Jove marched straight toward the stairs that would take him to the underground levels. His father would be held in the cells reserved for those awaiting their deadly fate. It should be empty save for the Stradat Lord Kapitan. Anyone else would be held at the Watch station.

A few guards milled about. On one of the upper floors, a few followed Stradat Loffler to stars knew where...probably to take a nap instead of doing something important. The capital was on edge, yet that mattered little to the elderly government leader. Granted, Jove wouldn't want to be holed up with Stradat Sarson discussing policy when she'd finally found a way to take down the Stradat Lord Kapitan, so he couldn't blame Loffler for escaping.

One of the doors to the west wing opened, and Saldr appeared. Just as Jove and Anderson made it to the stairs, the Yalv spotted him.

"Master Shackley!"

ALLI EARNEST

Jove paused, trying not to look annoyed. He had a purpose, and he would not be dissuaded from it by some magic hocus pocus he didn't care about. He'd also forgotten to ask about Miss Walker with everything going on.

The man looked more frazzled than he had during the sentencing that afternoon. His braid was unkempt and his cloak off kilter. "I need to speak with you."

Jove looked at the stairs, at Anderson, and back to the Yalv. "There's something I need to do first."

He didn't wait for an answer, only made his way down into the bowels of the Jayde Center. Saldr followed.

Flashing his papers at the guards at the bottom of the stairs, he entered the holding cells. A subtle scent of mildew permeated the cold, wet air. Jove shivered. The door shut with a clang.

A single hanging electric lantern lit the short corridor. Running along the sides were rows of metal bars. No privacy for those awaiting the end. A guard had followed them inside, as if Jove would be stupid enough to do something reckless.

Harlan sat, elbows on his knees, on his threadbare cot. Stripped of his medals, of his pride and honor, his hair was a mess, his shirt untucked. He glanced up with wearied eyes as the party approached his door.

"Come to say your goodbye, I see." He stood and walked slowly toward the door.

Jove dug his hands into his pockets to keep himself from reaching through bars and clawing his father. "Seems your impending death has brought out your sarcasm."

Harlan stopped at the door, his nose only inches from Jove's. They were the same height, same muscular structure. Yet his father looked so much like Zeke in that moment that Jove blinked, shaking his head to rid himself of his dead brother. His breathing picked up.

Harlan said nothing. His facial expression didn't change. It was like stone, chiseled and unaffected by time. Only his eyes hinted at his true feelings. Usually full of spite, water lined the edges now. It was almost imperceptible except to one who'd grown up under their careful watch.

"The key." Jove worked his jaw. "Give me the key."

The guard hesitated. "I have no authorization to unlock his

387

cell."

Jove pulled his hand out of his pocket and held it out. Heddie's parchment fell to the floor. He ignored it. "Give it to me."

"Go ahead, Bronson." Harlan said, looking directly at the soldier. "I've accepted my fate."

The key was cool in Jove's hand as he unlocked the door. Anderson bent down and grabbed the parchment, but Jove didn't care.

The bars of the door smooth under Jove's fingers as it opened with a loud creak. He stepped inside, his father retreating to give him room. A gesture of respect. Jove thought about spitting at his father's scuffed boots.

"What is this?" Anderson asked.

Jove didn't look back. "Something for Heddie. Haven't been able to crack it yet."

Harlan furrowed his brow. "A code?"

"It's Yalven," Anderson said, his voice soft.

Jove turned. "I would've recognized it if so."

His friend looked up, his dark eyes curious. "It looks like Petra's school work."

Saldr stepped up. "May I?"

Anderson handed it over. Saldr stared at the parchment, his eyes scrunched. "It's an old dialect, muddied with a good amount of dead Cerleze."

Harlan stepped up to the bars. "Can you read it?"

"It's addressed to Owen Christie. It says that he has disobeyed orders, that he has compromised the mission. They are sending his Chosen to take the Essence of...the Essence of Keys."

The parchment dropped from his fingers.

Cold shock flooded Jove's veins. He stared at the parchment. He couldn't decipher the letters there, but if what Saldr said was true...

Anderson cleared his throat. "But Christie left last autumn for a sabbatical."

Harlan shook his head, his severe face thoughtful. "The University deans came up with that lie. They've been searching for him in secret, hoping to find him, but if this is true..."

"This Owen Christie is dead." Saldr backed up until he

stumbled into the guard, Bronson, who hadn't moved. The soldier caught him. Saldr shook his head. "The Essence power that this speaks of has already passed to the Chosen."

Jove stared at him hard. "What are you saying? Is this the Essence you're looking for?"

Saldr's body flickered, but no one noticed except Jove. "The Essence of Keys has been passed down to the man you know as Ben Reiss. He massacred my people, destroyed my home, killed the Lord Elder. Yet, he is not the one I seek."

"No," Harlan spoke quietly. "The Cerls are looking for the other one. They're threatening to attack Kyvena directly to find him, thinking we're hiding him here."

"What?" Jove demanded.

"I've been meeting with Cerulene defectors in secret." Harlan backed up and eased himself onto his cot, forehead resting in his hands. "This was my chance to destroy Cerulene once and for all...now it's all for naught."

Jove merely stared at his father. Meeting with defectors...had that been the source of the affair rumors? Couldn't he at least have told Jove's mother? Out of all the pain Harlan had inflicted, this one could have been easily resolved by merely trusting his wife.

Jove hated him even more.

Anderson looked from the soldier, to Harlan, to Jove, to Saldr. "I don't know what you're talking about, but why is this important? What's this *Essence*?"

Before anyone could answer, the door to the cells opened. "Blessed stars, would ya keep it down?"

Stradat Loffler limped into the corridor, shutting the door behind him, the metal clanging. His usual guard was missing.

Why in the blazes is he here?

Saldr stiffened.

Jove gripped the key in his hand. The edges bit into his palm. He looked to his father, who hadn't taken his head out of his hands, to the ancient Stradat, who looked as vigorous as Jove had ever seen him. For once, his eyes were alert, focused on the world around him, instead of half closed.

Saldr shook his head. "How?"

"Simple relics, something you should know." Loffler laughed softly, holding up a bracelet. "You can only feel it now because I'm allowing you to."

Jove looked between them. When had the two interacted outside of treaty meetings? Because the way they glared at one another suggested a history Jove knew nothing about. "What's going on?"

Loffler looked toward him with those sleepy brown eyes— no, they weren't brown. They were golden. Jove had never noticed before. Loffler barely had them open long enough for anyone to take note of their strange color.

Saldr looked as if he'd seen a ghost. His eyes were nearly the exact same shade of brilliant gold as the ancient Stradat's.

Loffler perpetually looked to be in a state of dying. Jove had no clue how old he was. He'd been a Stradat for as long as Jove could remember...was there a chance that he could be...no, that was ridiculous.

Saldr stepped forward slowly, one hand going to the pouch at his waist—the pouch where he kept whatever that magic dust was. "He's the Essence of Spark."

"Almost." Loffler didn't move his eyes from Saldr.

No one spoke, only stared at the Stradat. There had to be a misunderstanding. Jove had spent countless hours with the man over the course of his career, particularly during his stint as High Guardsman. Shouldn't Jove have known? Felt something? Figured there was more to the man other than the fact he'd passed his prime ages ago?

The same could've been said of Owen Christie, who was now dead, his Essence power in the hands of Ben Reiss. Jove had trusted the latter, sent him on the mission where he'd led the Cerls to Myrrai and then attacked it months later. A traitor within the Watch.

Holy blasting stars.

"My father refused to pass the Essence power onto me, even if I was his Chosen." Loffler's hand found the bars of Harlan's cell. It looked as if he needed help to stand. "I took what I could, but it wasn't enough. The rest of my father's Essence power was, at last, reborn into a little boy over two decades ago...twenty-five years ago, to be exact. A boy a part of our ancient lineage, only just. It's taken me years to find him, and at last, Fate has blessed me kindly."

Twenty-five? Jove was twenty-five. Could it be?

He looked down at his hands. He stretched out the one that wasn't clenching the key. There wasn't anything out of the ordinary about it. A long scar crossed his palm from the time he and Zeke had tried to pry the sword from the wall above the dining hall's mantle. Nothing about his olive skin tone or his history in scars suggested anything other than what they were.

"You've known it for some time, haven't you?" Loffler's voice was soft, sounding much more like the man Jove knew. "Felt the spark beneath your skin?"

Jove was about to answer that he hadn't, until he looked up.

Loffler wasn't addressing him. He stared hard at...Anderson, who shook his head, but he didn't say anything. His eyes hadn't left the Stradat. No one else moved, no one made a noise. Not even Jove's father.

Anderson? Jove had never heard him say anything about having Yalven blood—no, no, that wasn't right. He'd said something about it at that horrid dinner party. Jove might've been drunk, but he could recall that moment with clarity.

Jove, Kase, Anderson, and Hallie had been arguing about the Yalvs wanting to play groggon. Anderson had been frustrated with the fact that the Yalvs would be taking even more opportunities away from his constituents. He'd felt badly about what they'd been through...

Especially as I have a bit of Yalven blood myself—back a few generations.

Jove's heart flew into his throat.

"I've set everything in motion. Jagamot will come. There is only one thing left." Loffler chuckled. "You."

Without warning, Loffler lunged, grabbing Anderson by the arm.

Several things happened at once. Saldr threw his dust in the air, shouting something Jove didn't recognize. Anderson screamed. What looked like purple lightning exploded from his skin once Loffler made contact with it. Someone tackled Jove. He fell, cracking his head against the stone floor. The strange lightning hit the guard, Bronson, in the chest. He collapsed.

But Jove couldn't do anything. The cell's metal bars glowed an ethereal purple. Then, he knew no more.

CHAPTER 37

LITTLE LARK

Hallie

THE LIGHT IN THE DUNGEON cell had never been warm, yet it played across Hallie's face like a perfect spring day in Kyvena.

Her head weighed too much; her whole body did. She'd slept too long. Why hadn't Caesar and Ajax come to fetch her yet? Not that she wanted them to. She'd much rather stay in her cell than face Correa again. Had they brought breakfast yet?

Her fingers clenched. The ground beneath her wasn't damp stone. It was soft, like a pillow. A bed. A *real* bed.

Stars. Tears seeped out her still-closed lids. It'd been so long since she'd last lay in an actual bed. Had it been the inn where she'd danced with the blond? The one Kase had dubbed Cornhead? How long had that been? Two weeks? Three? A lifetime ago?

"Hallie..."

She blinked. The light no longer bled onto grime-ridden walls. This ceiling was white, yellowed with age. Beams of dark oak interrupted the monotony every few feet and climbed up to a point at the tip of the far wall. Blue, red, and yellow light spangled it as sunlight filtered in from the stained-glass window she knew too well. A few tears slid down her cheeks, tickling her ears and falling gracelessly into her hair.

This was *her* room. Her old one.

Someone squeezed her hand. "Little lark? Can you hear me?"

Little lark.

She turned her head.

The man who sat in a chair beside her had more gray in his beard than when she'd left Stoneset, and hair still refused to grow upon the top of his head. The window painted colors on it and half of his face. His golden-brown eyes were glassy with unshed tears, though when Hallie smiled at him, a few wayward ones traced the soft lines in his cheeks.

Hallie sat up, ignoring the pain as her father moved to the edge of the bed. He pulled her into a hug, his hand smoothing back her hair as if she were seven once more and needed comforting after scraping her knee. Her own tears made her head pound even more, but she didn't care. Bits and pieces of the last few days trickled back to her, and with each memory, she gripped her father tighter.

"Papa, I..." He squeezed her tighter. "I'm so glad you're here."

Hallie thought she didn't have any more tears left to cry. It was all she'd done the last few days. Especially now that Kase...

She gasped, pulling back. She wiped her streaming nose and eyes. "Where's Kase? Is he all right?"

Her father held her face between his hands, his calloused thumbs wiping away stray tears. "He's fine."

Her eyes darted to the sides of the room. "Where is he? I have to make sure...why isn't he here?"

Her father dropped his hands and looked away. "I'll let him know you're awake."

"Wait. Will you stay a little longer?"

Because she had to let him know. She had to tell him. He'd never received her letters, and if there was a chance Correa was still alive...

"Why are we here?" she asked, pushing herself further up

and resting against the wall, a pillow scrunched under the small of her back. She still wore Kase's military jacket, the material bunching around her waist. "Why aren't we in the cavern? If Correa finds us, Papa..."

Her father didn't sit, only fiddled with his fingers as he swallowed, his throat bobbing with the action. "We didn't know if you or Kase would wake, or what was wrong. We didn't want to risk...besides, whatever happened at the Fort...your friend hasn't told us much, only that some sort of power was unleashed, allowing you two to escape. Though it was two Cerls who brought you to us at the smaller gate. Said they were helping you."

"Cerls helped us?" Hallie's stomach flew into her throat.

Her father shrugged. "We didn't ask questions, only took both you and Kase and got away from Achilles fast as we could."

"What did they look like?"

"Both tall and brawny. The one who seemed to be in charge had curly black hair."

Caesar and Ajax. They saved us.

"Are they still here?" Renewed tears bubbled in her swollen eyes. She rubbed them.

Her father walked toward the door. "No."

Maybe they couldn't come with them. Maybe they had to go back to Correa. Maybe they were prisoners like her. Hallie sent up silent words of thanks to the two guards. Hopefully, they knew. Hopefully, she'd get the chance to tell them in person how much she cared; but for now, she'd have to be content.

Hallie pulled her knees to her chest as her father turned, his hand on the knob. "We'll move to the cavern in the morning once you've rested some more. We can talk more there."

"Papa," Hallie said, her voice muffled by her knees. "Did you know we're Yalven?"

He froze.

"That's why they wanted me." Her voice choked on the last words. She cleared her throat and squeezed her knees tighter. "Why didn't you tell me? Why did you keep it from me?"

His hand slipped from the doorknob, but he didn't face her. "It's a burden I didn't want you to bear."

Hallie's face heated. "That's not fair."

Her father's only answer was silence. His shoulders slumped. Maybe this wasn't the best time to have this conversation. Maybe she should've waited until she'd gotten to the cavern. But she was so tired. She was so tired of being lied to, of being kept in the dark.

She was no longer a little lark afraid to fly.

"If you'd told me, maybe this wouldn't have happened. Any of it."

"I'm sorry." He didn't say anything other than that, only grasped the knob once more and turned it, opening to someone in the doorway.

The first thing she noticed were the tousled, windswept tawny curls, which stuck out even more as he ran a hand through them. His blue eyes met hers. Small, inconsequential cuts decorated parts of his face.

Her heart lurched. "Kase..."

Her father moved aside to let him in and swept out after, shutting the door with a soft thump.

Kase had barely moved beyond the door itself. He looked ragged and worn, if slightly cleaner than he had been in Achilles. His white shirt was too tight around his arms, showing the muscles there as he pushed the hair out of his face, though his eyes didn't leave the floor. The sunset outside had finally faded, leaving them in the onset of evening.

Stars, Hallie didn't like this side of Kase. At all.

"Why don't you sit?" Hallie's voice was rough, her throat raw from smoke. She settled herself against the wall behind her, trying not to wince at the pain in her head. "You must be nearly as beat as..."

But she trailed off as he sat gingerly in the chair, still refusing to look at her. She turned the gas lantern on her bedside table to its lowest setting. The golden light added a little color to Kase's ashen skin.

The silence grew thicker and thicker, like the smoke and flames from the fort. The flames had caught on the back of Kase's shirt when she'd woken up, but Ajax had doused them with his jacket. She vaguely remembered Kase passing out, and both of them being caught by Caesar below. But everything after that was a blur of loud noises and voices and shapes until she'd passed out herself.

Why had there been flames? Something had happened with the Lord Elder. Was that the reason for the inferno? Why had Caesar and Ajax helped them?

"So, this was your room?" Kase's voice was soft, like he was afraid if he spoke too loudly, he would break. "I expected more books."

He pulled at the cuffs of his shirt, which ended past his elbow. Hallie swallowed. "The only book I owned went with me to Kyvena. Most of what I read belonged to the schoolhouse." She played with a stray thread in the bed sheets. "Where did you get the shirt? It's a little too small for you."

"Yeah." He looked down at it and then back up at her. "It was the only shirt I could find around here. Niels only just returned with my pack, but I wanted to see you before..." He coughed. "My other one...the fire..." He stopped, his words choking off, before he took a deep breath again. "I'm sorry. I didn't mean to...to lose control like that. The flames coming toward me and the whole fort coming down around us..."

"Kase, look at me," Hallie whispered. He took a second or two before slowly raising his head. His eyes were red-rimmed. She chewed her lip. "You have nothing to be sorry about. If I hadn't been so stupid as to believe that telegram...if I'd only done something...*anything* else besides drag us all the way out here...then we wouldn't be in this mess. If anyone is to be sorry, it's me."

Kase turned away, running both hands through his hair, tugging at the ends. "I was ready to die at the end, only to be given a chance—a chance I nearly ruined because of...because of my stupid blasting weakness. When the fire burned toward us, my mind took me back to the Kyvena fire." He sounded like he was barely holding back tears. "All I could see were the flames and that stupid cigarette and Ana and..." He inhaled sharply. "I'm as useless as my father says I am."

Hallie's head shot up. "Kase..." She moved to the edge of the bed and grabbed his hand. He looked at her, tears clinging to his long lashes. She took his other hand, making him face her completely, and squeezed them. "I only know what you've told me about your father, but...but..."

She took a deep breath. "But you're far from useless. You're the...the best man I know."

"I'm not." Kase looked at their entwined hands and shook his head. "I've done awful things. Horrible things."

Hallie pulled her right hand out of his grasp and brushed his cheek. "You're human. We make mistakes, but it's how we fix them that reveals our true selves." She smiled when his eyes met hers. "If the Lord Elder hadn't responded, you'd be dead...and Achilles would still be in Cerulene's control with me as their tool. But you gave me the strength to force the Lord Elder to unleash his full power. You saved us, and once again, you saved me."

Though for how long, I don't know.

Kase squeezed her other hand. "But what do we do next? If they've attacked Kyvena..." He cleared his throat. "If there's anyone left, someone has to warn Jove and the Watch about everything—Correa, King Filip, the Essences."

Hallie wouldn't be going back to Kyvena any time soon. She didn't think she'd even make it through the Pass. "I'm scared, Kase."

A knock echoed on the door. Hallie looked up, dropping Kase's hand. "Come in."

Her father returned, a wooden chest in his arms. Hallie studied it for a moment, trying to piece together where she'd seen it before. The faded pattern along the bottom and the dust coating most of the outside betrayed its age.

It was the same one she'd found years ago but was unable to pick the lock.

"I should've let you read these earlier," her father paused, his mustache twitching. "But I didn't want to burden you. Especially after everything with Jack."

He set the chest at the end of the bed and fished a key from his pocket.

"Our family history isn't a happy one, and my mama would only let me read a few entries. I didn't care because Gran died when I was seven, and the end of her life wasn't pretty. I didn't want to know what she went through. Maybe it was cowardly of me, but anyway, here."

The key he held was unlike anything Hallie had ever seen before; too jagged and too small. It was also made from Zuprium.

He unlocked the chest and stared at the contents. "These

are Gran's journals from when she first left her people."

Hallie crawled to the foot of the bed, peeking over the top to find three leather-bound books, each cracking with age and kept closed with twine. She grabbed the top one and stared at the cover. It was simple, nothing to delineate what it was or who it had belonged to, but even then, it radiated with mystery and something that made Hallie's fingertips tingle.

The image of a glowing mountain door flashed in her vision. Warmth flooded her chest. The Lord Elder.

What does it mean?

Silence.

The chair creaked as Kase stood. "We can talk later."

Hallie blinked and looked up to find her father gone. Kase was heading toward the door. She set the book down. "It's okay if you stay."

Kase put his hands in his trouser pockets and shook his head. "Niels needs a break from watch duty. We don't know if Correa and the others made it out, but we shouldn't let our guard down."

She understood, but that didn't stop disappointment from settling on her shoulders. Kase shut the door behind him without looking back.

She took a few deep breaths to calm herself before turning back to the book in her lap. With careful hands, she unwound the twine holding the journal shut, opened it to the first page, and began to read in the dim lantern light.

Father and the Called knew as soon as I was born that I, Navara of Myrrai, would be Chosen. They say the day was cause for celebration, knowing that the power of the Essences would continue— that when the end of time came, we would be ready.

But I never wanted the power. I still don't believe Toro cares about me, a Chosen Yalven girl who only wanted to leave as soon as I knew a whole different world existed beyond the city of my birth. I wanted to truly live.

Father didn't understand at first, when he took the Essence of Time from his mother. He didn't understand the burden it placed upon him, upon all of Yalvara. The power to unwind time is the most powerful of them all, yet it is also the most painful.

I still remember the day I told him I didn't want to take on his

Essence. I was thirteen and had sat through a lecture where I learned of my eventual fate. I sprinted away before Chronal Edwr finished teaching, his shouts and curses trailing me, but I was faster. I found Father in the Great Hall and, even though I was too old to cry, soaked his embroidered robes with my tears.

The night of my Chosen ceremony, where I would take on Father's Essence at the age of 16, I ran. Pressing his relic, his timepiece with the carving of Myrrai on the cover, into my shaking hands, Father sent me through the Passage he created. He was the only one who could...

CHAPTER 38

I KNOW

Hallie

NIGHT WAS IN FULL SWING by the time Hallie left her room. She hadn't read much further in Navara's journals; the weight of those first words resonated too deeply. Navara had been only sixteen when she'd given up her destiny. Sixteen when she'd run away from home. Sixteen when she'd unknowingly sealed Hallie's fate nearly a century later.

Navara had gained her freedom only to imprison her great-granddaughter, yet Hallie couldn't blame her. She would do nearly anything to rid herself of the burden now on her shoulders.

After changing into some clean old clothes from her dusty wardrobe, she made her way on stockinged feet down the stairs and into the kitchen. The image of the glowing archway flashed in her mind once more. Navara had spoken of a Passage that she'd taken from Myrrai, one the Lord Elder had created. Was it the same? Warmth pulsed from her chest.

The Lord Elder.

He was trying to tell her something. Was it that she had to find this archway?

Another pulse.

Saldr's voice came back to her from what felt like an eternity ago in Kyvena.

And if there is a way to separate the two, the knowledge is lost in the great library of Myrrai.

She pushed the door open to the kitchen with a shaking hand. Someone had set a gas lantern in the hearth. In front stood three men entangled in a heavy discussion. The one on the far right was her father. On the other side stood Kase, the lantern light tracing his profile making her heart stutter.

But the figure in the center caused it to stop.

Niels.

His hair had grown since she'd last seen him, but his accent was still just as thick. "Not to be disrespectful, sir, but we need you here."

Her father rubbed his beard. "Lenore can handle anything while I'm gone."

"She's a decent apprentice, but you and I both know how flighty she can be."

Kase had changed into one of his own shirts, complete with a vest. Hallie relaxed a little. Seeing him in Jack's shirt earlier had been a shock. Not Kase's fault, but a shock nonetheless. He laced his hands behind his neck. "I need someone to get me through those tunnels quickly. Stowe is my best bet."

"And I told Zelda I'd be along to help her find our girl soon as I thought Lenore was ready."

Niels fell onto the low couch behind him with a defeated sigh. "All right, all right. But what if Hallie isn't ready to travel yet?"

"I'm sure a few rounds of my tonic will set her up right while we travel," her father said.

The image of the archway appeared again, followed by a weak pulse. She backed away from the men, but the movement caught Kase's eye at last.

He smiled a little. "Good to see you up."

The words cradled her like an embrace. The Kase from earlier was gone for now.

Her father turned, but the muscles in Niels' back scrunched. Hallie's heart hammered in her chest as she joined them. She took the chair next to Kase, who still stood in front of the lantern. Niels looked anywhere but at her.

Her father coughed. "Don't know how much you heard, but we're hoping you'll be up to a trip soon. We need to find your mama."

Hallie intertwined her fingers together. "I'm not going back to Kyvena."

Every eye was on her, and heat rose to her cheeks. Kase's hand flinched. Her father sat next to Niels, his eyes earnest and searching. "You haven't recovered yet, I know, but I have some—"

"It's not that. I need to find the Passage Navara used. Barring me traveling all the way to Tasava on a hovership, the only way I'm getting to Myrrai is through that. That's what the Lord Elder wants."

"Lord Elder?" Her father asked.

Niels kept staring into the floor like it was about to catch fire. Kase's voice was quiet as he spoke. "Do you even know where that is?"

She looked up and searched his eyes, willing him to understand something she didn't quite comprehend herself. "All I know is that it's in the Nardens. I can find it with the Lord Elder's help."

Her father shook his head. "I'm not losing you again."

The heat in her body rose even with her trying to tamp down her emotions. The Lord Elder could only handle so much. She didn't want what happened to Achilles to happen here. "You need to go to Mama. I need to find the Passage. It's the only way to figure out what's going on."

"What if you're walking into a trap?" Kase sat on the arm of her chair. "Just because Correa hasn't shown up here, doesn't mean he can't find you."

She'd tried to kill Correa, but it seemed her power clashed with his and brought the fort down. That was the only explanation she had for what happened. What if Kase was right? What if Correa survived and was looking for her now? She didn't have it in her to fight in her current state.

Hallie clenched her hands tighter. Her knuckles bled to

white. "I don't know what to expect, but after reading the journal...it's what I need to do."

She owed it to herself, Navara, and the Lord Elder to try.

"Are you sure?" Kase asked.

"I'm not changing my mind." Hallie released her hands and grabbed one of Kase's, squeezing it. "I think the journals and searching the library in Myrrai could help me...and...maybe even Ben."

"How do you know?"

Hallie shrugged. "I don't, but my gut tells me this is the right thing to do."

Kase chewed his cheek as he held her hand fast. "But I have to go to Kyvena."

"I know."

Niels' voice was soft, yet firm. "I'll go with you, Hals. If we don't find anything, we'll go to Kyvena."

"But—" her father started, but Niels interrupted.

"I know these mountains better than anybody." He tapped his thumbs together, purposefully refusing to make eye contact with anyone else. "If Hal thinks there's something here, then I believe her."

"Then I'll go, too," her father said, standing. He was an impressive figure against the backdrop of the dark kitchen with only the gas lantern for light.

"I need you to take me through the mine tunnels. You're the only one who can, Mr. Walker," Kase said.

Her father sighed and pulled Hallie out of her chair and into a hug. He held her tightly. "Come back to me, ya hear?" He released her and brushed stray hair from her eyes. "We'll leave first thing in the morning. Let's get you both a good night's rest."

He headed up the stairs. Niels rose. "I'll take first watch."

And then he was off, too.

He hadn't looked at her once during the entire conversation. Not a single time. Yet, he wanted to come with her to find something she wasn't sure even existed any longer? She looked over at Kase, who stepped around her and fell into the seat Niels had vacated. He laid his head against the back and stared straight up at the cedar beamed ceiling. "I don't like you going off without me."

She slid beside him, resting her head on his shoulder. He snaked an arm around her waist, and she cuddled closer. "We don't have a choice."

"You do."

She closed her eyes against the budding frustration. "Saldr said something about the library in Myrrai possibly holding answers. There's something in the ruins that can help. I've heard of Jagamot, but he's only mentioned in passing in all the texts we have at home. Same with the Essence powers."

Kase leaned his cheek on the top of her head. "Promise me that if you don't find anything, you'll come to Kyvena if it's even still standing?"

"Knowing you, I'll have to break you out of jail again."

He chuckled as he kissed her temple. They sat and talked in front of the light from the gas lantern until Hallie could barely keep her eyes open. She didn't want to leave him, but she knew that when morning broke, the stars would certainly fall.

Kase

THE MORNING CAME ALL TOO early for Kase's liking. With the knowledge that Hallie would be with Niels for stars knew how long, sleep evaded him. It was Cornhead from Laurent all over again, except this time, there was history between them. But she was right. He was needed in Kyvena, not gallivanting about the mountainside looking for something that probably no longer existed.

He rubbed his eyes and pushed himself onto his elbows. He and Hallie had stayed up for hours talking about everything except what awaited them the next day. Now, the goodbye he'd dreaded for weeks was finally here, and it was much worse than he'd anticipated.

But he had a duty. He could no longer run from his problems. He needed to face them head on and save what was left of Jayde.

He made sure his pack was prepared and headed downstairs. They'd make their way to the Stoneset cavern together, and then...and then Kase and Stowe would go through the tunnels.

He was the last one down. Stowe and Hallie argued in whispers by the door, and Niels sat on the couch, watching them with interest.

It was a shame Kase liked Niels. The way he was looking at Hallie made Kase's blood boil.

Of course, when Kase finally had a girl to take home to his mother, he would have stiff competition.

"We'd better head out," Kase said as he joined the others.

Hallie and her father paused, and she met Kase halfway. With a small smile, she took his hand and gave it a squeeze. He held her hand fast, her affection giving him confidence. Niels rose from the couch and stretched, yawning. Kase hated how muscular he was.

"We should take the hidden passage, just in case," Niels said.

They left the little inn and headed into the dawn. The sky had surrendered to a light gray as they entered the cottage that hid the tunnel. Stowe led the way down, and Niels brought up the rear. No one spoke as they traveled. Kase's hand was cold without Hallie's inside it.

With each step they took, Kase's stomach filled with dread. He and Hallie had been through a lifetime together the last few weeks, and yet, they would go their separate ways. He couldn't stop thinking about that...about how he was about to lose her, possibly forever.

Shocks, he was three seconds away from taking her hand and running away from all their problems. They could go to Tev Rubika and watch the world burn.

She might even say yes.

That was what kept Kase from following through with that idea.

At long last, they reached the end of the tunnel and entered the cavern. Even at this early hour, people milled about, the early vestiges of sunrise lightening the darker spaces. Several children ran to Hallie, cascading into her knees, hands flying around her waist. She laughed along with them. Kase couldn't help the smile traipsing across his face. She would make a great mother one day.

"Are you here to stay, Miss Hal? We sure missed you

reading to us!" one little boy asked, his gap-toothed grin betraying his age of no more than probably eleven.

Hallie just laughed, promising to read the children a story that night by the campfire if anyone had a book she could borrow.

Niels helped peel the children off her. He playfully chased a few of them, their laughter echoing off the stone. Hallie fell back to Kase, tucking herself under his arm. "Didn't realize how much I was missed."

Kase gave her shoulders a light squeeze. "As they should."

He didn't dare say anything else for fear he unleashed all the thoughts in his head. That would only make the next event of the morning even more difficult.

They reached Stowe's campsite, where the man busied himself with packing all sorts of tonics, salves, and poultices. A few more people came and spoke with Hallie and Niels. Kase hovered nearby, feeling very much out of place.

Too soon for Kase's liking, Stowe finished his packing, and the residents of Stoneset went their separate ways.

It was here. The goodbye.

They all walked to one of the cave entrances. The distant hills and village ruins were slowly illuminated by the light coming over the mountains. Kase chewed the inside of his cheek as Hallie turned to him, tears budding in her eyes. Stowe and Niels stood a little apart to give them some privacy. That didn't mean they weren't watching out of the corners of their eyes.

Hallie twisted her fingers in the hem of her untucked lacy shirt. She still wore his stolen military jacket. "I guess you'll be off?"

"How do you know where you'll be going?"

A soft breeze blew wayward strands of her hair about her face. She hadn't put it in a lady's bun since before Achilles. Kase found he liked her long braid. She tugged at the end. "We'll stay here a few days while I read through the rest of the journals. I'm sure something's in there that'll help."

Kase tried burying the jealousy that reared its head at that. She was doing something important and would follow him soon after. At least, that's what he told himself.

"I have something for you." Kase slid his pack off, digging

through it until the smooth surface of his pilot goggles met his fingers. He pulled them out before shouldering the pack once more. "I'm not sure you'll take good care of these after all the times you've mocked me."

She gave a choked laugh. "And the only time I flew a hover, I crashed."

Kase felt the stares of both Hallie's father and Niels as he laughed. "Talk to me once you've crashed twice on the same mission."

They stood in silence for a few more moments before Hallie's tears spilled over. "Will you not come with me?"

With a quick look at her father and Niels, he threw caution to the wind and pulled her in close. She folded into his embrace, burying her face into his borrowed jacket. He murmured his next words into her hair. "I'm the only one who has an inkling of what the Cerls want with the Essences. Your job is to figure out exactly what that is."

She stepped back, her eyes desperate. "But what if I can't? What if I lose myself again?"

"You won't."

"You can't know that."

"I do." Kase placed the goggles atop her head and clasped the strap. They didn't mess up her hair like they did his. He grabbed both sides of her face so she wouldn't miss a single word. "Because you're Hallie Walker, stubborn as the stars...and the one who'll save us all."

He wiped the tears cascading down her face. She smiled through them. "We'll find each other..." The words were ragged with her breathing. "...when this is over?"

He slid his hands from her cheeks, down her shoulders, her arms, lacing his fingers with hers. "I promise."

With one last squeeze for fear he might lose the will to leave for Kyvena, he dropped her hands and turned away. His footsteps were heavy, like his boots were crafted of stone. He'd reached her father when he peeked back one last time, to watch as she disappeared from view.

Yet she stood there smiling through her tears, eyes yearning. His goggles had slid sideways.

He didn't think, didn't tell himself that he was only making it harder for him to leave, only dropped his pack and sprinted back toward her. She met him halfway. He scooped her into his arms and captured her lips with his.

Electricity zipped through his body as she wrapped her arms around his neck. All he wanted was to drown in that moment, forget the outside world existed. His goggles fell from her hair and onto the cave floor below. She laughed against his lips. He pulled back to look her in the eyes.

"I love you," he whispered as he set her back onto the ground, saying the words he'd spoken only once before, when he'd found himself facing the end.

She wiped her eyes and nodded. "I know."

Turned out, Kase also liked romances fraught with space, laser swords, and overarching empires.

He laughed, kissing her again, focusing solely on the woman in his arms.

Hours later, as he and Stowe wound their way through the caves, he would remember and take heart.

They would be together at the end of it all. He would make sure of it. For the first time in his life, he had hope.

CHAPTER 39

HIS BROTHER'S COURAGE

Clara

EVERY FIBER OF CLARA'S BEING ached, even though it'd been days since giving birth. Samuel was the perfect baby. He smelled like rain and sugar and something she couldn't quite describe. He cried only in moments when he needed something and slept well most of the time.

Yet Clara still hurt.

In the early hours after her son's birth, Jove had returned to the room reeking of drink when he promised he'd stop. Clara tried to understand. She'd warred with herself—saying that it was no wonder her husband only wanted to drown out the pain he felt inside.

But she couldn't. She could only be so strong. Her son needed a whole father, not one drowning in alcohol and grief.

Les had returned from Harlan's sentencing hours before and locked herself in her chambers. Her sobs trickled through the walls. Jove had yet to appear.

Tears burned her eyes as she packed up everything she'd

need. She stuffed baby clothes and blankets into the leather pack Lizzie had fetched from the townhouse. Clara needed a few weeks at the Davey family estate; she needed to heal herself before she could heal her husband. She'd meet her mother outside the city gates. They'd catch a motorcoach to Crystalfell and be home within a week.

Clara wasn't strong enough to stay. The words she'd penned onto parchment an hour ago mocked her from the bedside table.

Jove,

We've gone to Crystalfell. Don't come until you're ready.

Clara

Hopefully, he'd be able to read her words through the tear-smudged ink. She wondered how soon he would drink himself into oblivion. She should've known she couldn't be strong enough for them both.

Tucking the ends of the blanket around her two-week-old son, the ache in her chest radiated down her arms. She squeezed her eyes shut and breathed deeply, relaxing her muscles with each exhale. In seconds that felt like an eternity, the pain receded.

She would be okay. Maybe she was wrong. Maybe Jove would finally realize what was right in front of him, that he didn't need alcohol to feel happy.

Maybe he would follow her, and all her pain would be for naught.

After slipping the leather pack onto sore shoulders, Clara picked up her slumbering son. He hadn't cared that his mother had swaddled him, only snuggled deeper into the blanket. She pressed the baby to her chest, taking in his scent and soft grunts of sleep. With a swift glance at the room and the bassinet, she stepped toward the door.

There was something else in the bassinet, tucked away on the side as if forgotten. She paused. Had it always been there? She laid Samuel on the rumpled bed sheets. Her fingers picked up the pin, blood-speckled, dusty, with the shape of the Jaydian symbol of a tree surrounded by a sun. The small ribbon below was just as filthy. *Lieutenant Colonel Ezekiel Shackley* graced the front in tiny letters no bigger than the tip of her fingernail.

She glanced toward the letter resting on the bedside table. The inked words watched her, judged her. With careful fingers, she attached the pin to Samuel's bundle, and then she left.

Babe in her arms, pack on her back, she was done being strong. She only hoped Jove could find his brother's courage.

EPILOGUE

THE ESSENCE OF KEYS

Jove

JOVE WOKE TO SCREAMS, DARKNESS, and burning on the side of his face. A murmured song with words he didn't recognize floated in the air. He brought his hand to the side of his face, but someone grabbed it.

The singing also stopped. "The Vasa has nearly finished its work, Master Shackley."

His jaw ached something fierce, but the burning was worse. He opened his eyes to find Saldr and his father sitting beside him. There was a golden light radiating from Jove's face. He blinked. The lantern hanging from the ceiling had gone out.

The golden light faded, and Jove sat up. His father's fingers were glowing too. Saldr put away his pouch. "Is there anywhere else you're hurting?"

Jove shook his head, amazed he no longer felt any pain. He touched his jaw. "Your magic?"

"Not magic. A gift from Toro."

Harlan's fingers dimmed at last. He looked at the cell bars, which were still emanating purple light. "And what in the blazes was that?"

"Unbridled power of an Essence, second only to that of the Lord Elder." Saldr stood, helping Jove up, then Harlan. "The Essence of Spark has been missing for nearly 900 years. And to think that it was split. May Toro have mercy on our souls."

Saldr strode from the cell, careful not to touch the glowing bars. Jove stared after him, unsure of what to make of his claim or the fact he'd used magic to heal him and his father. And what about Anderson being an Essence? Where was the man? Judging by the shouts and screams, Loffler was currently terrorizing people above. Was he with him?

He could do nothing against that power. He rubbed his jaw again. Who'd saved him from getting blasted by that lightning?

Harlan stretched his hand, not saying a word.

His father? Had he been the one to tackle him? Jove swallowed. There couldn't have been anyone else, yet Jove still didn't want to believe Harlan could have done something like that to protect him. It was out of character.

Saldr knelt beside the guard splayed a few feet outside the cell. Harlan squatted next to them, his fingers searching for a pulse in the man's neck. "Dead."

"Yes," Saldr whispered, "killed by the power of a god."

Jove's father cursed, his fingers clenching. "This is what I was trying to prevent by sending the *Eudora Jayde* to your people." His voice was low and dripping with spite. "Now that thing is loose. And it's kidnapped a future City Councilman!"

Saldr stood as Harlan closed the eyes of the guard, setting his hands across his chest. His father unbuckled the man's sword from his belt. "I will treat this with the respect it deserves." He tucked it inside his own belt.

"If he indeed has brought about the end, Jagamot, then we must hasten to stop him. The prophecies..." Saldr flickered. When he solidified, he took a deep breath. "The prophecies state all Essence wielders must give their lives to stop the end, as they are the slivers of Toro shattered in the Dawn. The only way to prevent the utter destruction of Yalvara is unite the Essence powers as one once more."

Karsi va si. We are one.

"One World. Are they working for the Cerls? The Yalvs?" Harlan barked, echoing Jove's thoughts.

Saldr wrung his hands. "I do not know. But we have spent too long down here. We must go above. I am one of the few who may be able to stop the Essence of Spark. Any other solutions are lost to the ruins of Myrrai."

"Then let's go," Jove said, pushing past them both and heading out of the holding cells. He didn't know what they were going to do, but Saldr still had that magic dust. Jove was still unsure of its power.

Not that he cared—only that it worked.

They could worry about the end of the world—or whatever Loffler had set into motion—afterward.

No one awaited them outside the door. The remaining guards were gone, the corridors dark. Light from Firstmoon and what looked like fire filtered in through the windows, allowing them to see dimly. Nothing glowed purple out here, but the lanterns hanging from the ceiling were dark. Jove didn't have time to stop and check on anyone who might be dead in the shadows.

The only reason he was still alive was because his father had tackled him. That fact stood out in his mind. If there hadn't been a crazed old man wielding ancient power on the loose, Jove might have been amazed at his father's heroics.

But alas, they needed to find Loffler and Anderson before more people suffered. Loffler didn't seem to be working for the Cerls, but Jove wasn't sure.

The group entered the foyer to mass chaos.

People were everywhere, torches in hand. Soldiers clashed with the populace, swords and blood flashing in the firelight.

Jove froze. Neither Loffler nor Anderson were anywhere to be seen, but the sheer size of the mob made it nearly impossible to tell. Where had they all come from anyway? Wasn't the upper gate closed?

A shot of cold went through Jove. The electricity. The gate ran on electricity...none of the lanterns were working...Saldr said Loffler possessed whatever powerful magic the Yalvs wielded...the electricity was out...just like it had when the First Settlers had landed on Yalvara.

Could it be? Could Loffler's Essence be the one...

Holy blasting, crashing stars.

"Karsi va si!" The people chanted, the Cerleze echoing off the walls.

One World.

Jove stumbled back into Saldr and his father. "The gate's failed. Loffler's power destroyed the electricity. We need to get out of here before—"

Saldr blinked out of existence and reappeared on the other side of Jove, throwing a cloud of dust at their would-be attacker. The man, who was dressed in a bloody apron, cleaver raised above his head, froze as soon as the dust landed.

Jove dragged his father away, Saldr following behind, breathing heavily. Harlan wrenched out of Jove's grip and led them down into the dungeons they'd left, making turns at random. Voices and footsteps followed. Any slip up, and they'd be butchered. The pouch at Saldr's waist was only so big.

"This way!" Harlan shouted as he flung open a wooden door and ascended the stairs behind it. Jove allowed Saldr to go in front of him before he slammed the door shut, locking it. It wouldn't hold for long, but it would buy them time.

At the top of the stairs, they found another door. Harlan opened it just as their pursuers hit the one at the bottom. The banging was amplified by the narrow stone walls. Harlan, Saldr, and Jove burst through the top door into an alleyway and the open air that smelled of smoke.

The city was burning.

It seemed One World had succeeded in their mission.

"You don't think..." Jove started, the flames reaching toward the sky reminding him of all he held dear. He didn't finish his sentence, only took off toward Shackley Manor.

He'd left Clara and Samuel there. His mother.

"Jove!"

Jove barely heard his father over the sound of his own heartbeat. The crushing in his lungs battled with the abject terror taking over his mind. He'd left them alone. *Alone.* Because he'd wanted to go out and drink himself into a stupor after the sentencing.

Tears streamed down his cheeks as he sprinted toward his childhood home. So lost in his goal, he didn't see the blue fire as it zinged through the air, cascading into his shoulder.

He screamed, flying forward and skidding on the cobblestones. White hot pain lanced out from his shoulder. Blood soaked his shirt. He couldn't move.

"You blasted *helviter!*" someone growled. Jove peeked up through his pain to find his father brandishing the dead soldier's sword. He sliced at the man holding a jagged-barreled, smoking pistol.

Not an electropistol. A Cerl weapon.

Holy stars.

The attacker lost his arm to Harlan's sword, the pistol tumbling from the disembodied hand. The man's gurgling scream was cut short by Harlan's next thrust. The pistol slid to Jove, who grabbed it in his good hand and pushed himself to his knees, cocking the weapon and firing at the other three men careening toward them. They dove out of the way, avoiding the fiery blue bullets.

Saldr appeared beside him, pressing dust onto Jove's wound. "I don't have enough to heal it, but I can...I can..."

He flickered again and wavered, falling to his knees. Dust stuck to his bloody fingers and smeared on his forehead as he wiped it. "I can't..."

Harlan finished off the other men, whom Jove had missed with his terrible aim. He wiped blood from his blade, his eyes hard and emotionless in the raging firelight.

Clara. Samuel. Mother.

Jove fought to stand, the pain in his shoulder reaching a crescendo, nearly bringing him to his knees once more. Above the crackling of the burning mansions, the sound of the populace still chanting One World's slogan, and the death screams, a roar rent the air.

Guttural. Earsplitting. Boneshaking.

Jove looked to the sky. Lit by the fires, the underbelly of an immense beast flew over them. Wind rushed through Jove's short hair. Scales glittered gold, talons reflected orange. The snout was long and large enough to swallow a man whole.

Atop the beast sat a man with light blond hair.

"The Essence of Keys." Saldr's voice overflowed with anguish.

Jove knew the man. He'd been a regular at state dinners when Kase hadn't wanted to come alone.

Yet his brother had assured him that he'd died, perished on the mission Jove had sent him on...only to be resurrected by the secrets Saldr had spilled to him mere hours before.

The man astride what Jove could only describe as a dragon was Ben Reiss.

Jove fell to his knees again; he could do no more but watch as the beast reached the Jayde Center. A fiery torrent blasted from the dragon's great maw and slammed into the glass dome from above, engulfing it.

The last thing Jove saw was the explosion of glass as the dome shattered.

CONTINUED IN BOOK 3

--

L O V E   T H I S   B O O K ?

Consider leaving an honest review where you purchased this book and on social media.

Join my newsletter for the latest updates:

Follow me on Instagram:

ACKNOWLEDGMENTS

As always, I'm so thankful for my entire family and their encouragement—especially Jason, Baby Boy, and Baby Girl (who, Lord willing, will arrive about a month after Realms' publication). Yes, I was exhausted trying to get this book to the finish line at 7-8 months pregnant, haha.

Thank you to my editors, Cassidy Clarke and Renee Dugan, for their superb feedback and enthusiasm for this book. Shoutout to my critique partners/early readers, Blake, Brittany, and Mary. All five of you helped shape this story into the book it is today, and YOU ROCK.

I also want to take a moment and give all the love to my cover artist, Deandra Scicluna. Have you seen the covers?! They are PERFECTION. Just wait, lovely reader, until you see book 3!

Thank you also to my wonderful proofreaders Arielle, Haven, and Blake. I appreciate you fixing up my misused commas and clunky sentences. My readers (and myself) are eternally grateful.

And thank you to you, reader. Your enthusiasm and love for book 1, *Cities of Smoke & Starlight*, made me want to finish off book 2 even more. I'm so thankful you took a leap of faith and read a story about a troubled pilot and bubbly scholar who fell in love when the world is falling apart around them. I'm so excited for you read book 3...

GLOSSARY

Abram Loffler: oldest Stradat, known for taking naps
Anderson Enright [inn-RIGHT] Petra's betrothed, friend of Jove, vying for election to the City Council
Ben Reiss [RYSS]: Watch agent, best friend of Kase (known as Skibs), in possession of the Essence of Keys
Called: Chronals called to a higher purpose of protecting Yalvara and the Gate, most wield vasa in some capacity, some are more powerful or have more sophisticated purposes than others (ie: Saldr the only one of his purpose)
Cerulene [SIR-oo-LEEN]: powerful kingdom on Yalvara, ruled by King Filip
Chosen: Certain Chronals/Yalvs/those of Yalven ancestry chosen to wield an Essence power
Chronal [KROW-nul]: Yalv with the capacity to wield vasa or become an Essence, tasked with protecting the Gate
Clara Shackley [CLAHR-uh]: wife of Jove
Dawn: beginning of time on Yalvara when Tovo was shattered to save humanity from Jagamot
Ebba Fleming [EBB-uh FLEM-ing]: mechanic
Ellis Carrington: Hallie's friend and classmate
Engineer Corp: group of brilliant minds in Jayde tasked with developing new technology/recovering old technological secrets from First Earth
Eravin Gray [air-uh-VIN]: leader of One World's Kyvena group, ex-best friend of Kase
Essence: term used to describe the five splintered powers of Tovo (Essences of Keys, Time, Souls, Spark, and Light)
Eudora McKenzie [YOU-dor-UH]: wife of General Samuel McKenzie, founded Jayde's Engineer Corp
Ezekiel Fairchild: brother to Les, executed for selling hover

secrets to Cerulene

First Earth: third planet from the sun in the Milky Way solar system, destroyed over 1000 years prior to *Cities of Smoke & Starlight*

Fiver: denomination of Jaydian money, equal to 5 pieces

Gate: powerful magical object that holds all timelines

General Correa [COR-ray-UH]: supreme military leader of Cerl forces, Essence of Light

General Samuel McKenzie: man who led the Life Ships, established Jayde on Yalvara, husband of Eudora

Great War: began as a conflict over resources, world-wide, ended with the disappearance of the Yalvs

Hallie Walker [HAA-lee; 'Hallie' rhymes with 'valley']: Yalven scholar at the University, hails from Stoneset

Harlan Shackley: the Stradat Lord Kapitan of Jayde, father of Kase, Jove, Zeke, and Ana, husband of Les

Heddie Koppen: Head Guardswoman of the Watch

High Council: Jayde's governing body consisting of the Stradats, the Lord Kapitan, and the High Guardsmen

High Guardsman/woman: head of the Watch

Hover: general term for aircraft using hover technology

Hover Bike: motorcycle-like vehicle used by the Crews to train new pilots on hover controls, cheap

Hover Crews: sometimes called simply 'Crews', force of hover ships, an offshoot of the Jaydian military

Hunder [HUN-dur]: denomination of Jaydian money, equal to 100 pieces

Jagamot [JAG-uh-mot]: great evil of Yalven lore

Jayde [JAYd]: nation ruled by an oligarchy called the High Council, founded by refugees of First Earth

Jove Shackley [JOHV]: oldest Shackley brother

Kase Shackley [KAEss SHACK-lee]: Senior Pilot, youngest son of the Stradat Lord Kapitan

King Filip: king of Cerulene, Essence of Souls

Kyvena [Kigh-VIN-uh]: capital of Jayde

Laurent [luh-RAHNT]: small village between Kyvena and Narden Pass

Les Shackley [LESS]: mother of Kase, Jove, Zeke, and Ana, wife of Harlan, sister to Ezekiel Fairchild

Life Ships: enormous vessels that carried remnants of humanity from First Earth to Yalvara

Lord Elder: leader of the Yalven nations

Lord Kapitan [KAP-ih-TIN]: high commander of the military

Millicent Sarson: female Stradat and ex-military general, intent on taking down Harlan Shackley

Myrrai [muh-RAE]: Yalven city, known as the realm of starlight

Nar: large village at the entrance to the Narden Pass

One World: group intent on uniting all Yalvara under one banner using whatever means necessary, considered anarchists

Owen Christie: Yalven professor at the University

Petra Lieber [Peh-TRAH Lee-BUR]: Hallie's friend and classmate

Relic: an item made from Zuprium to aid Essence wielders in controlling and focusing their power

Saldr [SAWL-der]: Yalven ambassador to Jayde, Vasa wielder, Called

Silver Coast: small coastal nation, used to be a part of Jayde

Sol Adrid [SOL uh-DRID]: capital of Cerulene

Stoneset: small mountain village in the Narden Range, on the other side of the Narden Pass

Stradat [straa-DIT]: highest elected official, three sit on the High Council

Tenner: denomination of Jaydian money, equal to 10 pieces

Tev Rubika [TEV ROO-bih-KUH]: oldest non-Yalven nation, dealing with civil war aftermath

Tovo [TOE-vo]: (known as Toro by Jaydians) Yalven god, his powers were split in the Dawn during the great battle with Jagamot

Vasa [VAH-suh]: Zuprium dust used by Called Yalven for different purposes, used mainly to manipulate time

Watch: Jayde's intelligence and police force

Yalvar Fuel [YAAL-var]: caustic resource found beneath the surface Yalvara, used in engines, being fazed out by the introduction of electricity

Yalvara [YAAL-var-UH]: planet near the edge of the Milky Way

Yalvs [YAALvs]: people native to Yalvara

Yarrow Barbary: trapper working the Narden Range

Zalina [zuh-LEE-nuh]: end of time

Zeke Shackley [ZEEK]: Lieutenant Colonel, medical specialist, middle Shackley brother, deceased

Zuprium [Zuh-PREE-um]: metal found on Yalvara that doesn't rust, is difficult to destroy, and when combined with electricity, creates   hover   capabilities,   sacred   to   Yalvs

ABOUT THE AUTHOR

ALLI EARNEST drinks way too much coffee and is obsessed with redwood candles, but growing up with two sisters, she's always been a tad overdramatic. It doesn't help that she enjoys books with dragons, wizards, and laser swords.

Graduating with a bachelor's degree in Middle Grades Education, Alli taught English Language Arts for five years and tried to convince thirteen-year-olds that Poe wasn't nearly as crazy as he sounded.

At present, Alli writes science-fiction and fantasy from an office filled with books and other collectibles. She's active on Instagram and TikTok, fangirling over her favorite books and documenting her author life. She lives in the southern US with her family.

www.alliearnest.com

Printed in Great Britain
by Amazon

38717429R00249